D0804826

# MEL ODOM

BOOK 2 ★ CALLED TO SERVE

# RENEGADE

Tyndale House Publishers, Inc.
Carol Stream, Illinois

Visit Tyndale online at www.tyndale.com.

Visit Mel Odom online at www.melodom.com.

*TYNDALE* and Tyndale's quill logo are registered trademarks of Tyndale House Publishers, Inc.

*Renegade*

Copyright © 2013 by Mel Odom. All rights reserved.

Cover photograph of truck shadow copyright © Chris Rainier/CORBIS. All rights reserved.

Cover photograph of soldier copyright © Daniel Bendjy/iStockphoto. All rights reserved.

Cover photograph of soldier silhouette copyright © Oleg Zabielin/iStockphoto. All rights reserved.

Designed by Ron Kaufmann

Edited by Caleb Sjogren

Published in association with the literary agency of Ethan Ellenberg Literary Agency, 548 Broadway, #5-E, New York, NY 10012.

Scripture quotation in chapters 12, 22, and 34 is taken from the *Holy Bible*, New Living Translation, copyright © 1996, 2004, 2007 by Tyndale House Foundation. Used by permission of Tyndale House Publishers, Inc., Carol Stream, Illinois 60188. All rights reserved.

Scripture quotation in chapter 14 is taken from the New King James Version.® Copyright © 1982 by Thomas Nelson, Inc. Used by permission. All rights reserved.

**Library of Congress Cataloging-in-Publication Data**

Odom, Mel.
   Renegade / Mel Odom.
      pages cm. — (Called to serve ; 2)
    ISBN 978-1-4143-4931-2 (sc)
1. Afghan War, 2001—Fiction. 2. United States. Marine Corps—Fiction. I. Title.
   PS3565.D53R48 2013
   813'.54—dc23                                  2013007140

Printed in the United States of America

| 19 | 18 | 17 | 16 | 15 | 14 | 13 |
|----|----|----|----|----|----|----|
| 7  | 6  | 5  | 4  | 3  | 2  | 1  |

*This book is for my wife and children, who
keep me strong and loved.*

*And to the soldiers, both the professionals
and the ones who have to drop their daily lives
to venture out to foreign and hostile lands.
God keep you and bring you home again.*

# ACKNOWLEDGMENTS

Jan Stob, as always, has been instrumental in keeping me at the keyboard.

Caleb Sjogren, new to me as an editor, has tucked the corners and smoothed everything out to make this book presentable. Congrats on the new baby! Yes, you will sleep again. Someday.

And to Tyndale, who allows me to bring these stories to wonderful readers.

# 1

**DRUG DEALERS** were like weeds. Even when they were pulled out by the roots, sometimes they came back.

Pike Morgan lounged in the night's shadows and watched the hustlers push their product. He'd already crossed paths with this particular group a few months back and drawn some unwelcome heat that his witness protection marshals hadn't been happy about. Pike was about to make them a lot less happy.

Of course, they wouldn't know until it was too late. He grinned at that thought and knew Petey would have been amused as well. It was at times like this, when he was about to beard enemies in their lairs, that Pike missed Petey the most.

All through juvie, through the back streets of Dallas, in the biker bars and strip clubs that dotted I-35 and I-20, Petey had always had Pike's back. Rough neighborhoods and dangerous situations had never been so bad when Petey had been with him.

Except for the time that Petey had gotten greedy and got himself killed. Petey had known that Pike would never have backed that particular play, so he'd gone alone, not telling Pike till he was in over his head. Pike had held on to Petey as he'd died, keeping the other man on his Harley in front of him while they'd raced to the nearest hospital.

Petey had bled out minutes before they'd arrived.

So now Pike was holed up, chafing under a whole list of witness protection rules—some he followed, and some he ignored—until after his testimony in the case against the men who had killed Petey. That was a trade-off he made to get those men because he couldn't get them on his own.

The drug dealers who had moved back into the neighborhood during his deployment in Somalia were another matter.

Standing against the wall of a warehouse that had been abandoned to urban decay, Pike watched the drug operation. He couldn't believe the Tulsa PD hadn't shut it down.

But the cops had to go by the book, and investigators didn't get many answers to questions. There wasn't a lot of trust for cops in this neighborhood, primarily Hispanic with some Asian families mixed in. In addition to the big crimes going down, there were a lot of little ones that had to stay secret as well. People who were there illegally, commerce that was handled under the table—all those things were done in the name of survival.

Achieving relative safety meant giving up the shadows that hid those other activities. People who were just getting by, who were marginalized, tended to get preyed on the most. Sadly, most of their predators came from the same families. That was another reason no one talked.

Pike wasn't there to talk. And he didn't mind taking action when officials couldn't. He liked action like that. Signing up for the Marines had been the closest he had come to getting back to the old ways, and that was too heavily supervised. Except when they were out in the field.

Somalia had offered a good run. But he was stateside again now and growing restless. Mechanic work only occupied a man so much.

And this was something that needed doing.

The drug delivery system was simple. Two Hispanic guys stood in an alley beside a derelict three-story apartment building and made contact with buyers, who drove up and never had to leave their cars. The guys in the alley negotiated the buy and took the money, which they put into a bucket that was lowered from a third-story window. The drugs were delivered back down the same way.

Police would have had a hard time dealing with the setup. In order to manage the takedown safely, they would need a lot of people. Those people would be seen coming, and the guys holding the drugs would vanish. All the police would have were the people on the ground. At best, they might have been able to capture enough crack to secure a misdemeanor conviction because no one could prove how much product was moving.

A twenty-year-old Camaro with a crumpled driver's-side front quarter panel rolled into the alley on busted shocks and doused its lights. Two young women sat in the front seats.

One of the young guns in the alley went over to take the order, leaning boldly into the window to flirt with the women. The other was puffing on a cigarette or reefer and watching the dialogue. The girls in the car laughed at the dealer's comments.

Pike decided to make use of the distraction. He reached down and picked up the five-gallon can of gasoline he'd brought with him, then started across the narrow two-lane. A light breeze stirred the trees along the street and created shifting shadows on the pavement. Pike made no noise as he walked.

He was dressed in black jeans, black military boots with crepe soles, and a black jacket to ward off the remnants of a winter chill that ghosted through the city. He carried three incendiary road flares in a pocket of his jacket and a telescoping baton attached to his belt. Black elastic gloves covered his hands and allowed him free movement.

The guys were so wrapped up in their potential for romance that they didn't see Pike till he'd already stepped into the alley. The man at the window came up hard-faced, putting on a show for the young women. He wore baggy pants, a Thunder basketball jersey, and a hoodie pulled up over a baseball cap. The hoodie was unzipped to show the Glock pistol tucked into his waistband.

"Hey, homes, what you doing here?" The guy's voice was loud, but Pike heard the tension in it, about to crack. The words were slurred just enough to tell Pike that he was high, too. That gave Pike an edge, but it also meant the guy would be more dangerous.

"Came looking for a taste." Pike didn't break stride, gaining another six feet.

The pusher pulled the gun and held it at his side. "You stop right there. This here's Sureños territory."

Pike read the papers. The Sureños were the local Hispanic crack dealers and sometimes feuded with the Bloods and the Crips over business.

"I know who you are. Just looking for a taste. Don't want no trouble." Pike knew he looked the part enough to sell it.

With his jacket open to the T-shirt underneath, the dragon tattoo wrapping his throat was partially visible. Since returning stateside, he'd let his hair and beard grow. His hair was shaggy, starting to brush his shoulders, and his beard was thick but he kept it cropped short. Mulvaney would have told him he looked too much like he had in the old days. Broad and swarthy, Pike knew he'd been marked by the streets he'd grown up in. On the surface, most people would assume he wasn't any better than the gangbanger in front of him.

Most days, Pike would have agreed with that assessment. But not when it came to drugs. That was one of the things Pike had never done, but he'd protected plenty of brother bikers who trafficked in things like that. Pike had always kept his hands clean, to his way of thinking. A man just had to know where his allegiances were. Too bad those could change without warning. If he'd been less of a survivor, he would have been dead a dozen times over.

Pike reached into his front pants pocket and took out a couple crumpled twenties. He let the slanting streetlight catch the bills. "I got money."

The man swaggered as he took a few steps closer. He was holding the gun and was in front of the young women, who stared raptly at them. He was shorter and lighter than Pike, but he figured the pistol made all the difference.

"An' I got a gun. So when I tell you to stand, you stand."

"Sure." Pike shrugged.

The man gave Pike a hard look. "I don't know you."

"Don't know you either. But I know who you are." Pike displayed the money again. "Unless you don't want to do business."

"You a cop?"

"I look like a cop?"

The man wrinkled his nose. "Don't know what you look like."

"Hey, Rudy." The voice came from the third-story window. "You okay down there?"

Rudy didn't look away from Pike. "Yeah, yeah. I got this." His eyes flicked to the gas can in Pike's hand. "You run outta gas?"

"Sure." Pike set the gas can down and held the twenties out again. "I got money."

When the man reached for the bills, Pike had to resist moving his hand away. Preventing the money from getting snatched would have been easy. But he let Rudy take the twenties.

"Now *I* got the money, homes, and it's gonna be the money I charge you to walk back outta this alley without getting shot."

Pike's left hand flashed out and clamped on to the gangbanger's gun hand, crimping the wrist almost to the point of breaking it. The Glock dropped from his slack grip, and Pike caught the weapon immediately in his right hand.

"Help! Help!" Driven by the pain in his wrist, Rudy collapsed to his knees. He cursed and clawed at Pike with his free hand.

Pike released the trapped hand, then snap-kicked Rudy in the face, sprawling him out unconscious in the alley. Spinning, cognizant of the other man pulling his weapon out as well as the frantic shouts spilling from the third-story window, Pike pointed the Glock and fired immediately, aiming by instinct.

The bullet caught the other man in the brachial nerves, and the man's pistol dropped from his numbed fingers. His mouth widened in alarm as he stumbled back.

Without pause, Pike raised his captured weapon to the third-story window and fired five times in rapid succession.

The rounds ricocheted from the brick exterior around the window, driving the guy there inside the building. Pike didn't want to kill anyone if he could help it. That would complicate things. All he wanted to do tonight was send a message.

The young women in the car sat frozen, staring at him. He slapped the car roof with the flat of his hand, hard enough that the noise echoed through the alley.

"Go!"

The driver put her foot on the accelerator. The engine coughed and wheezed, and for a moment Pike thought it was going to seize up and die. But the carburetor finally caught up with the increased fuel and the car sped away in a noisy, faintly sweet, blue carbon monoxide haze. The vehicle shot around the corner at the far end of the alley and disappeared.

Pike retrieved the gas can and headed for the door at the side of the building.

The man he'd shot in the shoulder scampered away, only pausing a second as if to think about going for the pistol lying on the ground. Pike ignored the man and focused on the door. He set the gas can down and tried the knob, finding it locked. Stepping back, he fired the pistol into the locking mechanism twice, reducing it to scrap metal.

He kicked the door open, picked up the gas can, and went inside, stepping immediately into the shadows beside the doorway so he wouldn't be easily seen. Footsteps clattered on the stairwell in the center of the floor. Empty units with doors torn from their moorings lined either side of the hallway.

Pike walked toward the stairwell, checking the rooms as he passed. No one else appeared to be in the building. He didn't think there would be with all the gang activity, but he wanted to be certain.

Two gangbangers halted halfway down the stairs. They raised their weapons and started firing. Bullets thudded into the walls beside Pike and dug divots out of the cheap carpet on the floor.

Without breaking stride, Pike took aim and fired. The bullets caught both men in the legs and they toppled down the stairs. By the time they started trying to get to their feet, Pike stood above them. He pointed his weapon at their faces.

"Drop the guns." He repeated the order in Spanish just in case either of them didn't speak English.

The two young men released their weapons, but they glared balefully at him through their fear.

"Sureños, right?"

"That's right, and you're gonna die for what you're doing tonight."

"That a fact?" Pike grinned. "You don't know me. But I know you. You tell that to your bosses. Tell them that if you come back here, I'm gonna find them and they'll never see me coming. You got all that? Or do I need to repeat it?"

Neither of them said anything.

Pike kicked the closest one in the head, hard enough to hurt. He was still attentive to any more activity on the stairs.

"Yeah, yeah. I heard you, man. I can remember."

"See that you do. I have to repeat myself, I'll carve it into you." Pike nodded toward the stairs. "How many more up there?"

"Three."

"What are they doing?"

"Packing the drugs and the money."

"Is there another way out of here?"

The guy hesitated and Pike kicked him in the head again, drawing an immediate string of curses.

"Is there another way?" Pike kept his voice level, calm.

"They can climb down from the window."

Pike gestured with the pistol. "Go. Get out of here."

Cursing, limping, the two gangbangers leaned on each other and staggered toward the door.

Pike picked up their pistols and stuffed them into his jacket. Then he uncapped the gas can and sloshed the contents over the floor. He took out a road flare, cracked it open as he backed away, and lobbed it into the pool of gas.

The flammable liquid caught fire at once and grabbed hold of the building like a live thing, crawling up the sides of the hallway as if ravenous. The darkness in the building melted as the flames grew stronger and taller.

Pike turned and ran from the building the way he had come. Outside, he glanced up at the third-story window but didn't see anyone scrambling through. He checked the loads in the Glock and discovered there were still seven rounds in the magazine. He sprinted toward the back of the building, spotting the two shadows of the limping men heading toward the street.

Rounding the rear of the building, Pike scanned the top floor and spied a rope dangling from another window on the third floor. A trio of gangbangers climbed awkwardly down it. They carried backpacks. A pimped-out SUV was parked halfway down the alley.

Pike pointed the pistol above the man at the top of the rope, then squeezed the trigger. The report reverberated between the buildings.

The man at the top let go in his panic and fell onto the next two. All three of them toppled to the pavement in a heap, then started clawing for their weapons.

Firing again, Pike stepped out so they could see him. "Lay the guns on the ground or I'll kill you."

Reluctantly, cursing, the men produced their weapons and placed them on the ground.

"Leave the backpacks."

"Homes, you don't know all the trouble you're getting into."

Pike trained his weapon on the man who had spoken. The gangbanger was the first to strip out of his backpack.

"Stay on the ground and crawl away."

Fearfully, the three men clambered across the ground. Sirens echoed in the distance. Pike didn't know if the sirens were coming to address the gunshots fired in the alley, but if they weren't, he knew it wouldn't be long.

Gray smoke rolled from the lower windows of the building where the glass had been broken out. Flames twisted and pushed the darkness inside the structure out into the alley.

Moving swiftly, keeping an eye on the three men to make sure they didn't pull out another weapon, Pike unzipped the backpacks. All three held money and drugs. Evidently the men had split up the haul. Satisfied, Pike grabbed the backpacks by the straps, lifted them from the ground, and headed for the sleek SUV. Firelight gleamed off the spinner caps.

"What are you doing, homes? That's my ride."

Pike didn't know which of the gangbangers had called out. He didn't care. Using the butt of the pistol, Pike broke the glass in the driver's-side window. The gangbanger cursed plaintively. Ignoring the cries, Pike hauled the backpacks up to the window and shoved them in.

Walking to the rear of the SUV, he pulled out a lockback knife and ducked down to slash the fuel line to the gas tank. Gasoline ran out onto the ground like ink, and the fumes filled Pike's nose. He started walking back the way he'd come. Taking another road flare from his pocket, he struck it and tossed it under the SUV into the pool of gasoline.

Flames whooshed to life and latched on to the vehicle.

"No! You didn't do that!"

Pike shot a look at the three men at the other end of the alley. "Tell the Sureños this neighborhood is off-limits."

The man cursed him.

Wheeling, Pike fired a round that cut the air over the man's head. The man dove to the ground, followed by his two buddies. At that point, the gas tank in the SUV exploded and the vehicle jumped off the ground slightly before settling back down. The interior was on fire as well, burning merrily. Most of the money and the drugs would burn before the fire department arrived, but he was willing to bet enough evidence would be left to get police investigators started on the operation. The neighborhood would be watched over for a time.

When Pike reached the unconscious man he'd left in the other alley, he caught the man's collar and dragged him into the street. He searched the man and found a throwaway cell phone. Opening the phone, Pike punched in 911.

"Nine-one-one operator. State the nature of your emergency."

"Fire." Leaving the phone connected, Pike dropped it onto the unconscious man and kept walking. Even if the neighbors didn't call in the fire, emergency units would be dispatched.

He walked away, feeling pretty good about the night's work.

# 2

AT 6:20 THE NEXT MORNING, Pike was taking bacon from a skillet when someone knocked on his apartment door. He was clad in a pair of faded, oil-stained jeans, barefoot and shirtless. He took the high-capacity Glock .45 from the counter beside the stove, set the skillet off the burner, and padded to the door.

He didn't peer through the peephole. A guy could catch a bullet in the brain that way as soon as the lens went dark and alerted a shooter on the other side of the door. Instead, he stood to the side of the door with the pistol in his fist.

"Who is it?"

"It's me, Mr. Pike. Hector."

Hector was the young boy from the neighborhood who had first asked Pike to help with Juan Mendoza, who was part of the Sureños. Hector's sister, Erendria, had gotten mixed up with the previous group Pike had "relocated."

"What are you doing here, Hector?" Pike kept from growling the question, but only just. The kid was good, hadn't taken up any bad ways, and he sometimes came by the garage where Pike worked. His mom worked a lot, and his sister was trying to manage community college and a job as well these days. She'd kept herself clean. Hector's father had run away shortly after he'd been born.

"I wanted to talk to you."

Pike still didn't reach for the door. "Shouldn't you be in school?"

"School's not till eight."

"Shouldn't you be getting ready for school?"

"I'm ready."

"Does your momma or your sister know you're here?"

"She's at work. Erendria is at college. She has *friends* she's studying with." The kid made *friends* sound like leprosy.

"Kinda early for her to study."

"I think she goes there for coffee and gossip. That's what my mom says."

Despite himself, Pike grinned sadly. Kid was caught between a working mom and a sister getting ready to take flight out into the world. That left him little family time.

"Can I come in?" There was a little whine in the boy's voice. Not enough to be annoying, and it was subtle enough that Pike knew Hector was trying to hide it.

"You alone?"

"Yeah."

Pike slipped the pistol into the back of his waistband and removed the lock bar he'd mounted in the floor, then unfastened the three locks on the door. When he opened it, Hector stood in the hallway.

The boy was nine going on ten. Hispanic and too thin for his age, dressed in a Batman T-shirt that was too big for him and hung almost to his knees, Hector was a good-looking kid with eyes that had seen too much. Innocence didn't count for much in the neighborhood. Pike understood that. Hector's black hair was unruly and his chin was too pointed. One of these days he'd be a good-looking young man, but he wasn't there yet.

Hector frowned at Pike. "You gonna ask me to come in?"

"You a vampire or something?"

Hector's frown grew deeper and he looked at Pike like he was loco. Then a smile cleared the frown in a heartbeat. "Oh, I get it. Because vampires have to be asked to come in."

Pike shrugged. "Door's open."

Hector walked inside. "My mom told me it's still polite to be asked into someone's house."

"I opened the door."

"I don't think that counts."

Pike bolted the door shut. Hector took notice of all the locks, but he didn't say anything. He took notice of the gun, too.

Around the neighborhood, Pike had a reputation as a guy not to be messed with. Occasionally he got involved in situations—domestic problems, thugs—but only because those events seemed to find him. He didn't go looking for trouble.

Well, mostly he didn't go looking for trouble. Last night had been the exception.

At the stove, Pike put the .45 back on the counter and replaced the skillet on the burner. He took the bacon grease that he'd saved and poured it into the skillet with the leavings from the last, getting a good half inch of grease in the bottom. He gestured Hector to the small kitchenette table with two mismatched chairs.

"Have you had breakfast?"

The boy sat. "Cereal. I can fix that myself."

"Can you eat again?"

Hector smiled. "Yes. But only if you have enough."

"I have enough. Eggs over easy work for you?"

"Yes."

Pike took eggs from the carton on the counter, cracked them, and dropped them into the grease. They sizzled upon impact and the whites started to color up almost immediately.

He cooked quickly and efficiently, the way he did everything.

When he finished, he filled two plates with eggs, bacon, and toast that he'd browned in the bacon grease–coated skillet at the end. After placing the plates on the table, he took grape jelly and hot sauce from the small refrigerator and put those on the table as well. He added two glasses of orange juice.

Pike sat, picked up his fork, and started to dig in. Then he noticed Hector staring at him expectantly, both hands clasped together on the table in front of him.

"Something wrong with the food?"

"No, the food looks very good. I was waiting."

"Waiting for what?"

"For you to say grace so that we may eat."

"Oh." Pike thought about that, even tried to remember the last time he'd said grace before a meal. It must have been sometime in juvie, but that had been a while ago.

He was twenty-nine now, and he and Petey had escaped at fourteen and started living on the streets. Mostly on the streets. Every now and again, they'd been busted on misdemeanors. Nothing serious enough to carry any real weight.

Pike nodded to Hector. "Why don't you say grace. I made breakfast."

"Sure." The boy beamed and bowed his head.

Pike did likewise, feeling foolish. He didn't believe in God, didn't even think he had during the bits and pieces of his childhood that he could remember. He didn't believe in anything beyond what he could do for himself, and he knew his limitations. That kept life simple.

Hector prayed quickly and fervently, and the words sounded familiar spilling from his lips. "God, bless this food we are about to eat. Bless Mr. Pike for cooking it. Thank you for watching over us. In Jesus' name we pray."

Pike was caught off guard as Hector abruptly raised his head. He felt odd for having sat there silent, but somehow hearing the kid pray hadn't been so bad.

"Okay, now we can eat." Hector picked up his fork and started moving food. For a little guy, he could put it away.

As he ate, Pike thought about the last time he'd eaten breakfast with someone. It had been in Somalia, with Lance Corporal—now Corporal—Bekah Shaw. He'd been part of her rifle team during the action over there. After his return to the States, he'd gone back to his routine at the apartment and the garage, but it always took a while to settle in. He enjoyed his time in the Marines as a reservist, but he liked his time alone as well.

Hector carefully spread grape jelly on his toast, then took a bite. A spot of jelly clung to his chin and he didn't notice.

Pike pointed to his own chin. "You got something there."

Hector picked up a paper napkin Pike had saved from a late-night Taco Bell run and wiped his chin. "Thank you."

"No prob." Pike bit into a piece of bacon, savored the flavor as he chewed, then swallowed. "So did you just come by for breakfast this morning?"

Hector shook his head. "No. I wanted to make sure you were all right."

"Why wouldn't I be all right?"

"The crack house burned last night."

Pike didn't say anything.

"I thought maybe you had something to do with that." Hector looked at him with those big brown eyes. "Did you?"

"Maybe there are some things you're better off not knowing."

"I can keep a secret."

"Yeah, me too."

They ate in silence for a little while, but Hector always had questions. Sometimes they were questions about his homework, which Pike occasionally helped him with down at the garage after school. Every now and again, Pike had gotten Monty—the garage owner—to help out. Monty had kids and knew more about homework. Pike knew how to do a lot, most of it self-taught, but he didn't always know how teachers wanted homework done. He could usually get the answer, just not the right way or in a way that Hector could understand.

"Where did you learn to cook?"

"In juvie." Pike wouldn't lie about that. The crack house was a different story. "You know what juvie is, right?"

Hector nodded. "Yeah. Where they put the bad kids."

"Yeah."

"You were a bad kid?"

"Partly. I didn't have any parents. So I got stuck in the orphanage and in foster homes. I didn't like them. After a while, they put me in juvie."

"Oh." Hector took another bite of eggs, chewed thoughtfully, and swallowed. "They taught you how to cook real good."

"Thanks."

Hector looked at him. "I'm glad you weren't hurt last night."

Pike thought a minute about how to best handle that. Finally he just nodded. "Me too. Now finish your breakfast. You don't want to be late for school."

# 3

**PIKE'S CELL PHONE** rang at 7:17 a.m. while he was at the bodega a few blocks from his apartment building. He'd gone in to pick up a newspaper and a cup of coffee to take to work. Monty was a master with engines, but his coffee-brewing skills lacked. Pike had never bothered to tell him.

As he stood in line for the cashier, Pike answered the phone.

Monty started speaking at once. "You in some kind of trouble, Pike?"

"No. Why?"

"I got two detectives here at the garage asking questions about you."

Feeling a little cornered, stepping back into the old days in a heartbeat, Pike looked through the advertisement-covered windows out onto the street. Everything seemed normal. "Are you sure they're cops?"

"Yeah. I been in some trouble before too, buddy. I know what cops are like. These are the real deal. I made them show me their badges and their IDs. Ain't my first rodeo."

"They say what they want?"

"You. They've been real interested in what time you normally come in. I told them around eight. They wanted to know where you lived. I didn't tell them that. I figured they could look that up at the DMV."

Pike knew that too. The detectives could have been knocking on his door that morning instead of Hector. That meant they'd chosen to meet him at his work. "They don't have anything on me, Monty. If they did, they'd have come to my apartment."

"That's what I figured, Bubba. This is just a roust. Shake you up a little. I just didn't know what for."

"Me neither." Pike didn't like lying to Monty, but he didn't want to involve the man in his problems either. "I'm at the bodega. You want me to bring you anything?"

"Yeah. A bomb. Mrs. Garcia brought that station wagon of hers back in and I gotta chase down another electrical problem. I'm beginning to think I'd be better off just getting her another car so I don't have to look at this one ever again. I swear, I don't need another project car."

"I'll be there in a few minutes. Fresh outta bombs. Anything else?"

"Nah, I'm good. And listen, Pike, if you need an attorney or something, I got a guy that's real good."

"I don't think it'll come to that, but that's good to know." Pike said good-bye and closed the phone. He took a deep breath and stepped up to the cashier.

The garage was located sixteen blocks from Pike's apartment. It was an easy enough walk, and he liked being able to see for himself what was going on in the neighborhood. Every place he'd ever been had its own rhythms. Getting to know them was just a matter of time.

He took different routes to the garage, never getting locked into any pattern, and he even got his coffee from seven different places, including the diner where Hector's mom worked. A routine could save lives, but it could also put them in jeopardy. The Marines taught discipline and order, but the streets taught Pike organic chaos. He split the difference most days, always changing it up.

He wore work boots with jeans, a sleeveless T-shirt from a Molly Hatchet concert, and a black nylon shell for the wind. He'd left his weapons at home. The cup of coffee kept his left hand warm. Wraparound sunglasses blocked out the morning sun.

The two police detectives stood just inside the open bay doors of the garage. They had on suits and looked official. Pike guessed the neighborhood was buzzing with fears of ICE. Immigration and Customs Enforcement made an appearance every so often, busting illegals sometimes but mostly looking for human-trafficking operations.

They stood a little straighter when they realized Pike was headed for them. Behind them, Monty's boom box blasted the Hollies' "Long Cool Woman." Monty was an oldies kind of guy, but it was an appreciation that he'd developed, not been born into. He was in his midthirties.

Mrs. Garcia's station wagon was in the first bay. Monty had gotten on it quick because Mrs. Garcia ferried four grandchildren around to school, dental and medical appointments, and extracurricular activities like soccer and dance. She was helping her son who had lost his wife to cancer. Her car had to move.

"Pike Morgan?" The older detective spoke first, taking the lead. Pike had had two other last names before that, stripped away just as quickly as they'd been given when he had been forced to move to the other two locations. They'd wanted to move him farther west. Oklahoma was as far from Texas as Pike had allowed them to move him. Getting into the Marine Reserve had caused the US Marshals a lot of headaches, but Pike had insisted, and he was still needed to testify in a couple ongoing court cases.

"Yeah." Pike came to a stop in front of the detectives and sipped his coffee.

"I'm Detective Tom Horner with the Tulsa Police Department."

He was well dressed, manicured, and had a clean haircut that looked like he'd just stepped out of a salon. Everything but the gray at his temples had been touched up. He looked to be in his late forties, a guy who watched what he ate and kept himself in shape. His right eye had a squint to it, like he'd gotten popped there and the swelling hadn't quite gone down. Horner nodded to his younger partner. "This is Detective Trey Winkle."

The other man was in his early thirties and balding a little, his scalp showing through his fair hair. He was full-faced and had a small, crooked scar across his chin that looked like something left over from a childhood accident.

"I see some ID?" Pike sipped his coffee and waited till the two detectives dug out their shields and IDs. They displayed them in quick flicks. Both sets looked legitimate. "What can I do for you?"

"We've got a few questions. Is there somewhere we can go?"

Pike met the man's gaze. "Here is fine."

Horner frowned a little at that, obviously not happy. Pike suspected the man was more unhappy over not being able to immediately seize control of the interview.

"All right. Can you tell us where you were last night?"

"My apartment."

"Is there someone who can verify that?"

"I was alone. I usually am. Except during those times that I'm not."

Horner smiled good-naturedly, like he was embarrassed and needed some help to make everything all right. "Well, that's a problem."

"Is it?" Pike blew on his coffee and took a sip.

"You don't have anyone who can corroborate your story."

"Does my story need corroboration?"

"We'd like to know where you were last night."

"I just told you."

Horner shrugged. "We'd like more proof than that."

"Why?"

Horner looked irritated and scratched the underside of his chin. "Peace of mind."

"Whose peace of mind?"

"Mine."

Pike grinned a little at that. "Didn't know you cared."

Some of Horner's good-natured attitude evaporated and he shifted, squaring up his shoulders and standing taller. "Maybe it would be better if we had this conversation downtown."

"Are you arresting me for something?"

Horner was quiet for a moment. "No."

"Then that question was an invitation I'm declining. I'm not going downtown with you, and we're done here. I've got people waiting to get their cars back." Pike stepped past the man.

Detective Winkle bristled and took a step toward Pike. Pike ignored the man, knowing his partner was calling the shots. Horner lifted a hand and waved the younger detective to heel. Winkle grimaced, but he stepped back.

Pike thought about pointing out how well trained the younger detective was, but he made himself pass on that. He had no reason to bait the police, even though his rebellious nature made him want to. He placed his coffee on the rear of the ancient station wagon.

At the front of the vehicle under the raised hood, Monty watched what was going on with a disapproving frown. He was a short man with broad shoulders and swarthy skin that broadcast his Hispanic heritage. He was fit and powerful, perhaps ten pounds over his best weight because his wife cooked well and Monty kept beer on ice in a cooler at the shop for after hours. He wore dark-blue shop pants, a lighter-blue uniform blouse with his name sewn on in red thread above the right pocket, and an OSU Cowboys ball cap. A gunslinger mustache framed his upper lip.

Horner wasn't quite ready to walk away. "Do you know about the crack house that got burned down last night?"

"Sure." Pike tapped the newspaper he'd laid beside his coffee. "It's in the news."

The story was on the front page.

"What do you know about it?"

"Just what's in the paper." Pike walked over to an upright toolbox, pulled out his keys, and opened it up to take out a tool belt. He laid the belt across his shoulder.

"Nothing else?"

"Anything else you think I should know?"

"Officers arrested a couple gangbangers last night who gave a description of a guy that looks a lot like you."

"Lots of guys look like me."

"I don't think so. Officers who work this beat have heard some rumors about you. Said you'd got in a couple scrapes, but they've never had a real beef with you. They also said there was another altercation involving a group of crack dealers a few months ago. They were beaten up pretty badly and got told to leave the neighborhood. I find that interesting."

Pike looked at the detective. "You know what I find interesting?"

Horner folded his arms across his chest.

"That the police department only knows about the drug-dealing operations after the fact. Probably makes a lot of people wonder how good you are at doing your job. They might even wonder why you're chasing after someone who put the gangbangers out of business instead of chasing after the guys putting drugs out in the neighborhood. From the story I read, the house that burned up can't be the only one in this neighborhood. Much less the whole city."

Crimson tinted Horner's face. "We'll be back to talk to you."

Pike shook his head. "Not without a good reason. Otherwise I'm gonna talk to an attorney about filing a harassment suit."

For a moment, Horner locked his gaze with Pike's. Then the detective jerked his head to his partner. Together, the detectives walked out of the building and got into their unmarked sedan at the curb in front of the garage.

"You know I make it a habit not to stick my nose into other people's business." Monty wiped his greasy hands with a red towel.

"I've always liked that about you." Pike joined Monty and stared into the car's engine space, tracking all the wires. Searching for a short was time-consuming and often frustrating. He wasn't looking forward to the job.

"So I'm not gonna ask you if you're the guy those cops are looking for. But you're also my friend, so I'm gonna tell you to be careful. The guy who burned that house down and rousted those drug dealers? He's made friends on both sides of the street. Personally, I like the idea that those guys are gone. Makes the neighborhood a little safer for my kids." Monty clapped Pike on the shoulder. "I just want you to be careful, amigo."

Pike nodded. "I always am." He stripped out of the Windbreaker and leaned on the car's fender. "Now let's see if we can get Mrs. Garcia's beast back on the road one more time."

# 4

**THE MIDDAY SUN BURNED DOWN** brightly on the Safed Koh mountains but didn't completely strip away the lingering chill that hugged the high peaks and narrow trails. Winter hadn't yet abandoned its grip on the land. Higher up, snow still covered the steep faces of the stony spires, and where Zalmai Yaqub had set up his trap, cold still radiated from the barren ground.

Yaqub lay prone on his stomach, elbows propped up to hold the binoculars he used to keep watch over the narrow passage that men and beasts of burden had trod over centuries of travel.

In his early forties, Yaqub had lived with war and strife all of his adult life. He had fought against the Russians with his father while little more than a boy, then against warlords and different governments that had tried to unite Afghanistan, and now against the Americans who thought they could do what their Soviet counterparts had not been able to do: break the country. He was lean and hard, capable of traveling overland on foot all day on only a mouthful of water if need be, and he knew a thousand ways to kill his enemies.

He wore a faded cloak over his gray *shalwar kameez*, the traditional long shirt and loose trousers of Afghan men. A turban covered his head, and his coal-black beard reached to midchest. Beside him, wrapped in a small blanket, the AK-47 assault rifle lay clean and ready.

A hundred and fifty meters away, looking like a smudge of shadow lying beside a big rock, Wali lifted his hand to signal the advance of their prey.

Yaqub signaled to his men, sending them all more closely to ground. He had trained them—every warrior who followed him— guided them in the ways of killing their enemies and worshiping their deity, taught them the need for their commitment not only to die for their beliefs but also to kill others with impunity. As their mullah, he had instructed them in the responsibility of *fard al-'ayn*, the individual duty concerning jihad. A man's duty to God was to smite his enemies, and these men they hunted today were great offenders because they had turned away from their faith to pursue profit instead.

Moving slowly, holding the binoculars in one hand, Yaqub uncovered the AK-47 with the other. Only a short distance away, Faisal prepared the RPG-7. The rocket launcher would deliver swift death, and Yaqub did not intend a show of mercy. Everyone would die.

At the bend of the pass, a man appeared. He was young and lean, his face wrapped against the chill breeze that skated through the passage like a hunting hawk. He carried an American-made M16, and Yaqub chose to resent the man even more for that. The Western nations had equipped their allies for years, always turning the Afghan people against each other and against outsiders who did not follow the Western beliefs. Many of the weapons that Yaqub's warriors carried had been captured during the war with the Russians. Al Qaeda armorers had learned to restore the rifles and keep them in peak condition.

Yaqub gently pulled the AK-47 into the ready position and flicked off the safety as the man continued his walk down the passage. Twenty meters behind the point man, the rest of the group followed, men and donkeys carrying the goods they intended to sell once across the Pakistani border.

The men were a mix of young and old. Yaqub was disappointed when he saw no Westerners among them. The men in the passage below were of the Northern Alliance, the collection of Afghan warlords that the Western powers had allied with.

The Northern Alliance was the weapon that the West had intended to keep aimed at the heart of al Qaeda. They were not friends of the West either, but the Northern Alliance did not like the true path of Islam. That way was too hard for the warlords, and they were weak warriors in Yaqub's eyes. They were not given to holy pursuits.

As Yaqub saw it, a man who claimed to be Muslim yet did not act on the war with the West at the first chance offered could only be put to death for failing his sacred duty.

The men came closer. The man on point never hesitated, but he also did not neglect his duty. His head swung from side to side, but he was tired from marching all night in the cold, and Yaqub's warriors were well hidden.

Fifty meters away, Yaqub slid his finger over the trigger and pulled through. The AK-47's recoil was so slight and the rifle so well balanced that he hardly felt any movement. He fired two rounds at the lead man, watching him drop in his tracks, then shifted the rifle again to pick up other targets as the group broke for cover.

A few meters away, Faisal lifted the RPG-7 and readied his shot. The rocket lunged from the launcher, straight toward a luckless animal as it fought to get its head against its handler. The man held on to the lead rope as the donkey struggled and the packs on its back beat against it.

Then they vanished in an explosion that ran a river of fiery destruction in both directions along the passageway for a moment.

"Faisal!" Yaqub ejected the empty magazine from his assault rifle and shoved a fresh one home. "Do not shoot the donkeys carrying the cargo! Leave those!"

"Forgive me, Zalmai. I shot too soon." Faisal laid the rocket launcher aside and picked up his rifle.

Knowing there was no use remonstrating the man for his mistake, Yaqub instead focused on shooting the caravan survivors. It would not matter if some of them escaped, and he was certain his men would not get them all now, but they were the enemies of his God and he did not want any of them to avoid the divine retribution he was delivering.

The caravan warriors knew they were in dire straits. They scattered like lambs, none of them attempting to gain control over the others and organize a defense.

Filled with the familiar bloodlust that fueled him, Yaqub rose to his feet and ran to the edge of the passageway as several of the caravan warriors tried to scale free of the kill box. He fired into them at point-blank range till the assault rifle cycled dry. Frustrated as the caravan men continued to rise, he dropped the AK-47 and gave ground before them.

"Faisal! To me!" Yaqub drew the Russian Tokarev holstered at his hip and fired it dry too, but by then, four men were almost on top of him.

"I cannot!"

A glance in the man's direction showed that Faisal was in danger of being overrun as well. He, too, had dropped his rifle and was pulling his pistols.

Beseeching God, calling for holy wrath, Yaqub freed the *pesh-kabz* at his waist. The thick blade was broad at the hilt but tapered down to a near-needle point. In its initial design, it had been forged to penetrate armor, capable of sliding between the rings or the plates and plunging into the man under the defenses. Permutations of the knife had been carried for centuries.

The knife remained deadly in the hands of a warrior who knew how to use it. Yaqub had learned his martial skills from his father, but several warriors over the years had contributed to his acumen.

Keeping the knife hidden at his side till the last moment, Yaqub continued stepping back before the onslaught of caravan warriors fleeing for their lives. Then he whipped the knife up into the nearest man's throat, feeling the warm blood spill over his hand and run along his arm to his elbow.

Fear and the knowledge of his unavoidable death widened the man's eyes. Setting himself, Yaqub put his weight behind his knife arm and pushed forward again, breaking the advance of the men. Yaqub grabbed the dying man's coat in his free hand and whipped him to the left, into the path of the man on that side, as he slid the knife free.

Twisting, stepping back again, Yaqub looked at the warrior on his right. The knife got the man's attention at once, and he brought up the American semiautomatic pistol. Fearlessly, Yaqub stepped forward into the man as his opponent's arm extended, getting inside the instinctive response. Yaqub set his feet even though the pistol blasted almost in his ear, swiveled his hips, and drove the *pesh-kabz* into the man's stomach.

Mortally wounded, the man folded over Yaqub's out-thrust arm. The dying man's hot breath and plaintive moan pushed into Yaqub's ear.

"Death is upon you, you weak, traitorous dog!" Yaqub plucked the pistol from the man's nerveless fingers, shoved his chest against the falling man to knock him away, and dragged the knife free as he raised his captured weapon.

Three men ran by Yaqub, avoiding the battle he waged upon them. He fired into their backs, emptying the pistol. They stumbled and fell, dead or dying, and he didn't care. A short distance away, Faisal was desperately fighting to stay on his feet. Gunshots rang out between him and the men trying to barrel over him.

One of the men fell as Yaqub let go of the pistol and stepped toward the scuffle. He moved in behind another of the men and thrust the long knife between the man's ribs. He shuddered and went down. Striding over the corpse, Yaqub grabbed the beard of another warrior, yanked his head around, and pierced the man's chin.

The next man turned to face Yaqub, whipping his rifle around, but the al Qaeda leader ducked beneath the blow and hacked at the inside of the man's back leg with the knife. The blow caused the man's leg to go slack. Yaqub grabbed the rifle and yanked it from the fallen man.

Managing the rifle one-handed, Yaqub aimed the weapon at the next man staggering up from the passage, then pulled the trigger. Nothing happened. Snarling an oath, Yaqub flung the rifle at the man and went to meet him.

The man came to a stumbling stop, though, and fell forward on his face, shot by another of Yaqub's warriors.

Breathing hard, the back of his throat alternately feeling frozen and too hot, Yaqub bent down and retrieved his rifle. He sheathed the *pesh-kabz* through his belt and shoved a fresh magazine into the AK-47. He walked to the edge of the passageway, knowing from the sporadic gunfire that the fighting was very nearly over.

He stood, swaying, over the narrow valley of carnage and looked down at the corpses and blood that lay strewn across the ground. He had lost men. He knew that. Losses were an acceptable part of his war. In his heart, he knew that he had been saved to continue the righteous work that had been laid before him. He would climb over the bodies of his enemies and the *kuffar* alike to reach the feet of God.

# 5

**PIKE SAT AT A TABLE** in the United States Marshals Office and tried not to be irritated. He stared at the shuttered window on the other side of the room and wished he were back at the garage instead of here. At least there he could have been doing something worthwhile. Talking didn't get much done, especially with the prosecutor assigned to the case that had brought him into the witness protection program.

"Is anything I'm telling you boring you, Mr. Morgan?"

Squelching an immediate and scathing response to federal district attorney David Clement, Pike eyed the man. "Pretty much everything you're saying is boring me."

Clement's face turned red and his ears burned. He was in his late thirties, a guy who still viewed himself as on the way up in his job field. As a result, he was aggressive and a true pain. He was twenty pounds too heavy, soft from sitting at a desk job and pushing papers most of his days.

Pike knew the type and didn't respect the man. During his juvie years, while shuttled out to various foster homes from the orphanage, Pike had seen far too many David Clements. They were happiest when they were checking boxes and filing paperwork. Men and women like Clement didn't want to get to know the people involved or the circumstances that had brought them together. They just lived to churn paper.

Clement sat there in shirtsleeves and a tie, his hair moussed into place. His expensive briefcase lay on the table to his right. His tablet PC occupied the space to his left. Those were standards that marked Clement's importance.

At least, they were supposed to be. Pike was bored of them as well.

Behind Clement, through the glass walls of the interview room, three US Marshals drank coffee and worked the phones at their desks. One of them was a woman Pike had seen before and thought was pretty good-looking. And she had a nice smile. He could tell from the smile that she went for bad boys. If she wasn't careful, that would cost her one day.

"You know, that's a pretty pitiful attitude you have there." Clement narrowed his gaze and tried to look tough.

Pike could hear the silent "mister" at the end of the declaration that the prosecutor left out at the last minute. The decision was a good one. Leaving it in would have irritated Pike further and probably prematurely ended the conversation.

Pike eyed the man. "How do you figure?"

"We're protecting you from people who want nothing more than to see you dead."

Pike folded his hands together on the table and barely resisted the impulse to reach across the space and grab the man by his shirtfront. At Pike's side, US Marshal Bill Dundee tensed up a bit and leaned forward. He was an older man, in his late fifties, and had a calm air about him that reminded Pike of Caleb Mulvaney, the Dallas homicide detective who had gotten Pike into protective services.

Dundee cleared his throat. "Maybe we could take a little break."

"Is that what you think?" Pike's voice was a low roar in the room. "That you're protecting me?"

Clement was fast on the uptake, obviously realizing he'd screwed up, but he was too stubborn or too stupid to let go of it. Like a dog that had shoved its head through a hole in the fence to get a bone but was unwilling to drop it when it wouldn't fit back through. "Of course we're protecting you. If not for the protection we provide, the Diablos would have killed you after they killed Peter Tull. You'd be dead by now."

For a moment, Pike wasn't in the interview room anymore. He was back in that roadside bar off Interstate 35 outside of Dallas trying to hold Petey together. Blood stink filled Pike's nose, something he'd become familiar with, and something he could never forget.

Petey was trying to talk again, trying to say he was sorry for getting them crossways with the Diablos. And Pike knew in his heart that if Petey had gotten away with his score and they'd gotten down to Mexico the way he'd thought they would, Petey would have been laughing, buying the beer and the women.

That was a nightmare that played through Pike's evenings on a regular basis. That scene was always there waiting for him, poised patiently to steal over him at a moment's notice. As he held his friend, Pike remembered all the good years, back when Petey hadn't gotten hooked on drugs and alcohol and playing against the odds. They'd been friends, sharing some of the same foster homes, sometimes at different times.

But all through that, they'd had each other's back.

A sack of venom broke open inside Pike's chest. He rose from the chair, surging to his feet like a lion, barely keeping himself on his side of the conference table.

"You're not protecting me! The only reason I came to you people was so I could get *all* the Diablos responsible for killing Petey! Now three years have come and gone. Months ago, I was told I was done with this, that those guys who killed Petey were going away forever. Now you're telling me that the prosecutor's office wants to open that case back up, that those guys have cut a deal and are gonna walk?"

Pike still couldn't believe that. Everything had been locked in. Now the legal team had dropped the ball and everything he'd done was for nothing.

"They're not going to walk." Clement strained to be calm, but his tone was so forced it was like he was talking to a child. "We've got a chance here to do some more good. To take down more of the Diablo organization, as well as some of the crime families they're in bed with. I promise you, those guys who killed your friend will *not* walk. That's not going to happen. We just need you to testify some more."

Pike cursed and slapped the table with his open hand, causing Clement and Dundee to flinch. "I didn't sign on to make a career out of this!"

"Yeah, you did. When you took on that new identity, you guaranteed your compliance."

"Then there's no more compliance." The back of Pike's neck felt hot.

"Their defense attorney is prepared to put guys on the stand who will say *they* killed your friend, not the men we put away."

"They're lying."

"We know that. But it will end up being your word against theirs in a court of appeals. What we have to do is work together. We need you to leverage a takedown of more of the Diablos. We've got to get the whole organization, not a handful of guys." Clement's face hardened. "You're going to do what we need you to do, Mr. Morgan. You're going to play ball the way we tell you to."

Teetering on the edge of control, Pike leaned across the table. "No, I'm not here for your *protection*."

Dundee stood at Pike's side. The marshal tried to take Pike by the arm.

Pike yanked his arm away, never shifting his gaze off the prosecutor. "Don't expect to come down here and order me around like I'm somebody that belongs to you." He regained control of his voice. "I don't. I've been my own since I can remember. You want to know the only man that's ever *protected* me, Counselor?"

Clement looked pale and stared down at the tabletop. In the background, on the other side of the glass walls, the marshals went on alert. Situations arose pretty quickly in the office as tempers flared.

"Petey, that's who. I had trouble, I didn't have to look over my shoulder. Petey was there."

*Until the day I wasn't there for him.* The thought hit Pike between the eyes like a sledgehammer. The guilt that he'd thought dead and buried for so long came screaming back like a Harley running straight dual exhaust, popping and snarling.

"Don't make the mistake of thinking you and these marshals are replacing Petey. You're not." Pike's chest tightened. "You're just a means to an end, brother. Nothing more. If you have a problem with me, we can call it quits right here. I'll go on my way and take care of this situation myself. I'm not a big fan of your department right now."

"Pike." Dundee spoke calmly. "That's not what he's saying. That's not what we want. They need you now more than ever."

Clement evidently grew some courage with Dundee standing between him and Pike. "Did you threaten to kill the Diablos? Is that what you just did?"

Pike leaned around Dundee. "I didn't threaten. That's a promise."

Clement looked at Dundee and shook his head. "My office can't deal with this attitude, Marshal. Surely you see that."

Dundee held up a hand. "Maybe you could just refrain from speaking for a moment, Counselor."

"Me?" Clement looked apoplectic. "Marshal, I'm not the one who just threatened to commit murder or walk out on this arrangement, and I'm *not* the one who burned down a crack house."

Dundee kept focused on Clement and spoke in a flat, no-nonsense voice. "Get some air, Mr. Clement."

For a moment the attorney looked like he was going to argue; then he cursed, pushed up from the table, and stalked out of the interview room.

Without a word, Dundee leaned a hip on the conference table and crossed his arms. He held his silence for a time, then looked at Pike. "If it was up to me, I'd give you a commendation for burning down the crack house."

Pike sat back in his chair and placed his hands behind his head. "I don't know what you're talking about." Denying knowledge of anything criminal was second nature to him.

Dundee smiled. "I didn't think you would, but this office has had to dissuade a determined homicide cop in Tulsa from looking at you for that crack house. And he's pretty certain you did it."

"Look, if you guys were going to pull the pin on that, we'd already be at it. Nobody got killed in that crack house. How many people did those dealers kill while they were in operation? How many teenage prostitutes did they put into business? No, that crack house was a blight. It had to go, and the local PD didn't seem overly concerned about it."

"It's not the crack house the DA is concerned about. They're afraid that the other Diablos are going to figure out where we've got you stashed if you raise your profile. If those guys do learn where you're at, you know you're a heartbeat away from becoming a dead man."

"I'm not worried about the Diablos."

"Yeah, I didn't figure you were. Clement out there thinks you've got some kind of death wish." Dundee silently studied Pike. "You don't, do you?"

"If I did, I'd have already been dead by now. You run the roads I do, dying gets to be pretty easy." *Just ask Petey.*

"Maybe. But Clement's boss isn't happy that you're serving in the Marines either. The Marshals Office had to work long and hard to close that deal. Being a Marine isn't exactly a low profile."

No, it wasn't, but being in the Marine Reserve—getting to go overseas to handle different theaters of action—had helped keep the edge off. Putting the crack houses out of business had helped too. If Pike could have, he probably would have joined the Marines full-time for a while because now that Petey was gone, he didn't know what to do with himself, but his record prevented him from a full-time bid at the moment. The Marines didn't know exactly who he was, and they were a selective breed. Pike respected that about them.

"I'm not a guy who's going to sit on his hands, Marshal." Pike kept his voice low and level, but the anger inside him still struggled to get out. He hated these meetings. They underscored his helplessness to get all of Petey's killers. "I told you that when Mulvaney brought me to you people."

Dundee chuckled. "That you did, Pike, but I guess we weren't expecting you the way you are. You're kind of raw."

"I say what I mean."

"A little tact might help."

Staring through the glass walls, Pike watched Clement as he spoke on his cell phone and gestured in short, explosive movements. The man clearly wasn't happy.

"Is the DA going to make a deal with the Diablos?" Pike asked the question almost offhandedly, like he didn't truly care. But the pure truth of the matter was that he only stayed put right now to make sure the Diablos who killed Petey got taken down. He thought he'd accomplished that, and now it was about to slip through his fingers.

"Yeah, he is if he has to. But it doesn't have to come to that, Pike. They need you to work with them some more, tell them more about the Diablos and their organization. If you do this—if you can deliver—they'll take the Diablos gang down."

"Then why hasn't that already been done?"

Dundee sighed. "Because the Diablo biker gang is turning out to be more connected than anyone had thought. Besides the drugs and prostitution rackets you told us about, that gang is tied in pretty tightly with human trafficking and the Mexican cocaine cartels. The Diablos are running product and money up I-35 and across I-40."

"So? Sounds like more reason to take them down."

"If the prosecutor was just after the Diablos, sure. But now he's not just after them. He wants more. Your testimony gives us some of the Diablos through the murder of your friend. Guys who are important to the organization, but they can be replaced. Subsequent investigation has netted us inroads to the trafficking networks, but the prosecutor has to have one to connect the other. You're the connection. That's why the prosecutor's office doesn't want you getting inadvertently burned by the Tulsa PD. We lose you, we lose the house of cards the prosecutor has been building for the last three years. Believe me, nobody wants to give that up."

Pike understood that because the situation had been explained to him dozens of times. In fact, he'd been counting on it to keep him from getting into any serious trouble.

"The prosecutor doesn't want those guys you put away back out on the street either. He's coming up on an election year, and he's not going to settle for getting the small players the Diablos want to dangle out there for him when there's so much more ripe fruit hanging on low branches to be plucked by anybody savvy enough to figure it out." Dundee shrugged. "So that means you have to cool your heels a little longer and let justice take its course."

"Any idea how soon that's going to be? Because justice has been dragging its tail for the last three years."

"All I'm told is soon. And to be ready so I don't have to get ready."

"The DA's getting greedy." Pike shook his head. "I've seen that happen too many times to guys with more on the ball. He's going to screw around and not be able to prove anything."

"No, he'll settle for what he can get soon. Like I said, we've got an election year coming up. He's going to want to put points on the board. Give this thing another few months, Pike. That's all I'm suggesting at this point. Another few months and you'll be done with this."

Pike took in a deep breath and let it out. Listening to Dundee made him feel good, and what the man said made sense, but Pike felt like ants were crawling all over his skin. He needed to be up and moving. The highway was calling.

And even when he was done with his part of the testimony against the Diablos, Petey would still be gone. Being done with his part didn't mean winning.

# 6

**THREE DAYS AFTER HE MASSACRED** the convoy in the Safed Koh mountains, Yaqub led the donkey train carrying the seized cargo down the city's war-torn streets without being challenged. Parachinar was under the auspices of the Kurram Agency, a part of the Federally Administered Tribal Areas of Pakistan. The military policed the city and neighboring regions and patrolled the border, but corruption ran deep.

For a portion of his cargo, Yaqub had tacit permission to conduct business within the city.

Once, Parachinar had been a beautiful place filled with orchards and breathtaking views of the surrounding snowcapped mountains. During that long-ago time, tribesmen had hiked down out of the mountains to winter their livestock. Goats and cattle grazed on the lush green grass that had filled the valley.

Before that, the Mogul emperors had traveled from Delhi, India, to while away lazy summers in Parachinar. That had been back when the land belonged to Afghanistan. These days, it was on the wrong side of the Durand Line, which had been drawn up in 1893 by the British and the Afghan emir, who had truly not had a choice in the matter. Those august beings had transferred the land to British India as a means of appeasement, but it hadn't settled harsh territorial feelings.

That division of land was still hotly contested by Afghanistan and Pakistan, who had later claimed the land. But these days, a loose border between countries benefited both.

Al Qaeda could cross the border into Pakistan and remain relatively secure from Western forces. The Pakistani government gave lip service to the United Nations and other countries about patrolling that border to stop drug trafficking and terrorists, but they didn't strain themselves doing it. In fact, they took considerable profits from those endeavors.

Potholes covered the street like a pestilent disease. Two- and three-story structures lined the thoroughfare, and occasionally Yaqub caught sight of armed men hiding inside rooms. Some of them would be corrupt policemen. Others would be greedy tribesmen looking for an easy mark they could profit from. Some of those would hope for material goods they could take and use or hawk, but others would be watching for information they could sell to the Kurram Agency or to Western intelligence officers on the other side of the Durand Line.

He walked with the AK-47 canted beside him, his eyes watchful and ever moving. Twice before, men in the city had made the mistake of thinking him an easy target. He'd left their bodies lying wherever they had hit the ground, and children had raced out of the shadows to loot the corpses in his wake.

Yaqub had no friends in Parachinar. Only people he did business with.

The air carried the stink of cooked meat and burned wood. Most of the traffic through the city was on foot. A few bicycles whished by on rubber tires, and donkey-drawn carts loaded with sale goods—produce as well as clothing—clattered by on wooden wheels.

Wali halted beside a three-story building that had once housed a hotel in better days. Reconstruction in the city was halfhearted and extremely slow. Spending money to resurrect targets for warring factions was foolish and wasteful, and it cut deeply into those corrupt profits. The hotel's outer wall had been blown away years ago, and canvas had been strung over the gaping hole. All the loose stones had been mined from the wall, stripping it down to the supports. Everyone wanted the extra stones to build with, but no one wanted to accidentally undermine the building and make it fall.

These days, Zulfigar and his sons and grandsons kept watch over the building after claiming it as their own. They defended their property with assault weapons and knives and had shed their own blood as well as that of anyone foolish enough to think they could take the building from them. Zulfigar rented the building out to travelers who stayed in the rooms in the top two floors, and he used the bottom floor as a catchall for anything he wanted to sell—usually things that found their way into his possession.

Yaqub nodded at Wali, and the young man immediately disappeared into the building. In a few minutes, he would be on the rooftop with a pair of binoculars, watching the streets for anyone who might be observing them. And he would be scouting for the American military drones as well. Pakistan enforced the border as much as they could against the Western powers, but the Americans still sent their unmanned aerial vehicles across the border to spy. The Americans knew al Qaeda went there to regroup and train, but they couldn't do much about it without risking an international incident.

Still, if the Americans had a confirmed target that was worth the risk, they would cross the border. Osama bin Laden had discovered that, and he had died for letting down his guard.

As Yaqub neared the canvas-covered wall, Zulfigar stepped out of it into view.

The man was old and fat, but still too mean and canny to die. He was a short man, barely over five feet, but he was almost as broad as he was tall. A fierce mustache and a beard white as the snow on the distant mountains stood out against his dark face. His two-tone brown *pakol* sat at a rakish angle on his head. His *shalwar kameez* covered him in layers of linen down to the American military boots he wore.

Three of Zulfigar's sons or grandsons stood in a loose semicircle behind the old man. They were not as trusting as their progenitor. They kept their weapons at the ready.

"Ah, Yaqub, you have returned safely." Zulfigar peered past Yaqub at the donkeys. "And with so many donkeys."

"I have been blessed by God with a bounty, my friend." Yaqub stopped and waved back at the smelly beasts. "Will my good fortune strain your generosity?"

"Of course not. I am charging you by the head, am I not?"

That hadn't been the agreement, but Yaqub ignored that. The opium cargo had been greater than he'd expected. He could afford to be lavish. He didn't intend to go into the drug business. That was only the means to an end.

Yaqub forced himself to smile. Things went better with Zulfigar if he smiled, and the old man had been useful over the years. "By the head is better than by the foot."

Zulfigar laughed joyously, then turned to the men behind him and ordered them to pull the canvas aside. As the first of the donkeys plodded into the building, he faced Yaqub again. "There is a stall we have set up in the back. Your donkeys will be safe."

"I won't be needing the donkeys. Perhaps you could broker a deal with someone in town to take them off my hands."

The old man pulled at his beard, as if thinking on the matter. Yaqub was certain Zulfigar was thinking more about how much he could charge Yaqub and still pad the amount he was going to sell the donkeys for.

"Yes, I can find you buyers. Some will want the donkeys to eat; others will want to use them as livestock. Are they good donkeys?"

Zulfigar walked over and began patting them with knowing hands as they marched by.

"They have been strong enough to walk through the mountains."

"Good. I should have little trouble finding buyers for such durable animals." Zulfigar glanced at Yaqub. "How soon can I sell them?"

"As soon as you wish."

Inside the building's bottom floor, Zulfigar called out to a half-dozen small boys sorting goods in one corner of the large room. Evidently a fresh load of merchandise had found its way to Zulfigar's door. The children listened attentively as he told them to scour the city for customers.

Once the children had rushed through the canvas and out onto the street, Zulfigar turned back to Yaqub. "How long will you be staying? We never discussed this."

"No more than three days. My business here will be over quickly." These days, Yaqub never dared stay overly long in any one place. The Americans had put a price on his head that was attractive to some who thought they might escape the wrath of the men who followed Yaqub. Zulfigar would never do such a thing because he could make a profit on Yaqub year after year. A one-time payoff wouldn't suit him.

"Have you eaten? That is a long walk down from the mountains."

"Not since morning."

"Then come. Let me feed you." Zulfigar headed toward the stairs.

"I will wait, my friend, until all of my men can be fed." Yaqub never took any special amenities. He lived the same way and with the same benefits his men did, and he fought on the front lines. This garnered their respect.

Zulfigar turned and nodded. "Of course. Give me a few minutes and I can arrange a meal for them as well."

"Thank you." Yaqub chose to be polite, though he knew the price of the meals he and his men took there would be added to Zulfigar's bill.

"While you are here, is anyone looking for you?"

"Of course. The Americans."

Zulfigar waved that away. "They are your enemy. They are always looking for you. Is there anyone new?"

"No. But I am meeting Russians tomorrow." It was better to get that information out of the way quickly. Zulfigar would know soon enough.

The old man's eyes gleamed, and he scowled. "Russians. You know what I say about Russians."

"Never trust the Russians." It was an old litany with Zulfigar. He remembered the days when the Russians had tried to conquer Afghanistan. Zulfigar had lost family in that war, his first wife and two children. "However, in this case I have something the Russians want, and they have something I want. We're making a trade."

Greedily, Zulfigar glanced at the wooden crates Yaqub's men were removing from the backs of the donkeys before the animals were herded into a makeshift pen in the back. Old straw covered the chipped parquet floor. "You already have a buyer for your cargo."

"Yes."

The old man shrugged. "That's too bad. I'm sure I could have found an interested party." And brokered a fee for that service as well.

"Consider it an easy profit, my friend. Since I already have a buyer, that responsibility is lifted from your shoulders. You will still get your cut for providing shelter for us."

"Good. Then because you are my good friend, I will tell you that there is an American CIA team here in the city."

Wariness thrummed through Yaqub. The old man had held back information from him before, thinking each time to sell it off when the time was right. Once before, the knowledge that Zulfigar withheld had resulted in bloodshed, though Yaqub had lost none of his men.

"It is all right, Yaqub. They do not look for you."

"Then what are they looking for?"

Zulfigar gave an exaggerated shrug. "They are Americans. Always nosy. Always poking about in things. It is their nature."

Yaqub thought about that. "How many of them are there?"

"Three. A small team only. They have two Pashtun guides, but the Americans are very good with the language themselves."

"You know where they are?"

Zulfigar grinned. "Of course."

"Perhaps we can come to an arrangement for that information as well."

"I'm sure we can, my friend."

★ ★ ★

At nine o'clock in the morning the next day, Yaqub met with the Russians in a building that was in much better condition than the one Zulfigar had claimed. He had met these Russians before, but Yaqub trusted no one. He was waiting for the day they turned on him, so he arrived at the meeting heavily armed.

Faisal and Wali accompanied him—the former because he spoke Russian much better than Yaqub, and the latter because he was death itself in a closed-in space.

Wali was twenty, but a faster man with a gun or a knife Yaqub had never seen. The young man had a killer instinct as well and never spoke unless he had something to say. He had an old burn scar that mottled the flesh on the left side of his face, and he'd never said where he had gotten it, though Yaqub had come to believe it was something from the man's childhood days. Wali's father was an evil man and had resented the fact that Yaqub had taken the son but not the sire.

"Yaqub, it is good to see you." Pavel Borisov was a giant of a man, six and a half feet tall and broad-shouldered. He had been *spetsnaz*, a member of the USSR's special forces. That had been before the Berlin

Wall fell and before Russia embraced capitalism. Since that time, he had gone into business for himself as a munitions broker, funneling Russia's overstocked arsenal off to terrorists and drug dealers.

A neatly trimmed mustache and goatee punctuated Borisov's lean, wolfish face. He wore clothing that let him blend into the city. His breath smelled of vodka and excess. Four armed men sat on the chairs along the back wall. All of them possessed military bearing and were focused on Yaqub and his two compatriots.

Borisov waved to one of the chairs in the small suite he had commandeered for the meeting. Yaqub sat at the table.

"I know you don't drink, but might I offer you some tea? I have a fresh pot."

"Thank you, no. I have breakfasted this morning. I would rather get to the business we have."

"Of course." Borisov spread his hands. "You have the opium?"

"I do." Yaqub reached under his shirt and took out a small paper-wrapped bundle. He unwrapped the contents and plopped the grayish-black ball onto the scarred table. The lump was almost as big as Yaqub's fist.

Borisov pointed at the lump. "May I?"

Yaqub nodded and dropped his hand into his lap, fingers only inches from the pistol he had hidden there.

Quietly, Borisov produced a clasp knife, opened it, and sliced off a small piece of the opium. The Russian took a small bottle from his pocket and set it on the table. He opened it, then lifted the eyedropper and let a few drops of the clear liquid fall onto the dark tar. Yaqub knew the liquid was Marquis reagent and was used to test for purity of drugs.

Within seconds, the opium lump turned a grayish, reddish brown.

Borisov smiled and looked at Yaqub. "Have you tested this?"

"No."

"It is very pure."

"Then it is worth the price we agreed upon."

The Russian put the bottle in his pocket and leaned back in his chair. "It depends on how much of this you have."

"Several kilos of it."

Borisov ran his fingers through his goatee and smiled. "Good, because what I have for you is very expensive. I think you will be pleased."

"I have enough to cover the price for the materials we agreed on."

"Show me."

Yaqub got up slowly from the table and walked to the window to his left, overlooking an alley two stories below. Four of Yaqub's men guarded a donkey-drawn cart. "Join me."

Borisov approached and peered out, cautiously pulling the curtain to one side. The Russian was not a trustful man and knew that he presented himself as a target. His men knew it too, and they shifted so they would be ready to bring their weapons to bear if need be.

Yaqub motioned with his hand and two of his men below pulled back the canvas tarp to reveal the small wooden boxes the opium had been packed in.

Licking his lips, Borisov nodded toward the cart. "All of the boxes contain opium?"

"Yes."

"Of the same grade?"

"It was all obtained in the same place. You would know about such things more than I would."

"All right." Borisov grinned. "You're very trusting these days, Yaqub. I can remember a time when you would have been much more cagey about trading goods."

Yaqub tapped the windowpane. "Not as trusting as you think, I am afraid."

Across the street, one of Yaqub's fighters briefly stepped into view. The young man held an RPG-7 on his shoulder and was locked onto the window where Yaqub stood.

Borisov stopped grinning and stepped back from the window. Both of them knew the RPG's missile could punch through the window and kill everyone inside.

"I trust, but only so far." Yaqub turned to the Russian. "Now show me what you have."

"Of course." Borisov snapped his fingers at one of the men, who quickly got up and retrieved a metal equipment box lying along the back wall.

Without a word, the man placed the box on the table, flipped the catches, and lifted the lid to reveal a long, slim tube. Below it was another, longer tube that tapered from one end to the other. The second tube was mounted on a pistol grip and measured almost two meters in length.

Drawn by the lethal beauty of the weapon, Yaqub slid his fingers across the greasy surface. The link between him and the destructive power of the device was almost divine. Still, he wanted more. He glanced at Borisov.

"I already have rocket launchers."

The Russian nodded but looked amused. "You do, but not like these. This is a *missile* launcher." He patted the weapon as if it were a faithful steed. "These are very hard to get, and my country would kill me if they knew I was selling them to you. Especially in exchange for opium."

Yaqub didn't know if Borisov was lying or not. Opium flowed across the Durand Line and into Pakistan almost as if by osmosis. From there it was processed into heroin and moved to other places, including Russia, which had a growing heroin problem.

"This is one of the latest man-portable infrared homing missiles designed as a surface-to-air attack weapon. It's called the 9K38 Igla, and once it has been locked onto a target, it fires a missile carrying over a kilo of explosives in its warhead." Borisov modeled an explosion with his hands, placing them together, then breaking them apart with outspread fingers. "Whatever aircraft it hits, that aircraft is coming down."

Excitement flared through Yaqub. Throughout his war against the Westerners, he had never gotten his hands on such a weapon. He kept himself calm.

"How far out can it be used?"

"Just over five kilometers." Borisov grinned. "When your people use those RPGs, which are fine weapons, they are practically in the teeth of your enemies. With the Igla, you're not." He paused. "I should imagine these would be quite the terror against an airfield."

"If you fire them from five kilometers out, the Americans can use their defensive systems. They have very good defensive systems."

Borisov frowned a little at that. "So you trade off. Get closer—not too close—and use them. The missiles travel at eight hundred meters per second."

"The closer my people are, the more likely they will be killed."

"Your people believe in your cause. They have proven time and again that they are ready, willing, and able to die for that cause."

"Yes, but replacing a trained warrior is difficult."

"Then don't waste one of them. The beauty of these missile launchers is that a child could operate one of them. Or an old man. Anyone strong enough to lift it and operate it."

Reaching into the box, Yaqub hefted the launcher into his arms. It was surprisingly light, weighing something over ten kilos. The excitement within him burned more brightly. He replaced the weapon within the box.

"How many of these do you have?"

Borisov held up three fingers. "For the opium you're offering, I'll give you three missile launchers."

Yaqub shook his head, knowing never to take the first offer where the Russians were concerned. They haggled as fiercely as a merchant in a souk. "It is not enough."

Stepping back, Borisov laughed. "Of course it's enough. I'm giving you the power to strike down your enemies, to blast them from the air and kill potentially hundreds of American soldiers. You can become even more feared than you already are."

"You want the opium that I have. I know this. I want the missile launchers, but three is not enough. I want more."

Borisov started to object, but Yaqub cut him off.

"You want to sell those weapons to me. You have been sitting on them here, nervously hoping that I would show up as we agreed, and you have been afraid that someone would find you with the missile launchers. As you have stated, your own countrymen would put you to death for offering these weapons for sale. Once I have them, you can no longer be apprehended with them." Yaqub saw the truth of that in the Russian's blue eyes.

"I have five Iglas."

Yaqub smiled. "For five Iglas, we have a deal."

A frown pulled at the Russian's wolflike features. "I have a deal. *You* have steal."

"There is one other matter I would require some assistance on."

Borisov's eyebrows rose. "You bargain this hard and you expect me to throw in more?"

"Perhaps it will benefit us both." Yaqub ran his hands over the missile launcher's case. "I have been told there is a CIA team in the city. I want them."

"You can kill them yourself. Why ask me?"

"Because I want to take these men alive. I have a use for them."

# 7

**"GUESS THE COPS** are still interested in you."

Lying on a creeper under a Chevy Silverado pickup with four-wheel drive, Pike caught the vehicle's edge and slid out into the open garage. Monty had put a hurricane fan in the corner to help circulate the air now that spring was starting to return to the city. In a few more weeks, working conditions in the garage would escalate north of miserable.

Monty stood between the Silverado and a Toyota Camry that was in for a brake job. The pickup needed a new transmission because the young driver couldn't stay away from off-roading with his buddies, and Daddy's wallet hadn't gone flat. Seeing how the truck and the father were being treated irritated Pike, so he was working on other vehicles in between to slow down the return time. The young driver was calling daily.

Pike didn't bother looking across the street to the small diner he and Monty sometimes ordered takeout from. Usually they ate what Monty's wife fixed them for lunch, but she knew they both enjoyed the diner's meat loaf Mondays.

The two-man detail assigned to watch over Pike had been there since he'd gotten back from his trip to Tulsa. They stuck out like sore thumbs. So much for whatever pull the federal prosecutor thought he had in the area. Pike hadn't bothered calling Dundee to let him know that whatever request had gone through the channels was being ignored. The crack house was still out of business, and repairs hadn't even started on the place, so everything was fine.

Pike wiped his hands on a grease rag. "Guess they are. Must be a slow day for crime fighters."

Monty handed Pike a cold beer from the chest they kept in the office. It was after three, and they would knock off in another couple hours. Monty had to coach a Little League baseball game. Pike figured he would hang out at the garage and tinker for a while on Mrs. Garcia's car because he didn't have anything else to do and he was restless. If he went back to his apartment, he'd be crawling the walls.

"I think they don't like you because they think you're doing what they can't."

Pike took a long drink but didn't say anything.

Monty hunkered down, sliding against the Toyota till he was in a sitting position. He rested his elbows on his drawn-up knees and dangled his beer can from his grease-stained fingers. He appeared hesitant, and that wasn't like Monty.

More attentive now because Pike liked the guy and what he brought to his family and to the community, Pike watched Monty struggle with his thoughts for a moment. Monty didn't usually do that. Usually he was a straight-ahead kind of thinker. Pike had watched Monty struggle more over figuring out his hitting lineup before a game than anything else. He kept his life on the straight and narrow. The garage owner had some bad stuff locked away in his closet from his younger years, but Pike didn't meet many people with clean hands.

"Something on your mind?"

Monty knuckled sweat from his eyebrow and grimaced. "Yeah. Shouldn't be, but there is."

"What?"

Taking a deep breath, Monty looked at Pike. "Those cops are talking like you lit up that crack house a few nights ago."

"Yeah."

"It's not my business—I know that."

Pike knew that too, but he also knew that Monty was about to make it his business.

"I don't want to ask, Pike, but I got to."

Pike took another sip of beer, relished the coolness of it against the dry heat and the taste of burned oil and hydraulic fluid that pervaded the garage, and thought about how he was going to answer. He respected Monty too much to lie.

"Do you really want to know?"

"Yeah, I think I need to. It's my family, Pike, and my garage. If those things are in the line of fire from some gangbangers, I need to know."

"Yeah, I burned it down."

"Figured you did when the cops come nosing around here, but I wanted to be sure."

"Now you're sure."

"Why?"

"It needed burning. People around here were getting hurt. Nobody seemed to be able to do anything to stop them. So I stopped them."

"You can't just do that."

"It's easier than you think."

"You could have been killed."

"I wasn't." Pike took another sip and felt like the ground was suddenly treacherous underfoot. There were two ways this conversation might go, and he wasn't holding out for a fairy-tale ending.

"I couldn't do what you did, Pike."

Pike didn't say anything.

"I knew about the crack house." Hurt showed in Monty's eyes. "I just kept trying to ignore it. Like everybody else around here. But I couldn't quit thinking about it. My kids are young right now, but I know that sooner or later they're gonna be old enough to be prey for those dealers. Thinking like that makes me sick."

Pike nodded.

"I've even called in to the police about the crack house. Twice. Reported what I was seeing. The police came around, but they never caught anybody doing anything. Exercise in futility. But I kept thinking about my kids and wondering what was going to happen. Then I found out that the place had burned up. I felt pretty good about it. Figured it was rival action between gangs, but it was all the same to me because it was out of business." Monty paused. "Then the police came around accusing you of setting that fire and running those guys out of the building."

"I didn't mean to bring any of this down on you, brother." Pike spoke softly and felt a big knot in his chest.

"I know, but I'm worried about it."

"You want me to pull up stakes, Monty?" Pike knew he had to ask the question, but he dreaded the answer. This garage and that apartment weren't home. He'd never had anyplace that he'd truly called home, but the idea of leaving everything was unsettling. "Is that what you're working up to? Because if it is, just say the word and I won't think badly of you for it."

Surprise twisted Monty's big face. "No, man, that's not what I'm getting at here. It's just that if the police suspect you burned that crack house down, them drug dealers are gonna get around to figuring things out too, you know?"

"Yeah."

"I don't want you to leave, Pike. I talked it over with my wife, told her what the cops suspected and what I thought was going on, and I asked her what she thought about everything too."

"She wants the kids safe. She wants you safe. That's understandable." Mentally, Pike started packing his tools, figuring out how much of them he could take today and how much would have to wait till he brought his truck down, and how much he'd have to just leave. The witness protection guys would be happy. They could tuck him in some other out-of-the-way place.

"Nope. That's not it either. She wants you to stay as much as I do. The garage is more profitable; I'm happier working; she don't have to worry about me getting hurt while I'm here on my own. Truth to tell, if you could help me figure out how to get Raheed out of his batting slump, life couldn't be better. But I want to make some changes around here."

Pike was lost. The conversation hadn't gone at all the way he thought it was going to go. "Changes?"

"Yeah, I'm gonna plow some of those profits we've been making into putting up a security system. Maybe a closed-circuit TV system. Thought maybe I'd up the security at my house, too. You know, in case somebody wants to try something there."

"I'm sorry, Monty." Pike felt bad at having forced his friend into a bunker mentality. That was the problem with being close to anybody outside his own skin. They paid a price too. He hadn't even thought about that when he'd gone into that crack house.

"Don't be, brother. I've been wanting to upgrade the security around the house anyway." Monty grinned. "With all the extra work you pull in, I bought a big-screen TV, some new game consoles for the kids, and I gave a few hundred dollars for a couple of really sweet big-barrel bats for the team. I got stuff I want to protect anyway. I just wanted you to know I'd be asking for help with the installs, if that's okay."

Pike didn't really know how to feel. On the one hand, he was glad he wasn't moving. On the other, Monty being this open with him made him nervous and uncomfortable. It reminded Pike of all the times in foster homes when other kids had wanted to be his friends. He'd learned the hard way that those kids belonged to the foster parents, and there was a big difference between a biological kid and a foster kid. At the end of his time there, they'd pack Pike's stuff in a little backpack and send him back into the system.

That had been when he was young enough to still be looking for a family. By the time he was ten, he'd quit looking and had known he was just a meal ticket for foster parents to occasionally punch. Till he got to be too uncontrollable. Then he'd stayed at the orphanage. At least that way he had consistency in his life that he hadn't had up till then.

Having Monty accept him in spite of the potential trouble he was bringing down on them was troublesome. Pike felt like he owed the man something, and he didn't like owing anyone anything.

"Yeah, I'll help."

Monty smiled. "I hope you're willing to work for beer and tamales, 'cause I can't pay you for your time."

"Then it's a good thing your wife makes good tamales."

"Don't forget the fried ice cream. She makes good fried ice cream too."

Pike saluted Monty with the beer can. "She does."

Monty nodded toward the Silverado. "You got that tranny ready to go?"

"Yeah."

"Want a hand with it?"

"Sure." Pike lobbed the empty beer can into a nearby trash bin, lay back on the creeper, and slid under the truck.

★   ★   ★

"Hey, looks like it's schooltime."

Looking up from under Mrs. Garcia's hood, Pike peered toward the front of the garage and saw Hector walking toward him and Monty. The boy had a troubled expression on his face.

"Now that's true unhappiness if I ever saw it." Monty wrapped more black electrician's tape on the piece of wiring they'd spliced into Mrs. Garcia's vehicle.

Pike grimaced. "It's that new math."

"Math." Monty shook his head and kept taping. "Better you than me, man. I'm good with history and geography, but I suck at math."

"I can tell from the way you tote up those accounts sometimes."

"I got a good wife. She can cook, wrangle kids, and keep my bookkeeping straight. She's a multitasker, is what she is."

Pike straightened up so Hector could see him. Immediately the boy changed directions and headed for him.

"Hector's good at figuring problems out and getting the answers, but he doesn't show all his work." Pike dipped out a handful of grease cleaner from a bucket on the worktable at the back of the garage and cleaned his hands. "Got an aptitude for it and the teacher doesn't have time to help him."

"Go on. I can finish up here. Then I gotta make some calls. Get some of these patched clunkers back to their owners."

"Thanks. I'm probably gonna be working late tonight, so I'll make up for any lost time."

"Sure. Go ahead. Maybe when Hector gets a little older, I can hire him to be my accountant. That'll make the missus happy."

"I'm going to take him over to the diner. We can get a table there and spread out."

Monty nodded.

"Hello, Mr. Pike." With a frustrated sigh, Hector held out his thick math book. "It is this thing again. My teacher is still unhappy with me." He opened the book and took out a sheaf of papers that had been marked up with enough red pencil that they looked like they were hemorrhaging.

"What's going on?"

"She says I work too fast and don't show the steps again." Hector sighed. "Showing all the steps is boring. The math is too easy."

"Sure, I get that. Mechanic work is too easy too. Remember me telling you that?"

"Yes."

"A mechanic has to be methodical in what he's doing. One step at a time. If he doesn't, he's liable to leave something out that's important and cause a bigger problem than he started with. We've been over this."

"I know." Hector looked forlorn. "This is why you take screws out of a part and put them in a small cup. So they stay together."

"That's right." Hector had been watching Pike work on cars for months. The kid was bright, always learning. "That's what you have to do when you take a math problem apart: keep all the bits and pieces in their proper places." Pike dropped his rag onto the worktable. "Let's go over to the diner. Get you a Coke. Then we'll take a look at those papers."

# 8

"**WHEN YOU GO** through the door, Hasan, there must be no hesitation. If you hesitate, you may well die. Do you understand?"

Hasan nodded, but Yaqub could see the fear in the boy's eyes. Hasan believed in God and he believed in Yaqub, but he did not yet believe in himself. That was the gift Yaqub intended to give him today.

The boy was fourteen, older than Yaqub had been when his father had first placed a rifle in his hands and taught him to kill the Russian soldiers who had invaded Afghanistan. Yaqub had only been eleven, but he had been blessed with a love of his God, a desire to see his enemies killed, and steady hands.

Leaning down so that his face was level with the boy's, Yaqub held Hasan's gaze with his own. "You will not hesitate, for I have chosen you to be one of my warriors. You are one of the few that I permit to follow me wherever I go. Do you understand this?"

"I understand." Hasan's voice cracked. "I will not fail you."

"You will not fail me because you will not fail God. Do you understand?"

The boy nodded.

"You serve God, as I do, and we have been given the task of ridding our country of the Westerners who would kill us and destroy our faith. This is not to be allowed."

"I will not allow it."

"Good, and know that if the time should come that you must give your life in pursuit of serving God, you will ascend immediately to heaven and know delights that will never be yours here in this world."

"I know these things, Mullah."

Yaqub smiled and once more stood straight. "Of course you do. I have taught them to you." He turned from the boy and stared at the building across the street where the CIA team was holed up.

It was early morning. The sun was only now lighting the sky in the east. Pedestrians filled Parachinar's streets, all of them wanting to finish their morning chores and shopping so they could get back inside and escape the chill that had fallen from the mountains.

Running the Americans to ground had taken only a few hours. Zulfigar's grandsons proved very adroit at scouting through the streets. The question remained, however, whether they had accomplished their goal without alerting their quarry.

The three Americans and their two Pashtun guides stayed to the shadows of the city, but they were foreigners and foreigners got noticed in Parachinar, no matter how desperately they tried to fit in. Yaqub still did not know what the CIA team's objective was, but that did not truly matter. His objective superseded their goal.

Now that he had the missile launchers, Yaqub needed the bait to set his trap. The American spies could serve as a distraction.

Standing inside a small store on the corner of the street across from the CIA agents, Yaqub saw Borisov step out onto the street. Once Yaqub had explained the Russian's part in the subterfuge, Borisov hadn't been enthusiastic, but he had agreed.

Yaqub turned to Hasan. "Remember, warrior, that you are doing God's work, that you are smiting his enemies."

"I will." Hasan seemed more calm now that the moment was upon them.

Yaqub remembered that feeling too, when the first Russian soldier had settled into the sights of the old single-shot rifle he had carried into battle. He could still remember the man's face—the young features before the bullet had struck him, and the bloody ruin that it had become. Over the years, his appetite for the blood of his enemies had only grown stronger.

"Do not meet their gaze, Hasan. Look at their hands, their bodies, the way they stand. Eyes can lie to you and make you the fool. But a man's body will reveal his truth to you."

"I know." The boy gave a small nod. "You have taught me."

"Today will be the proof of your ability to be a warrior in God's name."

"I know this also."

"Then do not fail. And do not kill the Americans unless you have to. I want them alive."

"It shall be as you say."

"Good. Then let's go."

Hasan, looking small and frail, followed Yaqub. Yaqub had chosen the boy for his task because he looked so vulnerable—not even the slightest hint of beard growth—and yet he was a crack shot, one of Wali's finest pupils. Yaqub had instructed the boy's faith, but Wali had coached him in handling guns and knives, intending him to be a bodyguard for their leader in public places. Hasan would be able to pass as his son, not another man.

Borisov stood his ground at the corner. "Five of them. Just as you said. Three American agents and two Pashtuns."

"Good. What have you told them?"

"That I was supplying you with munitions." Borisov started walking back into the building. "They were not surprised. I have history of doing such business. Sometimes I have sold to the CIA when agents needed weapons that would allow them to blend into the surrounding countryside."

"Do you know any of these men in the room?"

"No."

That was good. That meant they would not be able to read Borisov in any way.

"It occurs to me that I will need to have a reason for surviving this encounter." Borisov crossed the big room and headed up the narrow steps against one wall.

"If asked later, you can say that you were ransomed back to your companions."

"Just make sure that you really sell this. I do not want to appear on the CIA's terminate-on-sight lists."

"All will be well. Draw your weapon as we discussed. I will take care of the rest."

"Wali is across the street?"

"Yes. With a sniper rifle. No harm will come to you." Yaqub followed the Russian up the steps with Hasan at his heels.

Stomach knotting as he watched the action playing out from the control center in Creech Air Force Base, Captain David Carter presented a calm exterior to his cyber team. Everyone in the room knew what the stakes were. Zalmai Yaqub was near the top of the most wanted al Qaeda terrorists. If they could bring Yaqub down, alive or dead, it would be a feather in Carter's cap, a certain commendation in his file.

In his late thirties with neatly cropped brown hair and freckles, Carter was one of the oldest people in the room. Most of the cyber specialists piloting the unmanned aerial vehicles were just out of high school or in their early twenties.

When the UAV pilots weren't in the control center pulling reconnaissance, waiting for that instance when they got to fire a kill shot with either a rifle-equipped or bomb-equipped, they were usually piled in someone's house racking up kills in Halo, Counter-Strike, or other online video games. The gaming was good training for the jobs they held in the control center, and the United States Air Force had chosen these individuals for those very skills.

"Prentiss, do we have an ID on the individual with Yaqub?"

"Negative." Prentiss was twenty, a blonde who probably broke hearts all over the base. When she wasn't breaking hearts, she was shattering egos. She was rumored to be pure death on every console game known to man. With rapt attention, she studied the flat-screen panels in front of her.

She held a joystick in her steady hand, controlling the General Atomics MQ-9 Reaper flying high recon over Parachinar, Pakistan. The drone was relaying a satellite link from the CIA team embedded in the country.

Not so long ago, the Pakistanis had booted the CIA drone base out of Shamsi Airfield. The spy agency hadn't been set back. They were organizing new drone bases inside Afghanistan and farming some of their work out to the Air Force. Most of those assignments were scut work, but the apprehension of Yaqub was a career builder.

"I got a partial face as they entered ground zero. One of the CIA team sent me the image."

Ground zero was the building where the CIA team lay in wait for Yaqub.

The main screen in front of Prentiss was a top-down view from the Reaper. The UAV circled overhead at twelve thousand feet, less than half of its possible operational altitude. The onboard cameras were nothing short of spectacular. The cost of the MQ-9 was $36 million-plus per unit. With the present magnification, it was possible to easily scan the rooftops.

On the screen to Prentiss's right, a face was slowly taking shape. As she had said, the image was only a partial, shot from the side, but the computer program was extrapolating the data and slowly guessing what the other profile looked like based on the image. When it was finished, it would build the frontal view of the face; then that would be run through facial-recognition databases.

"He looks like a boy. Maybe ten years old." Prentiss spoke quickly, absorbed by the control of the UAV.

"You sure about the age?"

"Pretty sure. I have a younger brother about the same age."

Carter watched Yaqub, the Russian, and the boy disappear into the building. If the boy wasn't known now, he'd be known later. Everything they were getting, they were uploading to intelligence databases throughout the United States.

"Have we confirmed the Russian?"

"Affirmative. His name is Pavel Borisov. One-time *spetsnaz*–turned–black market weapons dealer. Apparently the Durand Line is one of the places he does regular business."

"And nobody's put a leash on this guy?"

"He's a killer. Runs with a hard crew."

"How did the CIA get onto him?"

"They aren't saying."

Carter accepted that. Silence on the CIA's end only meant that they did business with Borisov themselves. "The Russian just shows up to the CIA agents, says, 'I've got Yaqub—were you looking for him?'"

"That's pretty much it."

Although Carter had been in intelligence long enough to know that such things did happen, he'd also been in the business long enough to know that sure things could sometimes still go awry.

But that was why the Reaper program was so important. Even if Yaqub somehow got away, the man couldn't escape from UAV recon. The al Qaeda leader was hosed now. Yaqub just didn't know it.

# 9

**"DID THEY MAKE** you go to school in juvie? Or did you just learn how to cook while you were there?"

Startled, Pike took a moment to figure out his response. He and Hector sat in one of the booths at the diner. The boy's math book lay open in front of them, and Pike was studying one of the homework sheets that was bleeding red. He looked at Hector.

"They make you go to school in juvie."

"Real school or juvie school?"

"Both sometimes."

Hector's eyes rounded. "At the same time? Amigo, that's a lot of school!"

Surprising himself, Pike laughed. Sometimes that was how it went with Hector. The boy could make him laugh no matter how bad things were. And considering that the Tulsa PD plainclothes guys were still in the diner with them and that Monty was going to be spending money upgrading his house security, things were pretty bad.

"Not at the same time, buddy. Sometimes I went to regular school. Sometimes I went to juvie school."

"Which was better?"

"Regular school."

"Why?"

"Because there were girls in regular school."

Hector grimaced and stuck out his tongue. "Girls are loco."

"Trust me, there's gonna come a time when you don't mind so much."

"My sister is *muy* loco. She makes all the guys around her so mad, but they keep coming back. It is *estúpido*."

"That's what you've said." Pike turned back to the page of homework.

"What was juvie like?"

Pike was conscious of the boy's body warmth next to his. Normally he didn't like anyone invading his personal space, but having Hector around reminded him of how it had been when he and Petey were young. That was the only time he'd ever felt close to anyone. He didn't like the way Hector's being there, talking to him, kept bringing those memories back. Remembering those times was like juggling shards of glass. He'd put that old pain away.

"Juvie was a pain in the—" Pike stopped himself short, remembering who he was with. "Juvie was a pain. Why are you asking so many questions about that?"

"Because until you said it the other day, I didn't know where you were from."

"Oh."

"Tell me some stories."

"Stories about what?"

"About what it was like there. When you were little. Like me. My mom sometimes tells me stories about when she was a little girl."

"She probably has good stories to tell." Pike only remembered all the foster homes, the fights, the harsh authority, and the prophecies of doom and gloom that everyone wanted to promise him because of his attitude. The way he remembered it, his distant attitude—his willingness to be a loner—was the only thing that had gotten him through those times. He'd remained a loner. If he never made the mistake of depending on somebody, no one could disappoint him or hurt him, and even lies didn't matter because he didn't believe anything anyone ever told him.

"No, her stories are all boring. Except for the one when she had me in the hospital and brought me home."

"You like that one, do you?"

"Yeah. That's a good one. Very funny."

"I'll bet it is."

"You should come to dinner some night and let my mom tell it to you."

Thinking that might ever happen left Pike feeling awkward. He didn't like being around families. Monty had asked him over for dinner and even to Little League games on several occasions. Pike had always claimed prior commitments or a work thing he wanted to finish up. Gradually Monty had figured out that dinner with the family wasn't going to happen and had let it go. Nobody's feelings had gotten hurt. "Your mom and I both work late, Hector. I wouldn't want her to have to fix dinner for me. She comes home tired."

"She can make my sister fix dinner."

"I don't think your sister would be too happy about it either. Besides, like I said, I work a lot."

"You're not working now."

"Only because I'm helping you with your homework. People depend on me to get their cars fixed."

"Like Mrs. Garcia."

Pike nodded. "Yeah. Exactly like Mrs. Garcia." He slid the homework paper over to the boy. "Take a look at this problem and rework it."

Without complaint, Hector took the paper and reworked the problem. He wrote down the numbers without hesitation, speeding through the steps without missing one.

Pike looked over the work. "Good job. Why didn't you do this the first time?"

Hector lifted his thin shoulders and let them drop. "I don't know. It's easier doing math when you're here."

"Uh-huh."

Narrowing his eyes, Hector studied him suspiciously. "You sure you don't have any good stories from when you were a kid?"

"No."

"Not even one?"

"I lived. I got out of there. That's a pretty good story."

"The juvie people let you out?"

"No. I let myself out."

"How?"

Pike looked at the boy and put on a serious face. "One night I was very sneaky."

Hector laughed. "Like a ninja?"

"Just like a ninja. I escaped and never went back." Pike tapped the homework. "C'mon. We gotta pay attention here."

The server who had been taking care of them came back to their table. She brought a fresh soft drink for Hector and a glass of tea for Pike. She smiled as she put the glasses on the table. "Hi, Pike."

"Hi." Pike felt guilty because he didn't know the woman's name. With everything that had been going on the last few days, he was getting irritated at how his everyday life was becoming complicated and starting to chafe. Everybody was a lot more involved with him than he liked them to be. He wanted things to go back to the way they had been, when he was a stranger to the neighborhood and the neighborhood treated him like an outsider. Things had been less tense then.

The server nodded at the papers. "Math?"

"Yeah."

"I never liked math. Too many numbers, and when they started getting to be imaginary, I just got completely lost."

Hector looked up at her and grinned. "Math's okay, but I like reading best. Especially the imaginary parts."

"Is that right?" The server was about Pike's age, but she was too slim and too pale. She worked a lot of evening and night shifts. Pike had noticed her over the last few months. She usually stuck to the job, only talking to the other servers and to guests. He recognized the hurt child in her because he'd grown up around that and knew what to look for, but he didn't know her story. He just knew that there was a story. More than that, he didn't want to know her story. He'd heard it all before. It wasn't special to anybody but her. She'd learn.

"Yep. When I grow up, I'm going to write stories."

"Well, look at you." The server gave him a big smile. "I can tell people I knew you before you got to be a celebrity."

"Yep."

The waitress ruffled Hector's hair and looked at Pike. "Let me know if you need anything else."

He nodded, and she continued on her rounds. Getting special attention from the waitress bothered him. He liked coming into the diner, getting something to eat there or taking something to go in those Styrofoam containers. A business transaction without any strings, nothing social. He didn't want to be visible while he was there.

Hector hadn't given up. "Did you have a friend when you were in juvie?"

Pike considered the question, wanting to put an end to all the curiosity but not wanting to hurt Hector's feelings. "Maybe talking about juvie isn't such a good idea."

"Why?"

"A lot of people don't like guys who were in juvie."

"Why?"

"Because people think guys who went to juvie were bad guys."

"Why?"

"Because most of them are."

"You're not a bad guy." Hector smiled and shook his head as if that were the weirdest idea he'd ever heard. "You fix people's cars and you're in the Army."

"Marines." That correction was out of Pike's mouth before he knew it. He took more pride in being a Marine than he wanted to some days.

"Okay, Marines. But you're not a bad guy." Hector frowned and lowered his voice. "But we don't have to talk about juvie anymore."

"Good." Pike sipped his tea.

"You didn't answer the question."

"What question?"

"Did you have a friend when you were a kid?"

Pike thought about that and didn't want to shut the boy down again. "Yeah, I had a friend."

"What was his name?"

"Petey."

"That's a weird name."

Pike chuckled. "Yeah, I guess it was, but that was what everybody called him."

"Was he cool?"

"Big-time cool. Coolest guy I ever knew."

"Are you still friends?"

That hurt more than Pike expected it to, probably because Hector asked with such innocence and there was so much guilt associated with all of that, but Pike quickly covered it up. "Petey died."

A shocked and embarrassed look filled Hector's face. "I'm sorry. I shouldn't have been asking so many questions."

"No, it's okay." Pike told the boy that, but it really wasn't okay.

The argument with the witness protection program attorney was still fresh in his mind, and it had brought back those old memories of Petey lying there bleeding out in Pike's arms. Pike had tried in vain to stop the bleeding, but he didn't have enough hands and there hadn't been anyone else around. In the end, all he'd been able to do was hold Petey till he was gone, just slipped right through Pike's fingers while he was trying to get him to the hospital and left him alone all over again. No one ever stayed.

"Do you miss him?" Hector spoke only a little above a whisper.

"I do."

Hector hesitated for a moment, then plowed on with what was on his mind. "Does he talk to you?"

"No." Pike didn't know where the kid got that. Dead people didn't talk. They were dead; then they were in the ground or burned up, and they were gone forever. That was what being dead meant.

"I just wondered because my mom says that sometimes people you love talk to you when you need them most. She says her mom has talked to her even though she was already with the angels. That's part of the story of when I was born. My grandmother spoke to my mom and told her that I was going to be special."

"You are special, kiddo."

"You are too, Pike." Briefly, Hector looked at him as if expecting him to say something else, but Pike didn't know what to say. The whole conversation had made him uncomfortable and angry, and he felt like he had when he'd been trapped in juvie, just waiting till he had something he could fight back against.

"Let's get to your homework. It's late. Your mom will be home soon and she'll be worried about you. And I got Mrs. Garcia's car to work on some more."

"Okay." Hector turned his attention to the math.

At the front of the diner, the plainclothes detectives evidently decided that watching Pike teach math to a third grader was boring. Or maybe they were just getting off shift. They got up together, with a final look at Pike, and headed out the door.

For a few minutes, Hector worked quietly. Pike felt the old anger moving around inside him and tried to get it in hand, but it was whipping around like a broke-back rattler. He gazed at the boy and wondered how he could be so at peace with himself and his life when it was really hard. A missing father. An older sister who was about to leave the nest. A mother who worked too much because she had to in order to make ends meet. The kid's balance sheet was stacked against him.

Yet . . . here he was. Doing his homework. Learning from somebody his mother shouldn't even let him hang around with. Pike didn't know why Hector's mother let the boy come around the garage. He figured maybe she just didn't know what the kid was doing. She couldn't control Hector if she wasn't there.

The bell over the diner's door jangled, followed almost immediately by brief cursing from one of the female servers.

Pike glanced at the door and saw four men about his age enter the diner. They wore their hair long, trailing down their necks and brushing their shoulders. All four were clad in jeans, dirty baseball caps, and shirts with the sleeves torn off, their arms splotched with tattoos and their faces covered in beards and mustaches that had been allowed to grow untended.

One of them, a tall, rawboned man with pale skin that Pike guessed was a prison pallor, looked around the diner and spotted the server who had been taking care of Pike and Hector. The man wore his shirt open to midchest. An arrowhead necklace lay against the hollow of his throat. Two tattooed tears were on his cheek under his left eye.

The man looked at the server, who had drawn up into herself and frozen like a deer in headlights. She stared at the man like she couldn't believe he was standing there.

"I got out, Teresa, and you weren't there." The man smiled, but there was no humor in the expression. "Of course, I wasn't really expecting you to be. You ain't been to see me in over a year, and you said you wasn't coming back."

"Carl." Teresa's voice was strained, part hoarse whisper. "You ain't supposed to be here."

"Why? This here's a fine public establishment. Open to anybody that's got money in his pocket. I got money." Carl pulled out a wrinkled twenty-dollar bill.

Teresa shook her head, and unshed tears glimmered in her eyes. "You don't want to do this, Carl. Truly, you don't. You just got out."

Tendons strained in Carl's neck, and color flamed up from his chest to his face. "I *know* I just got out. Who do you think spent the last three years in that hole? Sure wasn't you. You pled out when the cops came snooping around. Let me go down by myself. You didn't mind spending all that money the meth brought in when I was cooking, though, did you?"

Tears leaked from Teresa's eyes, but she still didn't move a muscle.

Beside Pike, Hector got tense as a board. Instinctively, Pike dropped a protective arm over the boy's thin shoulders. "It's gonna be okay, kiddo."

Hector didn't say anything.

Carl grinned, and the expression looked like it had been carved onto his face. "Now I'm back, and I want to be fed. So get over here and take my order."

Teresa didn't move.

One of the other servers at the pass-through window turned to talk to someone. "Call the cops. Quick."

With one long stride, Carl crossed the space between himself and

Teresa. He wrapped a long-fingered, black-taloned hand around her elbow and yanked her toward the nearest table. "I said, get over here and take my order."

"No." Teresa fought back against him, but he was too strong. He dragged her to the table. Then she clawed his arm with her free hand, slicing streamers of blood along his forearm and wrist.

Carl cursed, released her, and backhanded her with surprising speed. The blow knocked her from her feet and she went down flat on her back. Blood trickled from the corner of her mouth and she cried, wrapping her arms around her head in a learned response as she curled up into a ball.

Pike was out of the booth and moving even as Carl drew back a boot to kick the woman. Carl saw him coming and grinned. "You shacked up with her? Coming over here to protect—?"

Without a word, Pike walked straight up to the man and hit him in the mouth. Talking to Carl would have only been a waste of time and left Pike open to an attack. The man had come into the diner looking for a fight and obviously wasn't going to leave until he had one.

The impact from Pike's blow staggered Carl and knocked him backward. Surprisingly, he remained on his feet, and Pike realized the man was made of sterner stuff than he'd first thought. He hadn't pulled his punch.

Watching the man, never taking his eyes from him, Pike reached down and helped Teresa to her feet. He pushed her toward the back of the diner and slipped into place between her and Carl.

The man stood there, and this time maniacal amusement lit his face. He wiped at the blood running from his nose and his burst lips. Crimson stained his teeth. "Well, now, that was a mistake. You wanted a piece of this? Now I'm gonna get me a piece of you." He pulled a lockback knife from his belt and flicked it open in a glimmer of steel. Light splintered from the razor-sharp edge.

Pike stood loose and easy, resting on the balls of his feet, his hands open at his sides.

"Got nothing to say?" Carl came forward and took a few swipes with the blade, obviously intending to scare Pike with the weapon.

Instead, Pike crossed the distance between them in one step, grabbed Carl's knife wrist in his left hand, and held it locked there. Then he punched Carl in the face three times in quick succession, finishing up with a jab to the throat that he pulled to keep from killing the man only because he didn't want to do something like that in front of Hector. Personally, Pike figured the man was a waste of breath. Erasing him from the face of the planet wouldn't be a bad thing.

Carl swayed drunkenly, his beer-tainted breath smelling harsh as kerosene. Pike grabbed the man's shirt, stepped into him again, and kneed him in the crotch. As Carl sagged, Pike controlled him with the captured wrist, twisting the arm till he shoved his opponent facedown on the floor. He took the knife away as Carl's three buddies started to move forward.

Pike glared at them and they froze, holding their hands up in surrender.

Then the front door banged open. As it turned out, the two plain-clothes detectives had evidently been talking in the parking lot and had seen the violence break out. They came in pointing guns and yelling, flashing badges. "Tulsa police! Down on the floor!"

One of them pointed his weapon at Pike.

Pike didn't argue. He placed the captured knife on the floor and slid it away. Then he lay down and waited for them to handcuff him. As he lay there feeling the steel cuffs bite into his flesh, he almost laughed. It was the first time all day that he'd felt like his old self.

# 10

BORISOV LED THE WAY to the room where the CIA agents lay in wait. Yaqub followed the man and felt himself calm almost to the point of numbness. He silently prayed and readied himself to take the lives of his enemies if the situation called for that, but he hoped that it did not. Live CIA agents were much better than dead ones.

One of the CIA men lounged at the end of the hallway just as Borisov had advised them. The man made an effort to not notice them, to continue looking out the nearby window. That wasn't a true reaction. A man who had been in the hallway with nothing but time on his hands would have looked to see who had arrived.

Borisov used his key to open the door. After all, this was supposed to be his room, the place where he was conducting business with Yaqub. The Russian stepped back from the open door and waved Yaqub inside.

Heart pounding smoothly behind his sternum and pulsing at his ears, Yaqub entered the room as though he suspected nothing.

Dressed in *shalwar kameez* and *pakols*, the two remaining CIA agents sat at a table in the center of the room. Though one of the men was black and the other man was heavily tanned, Yaqub could see their nationality stamped into their features. They had lived lives of comfort, and Yaqub despised them for that. Americans warred with impunity in Afghanistan, forcing everyone to heel under their tyranny and their godlessness. There was no disguise for that.

Their Pashtun guides sat on a couch against the wall to the left. The room was small and neat, but it had seen better days a long time ago. The stink of cigarettes and hashish clung to the yellowed walls.

Yaqub stopped only a few feet into the room. Hasan was just behind him. The al Qaeda leader let suspicion show on his face, knowing that in this next moment he might die, but God would have the virgins waiting for him for dying in this holiest of wars.

The CIA agents exploded into action, unable to keep themselves still. They pulled pistols from their clothing.

"Hold it right there, Yaqub! Raise your hands or you're a dead man!"

Even as weapons filled the Americans' hands, though, Hasan was faster still. As Yaqub raised his hands, the boy stepped slightly around the al Qaeda leader and fired immediately.

Yaqub kept himself still, trusting his faith and Hasan's skill. The boy proved to be spectacular. His bullets tore at the flesh of the Americans, punching into their legs and arms. A round struck one of the CIA agents in the hand.

The second man got off one shot before he went down, but he too fell as his wounded legs buckled under him.

Yaqub leaped forward and grabbed the pistol from the wounded man. As he stood, he turned the weapon on the Pashtun guides still seated on the couch. Neither of those men looked like they knew what they needed to do. Yaqub shot them both in the face, dropping their corpses to the couch.

Turning, Yaqub spotted Hasan lying on the floor, his brown eyes wide in surprise. Blood spread from the center of his chest, growing as Yaqub watched.

"Hasan!" Forgetting himself for a moment, thinking only of the boy's loss, Yaqub dropped to his knees beside Hasan. As he saw the spreading pool of blood, Yaqub knew there was nothing he could do. Hasan was dying. Crimson bubbles burst across the boy's lips as his face visibly paled during a shaky, forced breath.

Borisov cursed in his native language and clawed for the pistol in his pocket. He couldn't get it out before the last CIA agent filled the doorway. Almost as soon as the man appeared, though, he stumbled back and his right arm went limp, dropping the pistol he'd held in his hand. Blood gushed from a wound high up on his arm.

Reacting instantly, Borisov finished drawing his pistol, then swung the weapon in a backhanded blow that slammed against the CIA agent's forehead. Unconscious immediately, the man sank bonelessly to the ground.

"Mullah." Hasan's voice was so weak it was almost inaudible.

Resting his hand on the boy's shoulder, Yaqub knelt over him, leaning in close so he could hear him. "Yes."

"Did I only wound them?"

"You did. You were amazing, Hasan. Truly, God has blessed you."

With a final shudder, Hasan relaxed in death. His pupils bloomed in his eyes till there was no color left, and nothing of the boy remained in his body.

Praying, Yaqub closed the boy's eyes, then stood and looked through the window to see Wali leaving the opposite building and crossing the street.

One of the CIA agents moaned as he clutched his maimed hand.

Wali, Faisal, and more of Yaqub's men rushed into the room.

Yaqub pointed at the moaning man. "Get a tourniquet on his arm. I do not wish for him to bleed out now that we have him."

Faisal knelt to tend to the task himself, using a shoestring from the man's own footwear.

Quickly the CIA agents were gathered up by Yaqub's warriors and carried into the hallway. Wali stared at the dead boy.

"He did his job, Wali. There was no hesitation in him. You trained him well. Take pride in what you gave him."

Wali nodded, then leaned down and picked up the small corpse. He carried the dead boy out into the hallway too. He would not be left to be defiled by whomever the Americans recruited to investigate the incident.

Out in the hallway, Yaqub followed the others down the stairs. On the first floor, they did not leave the building and go out onto the street. They went into a back room, then down into one of the smuggler's tunnels that had been constructed beneath various buildings in the city. Townspeople also used them to escape structures that had been targeted.

Yaqub took one of the candles from a shelf built into the wall behind the short ladder that led into the tunnel. He lit it from Borisov's, then followed the big Russian through the darkness.

"Well, you have your CIA agents as you wished, Yaqub. I am curious, though, as to what you are going to do with them."

"You will see soon enough. The world will know."

"What do you mean, they're gone?"

Carter stood to one side of the control center and took the call from Langley over his headset. "I mean they're gone." This was Carter's first time to deal with CIA Special Agent in Charge Marshal Stivers, and he was definitely not a fan of the man. Instead of determining what could be done to find his team, Stivers seemed more intent on making sure the blame for their loss was placed elsewhere.

Of course, to be fair, there was a lot of stress on the CIA SAC now that one of his teams had been taken from a region they weren't officially allowed in. The Pakistanis had been adamant about clearing the spy agency out of the country.

"How could you people just lose my team?"

"With all respect, this was not our operation. We were picking up pieces from your agency. Your team got lost because you people lost them. We were trying to help you keep a visual on them. In the end, that wasn't possible." Carter glanced at the tablet he was carrying that linked him to information streaming in from the control center.

Prentiss was running recon on the area, watching as many of the streets as she could, but that was going to be wasted effort in the end. The city was too large for one drone to cover. A Reaper's usefulness, like any other tool in the military arsenal, was limited by available information.

"You probably know Parachinar as well as I do, Special Agent Stivers. All FATA lands are veritable smugglers' paradises. Black market goods and contraband filter through that region like grease through a goose." Carter wasn't exactly sure what that last meant, but it was something his grandfather had often said. "If you can get me a twenty on those men, I can get a bird in the air to keep track of them. When someone goes missing like this, it takes boots on the ground to locate them again."

With a final snarled curse, Stivers broke the connection.

Turning around, Carter faced the control center and studied the panel in front of Prentiss. The city lay revealed before them, but there was no clue where the CIA team had disappeared to.

On the screen to the right, the faces of the three agents were lined up. Carter and his team hadn't been given their names. That information was strictly need-to-know, and Carter had been informed that he didn't need to know. He'd accepted that.

Prentiss's shoulders had bowed with tension. That was a frequent problem with the cyber unit. Everything was at a distance. Sitting in Nevada, halfway around the world, the remote operators often forgot that the distance separated them from everything happening over there. Until something went wrong. Then that separation became painfully apparent.

"Take a moment, Prentiss. You're not going to find them by going blind staring at that monitor."

"I know." Prentiss took a deep breath and leaned back. "I know that losing them wasn't my fault. I've done this long enough that I realize we're limited in what we do. We're a backup measure at best and only occasionally strike-capable."

"That's right."

"But I still feel like there's something I should be doing."

"You're doing it. You're looking for those men."

Prentiss adjusted her headset. "I've got an electronic signal coming from inside that building. It's a video feed."

"Put it on-screen." Carter's phone rang and he automatically answered. "Carter."

Stivers spoke without preamble. "I've got a local team on-site at that structure. I need you to piggyback a signal through your bird."

"Can do. They've already pinged us. We're not going to be in real time with them. We're compressing and encrypting the data." Carter covered the mouthpiece and relayed the request to Prentiss.

Anger tainted Stivers's words. "I know the drill. Just get it to me. I've got analysts waiting on it."

Carter bit back a sharp retort. Evidently a guy didn't have to be polite at Langley. He just had to be good at what he did. Losing a team wasn't a measure of competency.

The data stream unpacked and showed on the panel, revealing the bloody room where the CIA team had evidently met whatever fate they'd encountered. Blood stained the walls. Two dead men sat slumped on a couch. When the man providing the video turned, a pool of blood was revealed on the floor near the door. Another was just outside the entrance.

There was no sign of the three faces on Prentiss's second panel, but the room had been turned into a charnel house.

Abruptly, the camera turned again, briefly catching the legs of another person in the room as well.

Prentiss looked up at Carter and mouthed, *Relaying*.

Carter nodded and spoke into the mouthpiece. "Are you getting this?"

"Looking at it now."

The camera view suddenly shifted again, lowering to the floor and increasing magnification. It took Carter a moment to figure out what the cameraman was focusing on; then—when he did figure it out—he wished he didn't know.

Two human fingers lay under the sofa the dead men sat on. One of them had been severed at the knuckle. The other at the second joint. Both amputated digits showed obvious trauma, not clean cuts.

Prentiss's reflection in the panel took on a more somber cast. Her mouth became a hard line. Without a word, she opened the drawer in front of her and slid a hand inside. From the time that he had worked with her, Carter knew she kept a Bible there—a touchstone for faith and family, she'd once told him. After a moment, she took her hand back out and seemed a little more composed.

On the panel, a man's hand appeared in front of the camera and scooped up the two amputated fingers.

Then the camera's digital upload ceased, clearing the panel so only the serene image of Parachinar's streets and surrounding snowcapped mountains stood revealed.

"That'll do, Carter. Thank you for your assistance." Stivers hung up before Carter could respond.

Prentiss looked at Carter as he punched off the phone. "Think those—" she paused—"belonged to one of the missing agents?"

"Yeah."

A shiver passed through Prentiss. "So who took the video?"

"Probably one of the CIA assets in the area. Somebody like those two Pashtuns who were dead in that room."

Prentiss hesitated. "I might be able to blow up some frames of those fingers, maybe pull the friction ridges and search through the system for who they belonged to."

Carter shook his head. "The CIA knows who they belong to. We're out of it, Prentiss. Unless they call us back in. Until then—" he nodded to her desk—"maybe you could say a prayer for those men."

"I already have been."

"Yeah. Me too. I think they're going to need it."

# 11

**ARMS CROSSED,** back against the wall, Pike sat on a hard bench bolted to the cinder-block wall. The cops and frequent visitors called the large community cell "genpop," short for "general population." The strong stench of unwashed bodies, vomit, and urine stained the air, but the smells were customary things to Pike. He'd spent plenty of days in places that were a lot worse than the jail he was currently in.

Two young black men still occasionally glared at Pike from their seats on the floor. Last night had been Friday, and the jail usually spiked in volume on weekend nights. More police were looking for collars in the streets, and more people were out in those streets.

One of the young guys had an eye that was nearly swollen shut. Pike had given him that when he and his buddy had tried to take Pike's space on the bench. The fight had been brief, over in seconds, and the jail's trustee had blown the incident off without writing it up.

As a result of the fight, the other black men in the cell gave Pike the stink eye too. He didn't take it personally. Color was one of the first divisive things in lockup. Race made it easy to figure out who "us" and "them" were.

Weakness was another way. A man who didn't fight for his own space was a victim waiting to happen several times over. In the orphanage, Pike had learned never to be a victim. Back then he'd packed batteries and bars of soap into tube socks to create makeshift blackjacks. That education had come at the hands of other kids who'd taken what little he'd had. He learned to fight, to look out for himself, and he'd never lost anything else except to sneak thieves who stole his stuff without revealing themselves.

Thieves were the worst because most of the time nobody knew who they were. Once their identity was found out, though, being a thief in a group home was the worst experience ever.

Things had been better after Pike had gotten to know Petey. Both of them were fighters and schemers. They'd used their fists, and they'd used their cunning. And they'd both read a lot of books. Pike favored histories because seeing how other people, other civilizations, handled adversity gave him insights into the person he wanted to be and how he could get there.

Petey had liked caper novels, books about heisters and boosters. He'd wanted to live outside the fringes when he grew up, be a hard-core criminal.

Pike had just wanted to survive. Still, there was something about them—about the way they thought and the way they handled themselves—that left them connected. Petey had been the first to show that desire.

When Pike was eleven, when the orphanage had almost given up on finding him a foster home that would stick, he had gotten cross-ways with five older boys who had formed a gang inside the group home. Two of them had taken a new kid's stuff. The kid had just lost his mom to an overdose and his dad to prison, and nobody in either parent's family wanted to take him. He was just another reject from the real world. He'd still cried himself to sleep most nights.

Later that day, Pike had cornered the two guys and told them to give the kid's stuff back. They'd refused. Pike beat them both down to the ground, then took the stuff back to the kid. It wasn't much. Just a book his mom had read to him sometimes and a ball cap he'd gotten from when his dad had taken him to a baseball game. The pack of Life Savers one of the administrators had given him was long gone, but there was no helping that.

The kid was grateful and tried to hang out with Pike sometimes. That hadn't worked, though. Pike was a loner, and the kid got farmed out to a foster home a couple days later.

After that, the three other guys who belonged to the same gang as the two Pike had beat up returned from their short-lived forays into foster homes. They brought swag back with them, things they'd stolen from the foster families—pocket change and a few dollars. They found out what Pike had done, and they came after him.

At the time, with five on one, Pike figured the guys were going to kill him. He'd been going down, and then Petey had come out of nowhere, yelling like some ancient Viking warrior.

Together, Pike and Petey had proved to be more than the gang could handle. The home administrators ended up pulling them off the five guys because Pike and Petey wanted to make sure those guys stayed beaten down and wouldn't try that again.

The home administrators had split up the gang anyway, and no way would those guys ever feel brave enough to come after Pike on their own. Pike had felt certain that would be the last he'd see of Petey, but somebody somewhere had decided to leave the boys together.

And that was how they'd finished up their tour through the orphanage: together. They'd shared comics, a few books, and chased after the same girls during the social activities the orphanage set up in an effort to integrate them into the straight world. That had been what they called it: the straight world. Petey and Pike hadn't cared for the straight world. There were too many rules and expectations, and they both already knew those were bad things.

Pike stretched his legs and smiled a little at the memories. Those had been good times. As good as they got in the orphanage, anyway. Getting to know Petey had changed Pike's life. He closed his eyes and breathed in and out, just the way he had back in the orphanage at night after lights-out. Sitting there on that bench in genpop, he felt more relaxed than he had in weeks.

★   ★   ★

After breakfast—a cold biscuit sandwich made with powdered eggs that stank and had an off taste—Pike got sprung. That surprised him because he'd figured with it being Friday night when he got popped, he'd be in jail for the weekend. Instead, shortly after nine o'clock, the trustee came for him and let him out.

The trustee was a young black guy who looked clean and neat but had eyes that said they'd seen too much. "Got your clothes in the changing room. Drop the jumpsuit in the laundry hamper, then go out the other door. There's a detective waiting for you."

"Who?"

The trustee shook his head. "I don't know. They just told me to give you the message."

"Thanks." Pike turned to go.

"Hey, Marine."

Surprised, Pike turned back to look at the young guy.

"I saw your file. I'm Marine Reserve too. I just got activated. You?"

Pike shook his head.

"You probably will be soon. Things are heating up in Afghanistan again. The tangos are on the warpath with a vengeance. You don't want to sit this one out, do you?"

"No, I don't." With the way he was feeling and how things were going, Pike needed a war.

"Keep it together, man. Sounds like you got picked up on a bogus beef. I hear nobody's filing any charges. You protected that woman. Ain't nobody gonna cry foul over that. Guy you busted up is shipping back to prison on Monday. Way I hear it, that couldn't happen to a more deserving guy."

Pike nodded and reached out to shake the young man's hand. "Good luck, Marine."

"You too." The young man's grip was sure and strong.

Dressed in yesterday's grease-stained clothes and wanting a shower and maybe a more substantive breakfast, Pike followed the paint line on the floor that would take him out of the jail. When he stopped at the property room to claim his personal effects, Detective Tom Horner stood there waiting on him.

The detective had on a suit and looked freshly shaved, his cheeks gleaming. He sipped from a Styrofoam cup, and the strong smell of coffee wafted to Pike's nose.

"Mr. Morgan."

"Detective Horner." Pike stepped to the property clerk's window.

"I thought maybe we'd have a word."

"Go ahead, but I'm not going to be here long."

Horner scowled, but he waved to the property clerk. "Get squared away here first."

Behind the bars, a young black woman with gold highlights in her hair and long blue nails looked at Pike, then at the computer monitor to one side. "Pike Morgan?"

Pike nodded and stood there as she reached for a manila envelope with his name written on it. She dumped the contents onto the counter in front of her, checked his driver's license, then took out the inventory list and checked the items. There wasn't much. Pike traveled light.

After he'd signed the inventory sheet, Pike turned and headed down the hallway, still following the painted line to the outside world. Horner fell into step beside him.

"No charges were filed against you."

"Good to know."

"If you hadn't hurt that man so badly last night, the detectives probably wouldn't have brought you in."

"They were just doing their jobs. I got no complaint. As far as hurting that guy, he came at me with a knife. Things could have gone a whole different way." Except that would have been even worse for Hector, and Pike knew it. During the night he'd worried about Hector, hoping the boy was doing all right in spite of everything that had happened.

"I know that. I also know that you were careful not to kill anybody at that crack house."

"I don't know anything about that."

"I got a phone call through the chief's office. I don't know who he talked to, but somebody wants me to give you a pass on this."

Pike didn't say anything.

"Nothing to say?"

"No."

"Who are you, Pike? Really?"

Pike looked at the man then. "Nobody you would want to know, Detective. Me and you, we ride separate sides of the road." He put his hand against the door and pushed through into the bright heat of the day. Taking his Oakleys, he slipped them on and kept walking into the parking lot.

"I came out here this morning to let you know I'm dropping the investigation into that crack house. Because I decided to, not because of that phone call. You want to know what changed my mind?"

Pike shrugged.

"The guys watching you yesterday said you were helping that kid with his math."

That stopped Pike in his tracks. He spun and faced the detective. "Let's make sure we have something straight. That kid stays out of whatever business you and I have."

Horner held his ground, his face serious. "I've got kids, Pike. I've helped them with their homework. These days I help them with decisions they make. They don't always listen, but I'm there when they need me. Something like that means a lot."

Pike nodded, but he didn't know what to say.

"I'm letting off the investigation into the crack house, but I'm going to step up the investigation into the people who put it into business. I'll make sure they get the message that the neighborhood there is off-limits."

The announcement made Pike feel strangely uneasy. The whole week was off-kilter, and he didn't like it. *Roll with the flow, bro.* Pike knew that was what Petey would have told him, and then he would have made fun of Pike for being weirded out by what was obviously just a run of good luck.

"That would be good. Some decent people in that neighborhood."

Horner looked at him. "I know. I want to help keep it that way. And if you'll let me, I'll give you a ride back to wherever you want to go."

"I'll make my own way." Before Horner could respond, Pike turned and walked away.

★　★　★

Since it was Saturday and a training weekend for the local Little League, Monty was off somewhere with his son and the team. The garage was locked up and it looked like everything there was fine.

Pike paid the taxi driver and got out. He grabbed the mail from the box, then passed through the security gate. Inside, he locked the gate behind him because the garage didn't take new business on Saturdays. As he crossed the graveled parking area, he checked to make sure all the cars were there. The Ford that had come in with a burned valve and the Subaru SUV that had needed a brake job were gone, but the owners had been scheduled to pick them up Friday evening.

As he walked toward the garage, Pike tried to recall seeing them in the lot when the cops loaded him into the back of the patrol car, but he couldn't. Monty had been gone. That much Pike had known because the security gate was locked down.

Slotting the key into the door, Pike let himself into the garage. Instantly the shadows trapped inside welcomed him into their embrace, and the worry and tension that was eating at him seemed to drop away a little. Heat filled the building, and he felt like he had to push his way through it as he went to the office.

He flicked on the light and ran through the sheets, making certain the Ford and the Subaru had made it back to their owners. Monty had signed off on both, paid in full. That meant the floor safe would have Pike's cut of those jobs. Pike left the money there because he didn't need it and didn't intend to do anything with it for the moment.

He dropped the wad of mail on Monty's desk and sorted through it quickly. Most of the contents were advertisements, coupons, and junk mail offering credit cards, money for college, and reduced auto insurance. But there was an official letter addressed to Pike Morgan. He always filled out the garage's address for personal correspondence.

The letter was from the Marine Corps and it was short and sweet, letting him know he'd been activated and was going to be shipped to Afghanistan from California with Charlie Company. More of the knot in Pike's gut loosened. He could shake loose from Tulsa in a matter of days.

He pocketed the letter, then noticed a Post-it note with Monty's handwriting affixed to the computer monitor.

*Hey, Pike. I called the jail. They said they were cutting you loose in the morning. So knowing you, you'll stop by here sometime Saturday. Dude, you ain't got nothing but bad luck following you around, seems like. If you need something, gimme a call.*

A number was listed at the bottom of the note. Pike recognized it as Monty's cell phone. The man didn't give that out to anybody except family, but he'd given it to Pike. Pike had never called it.

*Don't need nothing, Monty, but thanks anyway.* Pike plucked the note from the monitor, wadded it up in his hand, and fired it into the trash can beside the desk. The Post-it rolled off the hill of debris. Grimacing, Pike grabbed the trash can and took it outside to the Dumpster behind the building. Monty was a good mechanic, but he couldn't spot an overflowing trash can if his life depended on it.

Back in the building, Pike placed the empty trash can beside the desk and checked the sign-in sheet. Monty evidently had a couple people call in for the coming week. The workload looked light. New tires. Oil change. AC service. Nothing challenging.

Out in the service bay, Pike looked at Mrs. Garcia's car again and thought about climbing under the hood to take another stab at tracking down the elusive electrical problem. He glared at the car, suddenly realizing he knew too much of its history too.

Everything was too familiar, and it was going to be just as familiar the next day. He'd let things get too close to him, and he realized it for the first time. That scared him more than crack dealers with guns and detectives with handcuffs.

Unwilling to stay any longer, Pike decided to get breakfast, then figure out where his head was at. Something was wrong with him. He just didn't know what it was. But he knew someone he could talk to.

# 12

PIKE AVOIDED the diner across from the garage and walked three blocks to a little greasy spoon called Tina's. They made okay chicken-fried steaks and burgers and served breakfast all day. He didn't go there often because Monty didn't like the place. From what Pike had gathered, Tina was an ex-girlfriend, somebody he'd dated before he hooked up with his wife. Monty's wife didn't like him going there either.

This morning, Pike went there because no one knew him there. He ordered a big breakfast—biscuits and gravy, home fries, and sides of bacon and sausage—and devoured the meal, chasing it down with hot coffee. Maybe he'd stop for a six-pack of beer on the way back to his apartment. The food filled the hollow space in him that the egg biscuit hadn't touched, but it didn't settle the uneasiness that thrummed within him like a tuning fork.

He got a coffee to go, then hiked another four blocks to a small hotel that had a public telephone. This was one call he didn't want showing up on his cell records. He called Caleb Mulvaney, the detective sergeant who had investigated Petey's death and later helped Pike get into witness protection.

Mulvaney had been the first to point out that by providing testimony against the Diablos, Pike could bring down the whole outlaw biker organization instead of only getting a few of them before he got himself killed. Pike had countered that maybe the Diablos wouldn't be able to kill him and that maybe he could get them all. Mulvaney had just given him that look, that Mulvaney look. Pike hadn't been able to figure that look out—or how it weighed on him so heavy when the detective did it.

In the back of the hotel lobby, Pike called Mulvaney's number from memory. According to the agreement he'd signed with the Department of Justice, Pike wasn't supposed to have contact with anyone he knew from his old life. That included Mulvaney.

Surprising himself, Pike hadn't been able to walk away from Mulvaney. The detective had a quiet calm about himself that Pike had felt drawn to. The man had been the first on the scene after Petey was killed. Other police officers had tried to arrest Pike and take him away because he'd been carrying weapons that he didn't have permits for and because he had a dead guy in his lap. Mulvaney had intervened, telling them all to stand down until arrangements were made to take Petey's body away. Then Pike had gone willingly. He'd just wanted to do right by Petey. Mulvaney had read that without a word being said.

Mostly, though, Pike went because he no longer had anywhere else to go.

At his end, Mulvaney answered and then hung up the phone. Both of them were careful about the connection that existed between them. The US Marshals knew they stayed in touch and had decided to look the other way for the most part because Pike and Mulvaney were both more stubborn than the marshals were persistent. But with the Diablos still lurking around, it was better to be careful.

Fifteen minutes later, while Pike was watching kids skateboarding in an alley across the street, the pay phone rang.

"Hey. Everything okay, hoss?" Mulvaney had a raspy voice that sounded like it came from the bottom of a well.

"Yeah. Why wouldn't it be?"

"Heard you were getting grief from the attorney."

"They don't want to push me too hard. I got more to give them than they can take away from me, and they know it."

"You torched a crack house? Seriously?"

Pike grinned at that. Mulvaney had that effect on him. The guy was old enough to be his dad, which was a creepy thought every time it crossed Pike's mind, but he stayed cool about things. "New building. Same guys."

"Dealers are like roaches, kid. You shine a light on them, they scatter, find a new hole, and set up shop."

"Gonna be hard to set up shop in this one again. It's extra toasty."

"That's what I heard. You gotta get a new hobby."

"Nothing else lets me work out my aggressions as well."

"Work out your aggressions, huh?"

Pike leaned a shoulder into the wall, relaxing a little as he talked to Mulvaney the way he always did. "Something a counselor told me once. Said it was something I needed to work on."

"I don't think torching crack houses was on the list for viable exercises."

"It should be. Improves the community. Makes you feel better."

Mulvaney laughed. "So what's going on?"

"What do you mean?"

"Why did you call?"

"I gotta have a reason?"

"Kid, you *always* have a reason."

Pike thought about that, silent for a moment while he gave the question consideration. "I'm shipping out next week."

"Okay. You nervous?"

"Nope. Looking forward to it, actually."

"So you can work out more aggressions."

"Gonna be plenty of chances from what I'm hearing in the news. Lots of bombings and attacks over there."

"Al Qaeda's gearing up, thinking the United States is going to keep pulling soldiers out of the area. The terrorists want to be able to step into the vacuum."

"Yeah, well, the Taliban's not gonna want that to happen so easily. Neither will the warlords." Pike knew what to expect. "Once America pulls out of Afghanistan, there's gonna be a major land grab. The Afghan police ain't ready to pick up the pieces. Russia's waiting in the wings, so it'll be interesting to see how that goes down. Especially since Pakistan is part of the mix. Kinda feels like throwing gasoline on a fire sometimes."

"You do what you can, kid. Same as with burning crack houses."

They were comfortably silent for a time, which was one of the things Pike really respected and enjoyed with the old warhorse. Mulvaney didn't talk just to hear himself talk.

"So what's got you bothered, Pike? I can hear in your voice that things with you aren't quite right."

"I spent the night in jail."

"I hadn't heard about that, but that's not new for you. I don't see any life-changing experience there."

"It kind of was. Kinda has to do with me burning down crack houses."

"So tell me."

"There's this diner across the street from the garage where I work."

"With Monty. Yeah, I remember."

"You remember Monty?" Mulvaney's memory surprised Pike, though he knew it shouldn't have. He was a decorated detective and knew his stuff.

"When you call, you mention Monty. Nice guy. Wife and kids. Coaches Little League ball. I tell you, my hat's off to any guy willing to do that job. Those guys should be licensed to carry anything short of WMDs."

The fact that Mulvaney remembered Monty bothered Pike. A lot. He hadn't realized he'd talked about Monty so much.

Mulvaney prompted him. "Anyway, this diner. Keep going."

"I was there last night helping Hector with his math homework." Suspicious, Pike hesitated. "You know about Hector, too?"

"Yeah."

"I talk about him?"

"More than you talk about Monty, if you want to know. Thing that surprises me is that you can help the kid with his math homework."

Pike ignored that. "So I'm helping him with his homework. The server comes by, checks on us. She knows my name."

"Your whole name?" Mulvaney sounded a little worried for a fleeting instant.

"No. Just Pike."

Mulvaney chuckled. "Doesn't take a detective to figure that out. She knows you because you go in there so much."

"Yeah. And that bothers me."

"What bothers you?"

"Her knowing my name bothers me. I didn't know hers till last night."

"Pike, I'm gonna tell you this and you'd better not bust me for my man points for saying so, but you're a good-looking guy. Women are gonna notice you, and once they've noticed, they're gonna remember you. Especially if you're polite. She probably knows your name and how you want your burger, whether you like mustard or mayo. I don't see a problem."

"I don't like it."

"You don't like what?"

Thinking about how to best put it, Pike shook his head in disgust. His reasoning sounded foolish even to him. "People knowing me. Knowing my business."

"Anybody know you're in witness protection?"

"No."

"Then they don't know your business. They just know your name. Only your first name at that. They don't know you."

"They know me more than I want them to. There's a police detective who knows me now."

"That's your fault. You don't want to be noticed by the police, don't break the law. Or at least have the decency to cover it up."

Pike ignored the interruption and continued his list of things that bothered him. "Hector comes to me for homework."

"Because he's got nobody else and he figures you're safe. It's your fault for being somebody he trusts. Man, that'll teach you."

"Now this diner knows me because I punched out the server's ex-convict ex-husband."

"That's what landed you in jail last night?"

"Yep."

"They should have hung a medal on you."

"I'm thinking around Tulsa they run shy on medals for beating the snot out of ex-husbands. From what I've seen, could be a full-duty detail if somebody wants to take up the cause."

"For them to put you in jail, you must have beat the guy pretty good."

"He pulled a knife. He had friends. When I beat him down, I wanted to make sure none of that was going to be a problem. He hit the floor and stayed there until they carted him off."

"I see. But you're not worried about the ex-convict?"

"He's gonna be a convict again. Violating his parole. They're sticking him back in the big house with new charges pending."

"Then he's not the problem. The problem is that you're not invisible in the neighborhood."

"Yeah."

"Why does that bother you?"

Pike was quiet for a bit, thinking about it. "Because I don't like to run a high profile."

"Usually you don't hang around one place to get a profile. Do you realize you've lived in that neighborhood for almost three years? Except for the time you've been on active duty."

Actually, Pike hadn't thought about the time involved. "Hector used to be a lot smaller."

"I'll bet he was. I also think Hector's part of the problem."

"Hector's not a problem. He's just a kid."

"Right. A kid that you help with his math homework."

"So I fix a few kids' bicycle flats. I like working with my hands."

"Bet it doesn't take as long to patch a bicycle tube as it does to do long division." Mulvaney was laughing.

"You think something is funny?"

"Yeah, I do. You. I think you're funny. But it's sad, too, because what's going on is that you're starting to notice how much you like it there."

"I don't like it here. It's just a place to hang until we put the Diablos away."

"Keep telling yourself that."

"I will."

"Because I think what's really going on is, after three years—longer than you've lived in any one place since you got out of the orphanage—you're figuring out that you like living there and you're starting to get afraid that somebody's gonna come along and take you away from all those people."

The uncomfortable feeling squirmed through Pike again, and he suspected Mulvaney was closer to the truth than he wanted to admit. "These people will do just fine without me."

"Really? Hector gonna learn math on his own?"

"He's a smart kid. I think he's deliberately having problems with his math so he can get me to help him. I sit down with him, he's awesome, and I'm not a teacher."

"Don't sell yourself short as a teacher. The kid wants somebody he can look up to."

"You and I both know I'm not the guy for that."

"Probably not, but you're all he's got right now. Another thing: if you leave, is the crack house gonna burn itself down?"

"Detective Horner's gonna be looking into that now."

"Detective Horner, huh? Haven't made it to a first-name basis yet?"

Irritated, Pike frowned. "Maybe now isn't a good time to talk about this."

"I'm fine with it. You're not bothering me."

"It's bothering me. Talking to you isn't helping." Pike shifted against the wall, trying in vain to find a comfortable spot. The conversation wasn't going the way he'd thought it would.

"I wish I could fix this for you, kid, but this is something you gotta figure out for yourself. Once you think it through, get it set in your mind, you'll know what to do."

"I'm thinking it would probably be better if I let the marshals move me." The words sounded hollow and wrong to Pike, but he didn't take them back.

"After you fought with them to stay there?"

"If I change my mind, they'll be happy."

Mulvaney's voice lowered and grew more serious. "Yeah, I think you're right about that. But what about you, Pike? Are you gonna be happy?"

"I don't know."

"Well, if you want some advice—"

"That's why I called, but you've made everything confusing."

"You were already confused. If I was you, I wouldn't do anything until I was sure what I wanted to do."

"I don't like waiting. I want to have a plan now."

"You're getting reactivated. You can't move anyway. A few days, you'll be out of there. Moving will mean a new identity, and it'll mean Lance Corporal Pike Morgan will no longer be a Marine."

"Private."

"I thought you made lance corporal during the Somalia mission."

"I did. It lasted till I got back to the States. Didn't make it through my first week before a shavetail second lieutenant with an attitude busted me back down."

"You're sure the lieutenant had the attitude?"

"That's how I remember it."

Mulvaney sighed. "The bottom line is this: are you ready to leave the corps? Because that's what you'll have to do if you let WitSec move you. The military will have your fingerprints on file. You won't get back in under another name."

"No. I don't want out of the corps." That was one thing Pike was certain of. He enjoyed being a Marine even though he didn't care for the authority so much.

"Then go. Be safe. Wait to see how you feel when you get back."

Pike watched the kids on skateboards in the alley and wondered if Hector knew them. Then he wondered if those kids would be a good influence or a bad influence on Hector. Realizing he was even thinking about that bothered him a lot. Hector had his mom to worry about him. The kid's upbringing was none of Pike's business.

"I appreciate the advice, Mulvaney."

"You're welcome, and I wish it was easier for you. The way you grew up, Pike, there were a lot of things unfinished about you, a lot of things that you were never shown and that never got done." Pike could hear Mulvaney take a drag on his cigar. "Do you ever read that Bible I gave you?"

"Cut me some slack. I don't need another go-to-church speech."

"I'm not going to give you one . . . but you should find a solid church. A lot of your questions might get answered there."

Pike didn't say anything, but he figured that was highly unlikely. Church hadn't stuck when he'd been in the orphanage, when he'd needed to believe in something. Now he didn't need anything outside of his own skin.

"You got a long plane flight coming up soon. Pack that Bible. There's a section you should read. You got a pen?"

"I'll remember."

Mulvaney sighed. "Seriously, kid, this is something you should check into."

"I'll look. I'm good at remembering things. Don't bust my hump."

"First chapter of Philippians. I forget the exact verse, but it goes like this: 'I am certain that God, who began the good work within you, will continue his work until it is finally finished on the day when Christ Jesus returns.' You know what that says to me? Means we're all a work in progress, Pike. Me. You. Everybody. What you're going through now? This is just another step in whatever mission God put you on."

"Yeah, well, if that's true, maybe he could have made the signposts clearer."

Mulvaney chuckled again. "See? That's what you don't understand. No matter what you do, you're getting pushed along. You got free will. You can choose to ignore what's going on in your life, ignore what you're supposed to do, but you're still on the path."

"I'm pretty sure God didn't intend for me to burn down crack houses."

"Between you and me, Pike, I think God's a little more flexible about how some things get done."

# 13

**"GO LONG!** Go *long*!"

Sitting on a blanket spread out under a tall oak tree, United States Marine Corporal Bekah Shaw watched her son fading back to pass the junior-size football he held. He was lean and tan and had a shock of thick black hair that heralded back to the Cherokee blood that ran in the Shaw family. Bekah's brunette hair was lighter in comparison.

Travis's birthday had been last month. He'd turned seven, and he'd grown taller since Christmas. He was already almost out of the jeans she'd put under the tree. He wore a pair of them now, as well as a bright-orange Oklahoma State University jersey that Heath had gotten for him.

*Lieutenant Bridger.* Bekah mentally corrected herself, reminding herself that Heath was her commanding officer. That line had kind of blurred over the last few months since they'd returned from Somalia. She'd gotten the promotion to full corporal, and the friendship she'd struck up with Heath had grown stronger.

Maybe it was even threatening to become something more. Bekah tried not to think about that. She wasn't ready to deal with someone else in her life. Right now Travis kept her days pretty full. That and the new job as an office administrator for an attorney in Norman, Oklahoma.

She had her suspicions about how that job had come about. In his civilian life, Heath was an attorney. At one point, she'd asked him if he arranged the job for her, and he'd told her that if she hadn't qualified, she wouldn't have gotten it.

Bekah hadn't been happy with the answer because she didn't take handouts. She came from poor people who worked hard for what they had. Finally, though, she'd realized that she was working hard in the new job and that she was there because she deserved it.

In the end, she gave those worries over to God. That was one of the other new things in her life: knowing when to leave burdens in God's hands to let him take care of them while she tended to things as best she could. That insight had come to her while she was over in Somalia, trying to save lives and stay alive herself.

It was something her granny had been trying to get her to learn for years. Bekah had just never quite understood that. When she'd returned from the deployment, though, she'd carried with her a peace that she'd never known.

The commute to the law office was an hour each way from where she lived in Callum's Creek, but she only had to make the drive three days a week. On Mondays and Tuesdays, she worked from home, making calls, setting up meetings, and billing clients. The work was hard, but it didn't take her away from Travis too much, and the pay helped her square away her bills.

Now she could sit in the small park in Callum's Creek under a tree and not worry about her paycheck stretching to the next one. That was a good feeling.

Out on the green grass, in the heat of the day, with a brilliant blue sky above, still dressed in the slacks and dress shirt he'd worn when he went to church with her that morning, Heath Bridger went "long." The distance wasn't much over ten yards. Travis's arm wasn't that strong yet. But he was improving.

Six feet four and lean, Heath had light-gray eyes—wolf's eyes,

Bekah's granddaddy had called this color. Orange-lensed Oakley sunglasses covered his eyes now, but Bekah remembered how they looked. He moved with poise and speed on an athletic build—broad shoulders and narrow hips. Back in his college years at OSU, he'd quarterbacked the football team with the same laser focus that he exhibited when he commanded Marines in the field. His short dark-blond hair was cut to military length and stood out against his bronzed skin.

"I'm open!" Raising his arm, Heath jogged steadily, looking over his shoulder at Travis.

Her son backpedaled like he was being pursued by blitzing linemen who had sliced through his defenders. He had natural athletic grace, passed down from his daddy, though thankfully he'd gotten none of his daddy's mean-spirited ways that Bekah could see.

Billy Roy Briggs had been the high school's star pitcher, and he'd married Bekah right after graduation. She'd loved him, but she came to realize that he'd never truly cared about her.

Travis drew his arm back and threw the football. The pass was a good spiral—Heath had been working with him on that—but Travis's aim was off. The football was going to sail behind its intended receiver.

Twisting gracefully, Heath somehow managed to plant a foot, find traction, and reverse direction. He stretched and caught the football on his fingertips. He pulled it in and raced a few feet forward, then held the ball up and roared with pride. "Touchdown! And the crowd goes wild!"

"Touchdown! Touchdown!" Travis ran after Heath with his arms spread wide. "The crowd goes wild!"

Turning, Heath leaned down and caught the boy around the waist, lifting him high and performing some kind of victory dance.

"Well, they scored again." Granny sat in the shade beside Bekah, sharing the blanket they'd brought for the picnic. The older woman was in her late sixties and probably thinner than she should have been.

Her white hair was cut short because she didn't like having to fool with it. Living on a ranch, with plenty of constant upkeep, Granny tried to keep her life simple. She sipped sweet tea from a Mason jar. Her Sunday dress was neatly arranged around her. "I reckon the two of them are pert near unbeatable."

Out on the grassy field, Heath and Travis kept up their victory dance.

Bekah shook her head. "They're dorks is what they are."

Granny sipped her tea. "They're men with a ball. They're not going to be anything other than dorks. Give them fishing poles, they'll turn into big fibbers. You can't hold that against them. They just can't help themselves."

Bekah laughed at that, then turned her attention back to the picnic basket she and Granny had packed for their lunch. She put out plastic containers of fried chicken, potato salad, coleslaw, a jar of bread-and-butter pickles she and Granny had canned just a few days ago, and a loaf of homemade bread. She added a squeeze bottle of honey because Travis liked honey on his bread.

"You're leaving on Tuesday, right?" Granny was talking about the order that Bekah had received for her to report to Charlie Company First Battalion, Twenty-Third Marines in Twentynine Palms. They were based out of Houston, Texas, but had Oklahoma divisions.

"Yes." Bekah still didn't like leaving her son behind while she went overseas, but she'd gotten better at accepting that. She'd made a difference in Somalia. Rather, God had made that difference through her. Her life was a trade-off. She was a good mom and she was a good Marine. Those roles didn't overlap, but they were both necessary functions. Dividing her time was what hurt the most, but she couldn't walk away from either role no matter how hard it got.

She was needed, and she knew it. The hardest part to manage was the feeling of unfinished business in both areas of her life.

"Are you going to be ready for this again?" Granny's attention was still on her great-grandson and Heath.

"Yes. Better than last time. I don't have so much hanging over my head." The last time Bekah had deployed was a nightmare. So many things went wrong.

"You know, if this job at the attorney's office holds up for a while, you could think about leaving the Marines."

Bekah took in a breath and let it out. "I'm not ready for that yet. I get insurance through the Reserve." That had been the primary reason she had signed up with the Marines instead of one of the other branches. Marines were always first in, and they stayed on the federal payroll instead of rotating back to state funding when they weren't deployed. She and Travis needed the insurance. "And then there's the matter of Travis's education. I'm saving a big chunk of my pay for his college now. I don't have enough to see him through yet."

Granny leaned over and wrapped an arm around her. For just an instant, Bekah felt like that child she'd been, the one who had been raised by her grandparents after she was orphaned.

"I understand that, baby girl. I just wanted to make sure you didn't feel like you were getting pressured into this."

Bekah hugged the older woman to her, feeling the wiry muscle that hard work had put on her thin frame. "I love being a Marine, Granny. And I really feel that this is part of what God has planned for me."

Granny kissed her on the cheek. "I'm glad to hear you say that." She released her. "Now why don't you call those two dorks over here so we can eat."

★　★　★

Travis, on his knees on the blanket, his hands clasped before him, said grace before the meal. When he finished, Bekah squeezed his shoulder and told him he'd done a good job. Then she passed out paper plates while Granny poured sweet tea into Mason jars and handed them around.

Heath sat cross-legged with his plate in his lap. He was fastidious when he ate, making sure he didn't get food on his clothes. She felt a little uncomfortable watching him. Heath's father was a rich attorney in Texas with multiple offices, including two in Oklahoma. Heath worked at one of them. He was used to dining in five-star restaurants.

Yet, here he was.

Over the last few months, he'd called regularly, asking about Travis, about Granny, about the new job, about things on the ranch, and about how she was doing. Sometimes, after they'd talked for an hour or more, she couldn't remember everything they had talked about. He didn't talk too much about his caseload, but her experience in the attorney's office gave her a better idea of the stresses Heath was constantly under.

And she knew there was one case that was troubling him something fierce. Bekah had politely tried to drag it out of him, but Heath had blocked her every attempt, always a gentleman, always with a smile.

"What are you thinking about?"

Bekah suddenly realized Heath was talking to her. "Nothing, really."

"*Nothing* must take a lot of concentration."

She smiled at him. He wasn't the only one with a killer smile. "You'd be surprised."

"I appreciate you asking me along today." Heath looked out at the park. "It's pretty here. And quiet."

"It's pretty because you haven't seen it all your life, and it's quiet because everybody else in Callum's Creek is sitting in the air-conditioning."

"Air-conditioning's overrated if you ask me." Granny blotted perspiration from her neck with a tissue. "Makes folks soft. If you want to enjoy the world, you got to get out in it. That's what I think. Staying home under the air conditioner ain't gonna cut it."

Heath grinned at the woman and bit into a sweet pickle. "The places they send Bekah and me to don't have much air-conditioning."

"I suppose not." Granny paused. "I was just talking to Bekah about the two of you taking off on Tuesday."

From the corner of her eye, Bekah noticed Travis's sudden frown. He wasn't complaining about her leaving, but he didn't much care for it. They usually didn't bring it up. As hard as the separation was on her, Bekah knew it was harder on her son. If he had a father in the picture, it might be different. Going to school, knowing you didn't have a parent to call on if you got sick or scared, was hard. Bekah had grown up with both her grandparents only minutes away. Sometimes weeks passed before she could get a phone call to Travis.

From the way things were looking in Afghanistan, Charlie Company might be in the mountains, well away from the cities and phone service. At least there were letters. Travis had gotten a lot better about writing.

Granny went on. "I was thinking I might take Little Travis fishing this afternoon, leave the two of you some time to relax."

Since Bekah had named her son after her grandfather, they'd called him Little Travis. Even though her granddaddy had passed on, they still sometimes called her son Little Travis out of habit. Travis looked a little happier than he had, but Bekah knew he wasn't. He loved his great-granny and he loved fishing, but he didn't want to be away from his mother.

Or Heath.

Bekah wished she knew whether she should nip that relationship in the bud. When Heath moved on—and she was pretty sure he would because there was no comparison between her and the sophisticated women she figured he was out with when he wasn't slumming in Callum's Creek—Travis was going to be devastated. She knew she wasn't going to be any too happy about it herself.

She also wished Granny would have talked to her about fishing or about spiriting Travis away. That came out of left field and made Bekah feel really uncomfortable. Though they'd had some one-on-one time in Somalia, she and Heath hadn't really spent any time by themselves stateside. She didn't think she was ready for that with him, and from the pensive look on his face, he wasn't exactly thrilled about the idea either.

*Then why did you come out here today?* Bekah felt confused and hurt and mad all at the same time.

"Actually, much as I would enjoy that—or even the fishing—I've got to take a rain check." Heath picked at his plate. "Since we're getting activated, I've got a few matters to attend to."

"Gotta get your ducks in a row." Granny nodded. "I totally understand."

Heath hesitated a moment longer, then evidently came to a decision. "One of my clients is on death row. I'm trying to get that sentence commuted to life imprisonment."

"Somebody's gonna die?" Travis looked dismayed.

The boy's question startled Heath, and Bekah knew that he hadn't considered what Travis was going to think. He smiled reassuringly at the boy.

"No. Nobody's going to die. I'm going to save him. He's a good man."

"Then why's he on death row?"

"Travis." Bekah tried to warn her son off the subject, thinking that Heath probably didn't want to talk about it.

Heath answered anyway. "Because he made a mistake. He's not a bad man, but he was bad once. He hurt somebody." He rolled the football over to Travis. "But it's not something you need to worry about. Okay?"

"Okay." Travis held on to the ball. "Want to throw the football some more?"

Heath grinned. "Sure."

★　　★　　★

Later, when they were packing up the picnic things, Heath helped Bekah shake the grass and dirt off the blanket and fold it together. When they finished, their hands were touching and she was standing right there in front of him. She took in the scent of him, the lingering bits of the cologne he'd worn and the masculine sweat he'd worked up chasing Travis and the football.

"I'm sorry this evening didn't work out. Hope you're not too disappointed."

Bekah studied him, thinking he was just being polite. "It's okay. Granny sprang that ambush on me, too."

"Oh." Heath looked disconcerted and a little troubled.

"She means well, but I don't want her thinking for me."

"Understood."

From his tone, Bekah didn't think Heath understood. And then she realized she didn't know what he thought he understood. That bothered her because suddenly she wanted to know. But she wasn't going to ask. That would make everything that much more confusing.

"At least you'll get to go fishing."

"I will."

"I didn't know you liked fishing."

"My granddaddy used to take me when I was younger than Travis. He liked to fish and tell stories. We didn't always come back with fish, but I got to hear lots of stories. Some of them were the same, but I didn't mind."

Heath smiled. "Sounds nice."

"It was. I miss that. It hurts me to know that Travis missed out. He was around for some of that, but he's not going to remember."

"Maybe he'll surprise you."

"I hope so." Bekah took the blanket from him. "Can you get the picnic basket?"

"Sure." Heath managed the task easily, following her to her truck and putting it in the bed. The Chevy pickup was over twenty years old and still showed primer and Bondo scars where she'd removed rusted places since she'd been home. She'd intended to paint the quarter panels, but the last few months had just been too busy.

Heath acted awkward and gave her a strange smile. "If it's okay, I think I'll head back now. Let you get to your fishing."

"Yeah. That will be fine."

"I'll say my good-byes and go."

She nodded.

Heath looked at her. "It was good to see you today, Bekah. I meant what I said about appreciating you asking me out for this."

"Anytime." Bekah stood with her back against the door of the truck, watched him tell Granny good-bye, then hug Travis briefly. Her son hung on to him tightly, squeezing Heath with fierce determination. That part almost broke Bekah's heart. Her son wanted a daddy, and there wasn't anything she could do about that.

Then Heath placed Travis in the car seat, didn't have to listen to her son tell him that he was too big to use it, and walked to the sleek black Porsche Boxster. Travis had known what the sports car was called before Bekah did because he had bought a Hot Wheels car like it after seeing Heath's.

Standing there beside her pickup, Bekah waved good-bye to Heath, certain that he was returning to a life she would never be able to comprehend. Or fit into.

# 14

AT 8:30 MONDAY MORNING, Heath Bridger—attorney-at-law today, not Marine lieutenant—sat at a conference table in Oklahoma State Penitentiary. Nervous tension knotted his stomach as he waited for his client. The last few visits hadn't gone well, and Heath was hoping to change that today. He didn't know how long his deployment to Afghanistan would take, and he wanted to turn the corner on Darnell Lester's case before he left.

With the man, not the judge. In this instance, the man was the problem, not the legal system. Heath felt certain he could swing the commutation. He just wanted Darnell's permission to push for the change. He didn't *need* the permission. As the man's defense attorney, Heath was required by law to give Darnell the best representation he could. But it would be better if they were in agreement as to what that representation entailed.

The door opened. Heath sat up straighter and squared his shoulders. Today he wasn't there to listen to what Darnell wanted to do. Today he was going to tell the man what he needed to do to save what was left of his life.

"Good morning, Counselor." Dressed in an orange prison jumpsuit, wrists chained to his waist and his ankles shackled, Darnell shuffled through the door under the prison guard's watchful gaze.

He carried a worn Bible in his right hand. There were no bookmarks. Darnell knew his Bible.

"Good morning, Darnell." Heath glanced at the guard. "Take the cuffs off."

The guard was young, probably continuing to feel the self-importance of his role as protector of the innocent and punisher of the evil. There was evil in prison. Heath had seen it. His father had represented some of those men—and women. Heath had been tangentially involved in some of his father's cases with those people, but Lionel Bridger didn't let anyone touch defenses where he chose to be lead counsel.

"That probably wouldn't be a good idea. They told me this guy killed a cop."

Darnell ignored the comment. He had killed a police officer, and he'd been sentenced to death for it. Hearing it spoken out loud like that clearly wasn't new to him anymore. He wasn't going to show any sensitivity to that declaration. His guilt was a private thing, and Heath had noticed that.

"Guard." Heath put his military voice into play, assuming instant authority. "I'm here to see my client. Either you take those cuffs off or I'll get your supervisor to do it."

The guard cursed and took out his key. Evidently he didn't want to bother his supervisor. "It's your funeral."

Darnell swapped looks with Heath and smiled a little at the guard's rough prediction, but he didn't let the guard see the look of amusement. Guards could sometimes exercise a lot of control behind bars and make a bad stay even worse.

Cuffs in hand, the guard left the room.

Heath stood and waved Darnell to the seat on the other side of the narrow table. "Sorry about that."

"He's a pup. Got a lot of bark on him. He stays in here long enough, it'll get sanded off. Prison don't just break the prisoners. Breaks the guards, too. Seen it happen." Darnell put his Bible on the table, then sat and studied Heath with idle curiosity. He laced his fingers together in front of him. "Surprised to see you this morning."

"You didn't have me penciled into your schedule."

Shaking his head, Darnell smiled faintly. "No, Counselor, I did not."

"I'm glad you could make time for me."

Darnell grinned broadly. At fifty-four years old, the man still had a lot of life ahead of him, good years if he wanted them, but the last fourteen years of incarceration had nearly crushed him. He'd been a soldier in the United States Army during the First Gulf War, and he'd come away shattered by the things he'd seen.

The US military had fared well in that encounter, didn't have losses like they did in the Second Gulf War, but the men had seen things over there that had scarred them for life. Heath knew about those things, and he'd seen for himself the changes a soldier went through when encountering violence and an implacable enemy.

Then, after all that carnage, a soldier was supposed to reenter into society and integrate more or less on his or her own. That didn't work a lot of the time, and that integration had failed miserably with Darnell.

The man had come back to find himself divorced and jobless, untrained for anything that would make him a decent living, surrounded by people who had no understanding of what he'd gone through. The only thing he'd clung to in those years had been his daughter, Deshondra. He'd maintained contact with her, providing love and comfort for her to the best of his ability and even a home for her during her junior high and high school years when living with her mother was no longer an option. During those years, Darnell had functioned better. It was after Deshondra left for college that Darnell had fallen again. He'd learned to live right for her and couldn't do it for himself.

In Heath's book, Darnell was a good man. At least, the man he'd met in prison was. The one before had been broken and without a core.

Darnell was thin and long, underweight for his build. Heath had seen pictures of the man from when he was younger. That Darnell Lester, the one who had stood so proudly in his Army uniform, was a buff guy. The wreckage of what had been remained in the knobby shoulders and broad chest. Time had turned his hair cottony gray and left him bald on top. His right eye was pale blue, contrasting sharply with the one on the left. Burn scarring mottled both his arms, marking the black skin pink and white in splotchy patches. He'd come home wounded, gotten hooked on pain meds, and lived with that monkey on his back for years before he killed a police officer during a convenience store robbery.

"Gotta admit, I was curious why you set up this meeting. Thought we had everything wrapped up last time."

"*You* had everything wrapped up the last time we met. Not me."

Sighing wearily, Darnell shook his head. "If this is about that sentence commutation—"

"It is."

"—then I don't want to hear it." Some of Darnell's good-natured demeanor dropped away. "I been in here for fourteen years, Heath. I'm ready to go home to my Lord now. I got no fear of that needle. Gonna pay for taking that man's life an' be done with all of this."

"Because you want to get out of prison?"

"Ain't just prison, Counselor." For the first time, Darnell had an edge in his voice. Anger smoldered in his good eye. His other eye had been blinded in the violence that had occurred during his arrest all those years ago. "I got innocent blood on my hands. Time to wash it off."

"How can you have blood on your hands?" Heath stayed on the attack, not backing down. Part of him was afraid he was going to break the man, though. He didn't want that. Darnell had made his peace with his life inside prison. Ripping that away would be horrific and inexcusable.

But if he had to bruise the man, fracture him, and even come close to destroying him to save his life, Heath was going to do it.

"I got blood on my hands the day I killed that man. Shot him deader than dead."

"You carry your Bible around, and over the months I've known you, you've quoted Scripture at me time and again. Seems to me you've mentioned that Jesus died on the cross for our sins. That whatever evil we did in this life was paid for by his blood once we accepted him."

"It is."

"Have you accepted Christ?"

"As my blessed Savior, of course I have." Indignation underscored Darnell's retort.

"Then what makes your sin so special that you figure you get to hang on to it?"

"I ain't hanging on to it. What's done is done. There ain't no correcting it."

"True. I'm not here to try to absolve you of that shooting. You killed a man, and there's no court I know of that will reverse the decision to punish you. But I believe they will reverse what form your punishment should take. I'm here to stop the lethal injection the state is getting ready to hot-line into your arm."

Darnell squinted his good eye at Heath. "That was ordered in a court of law."

"Yeah, and I think I can get it commuted in another court of law."

"I told you, I don't want you to do that."

"Because you want to die."

"Everybody dies, Counselor. That's the price we pay for being born. I ain't afraid to die."

Heath was silent for a moment; then when he spoke again, it was in a soft voice. "I know you're not afraid to die, Darnell. I see that in you. But I also think maybe you're afraid of living."

Darnell snorted derisively and started to get up. "Too early in the morning for this. Even in here, I got better things to do with my time."

"You say you found Jesus in here."

Half out of his seat, Darnell froze. "I did."

"Then you need to walk the walk."

Darnell's nostrils flared in anger. His fists clenched on the tabletop. "You're pushing too hard."

"Am I? I talked to your daughter about this, and she's in agreement with me. She doesn't want you to die any more than I do. She says she needs you in her life."

Darnell's voice turned hoarse. "I ain't in her life. I'm in *here*."

Heath nodded. "And being in here is hard. I know that. I can't imagine what it's been like living here for fourteen years, being around the kind of men you have to be around, guards as well as prisoners. That kind of hard living takes a toll."

"Then you should understand why I'm ready to get out of here."

"I do, and under other circumstances—if you didn't have Deshondra and your grandchildren who want to have you in their lives—maybe I'd agree with you. But they *do* want you, and I think you deserve better than you've gotten."

"I've got all I need."

Heath returned the older man's gaze full measure. "Since the first day I met you, you told me you were a believer. That you'd gotten in here and found your faith."

"I did. And you need to be careful about what you say next."

"All that quoting led me to the Bible myself."

Darnell smiled, and some of the smoldering anger dissipated. "Ain't that a blessing."

"Are you familiar with Psalm 37:23?"

After a moment's hesitation, Darnell sat down and started to open his Bible.

"Look it up if you want, but I can tell you what it says."

Darnell stopped searching through the Bible and looked at Heath.

"The psalm says, 'The steps of a good man are ordered by the Lord, and He delights in his way.'"

Stubbornly, Darnell turned his attention back to the Bible and found the psalm. He read silently, lips moving as he tracked his forefinger across the page.

"That passage says God wants to guide a person's steps after that person has gone to God for assistance. It says if you're going to follow the will of God, then God will be happy. It doesn't say the way will be easy. Just that the way will be there."

Darnell sat there quietly.

"You weren't following God's path when you killed that police officer, Darnell, but since you've been in here, since you've come to your faith, you've tried to follow the course laid out for you. You've gotten closer to your daughter, been the kind of father—she tells me—that she can count on. You've been the best grandfather you could be under your circumstances. Your grandchildren love you. The warden tells me you've helped a lot of fellow inmates with their own struggles and to find the faith they need to get them through their time here. You . . . have made a difference while you've been living in these walls. That's the man I want to save. That's the man Deshondra asked me to save."

Unshed tears glimmered in Darnell's good eye.

Heath reached into his briefcase and took out the file he'd prepped. Flipping it open, he revealed a still that had been taken from inside the convenience store that morning when Darnell killed the off-duty police officer who'd tried to stop the robbery.

The Darnell in the photograph was down to skin and bone, burned out on the drugs he'd been using and by his inability to take care of himself. The photograph was black-and-white and grainy, but it was still clear enough to see the wide-eyed fear on the younger Darnell's face. The image had been taken only seconds before Darnell fired the shot that killed Keith Jointer. The scars on Darnell's arms showed as plain as day.

"This man—" Heath tapped the photograph—"was lost and without direction that morning. He was still trapped back in that war. He wasn't going anywhere . . . except to prison. This is the man that jury gave the death sentence to." He paused. "That's not the man here in this room with me."

Darnell shook his head. "You don't know how hard it is in here."

"No, I don't. But this is the way you've been given, Darnell."

Looking up at Heath, Darnell remained silent for a moment, but his gaze brimmed with challenge. "Do you believe this is God's will for me? To stay in this place an' be miserable?"

"It's not up to me to believe. It's about what you believe. You know, I can cite a number of case-law studies on nearly every legal matter that might come up. I'm good at what I do. But that's the first time I've ever consulted the Bible about one of my cases." Heath willed the man to believe him.

Silence hung thick and palpable in the conference room.

"So what do you believe, Darnell? Do you think God has truly made a difference in your life? Do you think he wants you to be a father to Deshondra? A grandfather to Trashae and Keywon?"

Darnell looked at his Bible and gently smoothed the scuffed

cover. "I'm still a relatively young man, Heath. Still got a big part of my three score and ten years ahead of me. I could be in this place another twenty years. That's hard time."

"Twenty years." Heath spoke softly. "Time enough to see your grandchildren through college, time enough to make a difference in their lives the way you have in Deshondra's. Time enough to be there in your daughter's life when she needs you. Maybe even time enough to become a great-grandfather."

"I'd just be a shadow to Deshondra's family."

"Darnell, have you ever looked at your shadow in the early morning or the late evening, when the sun sits on the edge of the world? When you look at it then, your shadow gets awfully long, bigger than you ever thought it could."

"Do you think I can make a difference in my daughter's family? Even from in here?"

"You already have, Darnell. Deshondra wants me to fight for you as hard as I can, and I promised that I would. I don't go back on promises. If I have to, I'll quit working for you and work for her; I'll fight you if I have to."

Darnell chuckled. "You like a good fight?"

"No, but I've never run from one either. And if you want to know if that's an idle threat, Deshondra's waiting outside to tell you the same thing."

"She is?"

Heath nodded. "She wanted to come in with me. I asked her to let me talk to you first, see if we couldn't come to some agreement."

Darnell huffed, but Heath could see it was resignation, not resistance. "All right, Counselor. Do the best that you can do to get my sentence commuted."

Heath offered his hand, smiling broadly. "I will. That's going to be easier to sell than selling it to you."

Darnell wrapped both hands around Heath's, holding him tight. "I gotta warn you of something, Counselor."

"What?"

"You went to the Bible to find an argument for me, an' maybe you're feeling pretty good about that, but I want you to know that anytime you go into the Good Book for your own purposes, God's Word has got a way of seeping into you. Whether you want it or not, you're gonna be changed. I know that for a fact. Seen it happen. My best advice is to accept what's coming."

"Sure." Heath stood and went to the door to summon the guard to bring Deshondra into the room, but Darnell's confident tone haunted him and he felt a chill. He told himself it was just the air-conditioning cycling on, that he'd stepped into the path of the vent, but something he couldn't put words to nagged at him.

# 15

**"PIKE, YOU GOT COMPANY, AMIGO."**

Shoving the starter aside from underneath the vehicle, Pike gazed up through the front end of the Chrysler sedan at Monty, who was removing the radiator fan. The Chrysler had come in needing a ring job and had to turn around quick. They were double-teaming the car to get it out by five.

Face covered in sweat and grease, Monty nodded toward the front of the garage.

Sliding around on the creeper, Pike twisted his head so he could see the garage doors.

Hector stood there holding his bike and looking apprehensive. His backpack was slung over his shoulder, heavy with books.

Pike hadn't seen him since the fight in the diner. Given everything that had happened, Pike figured Hector's mom had told the boy to stay away from the garage for a while. For a moment, Pike stayed on the creeper and looked back at Hector. Usually, once the boy was certain that he or Monty knew he was there, he would come on in. They had rules about him walking around the cars and the equipment and he understood them.

Hector didn't budge. Behind him, out on the street, cars whisked by.

Monty spoke softly. "He ain't coming in."

"Why?"

"If you wanna know, you're gonna have to ask him." Monty flicked his eyes up to the front of the garage. "You wait too long, he'll pull up stakes and go. Whatever's bothering him? It's bothering him pretty hard."

For a minute, Pike thought he'd just let it go. If Hector wanted to bug out, that was his business. He wasn't going to stop him.

Monty fitted a wrench onto one of the tappet covers and started cranking. "You know I don't make a habit out of telling you how to run your business, Pike—"

Monty seemed to be saying that a lot lately. Maybe it *was* turning into a habit. "And I've always appreciated that about you."

"—but that kid wants to talk to you something fierce, and whatever's on his mind is holding him back."

"Might be better for him if he stopped coming around."

"Yeah, you're probably right." Monty twisted a screw free of the housing with more effort than was required. "He's just a kid, right? He knows what's good for him. And it don't matter if he gets his heart broke."

"I ain't done nothing to him."

Monty shrugged. "Doesn't matter anyway. He's gone."

Pike glanced at the bay doors and saw that they were empty. Cursing, he tossed his wrench aside and slid out from under the car. He got to his feet and jogged to the front of the garage.

Fifteen feet from the bay doors, Hector was walking his bike to the corner.

Pike took a red rag from his pocket and wiped his hands. Looking at Hector walking beside his bike with his head hanging down made Pike think of all the kids in the orphanage who'd gotten busted up, who no longer believed that they'd get adopted by a family and know what it was like to have a mom and dad. When he spoke, he had to push through the thickness at the back of his throat.

"Hey. Hector."

The boy paused and looked back over one narrow shoulder. He seemed uncertain and troubled.

"You got a flat tire?"

Hector shook his head.

"Chain slipping?"

Another head shake.

"You got homework?"

"Not today."

"Okay, then maybe you got time to drink a soda?"

For the first time in a long time, Hector hesitated. That pause hit Pike like a hard right cross.

"Look . . . Hector . . . if something's wrong, maybe I can help."

The boy ducked his head, and for a moment Pike thought he was just going to push on and walk away from him. Before he knew what he was doing, Pike was walking toward Hector. When he reached the boy, he knelt down on the other side of the bicycle, giving Hector his space, not invading his bubble.

"What's going on, buddy?" Seeing the pain written on the boy's face, Pike felt himself grow cold and still inside.

Tears glimmered in Hector's eyes, and his voice was a hoarse whisper. "You hit that man so hard."

"I know. I did."

"He was all bloody. I thought you had killed him."

Pike shook his head, looking into the boy's eyes. "I didn't kill him."

"You're a soldier. A Marine."

"Yeah."

"You kill people."

Unwilling to lie to the boy, Pike nodded. "Sometimes I do."

Hector's shoulders trembled. "I know about the war. I see it on television. I know that you have to kill men over there so they do not kill you."

"Or my friends, yeah. That's the way war works, kid."

"That night in the diner, that was not war, Mr. Pike."

"No, no, it wasn't. But that man hurt that woman, and he pulled a knife on me. You didn't want her to go on being hurt, did you? Because I've seen men like him. Once they start hurting somebody, they can't hardly give it up."

"I know. I have seen such men." A tear trickled down Hector's cheek. "That night, when I saw you, I saw such a man in you. I didn't think I would ever see it. Not in you."

Pike took in a breath and let it out. He stopped kneeling and sat down, draping his arms over his knees, looking at the boy on the other side of the bicycle that had become a barrier between them. He wondered if Hector wanted the bike there as a defense.

"I'm sorry you had to see that, Hector. Truly, I am. You see enough bad things in this neighborhood." Although Pike was sorry about it, he also knew that the situation with the woman in the diner could have gotten much worse. The man had been out of control.

"You just kept hitting him."

"I didn't kill him. That was my choice."

"You are a violent man."

Pike nodded. "I have been. I try not to be these days. But violence is what I know best."

"Because of juvie?"

Pike frowned. "Part of it's from juvie, but part of it—" He shook his head, feeling the afternoon heat baking into him as he sat on the concrete skirt. "Part of it's just who I am."

The boy wiped the tears from his face. "I'm afraid."

Shock poured like cold acid through Pike's stomach. "Of me?"

Hector shook his head. "Not you. I don't think you would ever hurt me. Not this part of you, but now I know that there is another part."

"I wouldn't. I promise." Pike had to resist reaching out to the boy, but he knew that would be the wrong move.

"I'm also afraid that I will never get to see you again."

"Why?"

"Because my mother will learn about the fight at the diner, she will learn that I was there, and then she will tell me I have to stay away from you."

Pike put on a smile he didn't feel, but he did it to relax the boy. "You're probably right about that. I was never the kid moms wanted their kids to play with." He shifted, sitting up a little straighter. "I'll tell you something else."

"What?"

"Your mom shouldn't learn about the fight from gossip in the laundry mat. You need to tell her."

"I know. I know that would be the right thing to do, but I don't want to."

"Something like this, Hector, you don't want to hide from your mom. It'll only make things worse."

"How do you know? You didn't have a mom."

"No, I didn't." Pike gazed into those liquid brown eyes. "But if I had a kid, I wouldn't want him to hide something like this from me. Do you understand?"

"Yes."

"Then that's why you have to tell your mom."

"And if she tells me to stay away?"

"You'll stay away. You'll do what she says. That's how it will be."

Hector nodded glumly.

"You'll do it tonight. When she gets home. You've worried about this by yourself for too long. All right?"

"Yes. I will."

Effortlessly, Pike stood and looked down at the boy. "How about that soda?"

"No thank you. I have to get home. There are things my mom asked me to do. If I am going to tell her about that night, it would be better if I had those things done."

"Sounds good. How about a soda for the road, then?"

"All right."

Pike went back into the garage and got a can of soda. Hector followed him as far as the garage entrance, took the soda, and said adios. Pike watched the boy to make sure he made it safely across the street even though he'd been doing it on his own for a long time.

Returning to the job at hand, Pike lay on the creeper and slid under the car.

Monty wiped sweat from his face with his arm and looked down at Pike. "Everything okay?"

"Everything's fine. Hector's mom doesn't know about the fight at the diner. Kid's afraid she'll have a cow."

"Any self-respecting mother would."

"Yeah."

"There's nothing you could have done about it, Pike. It was what it was."

"I know." As he worked, Pike thought about what the garage would be like without Hector coming around. He didn't like the feeling. He tried to tell himself that he could do without the interruptions and the homework and the constant need to watch his language.

"Surprising how much a kid can get under your skin, isn't it?"

"He's not under my skin."

"Keep telling yourself that."

Pike focused on removing the header and pushed everything else out of his mind. That only lasted for a while.

★  ★  ★

On Tuesday morning, Pike got up to go to the airport. He showered and dressed; then he shaved his beard growth off, got his face slick and clean, and stared at his face in the mirror. His hair was a lot shorter, courtesy of a visit to the barber a few blocks over who kept his shop open till seven, and there was a shadow of untanned flesh close to his hair.

He looked squared away, Marine ready, and he felt that call to battle dawning within him. That was where he lived, out there where the good guys could be told from the bad guys because they wore different uniforms.

For the most part. There were always surprises.

*Get moving, Pike. The sooner you're shut of this place, the happier you're gonna be. The last thing you need is a bunch of confusion in your head.*

His sleep had been troubled last night. Normally before he shipped out, he slept like a baby. Trying to live around other people in the neighborhood was harder than living with Marines, though that was hard enough.

He'd stayed up late watching Charlie Sheen in *Beyond the Law*. That movie was one he and Petey had liked. None of the Hollywood movies ever really got what being a biker meant, but that one was close. And they'd liked Brian Bosworth in *Stone Cold*.

On his way through the apartment, he checked everything again. It was weird having a house. He and Petey had just flopped in several places, never staying anywhere too long, keeping one step ahead of the biker gangs, the police, and the jealous women. They'd made their own way, and there hadn't been anything to take care of but their bikes.

*That was better than this.* Pike told himself that as he checked to make sure the windows were locked. He didn't have anything in the apartment he was particularly attached to, but he didn't like the idea of coming back off a tour and discovering someone had ransacked his place either.

His clothes were all washed. Everything he'd worn last night was clean and put away. He shut the door behind him, engaging all the locks, and headed down the stairs with his duffel over his shoulder.

Out on the street, he walked toward the corner, intending to splurge and take a taxi to the airport. His truck was safely locked up at the garage. The air was clean and fresh, carrying just a hint of a chill with it.

He'd almost reached the corner when he heard his name called out. "Pike! *Pike!*"

Turning, Pike saw Hector riding his bike toward him. The boy rode swiftly and didn't brake in time. Pike had to step back and grab the handlebars to keep Hector from crashing into him.

"I thought I had missed you." Hector looked up at Pike and clambered off the bicycle.

"I thought you were gonna run over me."

Hector shook his head and adjusted his backpack. His eyes took in Pike's duffel. "You're leaving."

"Got called up again. I'll be gone a few months."

"You'll be back?"

That was one of the things that had bothered Pike. With all the stress over living in Tulsa, it would be easier to just leave. There wasn't anything here that he couldn't walk away from. Even Monty had shaken his hand and told him good-bye like he was never going to see him again.

*Or maybe he was just thinking I was gonna eat a bullet.*

"When I can." It was as close to a noncommittal answer as Pike could give without lying.

"I talked to my mom last night."

"That's good." Pike's gut clenched a little.

"She was upset."

"Under the circumstances, I think that's understandable."

"I know. She told me she didn't like it that I was there when it happened, but she told me she understood, that it was good that a man like you would stand up for a woman and help her."

That surprised Pike.

"I also told her about the way you hit that man, the way you kept hitting him, and I thought you were going to kill him. I told her I became very afraid."

Pike didn't say anything.

"My mom says she has known men like you. Men who sometimes get lost. She says sometimes they get lost because of war, like she said her father did in the Vietnam War, and sometimes they just get lost because they never find their way."

"Your mom is pretty smart."

"I also told her I would understand if she wanted me to stay away from you, but she asked me if I wanted to stay away from you. I told her I didn't want to be scared like that again."

"I understand too, kid. It'll be okay."

Hector's eyes were wide with innocence and some anxiety. "She told me to remember how you help me with my bike. How you help me with my homework. And how I shared breakfast with you. She told me to think about you when you're not lost. She said that's what she had to do with her father. She said that sometimes he scared her, but he was good to her, and on the bad days she remembered that."

Pike waited, not knowing what to say.

Reaching into his pocket, Hector pulled out a chain with a small compass no bigger than a fifty-cent piece. "When I first started walking home from school, I was afraid I would get lost. Mom walked me home and showed me where to turn, but she also got me this compass." He held it up. "You know how to use a compass?"

"Yeah." Pike's voice felt tight.

"Good. Mom said you would. She said the Marines would have taught you." Hector placed the compass in one of Pike's hands, then curled his fingers tightly over it.

"I can't take your compass, Hector."

"I want you to have it. I know how to get home from school." He looked up at Pike, holding on to Pike's big fist with his two small hands. "When you go away, I don't want you to get lost. I want you to come back safely."

"All right."

Hector took his hands back and got on his bike. "I've got to go to school."

"I gotta go too."

Hector started pedaling away, but he turned to look over his shoulder. "Come back, Pike. Do not get lost."

Gently, Pike shoved the compass into his pants pocket. He watched Hector till he was out of sight, then hailed a passing cab. He shoved the duffel into the trunk and slid into the rear seat. Once the cab was moving, Pike lay back and closed his eyes, psyching himself up, feeling the life he'd had there in the neighborhood fall away from him as he mentally armored up for the waiting war.

# 16

BY THE TIME CHARLIE COMPANY arrived in Kandahar, Pike was eager to get down to business as usual.

He was also relieved to see that his unit's gunney was familiar to him.

Gunnery Sergeant Francis Towers stood six and a half feet tall and was powerfully built, a man constructed for the Marines and for the battlefield. His skin was coal black and his general attitude could be intimidating for anybody who stood in his way, and since Gunney Towers didn't dawdle, a lot of people ran the risk of getting in his way.

"Pike, isn't it?" His voice was a deep bass that could carry over mortar fire on a battlefield or dress down a company of raw recruits. As a seasoned full-time Marine, he'd been cycled into Charlie Company as a liaison for one of the lieutenants.

Pike stood straight for inspection in front of the line of Humvees Charlie Company had been assigned for patrols in the city. They were taking to the streets this morning.

Despite the fact that as a kid Pike had never cared for authority, and he didn't like a lot of it in the Marines, he liked Gunney Towers's no-nonsense approach. "Yeah, Gunney."

Stopping in front of Pike, Towers glared down at Pike's rank designation. The private's stripes were Velcroed on, and he'd be pulling those when he moved out onto the street. "Thought you was a lance corporal after that hitch in Somalia. I remember signing the paperwork."

"I was."

"Then why are you wearing private's stripes again?"

"Because I earned them."

Towers snorted and shook his head. "Guess the reason for that will be in your field service report."

"Yes."

"You do know that the brass expects you to advance in the corps, don't you, son?"

"I do."

"An advancing Marine is a battle-ready Marine."

"Yeah, but sometimes you draw the line, Gunney."

Towers squinted at Pike. "You got crossways with an officer, didn't you?"

"Actually, he got crossways with me. He didn't want to apologize."

"You're a hardhead."

Pike shrugged. "It's not an endearing trait, Gunney, but it's kept me alive."

"Maybe you ain't no lance corporal, Marine, but you're an experienced and combat-ready veteran. When you're out here with me, I expect you to act like one."

"Roger that."

"Because we got a bunch of raw guys to whip into shape. I need you to help me keep them alive."

Pike nodded, feeling some of that pride of being part of Charlie Company begin to fill him. That was one of the benefits of being a Marine that he hadn't expected when Mulvaney talked him into signing up. Pike hadn't been interested in joining the Marines till the marshals started having a cow over it; then being able to join became a deal breaker.

He kept his pride carefully measured, though. It wasn't something he told many people about. He knew he could walk away from it if he needed to, but he enjoyed the thrill of being there. It was almost like the feeling he had when he was working at the garage and watched someone drive off in a vehicle he'd repaired. Something was fixed when he finished up.

Gunney Towers kept moving down the line, inspecting the troops. His voice boomed out, and men and women in the unit came to attention. The newbies shivered in their combat boots.

"Pike."

Turning toward the voice, Pike recognized Corporal Bekah Shaw. Her battle-dress uniform consisted of Kevlar with reinforced bullet-proof plates that felt like lead. A combat harness with an ammo rack, grenades, and webbing containing other equipment covered that. Her load-bearing equipment also carried a water bladder for personal hydration. Large goggles fit across her helmet, not pulled over her face yet. Her MBITR inter-/intra-team radio hung at her shoulder. She shouldered an M4A1 assault rifle like the one Pike carried.

"Shaw. I never saw you to congratulate you on the promotion, so congrats." She was one of the few Pike acknowledged on a personal level. The rest of the time he was all business.

Bekah smiled. "Thanks. Gunney put you with me. We're supposed to train the two people in our group." She eyed two Marines standing only a short distance away. "Private Ezekiel Weathers."

The tall blond-haired kid looked like he was all of eighteen years old, straight off the baseball field from whatever podunk high school he'd attended. His cheeks were tanned but too smooth to have much beard growth. Nervous tension tightened his jaw, and edgy alertness quivered in his blue eyes. He stepped forward and snapped into parade rest.

"It's just Zeke, ma'am. Only my momma calls me Ezekiel."

"Don't *ma'am* me, Zeke. I'm a Marine, same as you."

Zeke dipped his head. "Sure. Sorry."

"Where are you from, Zeke?"

"I was born in Randall, Minnesota, but I moved around a lot. Finished up high school and wanted to go on into college. Signed with the Reserve to help pay my tuition." Zeke grinned good-naturedly. "Didn't count on getting called up so soon."

"We live in fast times. Try to stay up."

"I will."

Bekah glanced at the other Marine standing there. His round face and thick shock of black hair marked him as Asian as much as his butternut complexion, and he had a deliberate hard-guy expression that he was working on. Wraparound sunglasses hid his eyes, and a toothpick stuck out between his lips.

"Private Johnny Cho. From Los Angeles."

"Everybody just calls me Cho." He smiled a little but worked on looking cool. The toothpick slid from one side of his mouth to the other.

Pike ignored the man's attitude. Acting cool went away in a hurry during battle. How a guy—even a Marine—behaved under fire wasn't determined until the rubber met the road.

Bekah glanced at Pike. She had her hair pulled back and looked good. She wore wraparound sunglasses and had a little tan, but it was from being outside, not fake-baking. Pike didn't know much about her other than she was from Oklahoma and had a kid. That reminded him of Hector and the compass in his BDUs.

Something about her was different this time out, though Pike couldn't put his finger on it. She acted more confident, more together, and he didn't think it was a boost in rank that caused it.

"We've been assigned to two-man teams. We're supposed to sweep the city, look for tangos, and otherwise present a presence to shore up the local Afghan National Police."

Pike didn't say anything. The assignment was what he expected. He wasn't a big fan of the ANP. Most of the local militia guys still weren't trained well enough to keep themselves alive against everything the Taliban and al Qaeda threw at them.

Bekah continued. "Since you and I have combat experience, I'm going to split us up with the new people."

"Sure."

"Pick whoever you want."

Without hesitation, Pike nodded toward Cho. "New guy number two."

Cho frowned at that. "The name's Cho."

Pike ignored him. A Marine learned how to work within a group without the need for individuality during working times, or that Marine ended up dead. It had been the same way in the group home. Somebody went along to get along. That was just how things worked. Downtime was different.

Bekah called the new guys in for a radio check, which Cho again resented.

"Hey, we got this, Shaw. This isn't the first time we've been on maneuvers."

Bekah faced the man directly. "It's your first time in the sandbox, and it's your first time working under my lead. So it is your *first* time. Got that? Otherwise I'll check to see if they need another Marine on mess detail. That can be your first day here if I say so."

Nostrils pinching, Cho dipped his chin. "First time. Got it."

"Good." Bekah nodded toward Pike. "You move when he says move. You do that, you may end up intact at the end of the day."

Cho nodded, but he wouldn't look at Bekah.

"Okay, Marines, let's saddle up."

Pike turned and headed toward one of the Humvees. Cho moved

more quickly and headed for the driver's seat. Pike growled. "Don't even think about it."

Cursing beneath his breath, Cho altered course.

Pike slid into the driver's seat and adjusted it for legroom.

Cho took his helmet off and started to place it on the floorboard.

Pike slid the checklist from between the seats, looked over the radio freqs they'd be using, and glanced at the streets they'd been assigned. He'd already studied the maps earlier that day over breakfast in the mess hall. "Pick up the helmet and get it on."

"It's hot."

"It's gonna get hotter."

Cho grabbed the helmet and put it on, leaving the chin strap undone.

"Secure the helmet."

Cho didn't move.

Pike lifted his eyes to the other man. "I tell you again, I'm gonna haul you out of this Humvee and work you over."

"Touch me and they'll put you in the brig."

"I like the brig. I don't have to put up with annoying wannabe Marines too stupid to live. There's a reason I've got as much time in this uniform as I do and I'm still wearing these private's stripes. The corps likes the job that I do well enough that they put up with me. You don't have that luxury, and I guarantee you'll spend longer on med leave than I do in the brig."

Cho fastened the helmet strap.

After folding the street map and putting it away, Pike hit the starter and listened to the engine rumble to life. He'd already checked the two that were assigned to his squad. Both of the vehicles needed some tinkering, but they appeared to be in good shape. Later he'd find out if the assigned vehicles would be theirs for the duration or go into rotation. If his squad was keeping them, he was going to poke around some more and take a better look at what kind of shape they were in.

Stiff and rebellious, and thankfully quiet about it, Cho deliberately focused on the line of vehicles threading out of the motor pool. Pike shoved the transmission into gear and let out the clutch, pulling in after Bekah.

Zeke waved at them like he was a kid going on a trip.

"Dumb cracker."

Pike drove with one hand, not liking the looseness he felt in the steering. That would definitely have to be fixed. "He's young, naive; you're stupid because you think you know it all."

Cho bristled, his shoulders straightening like he was going to say something. But he didn't.

Pike wasn't entirely happy about his teammate's reticence. The flight over and the training hadn't had enough physical aspects to get Pike relaxed. He kept driving, though, knowing from the uptick in violence against NATO military personnel that it wouldn't be long before he was in the thick of a fight.

# 17

DESPITE THE CONSTANT THREAT of attack by the Taliban or al Qaeda, Kandahar's citizenry struggled through their daily lives. Jobs still had to be done; children had to be fed. Despite the fear that hung over the city, people kept moving.

Behind the Humvee's steering wheel, only a few feet from the bumper of Bekah's vehicle, Pike looked out at the neighborhood and respected the courage it took for those people to get up every morning. Several of the buildings showed scars—recent damage as well as old. A few of them had burned-out rooms where soot tattooed the sides of the building above the windows in twisting paths of destruction. Other structures were in the process of being rebuilt.

A few minutes later, the two Humvees rolled by the squat, gray two-story stone building that housed the Kandahar prison. Only a few years ago, the prison had been attacked by the Taliban. A suicide bomber had blasted the wall open, and other tangos had unloaded a unified rocket-launcher attack on the guards that had left several dead. As many as a thousand prisoners, many of them Taliban, had escaped. On the other side of the road, farther back, pomegranate orchards stood tall. The trees had provided cover for the insurgents, and the escapees had fled into them, quickly disappearing.

Now the prison stood again. Razor wire ran along the top of the stone walls and guards walked their posts. White police vans with red stripes and light bars mounted on top were parked outside on the street. The uniformed ANP watched the Marine convoy go by but didn't acknowledge them. The men stood hard-faced and unreadable.

Traffic forced Pike to stay on his toes, constantly tapping the brake, shifting the transmission up and down as the uneven pace continued. Yellow cabs zipped daringly among the other vehicles, but they gave a wide berth to the Marine Humvees. Pike knew that wasn't out of respect. It was because the drivers saw the Humvees as potential targets and didn't want to be caught in the blast radius of a rocket attack.

Wagons, some pulled by people on bicycles or on foot and some by small donkeys, trundled along the street and created hazards. Several of the wagons were loaded with goods, including poultry and other livestock. More people rode refurbished bicycles or scooters.

Several minutes later, the Marines reached the market area and Pike's senses went on full alert. In a crowded street, the Marine vehicles were most vulnerable to attack.

Vendors had set up alongside the street under canvas tarps they'd hung from the bombed-out buildings behind them. Sticks held the tarps at an angle and provided some shade from the hot morning sun. Despite the heat, men wore traditional clothing that covered their bodies, and many of the women wore burqas. Women remained a target for the Taliban.

Shoppers pored over fruits and vegetables, chickens and goats, and racks of clothing. Merchants talked to the people or sat on folding chairs in a good position to watch over their goods.

The desperation that radiated off the street reminded Pike of the Tulsa neighborhood where he lived. He'd never noticed the resemblance before, but that small patch of Tulsa wasn't far removed from Kandahar when it came to hard living and distressed people. Maybe it was like that everywhere. The Tulsa neighborhood just didn't have the same kind of in-your-face physical threat level.

"Man, how can they live like that?" Cho peered out the window with a look of disdain. "Raggedy clothes, dirty, buying stuff out of carts instead of stores, taking home live chickens." Cho shook his head again. "That's a harsh way to live."

"Where'd you grow up in Los Angeles?"

"Wilshire."

"Next door to Koreatown." Petey had wanted to see California. He and Pike had done business there for a time, till things got crazy with the Mongols.

"Yeah, but I never went to Koreatown except to sightsee." Cho shook his head. "Old people with old ways live there. My grandparents lived there for a while; then they got out and bought a laundry. My old man went to college and became a stock trader. He stayed around Wilshire because my grandparents live there, but we have a nice house. Swimming pool. Guest house."

*We* have a nice house. Pike smiled at that. Cho wasn't even out of his parents' house yet. "These people don't live in nice houses because they can't afford to and because nice houses tend to be a tango target. Probably a lot of those people you see out there are squatting somewhere—an alley, a condemned building—getting by day to day and hoping they don't get caught in a cross fire between Taliban, al Qaeda, the ANP, or us. Or get slammed by a bomb blast that was aimed at someone or something else."

A man and his wife, each carrying a child, hurried across the street when traffic came to a standstill. Ahead, Bekah braked for them, allowing the couple time to cross with their kids.

"If I had to live like this, I'd move."

"And go where?" Pike shifted as they got under way again. He tried to swallow the instant anger he felt at the younger man, reminding himself that Cho hadn't seen much of the world. Cho looked out the window and shrugged. "I don't know. Someplace other than here."

"Anywhere else isn't home. And a lot of the country is worse than here." In some ways, moving in Afghanistan was a lot like moving from foster home to foster home. No matter where a displaced kid in the system went, it would never be home.

"Then move to a different country. They gotta think of their kids."

"Ain't that easy. How do you suppose they'd get their papers?"

"I just got here. I don't have any answers."

"They've been here all their lives. They don't have any answers either. Until they get them, they still have families to feed. Don't you look down on them just because they're struggling. You don't have that right."

Stung, Cho looked back out the window.

Pike turned right at the corner, following Bekah. Looking at Cho's profile, Pike felt a little sympathy for the younger man, but mostly he knew that Cho needed instruction. It was kind of like helping Hector with his math homework, only Cho didn't want the education. "So instead of blaming these people, shut up and pay attention. Staying alive may depend a lot on what you learn and how fast you learn it."

Cho didn't say anything, but he gave a slight nod.

Movement on the left side of the street caught Pike's attention. Adrenaline surged through his body and his senses went on high alert when he saw a man dressed in a turban and wearing a dirt-stained *shalwar kameez* lift a long tube from a cart pulled by a donkey. Small chicken coops filled the cart, stacked as tall as the man who pulled the rocket launcher to his shoulder.

Pike hit his radio. "Bekah! Rocket-armed tango at nine o'clock!" Then he reached for the M4A1 as Cho came alive beside him.

Cho started to get out of the Humvee.

Leaning through the window, Pike leveled the assault rifle. "Stay in the vehicle, kid."

Ahead, Bekah's Humvee was mired in traffic, pinned by the press of human bodies and other vehicles.

Bekah's voice remained surprisingly calm. "I don't see him, Pike."

"Get out of there." With the iron sights resting on the man with the launcher, Pike started to pull the trigger, then had to hold up as a young Afghan male stepped into his line of fire and the tango moved behind a row of chicken coops. Pike cursed but held his target, tracking through the poultry and the pens. "I don't have a confirmed shot."

Bekah cut her wheels hard to the right and barreled into an old sedan, shouldering the smaller vehicle to the side. Metal screamed as the vehicles traded paint, but the Humvee slid through.

The rocket leaped from the launcher, spitting out a black contrail as it spun toward the Humvee. Instead of hitting the Marine vehicle, though, the warhead slammed into one of the bright-yellow cabs that chose that moment to dodge out around stalled oncoming traffic. The cab caught the rocket in the right wheel. The RPG operator obviously wasn't greatly skilled with his weapon of choice.

The resulting explosion shredded the cab's wheel assembly and overturned the vehicle into Bekah's Humvee. Trapped between the lines of buildings on both sides of the street, the sound of the explosion rolled over the immediate vicinity with thunderous force. Some people ran, but others threw themselves onto the ground.

With the tango in full view now, Pike held the rifle steady and put two quick rounds into the man.

Scanning the neighborhood, Pike switched over to the base freq. "Indigo Dispatch, this is Indigo Nine. Request backup. We've been hit by a tango attack."

"Roger that, Indigo Nine. Are you operational?"

"Affirmative."

"How many tangos?"

"Can't confirm that."

A man pushed himself up off the ground thirty feet from Pike's Humvee. The guy was young, only the beginning of a beard on his face, probably just into his teens. He stared hard at Pike and lifted a pistol. The young man's voice was hoarse, filled with hate and fear. *"Allahu Akbar!"*

Pike reached for Cho, wrapping a hand behind the other Marine's head and shoving him down as he ducked as well. A short, rapid torrent of bullets slammed into the Humvee, but thankfully none of them came through.

Once the bullets stopped, Pike rose and shoved his M4A1's barrel through the open passenger window, lining up his shot. The young man tossed his weapon aside and took a small detonator from his clothing. He screamed louder as he ran toward the Humvee.

*"Allahu Akbar!"*

Pike fired immediately, pumping four shots into the terrorist's center mass. Brass spun from the M4A1 and bounced inside the Humvee.

Stumbling, the tango went down to one knee and pressed his free hand to his chest. He looked surprised at the blood that covered his palm and fingers.

Cho stared at the dying young man. "You shot a kid! That was just a kid!"

Knowing the man was still a threat with the detonator, Pike fired again, wishing he had a heavier caliber with knockdown power. The final bullet caught the tango in the face, but not before he pressed the detonator.

The bomb erupted in a wave of concussive force and shrapnel.

"I'm hit! *I'm hit!*" Cho clapped a hand to his face and pulled it down to look at the blood now on his hand.

Roughly, Pike grabbed the man's chin and swung his head around to survey the damage. A piece of shrapnel about the size of a thumbnail jutted from Cho's face. When Pike touched the metal to see how deeply it had gone, it fell away, leaving a puckered area that was already starting to swell and blister from the heat. Blood spatter was smeared across the side of the Marine's face.

Turning his attention back to the street, Pike picked up his rifle again. "It's not your blood. You're fine."

Tentatively, Cho worked his jaw as if trying to convince himself he was all right.

"Bekah." Pike raked the street and immediately picked up more activity. Three windows on the opposite side of the street suddenly sprouted rifle barrels. Gut clenching, realizing how vulnerable they were on the street, Pike lined up on one of the shooters as the man opened fire indiscriminately on the market. Squeezing the trigger, Pike bracketed the rifleman and put a trio of bullets into the man's chest before he fell back inside.

Ahead, Bekah's Humvee struggled to move forward, but the blast and the cab had knocked it up on two wheels. The tires on the right side screamed, and rubber burned, giving off thick, black smoke. The vehicle wasn't moving.

A note of panic edged Bekah's response. "We're pinned. We can't move."

"Then hang on. I'm gonna move you." Pike dropped his weapon between the seats, grabbed the steering wheel in both hands, and let out the clutch. He covered the distance between the two vehicles, leaning on the horn to get people moving out of the way. He lined up behind Bekah's Humvee as bullets ricocheted from the buildings and the vehicles. Rounds tore through the Humvee's roof. At least one of the bullets caromed off Pike's helmet, smacking him hard enough to dip his head.

Lining up behind the other Humvee, he stomped the accelerator.

The bumpers met with a muffled clang, then continued to grind as Pike powered forward. Grudgingly, the trapped Humvee rolled. Metal screamed as the Marine vehicle grated against the stone building.

The stricken cab bumped and jostled and shifted as Pike kept the accelerator down. As the vehicle banged against Pike's Humvee, he spotted the dead men inside the cab. Evidently shrapnel had torn through the front of the vehicle and shredded the driver and his passenger.

Two more explosions rocked the street. Glancing in his rearview and side mirrors, Pike spotted two blast zones that had knocked people flat in a circular radius around the detonations. The bombs killed indiscriminately, leaving men, women, and children scattered in their wake.

Cho cursed, equal parts anger and fear.

Pike kept his voice level as he continued shoving the other Humvee forward. "Keep watch, Cho. Don't hesitate to shoot."

Looking pale, his toothpick no longer in sight, Cho nodded. "Okay."

A moment later, Bekah's Humvee dropped onto all four wheels and the tires gripped the street. Pike followed her back into the traffic and roared through the maze of stalled and confused cars. He clipped several of the vehicles as he passed, but most of them had been abandoned.

"Here!" Bekah pulled her vehicle to a halt at the mouth of an alley that was barely wide enough to admit the Humvee.

Pike swung in at a right angle behind her, creating a temporary bulwark against any enemies who might pursue them.

Bekah got out of the Humvee with her rifle at the ready. She scanned the surroundings, talking rapidly. "Indigo Dispatch, this is Indigo Nine Leader. We're going to form a line here, see what we can do to help contain this situation. We're not the only target. The tangos are firing on the civilians." She looked over her shoulder at Pike and pointed at the fire escape snaking up the side of the nearby buildings. "Take Cho. Grab the high ground."

Pike nodded and moved at once, but he didn't like leaving Bekah behind with a green Marine. However, having a sniper spot would go a long way toward helping. He ran up the iron steps, his boots ringing rapidly. Cho's weight slammed down on the stairs right behind Pike, and Pike hoped the fire escape would hold as it shifted and swayed beneath them.

"Roger that, Indigo Nine Leader. Indigo One, Three, and Four are en route. ETA is two minutes."

Pike ran harder. Two minutes could be several lifetimes in a battle.

# 18

**TENDRILS OF SMOKE** climbed into the air southwest of where Yaqub sat in the SUV his men had stolen less than an hour ago. Through the bug-smeared window, he kept watch over the Noor Jahan Hotel, where American journalists often congregated to file their reports and receive information from military liaisons.

The structure was three stories tall and had red-tiled roofs. Flags fluttered above the hotel. A dozen cars were parked in the dirt lot in front of the building. Nearly all of them were SUVs and minivans used by the reporters.

Several reporters ran from the hotel to their vehicles. Most of them were young men pursuing fame available to those who reported from the battlefield. The Westerners loved beating their breasts, so certain of their military superiority even after so many years.

In disgust, Yaqub watched those men fling open their doors and clamber aboard. Today they would not be broadcasting messages. Today they would *be* a message.

Dismissing the young men, Yaqub kept watch through his binoculars for the man he awaited. But when the last of the reporters had driven away in their vehicles, the man had not appeared.

Yaqub turned to Wali. The young scout sat in the driver's seat. "Wali, you are certain Jonathan Sebastian arrived at the hotel?"

"Yes. He is here."

"Then he did not leave the building."

"Perhaps he is not as willing to risk getting killed as his younger counterparts. He has achieved his fame and fortune."

Yaqub opened his door and stepped out. "Then if Sebastian is content to do his coverage of the news from this place, our mission here will be even simpler." He strode across the dirt parking lot toward the hotel.

Wali stepped into position beside Yaqub, followed by four other men.

Lifting the radio from his pocket, Yaqub spoke briefly. "Faisal, send our warriors after the journalists."

"At once."

Yaqub continued walking without being contested all the way into the hotel. In the lobby, a handful of men stood watching breaking news on a laptop on a coffee table. From the dialogue exchanged between them, Yaqub knew they were Westerners, probably Americans, British, and others who felt they had a vested interest in the future of Afghanistan. They were probably planning on bringing their Western ungodly ways to the country—and on taking advantage of the low labor cost that would be available in a recovering country.

Around the lobby, bellboys and the managers behind the desk took immediate notice of Yaqub and his entourage, sensing that something was wrong.

*They look like lambs that have discovered a wolf among them.* The thought brought Yaqub pleasure. He drew the silencer-equipped Makarov pistol from hiding and pointed to the group of men surrounding the laptop. "Kill them."

One of the men turned and guessed at what was coming. He tried to yell a warning to the other men and flee at the same time.

Scarcely had the breath left his mouth than Wali pulled out the silenced Ingram MAC-10 he carried and opened fire.

The machine pistol spat a spray of bullets that chopped down the men and shattered the laptop. The silencer nearly muffled all sounds of the shots. Wali ejected the spent magazine and fed in a fresh one.

Two of Yaqub's men separated from the group and walked through the journalists. Some of them still moved. Using silenced pistols, the two men shot each of their targets through the head whether they were moving or not.

Behind the hotel desk, a closed-circuit television camera recorded everything, exactly as Yaqub wanted. Two men worked behind the hotel desk. The younger one ran for the door.

Yaqub shot the runner three times. Staggering, the younger clerk grabbed for the desk and managed to knock down an advertisement. Yaqub leaned over the counter, pointed his pistol at the younger man lying on the floor, and shot him through the head. The man went slack.

Face cold and neutral, knowing that the surviving man was afraid of him, Yaqub stepped closer to him. "Do not run."

The man trembled visibly, and sweat broke out upon his brow. "I will not run."

"There is an American staying here. His name is Jonathan Sebastian."

The clerk's voice cracked and he had to clear it to continue speaking. "Yes, he is here."

"What room?"

"I will need to look at the computer."

"Do so."

Fumbling, the man tapped the keyboard, studied the results, and looked back at Yaqub. "He is in suite 317. Third floor, then to the left." He trembled. "Please, I ask in God's name, do not kill me."

"God will not protect you. You should have been making war

on the Americans, not serving them. I am God's vengeance." Yaqub pointed his pistol and squeezed off two rounds in quick succession. The clerk was dead before he hit the floor.

Taking aim again, Yaqub looked up into the security camera, then squeezed the trigger once more and reduced it to scrap metal. Sparks flew for a moment as pieces rained down.

Yaqub turned from the desk and swapped out magazines in his weapon. He led the way to the elevator and the others followed.

★   ★   ★

Paul Schofield sat tensely in the SUV as it raced down narrow streets toward the area where black smoke streamed into the sky. He was twenty-two years old, barely out of journalism school, and had hoped the assignment to Afghanistan would be a route to easy money. All he needed was a little fame, a little notoriety, and he'd be able to write his own ticket.

At least, that was what his journalism professor had told him. *"Get out there in the soup. Don't be afraid to make a difference. Take risks. That's how you get ahead in this business. You can't just report the news these days. You have to* be *the news."*

That was his line of thinking until three days ago, the first time Schofield had seen dead people anywhere other than in a funeral home. Seeing a corpse on the street was a lot different from seeing a body a mortician had worked on. Paul's grandmother had looked better the day they had buried her than she had the last few days in the hospital.

But the four people Paul had seen three days ago had been IED victims. Paul didn't even know what the improvised explosive device had been rigged up to look like. All he could remember was the blood and the stink and the way the bodies had been torn to pieces. It had looked like a lot of the video games he had played in high school and college, almost familiar, only all too immediate. But in the games, he hadn't been able to *smell* the carnage.

That odor haunted Schofield, and his appetite hadn't yet completely recovered. He was beginning to think it never would.

"You okay, Paul?" Carter Pierce turned toward him from the middle seats of the SUV. He was tall and dark-haired with eyes that could cut right through a person. His profile was absolutely photogenic, a Bruce Campbell kind of chin. A guy could make a lot of money with a jawline like that.

"I'm fine." Paul wished his voice didn't sound like a croak, but something was caught there.

"You look kinda sick to me."

"I said I was fine." Schofield had always hated being the new guy. In junior high gym, that meant getting picked last. In college, it meant being the guy none of the professors remembered. In Afghanistan, it meant being the brunt of everybody's sometimes-cruel observations about how shocked he was at what he was seeing.

"I was just thinking that if you decided to hurl inside here, the way you did when you saw that IED site, there's not a lot of room in an SUV." Pierce brushed at his jacket lapels. "I don't want your weak stomach to mess with my close-up." The two reporters in the backseat smirked at Paul's expense.

"Hey, Pierce." That was Brett Snyder, a stringer for the Associated Press and a four-year veteran of the conflict in Afghanistan, the guy among them with the most time in. He was divorced and had a drinking problem that nobody was supposed to talk about but everybody did. He was also more sympathetic than the others. When he wasn't half in the bag. "Shut up and leave the kid alone."

"Hey, it's a concern. I want to look good." Pierce slumped back in his seat. "Don't want to spend the rest of the morning smelling like puke either."

"Do what I told you to do."

Paul was relieved, and he knew that Pierce would do as Snyder ordered. Snyder was the go-to guy with all the contacts in the American military, the UN, the ANP, and the ANA. If a reporter wanted to talk to somebody in those camps, it was better to go through Snyder to get there. He had the juice to make things happen.

Pierce looked at the window and checked his appearance, smoothing his perfect hair, breathing into his palm to check his breath.

The SUV swerved and the tires screamed as the vehicle floated around a sudden turn. The black smoke was closer now, thicker and more foreboding.

*That would be an awesome shot if I could get it.* Schofield imagined himself standing in the foreground of the shot, one hand in his pocket as if he were relaxed while carnage reigned through the rest of the city.

Harsh ratcheting sounds came from outside the SUV, penetrating the constant feed from the military band radio. The soldiers spoke in cryptic responses. Schofield was picking up the militaryspeak, but a lot of it remained Greek to him. Still, the intensity in the voices, knowing that guys were out there laying their lives on the line, excited him.

All he needed was one of those soldiers telling him the story of today. That story could make Schofield's day.

A rapid-fire popping noise increased in decibel level. Schofield recognized the noise as motorcycle engines. They were two-stroke dirt bikes. He'd ridden those back in New Mexico, where he'd grown up. He turned in his seat and looked behind them.

Four motorcycle riders wearing scarves, turbans, and backpacks roared up the street toward them.

In the front passenger seat, Snyder turned and cursed. He slapped the driver on the shoulder. "Get us out of here!"

Pierce sat up straighter as he gripped the seat in front of him.

The SUV driver wove back and forth across the street, barely controlling the vehicle as it careened between the ramshackle buildings and ruined structures.

Schofield's stomach spasmed, and he knew he was going to be sick. He couldn't help himself. He hunkered low in the seat, thinking that the motorcyclists were going to pull out their rifles any minute and start shooting the SUV. Or maybe they had rocket launchers. Schofield had seen vivid proof of how destructive those weapons could be.

Instead, the drivers spread out, each one matching speed with the journalists' SUVs.

"Turn right! Turn right now!" Snyder pointed at the coming intersection. He was holding tightly to his seat belt with his other hand.

The driver responded immediately, tapping the brake to slow down, then clawing at the steering wheel to turn the vehicle.

Paralyzed with fear, Schofield watched the motorcyclist who had targeted their vehicle. The rider maneuvered his machine with surprisingly expert precision. He cut back to the right, sweeping behind the SUV as it turned, then seizing the inside track as they rounded the corner. In a split second, the motorcyclist was once more beside them.

Snyder cursed again. Beside the window where the motorcyclist was, Pierce suddenly tried to claw his way over the top of Schofield. Events became very confused as Schofield instinctively fought being manhandled by the other reporter, slapping and pushing at Pierce to force him to stay where he was.

Then, while the SUV was still nearly out of control in the turn, fighting for balance, the motorcyclist blew up. Blood painted the side of the SUV, and shrapnel shattered the windows and peppered the vehicle as the concussive impact added to the centrifugal force already pulling at them through the turn.

Losing traction, giving in to the laws of physics, the SUV flipped onto its side and skidded along the street until it crashed into a knot of people. On the other side of the windshield, two men struggled against the vehicle's weight as it pinned them against a building. One of the men suddenly vomited blood and collapsed. The other screamed in pain.

Down the street, bodies lay on the ground in one of the market areas. Black smoke continued to plume in the sky. Schofield realized then that they had reached ground zero of the firefight. The steady stream of small-arms fire dimmed when louder explosions crashed over the area.

"Out! Get out of the vehicle!" Snyder tried to follow his own advice by disengaging the seat belt and struggling to pull himself through the broken passenger window.

Schofield instantly became aware of Pierce's deadweight lying on him. He looked at the other reporter and stared into the man's open, unseeing eyes. A scream caught in the back of Schofield's throat and wouldn't rip free.

Snyder was halfway out the broken window when harsh cracks sounded close by. The man stiffened, then dropped back into the SUV.

"Move! Out of the way!" The man behind Schofield fought to get out from under his weight. Schofield tried to explain that he was trapped by his seat belt and by Pierce's corpse, but he couldn't speak.

Then, abruptly, a young, cold face appeared in the broken window. For a moment, Schofield thought maybe someone had come to rescue them. Someone wearing the digital camouflage of the United States military or even someone from the UN forces would have been more calming.

The man said something, but Schofield didn't understand the language. He understood the AK-47 that was thrust inside the SUV, though. Before he had time to even try to get away, the man opened fire.

# 19

**ON THE ROOFTOP,** Pike surveyed the battlefield as adrenaline cascaded through him. He stayed low and kept the M4A1 pulled tight to his shoulder as he sought out targets that tried to close on Bekah and Zeke's position at the Humvees. A turban-wearing man carrying an AK-47 fired steadily at the Marines as he approached in a crouch from the abandoned vehicles in the street.

Pinned down by the steady stream of rifle fire, Bekah and Zeke couldn't respond.

Pike targeted the man's head and shoulders from three stories up and squeezed the trigger, riding out the recoil and firing again and again. The al Qaeda gunner dropped in the street.

At the end of the block, an SUV and a motorcycle came around the corner. In the next instant, the motorcyclist exploded and the SUV rolled over, sliding into a building and taking out civilians along the way. A man tried to scramble from the doomed vehicle, but bullets struck him and he dropped back inside.

One of the terrorists chewing through the civilians turned his attention to the stricken SUV. Pike tried to bracket the man with his rifle, but he couldn't get a clear shot between stalled vehicles and civilians still on the street.

The al Qaeda gunner strode to the side of the SUV and peered inside. Pike got his sights set on the man as the tango shoved his rifle barrel into the vehicle and started hosing the occupants. Pike squeezed the trigger and readied himself for a second shot. The al Qaeda warrior dropped to the street in a half crouch, wounded but still in play. Pike shot the man twice more, leaving him stretched out beside the SUV.

In the intersection behind the overturned SUV, another similar vehicle streaked by with a motorcyclist drawing even beside it. Before the SUV cleared the intersection, the motorcyclist exploded and the resulting blast blew the larger vehicle sideways as the tires shredded.

*Let it go.* Pike blinked and refocused on the street in front of Bekah and Zeke. *Save your team.*

A half-dozen tangos converged on the Marines' position from all sides. Pike fired relentlessly, but the targets were too fast. Two of them were in the street, but four others closed on Bekah and Zeke.

"Bekah, get out of there. You can't hold that position."

Below, Bekah grabbed Zeke's arm and pulled him back toward the building behind them.

Bullets slapped into the roof beside Pike, grabbing his attention immediately as he rolled for cover. He flailed out with his free hand and grabbed Cho's collar, pulling the man into motion. Together, they ran across the roof.

From the corner of his eye, Pike spotted three tangos on the next rooftop. Evidently they'd abandoned their posts inside the building and come to the high ground. Or maybe they'd been there and he just hadn't noticed in all the confusion. One of the attackers swung up an RPG.

Cho stumbled and nearly fell. Fisting the younger man's BDUs, thinking maybe he was moving too late after all, Pike kept Cho on his feet as they ran for the fire escape.

★　★　★

"Keep moving, Marine." Bekah pushed Zeke ahead of her toward the doorway of the building. She hated leaving the Humvees behind. Mobility was one of a Marine's greatest assets in battle.

She stumbled just for a moment as a bullet slammed into her Kevlar between her shoulder blades. The armor kept the round from penetrating, but the hydrostatic shock of the impact knocked the breath from her. She ran through the doorway on Zeke's heels, then turned around, taking advantage of the shelter offered by the doorframe.

She raised her rifle to her shoulder and aimed at the al Qaeda fighter closing in on her. "Take cover."

Mechanically, but slower than Bekah wanted, Zeke followed commands that had been drilled into him. He planted himself on the other side of the doorway, back against the wall, and brought his rifle up.

Thinking of Travis and her granny—and how much she wanted to stay alive to go back home to them—Bekah fired her weapon in short, controlled bursts. One of the al Qaeda warriors pulled up, staggered, then dropped. The others hunted for cover around the Humvees, and Bekah found herself shooting her own vehicle while trying to target her enemy.

Zeke stood frozen. His eyes moved restlessly and perspiration trickled down his chin and neck, but he never budged.

"Return fire, Marine. I'm reloading." Bekah withdrew from the doorway and cleared the spent magazine, ramming it home in her ammo rack. One of the tangos surged forward as soon as Bekah pulled back. "Do it now." *Or we're going to be overrun.* Bekah grabbed for the next magazine, trying in vain to dispel thoughts of Granny having to explain to Travis why Mommy wasn't coming home anymore.

Zeke held the trigger down and bullets sprayed wildly, kicking up roadway chunks in front of the approaching al Qaeda warrior and rising to slam into the Humvees. The young Marine's weapon cycled dry in seconds. He squeezed the trigger again.

Bekah slammed the new magazine in place and slapped the release, stripping the first round from the clip and seating it. "Reload, Marine." She struggled to keep her voice calm, keep her mind off Travis and Granny, and speak over the destruction taking place on the street around them. "Set your weapon for three-round burst."

"Right, right. Three-round burst." Zeke wheeled back inside the doorway and dumped the empty magazine. It slid through his fingers and dropped to the floor. He started to reach for it.

*"Reload!"* Bekah targeted the tango scrambling once more for cover and squeezed the trigger. The rounds caught the man in the back, and he sprawled onto the pavement.

Zeke grabbed a magazine and shoved it home on the third attempt. "Three-round burst. Set."

*If you survive this, you're going to work with him on his responses.* Bekah ducked inside as a fusillade of bullets chipped at the stone walls around the doorway and whizzed by her.

The Humvees were a problem. Bekah hadn't thought about the al Qaeda warriors using them for cover. She hadn't thought there would be so many of them either. The citizens in the street had cleared out, leaving only their dead behind. Thankfully, they'd taken their wounded with them as far as Bekah could tell.

She freed a fragmentation grenade from her combat harness, shifted hands with her assault rifle, and yanked the pin. Holding the spoon in place, she showed the munition to Zeke. "Fire in the hole!"

He nodded and pulled back, his face so pale she thought he might pass out.

Squatting, Bekah rolled the grenade into the street, giving it just enough propulsion to place it under the Humvees. Then she ducked back and changed hands with the M4A1 again, counting down. *Three, two, one . . .*

The grenade exploded and shrapnel hammered the wall behind Bekah and tore through the door into the room. Whirling, she leaned around the doorframe again and peered out over the gunsights.

Two tangos were on the ground, their feet torn and bloody from the shrapnel that had ripped their legs from under them. They struggled to get to their feet and raise their weapons at the same time. Bekah thought of the civilians lying beyond them who were dead, cut down viciously with no quarter given. Her heart hardened, and she vowed that her young son would never see the part of her that was in action today. She pulled the trigger, killing both men.

She swept the area over the rifle sights, realizing then that the shrapnel had also taken out the tires on her Humvee. The vehicle listed sadly, like an old, arthritic dog, covered in scars from the earlier collision and the rough ride against the wall.

For the moment, no one fired at her, but she heard small-arms fire from above. Almost immediately, a loud explosion rang out. She switched over to her comm.

"Pike!"

There was no answer.

*"Pike!"*

Pike didn't hesitate at the roof's edge. Cho tried to hold up, but Pike kept his grip and muscled the other Marine over the side with him. He'd judged the fire escape's location from memory. There were no markers along the roof.

His memory wasn't quite spot-on. He saw in a rush that he was going to miss the steps and the landing one floor below him. That left a long fall that would break his legs even if he survived it. He released his hold on the other Marine and prepared to catch himself if he could.

Cho was on the mark, falling in a painful collapse at the bottom of the steps just short of the landing.

Flailing with his free hand, not willing to lose hold of his rifle, Pike caught the railing in an iron grip. His shoulder threatened to come apart as his body weight hit the end of his arm. For a moment he thought his hold was going to slip, but he clung fast, feeling the rusted metal bite into his palm like rat's teeth.

He pendulumed and slammed into the landing. His helmet kept him from breaking his skull, but the impact banged his goggles into his right cheek hard enough to split the skin. Warm blood tracked down his face. He yelled in pain and frustration as he slung his rifle over his right shoulder and swung his other hand up to grip the railing as well.

The roof's edge exploded above him, and he knew the al Qaeda warrior with the RPG had fired low. Stone and mortar rained down on Pike and Cho, causing them both to duck their heads. A few large pieces thudded off Pike's helmet and hammered his back and shoulders. Bright pain seared through him, but he held on. The blast had left him mostly deafened.

Smoke drifted over him, and he realized the fire escape was no longer flush against the building. The metal latticework vibrated as it gaped two feet from the wall. Pike hung crookedly, nothing below him.

"Cho!"

The other Marine lay with his hands over his head.

Pike didn't know if the man was dead or unconscious. *"Cho!"*

"Yeah." Cho shifted, then started coughing violently.

"Get up or you're a dead man." Pike swung hand over hand along the fire escape till he was mostly above the second-story landing. He rocked forward once to build some momentum; then on the second forward progression, he let go.

Cho forced himself to his feet and started down the steps, leaning to one side because of the incline and maybe because of some disorientation he was feeling.

Pike landed safely, but his back and helmet collided against the railing with enough force to knock the wind out of him and temporarily send his senses reeling. He dropped to his knees, certain that the fire escape was going to buckle beneath him at any moment. He slid his M4A1 from his shoulder and pointed toward the collapsed section of the roofline as smoke and dust frosted him.

Cho joined Pike on the lower landing just as the first al Qaeda warrior peered over the edge a few feet from the broken area. Firing instinctively, Pike bracketed the tango with two three-round bursts that drove the man backward. Reaching to his combat harness, Pike ripped a grenade free, yanked the pin, and heaved it on top of the building.

"Pike!" Bekah repeated his name over the MBITR, but Pike could barely hear it.

He got to his feet and raced after Cho. Two tangos stood at the roof's edge and fired down at them. Bullets whined off the fire escape railing. Ahead of Pike, Cho stumbled but kept going, whipping around the next turn as the steps shivered beneath them.

"I'm here."

On top of the building the grenade exploded, and the gunfire from above came to an immediate stop. One of the tangos fell over the side and plummeted to the alley below, screaming all the way to that final sudden impact.

Pike made the next turn and glanced at both ends of the alley, making certain of his bearings and trying to gauge the danger they might be fleeing into. "Where are you?"

"Inside the building."

"Good to go?"

"Yes."

"Rendezvous there? I had to give up the rooftop to encroaching hostiles."

"Yes. We've got tangos still trolling the streets."

"Guys are real believers." Pike reached the alley and sprinted past Cho, who had stood undecided for a moment. The Marine didn't hesitate falling in after Pike, though.

"This is an all-out push."

"Our lucky day," Pike muttered. "What about support?" With everything that had been going on during his time on the roof, Pike had lost track of the other Marine units en route.

"Inbound. Should be here any minute."

The action on the street had intensified. Al Qaeda warriors had swarmed the Humvees, drawn to the Marine vehicles like flies to an ice cream social. Rounds screamed along the alley, ricocheting from the building walls.

Pike knew rounding the corner even behind the shelter of the Humvees was going to be risky. He paused at a doorway in the alley thirty feet from the corner and tried the doorknob. It was locked.

"Coming through the back door."

"Affirmative. We have not cleared that area."

"Roger that." Stepping back from the door, Pike rammed his boot twice beside the lock before the door splintered and gave way. He rushed into the gloomy shadows that filled the building.

The building had been a laundry at one time. Ancient machines covered in rust lined the walls and filled the center of the open area. Several of the units were in pieces, scattered across other washers— evidently the work of scavengers. Laundry bags lay in disarray, all of them picked over. Everything in the room had been burned, and the air remained thick with the stink of old smoke. Pike didn't know if the building was the site of a bombing or if the area had gone up in flames through the predations of an arsonist. All that was left was ruins.

He went forward, jogging through the debris. He pulled up the scarf around his neck to cover his mouth and nose so he wouldn't suck up too much dust and ash. The fabric blunted the smoke stench only somewhat.

The door at the end of the room had charred but hadn't burned down. Pike figured a fire brigade had arrived in time, or maybe the plumbing had saved what was left of the room. Scorch marks and smoke damage webbed the walls. The fire had eaten through the roof and laid bare the electrical wires, which looked leprous without their protective coating in many places.

Pike smashed his foot into the door and it shuddered open, revealing three al Qaeda warriors in the hallway. They'd evidently been creeping toward Bekah's position. Less than four feet away, the tangos shook off their surprise and started lifting their weapons.

Knowing Cho was behind him and any kind of retreat would leave them flat-footed—and that exchanging shots in the hallway wasn't in his favor—Pike lowered his head and charged. His helmet caught the lead tango in the face, breaking his nose. Pike kept driving, digging in with his combat boots, bulling the man's weight backward into the next man.

Levering his left hand up between them, Pike gripped the smaller man's clothing in his fist, headbutted him again, and lifted the M4A1 into firing position. The al Qaeda warrior behind the first man opened fire, striking his own man in his fear.

Pike fired two three-round bursts into the shooter's chest, then bulldozed the two men again. The first man took down the second, leaving them both tangled on the ground.

The third al Qaeda warrior opened fire, but Pike ducked and

threw himself forward, propelling off the bodies of the first two men, feeling them give beneath his weight. He struck the last tango in the stomach, driving the man to the ground. Rising to his knees, still astride his enemy, Pike ripped his KA-BAR free of his combat harness, gripped it tightly, and plunged it into the man's neck.

Breathing hard from the exertion and from the adrenaline thundering through him, Pike stood in the gloom and surveyed the dead men. He gripped his M4A1, then unclipped his flashlight and directed the beam through the hallway. At the end of the run, the corridor twisted to the right, probably leading to units on the other side of the building.

"Pike?" Gunshots punctuated Bekah's transmission.

"On our way. Ran into rats in the walls." Pike put his flashlight away and walked back to the doorway that led to the section where he guessed Bekah and Zeke had holed up. He opened the door, grateful that it opened easily enough with a squeal of rusty hinges, and resentful because it didn't offer much in the way of protection. Several splintered holes in the surface that let light through underscored its weakness.

Pike and Cho stepped through into another section of the building that had been a shop of some kind, probably a grocery store. Empty shelves lined the walls, but empty cans and boxes that had once contained foodstuffs were among the debris littered over the floor. Posters advertising products occupied some of the wall space.

Bekah and Zeke stood at the doorway, firing unevenly. Bekah called out orders to the green Marine, managing the rhythm of suppressive fire as much as she was able.

Pike paused just long enough to find a broken board and ram it under the interior door's edge so that anyone trying to get into the room would have a hard time and his team would at least have some kind of warning before that happened. Of course, shooting through the door remained just as easy.

"Cho. On me." Pike advanced to the empty space at the front of the shop that had once been occupied by a large plate-glass window. He waved Cho to the right side, setting up on the left and pulling the M4A1 to his shoulder.

The al Qaeda fighters had concentrated their efforts on the Marine vehicles. Drawn by the scent of blood, certain of their place in heaven for dying in their jihad, they came on. Pike counted at least seven of them as he snapped off shots to break an advance across the street. Snipers still occupied the upper floors of buildings across the street, adding to the danger.

Movement at the end of the street to Pike's right drew his attention to the three Marine Humvees rolling into the area. Fifty-cal machine gunners on the Humvees' rear decks took aim, and the heavy-caliber fire pealed along the street.

Still, the sniper nests along the buildings on the other side of the street remained dangerous. Pike hated the idea that the Marines were headed into that deadly line of fire. He pulled back from the window.

Bekah keyed her radio. "Indigo teams, be advised that you have snipers in buildings on the west side of the street." She shifted as she spoke, trying to elevate her weapon to target the snipers. Even then, the 5.56mm rounds weren't going to do much damage unless she hit the tangos. "Hold your positions or you're going to roll into them."

Pike tapped Bekah on the shoulder. "Cover me."

She glanced at him, worry etched into her face. "Where are you going? Heath's out there."

*Heath? Not Lieutenant Bridger?* The casual reference didn't surprise Pike. He'd picked up on some of the undercurrent of attraction between Bekah and the lieutenant when they were together in Somalia. He was surprised she had gotten so at ease with the officer because they came from different worlds. There was scuttlebutt up and down the grapevine that Heath Bridger had done some legal work for her in civilian life, but nothing more.

Pike nodded and brushed sweat from his eyebrows, not surprised that his hand came away stained with blood. "I know. And if they keep coming, they're gonna roll right under those enemy guns. I'm gonna even up the odds a little."

"How?"

Hunkered behind Bekah, Pike nodded at the Humvees. "I'm gonna grab one of those fifties and chase those snipers back into their holes."

"You can't go out there."

"I'm going. I need you to keep them ducking." Then Pike was in motion, staying low and running for all he was worth.

# 20

WHEN THE ELEVATOR STOPPED at the third floor, Yaqub stepped out of the cage with his pistol at the ready. Two Westerners, a man and a woman, halted in the hallway and gazed at him with glassy eyes. Neither of them was Jonathan Sebastian. Before they could move, Yaqub shot them both and walked past their bodies.

He glanced at the numbers as he passed them, finding room 317 two more doors ahead. Stopping beside the door, he waved to Wali.

The younger man moved forward, tried the lock, and shook his head. He stepped back and lowered his pistol, firing three rounds into the mechanism. Metal pieces dropped to the floor. Before the sounds of the silenced shots faded, Wali threw his shoulder against the door and followed it inside.

Yaqub trailed on the young warrior's heels, scanning the room immediately.

Frozen in surprise, Jonathan Sebastian sat on the bed's edge. The man was in his late forties, an industry legend in international news. He had made his name covering the first war in Iraq over twenty years ago. That long history and the name recognition Sebastian enjoyed as a journalist were what had drawn Yaqub to the man, though he radiated a sense of pompous self-worth that Yaqub found repugnant. His hair was perfectly coiffed, and Yaqub knew from the information he had on the reporter that Sebastian had allowed himself to go gray because the vain man believed it would give him even more appeal to his viewers. The reporter was lean and in shape, and Yaqub knew that he had a personal trainer. He wore suit trousers and went barefoot. His tie hung at half-mast and his suit coat lay on the bed within easy reach.

Another man stood at the window watching the curling black smoke coming from the city. He was half Sebastian's age, smaller, and looked immediately frightened. He held a small digital camera and had evidently been taking pictures of the destruction.

Wali kept his weapon at the ready as he went forward and quickly searched both men for weapons.

Yaqub lowered the Makarov. "Jonathan Sebastian."

"Yes." Sebastian looked scared and confused.

A trace of pride sailed through Yaqub at the other man's reaction. It was good to incite fear in one's enemies, but it was even better to do so to the people who spread the news. "Do you know who I am?"

Sebastian glanced at the other man, who had taken a cowering step back till he reached the wall. He stood there, obviously wishing he were anywhere else.

"He's Zalmai Yaqub, sir." The man's voice broke.

Sebastian nodded as he turned toward Yaqub. "I met you when you were a boy."

"I am no longer a boy."

"I interviewed your father, you know. Back when such a thing was still possible. Before the CIA strike."

"So I was told. My father remembers you well. He will be pleased to see you again."

"I thought your father was dead."

"No. Get dressed. You're coming with me."

"Where?"

"To the biggest story you have ever covered. One that will build your career even more than it already is."

Sebastian sat still. "What if I don't want to go?"

"You don't have a choice. Get up. Put your clothes on or I'll have someone dress you. We don't have time for them to be gentle."

Reluctantly Sebastian stood. His face didn't reveal anything, but the man had to be factoring in his chances for rescue. "You can't just take me. Somebody like me, someone will come looking."

"I know. I am counting on that. If you do not come with me, I will kill you and find someone else to relay this story. I would prefer you, but I refuse to argue. I do not have time." Yaqub shifted the Makarov in his hand meaningfully. "Neither do you."

Sebastian put on his shoes and picked up his coat. He nodded to the younger man. "What about Kimball?"

"He will not be joining us."

Kimball appeared relieved, almost sagging with the emotion.

"He's my cameraman."

Yaqub smiled at the American, conscious of the time slipping away. By now the attack on the hotel would have been reported. With all the action already transpiring in the city, a military force might even now be on its way.

"I have cameramen." Yaqub turned to Kimball. "You have a camera."

The man looked at the device as if it had somehow betrayed him. "Yes." He had to clear his throat to get that out.

Yaqub stood beside Sebastian. "Take our picture."

Hesitantly the man lifted the camera and tried to hold it steady. His hands trembled violently, but he managed to take the shot.

"Another."

The man triggered the camera once more.

Yaqub held out his hand. "Please. Give the camera to me."

Still shaking, the man placed the camera in Yaqub's palm. Yaqub stepped back and nodded to Wali.

Adjusting the machine pistol he carried, alerting the American enough to make him raise his hands in his own defense, Wali sprayed him with bullets.

Sebastian cursed hoarsely, but there was no anger in his words, only a raspy fear and the understanding that his life was no longer his own. Fearfully he stared at Yaqub.

"Let us go." The al Qaeda leader placed the camera on the desk in the corner of the room, where it would be found during the subsequent investigation, then turned and headed through the doorway into the hall. Wali pushed the journalist into motion and followed.

★ ★ ★

Yaqub crossed the parking area without incident. He spotted some of the journalists hiding on the premises, talking on satellite phones and taking pictures or videos with their devices. Yaqub didn't care.

He stepped into the back of the SUV while Wali shoved Sebastian into the other side of the vehicle. Yaqub kept the Makarov in his lap and gazed out the window.

"What do you want with me?" Sebastian's fear almost shredded his words.

"You have an important job ahead of you. You are going to be my chronicler, Mr. Sebastian." Yaqub turned to the man and smiled. "You should be very grateful. The story you are about to reveal to the world is going to make you legendary in your circles. Your name—the things you will host—will always be remembered in your country."

"What are you talking about?"

The driver started the SUV and put the vehicle into gear.

"The Americans killed Osama bin Laden. He built al Qaeda into the force that it is, ignited the fire of jihad against the West, but no one has done as much since his death. My people need a champion, and I intend to give them one. I intend to be that champion. I am going to pick up that holy war and drive the infidels from Afghanistan while they linger in their indecision and growing weakness. Then I am going to attack them in their homelands. Since bin Laden's death, many have gone into hiding, but they still strike in this country. They are largely ineffectual because they are separate in their efforts. I will unite them, forge them into the weapon that God intended them to be. They will see what I am capable of, and they will flock to me. Blood will run in rivers in Afghanistan." As he spoke, the certainty of his future and his calling swelled inside Yaqub. God had called him forth to do this. His father had told him that, and now he believed it to be true.

Sebastian shook his head. "You're painting a target on yourself. The military will hunt you down the way they did bin Laden."

"No." Yaqub's voice exploded out of him, and he strove to control his anger. He wanted to slit the throat of the man for voicing doubt in front of his followers. It took effort to remember that he needed the man. "No, that will not happen. The West has grown sicker of this war than they are afraid of al Qaeda. I will teach them to fear the jihad again. Already many Afghans are turning against them. There will be more. The American president will see how much it will cost to continue this war. He will pull the troops from Afghanistan, and I will consolidate the warriors who will follow me."

"You won't get the Pentagon to back off."

"I will. The Pentagon does not lose its sons. The American people do, and they have no stomach for a continuance of the war. Allies of the American effort are withdrawing. Already the Americans have overstepped themselves in Pakistan by putting illegal CIA bases in that country. They have undone political alliances there. The Russians are furious with the Americans and British for allowing the opium trade to continue among the warlords they have agreements with, because the drugs are pouring into their country. No one is happy with the way the Americans are conducting this war these days—with the deals they are making—and the effects transgress the borders of this country. I will further discourage them. They are weak. They will give in."

"How do you plan to do that?"

"By killing their soldiers. Every corpse that goes home to a grieving Western family is a butcher's bill for the cost of this war." Yaqub shook his head. "Our young are raised to be warriors. They willingly give their lives in our holy war because they know the rewards they will reap in heaven. They believe in *fard al-'ayn*, the personal obligation of the Muslim man to God. Your countrymen do not surrender themselves so enthusiastically."

Sebastian said nothing.

"That is why al Qaeda will win. That is why I will win."

The driver took evasive action without warning.

Glancing forward, Yaqub spotted two ANP pickups speeding toward them. The driver had shifted to allow the Afghan police passage on the street. At first Yaqub thought they might escape unnoticed, but the pickups quickly turned around, throwing out rooster tails of dirt as they reversed direction.

The PA on one of the trucks blared out orders in Pashto behind them. "You there! Stop!" The command was repeated in English, French, and Arabic.

Shifting in his seat, Yaqub watched as the SUV behind the one he was riding in braked and slowed down. The driver wove back and forth across the street, keeping the ANP vehicles behind him. The man operating the 7.62mm machine gun mounted on the rear deck of the lead ANP truck opened fire. Bullets struck the SUV, shattering the rear glass and splashing blood inside the vehicle.

The driver jerked the wheel and managed to bring the SUV to a rocky stop sideways in the narrow street, blocking both ANP pickups. The machine gunners aboard the two trucks opened their weapons full throttle as their drivers pulled into overlapping fields of fire.

Two al Qaeda warriors stumbled out of the SUV, taking advantage of the protection offered by their vehicle but already in dire straits. One of them hauled out an RPG, then lay on the ground and brought the weapon to his shoulder under the SUV. An instant later, the warhead streaked away and smashed into the pickup on the right. The ANP vehicle bucked up a couple feet, like a horse trying to rear on its hind legs, then crashed back down. The blast left the front end smashed and warped, and gray smoke wisped from the vehicle.

The surviving machine gunner laid down a vicious strafing attack that chewed through the pavement and tracked back to the al Qaeda warrior scrambling to get out from under the SUV. Bullets ripped him apart before he could take cover. His body quivered and went still beneath the vehicle.

The second ANP pickup skirted the first, then turned down an alley to the left.

Wali calmly tapped the driver on the shoulder. "Take the next alley to the left. They are coming up the side street in an effort to intercept us on the next cross street ahead."

A feeling of ease dawned inside Yaqub. Wali was a master of terrain and always planned out their missions.

The driver nodded and braked the SUV. Then he turned the vehicle sharply and headed into the alley as instructed. The vehicle ahead of them continued forward, following the path they had chosen in anticipation of the kidnapping.

Yaqub sat quietly, trusting Wali because he guessed what the younger warrior was planning. It was a daring move and not without risk. He took pride in the young man, wishing more like him would join his ranks. Eventually they would.

The mouth of the alley came closer.

"Now." Wali readied his AK-47 and peered ahead. "Turn right. Quickly, *quickly*."

Obeying, the driver hauled the wheel to the right. The acceleration caused the SUV to skid; then the tires found purchase again. The heavy vehicle rocked on its suspension for a moment, then straightened out.

Ahead of them, the ANP pickup rounded the next corner at the cross street.

"Quickly." Wali kept the AK-47 in one hand and placed his free hand on his seat belt release. "Turn the corner. Go after them. Ram them from behind when you can. Do you hear me?"

"I hear." The driver hauled on the steering wheel again, turning the SUV sharply.

On the cross street, the ANP pulled to a halt at the corner as the lead SUV flashed by. The driver of that vehicle had slowed, doubtless looking for Yaqub's SUV. The machine gunner on the pickup's rear deck hesitated but tracked the first SUV with his weapon.

"Ram them. *Now!*" Wali braced his feet against the floor.

Yaqub braced himself as well and held on to the Makarov.

The SUV's front end was reinforced with rebar welded over the bumper to protect the engine. When the two vehicles slammed into each other, the SUV's greater weight knocked the ANP pickup forward. On the rear deck, the machine gunner staggered, then held on to the weapon in an effort not to get knocked over the side. Not so lucky, his companion spilled into the street.

Wali opened his door as they neared the hapless policeman. Disoriented, doubtless in shock, the man shoved his head up just in time to catch Wali's door in the face. The thump resounded in the SUV, and the man's body rolled limply to the side.

"Keep pushing them! Keep pushing!" Wali screamed into the driver's ear.

Unable to regain control of the vehicle, the ANP driver tried to speed up and get away. The SUV had more power and closed rapidly as the driver struggled to cut to the right. The larger vehicle caught the pickup on the right rear corner, pushed its rear tires so they lost traction, and turned it sideways across the front of the SUV.

They crossed the narrow street and slammed into the front of a shoe store, causing the people inside to duck away from the large plate-glass windows. Jagged shards dropped from the windows and cascaded in pieces across the pickup. The smaller vehicle crushed inward as the SUV bore down on it. Three policemen screamed on the other side of the fractured glass.

"Enough." Wali released his seat belt. "Back away and stop."

With a wrenching howl of twisted metal, the driver reversed the SUV about ten feet, then came to a rocking halt. Wali got out on one side and Yaqub stepped from the SUV on the other.

Some of the people inside the shoe shop had started forward, perhaps thinking that an accident had occurred instead of an ambush. Yaqub fired into them, wounding some of them and driving them all back.

Mercilessly, Wali shot the injured man in the pickup bed, then went forward and gunned down the driver and one of the passengers as well. All three of the men inside had been trapped by the crushed doors. The last man attempted to crawl from the door window, slicing his hands and forearms on the broken glass.

Yaqub walked toward the survivor, relishing the terror he saw in the man's eyes. The man hung there, trapped by the dead man on his legs and his injuries resulting from the crash.

The man sucked in air as he stared helplessly at Yaqub. "No. Please. Have mercy. I ask this in God's name." He prayed frantically, his voice breaking with his fear.

"You are a traitor to God. He does not hear your prayers. And I will not listen to them." Yaqub looked around at the bystanders, knowing he commanded their attention too. Then he held the pistol only inches from the man's head and pulled the trigger.

The policeman relaxed in death as blood wept down the side of the wrecked pickup.

Yaqub returned to the SUV. Sebastian looked pale and sickly and had managed to free himself from his seat belt. He froze in place with one leg out the door when Yaqub pointed the pistol at him.

"Get back inside or die here on the street." Yaqub glared at the man.

Trembling, Sebastian crawled into the SUV. Yaqub joined him; then the driver got under way again, once more rushing through the streets like a black shark.

# 21

**BULLETS FROM THE SNIPERS** across the street pelted the Humvee as Pike hauled himself into the back of the vehicle. He slung the M4A1 over his shoulder and tucked in behind the big .50-cal machine gun. More rounds flattened against the defensive shroud that flared around the weapon. Under his weight, the deck listed sideways on the shredded tires as he moved.

After checking the belt feed and finding nothing amiss, Pike settled in behind the big gun. As he spun the muzzle around toward the buildings on the other side of the street, a rocket struck the street only a few feet in front of him. Broken rock beat against the Humvee, shaking it slightly as smaller debris bounced from Pike's armor and stung his face and hands.

Pike opened fire and felt the heavy machine gun jerking and rising, climbing from the muzzle velocity. He corrected the gun's natural upward inclination and stitched a jagged line across the buildings where the al Qaeda snipers lay in hiding.

Spent cartridges ejected out of the gun like brass rain. The .50-cal round had been designed as a tank buster, the solid core capable of penetrating armor and going on to kill targets within a steel-clad vehicle.

The rounds did their job now, chopping through wood, punching through stone, and destroying the enemy combatants on the other side. Pike didn't let up till the belt had nearly cycled through. Ears ringing from the basso explosions, sweat running down his face and neck, Pike abandoned the machine gun only long enough to grab the next ammunition belt from the ammo box and connect it to the last. Then he was back at the gun, scouting for whatever survivors might still be at their posts.

"Pike, hold your fire." Heath Bridger's voice was sharp, but he was in control.

"Roger that. Holding fire, but I'm locked and loaded." Pike sat sweltering behind the machine gun. He kept watch anxiously as Marines debarked from the Humvees and spread out to contain the situation.

★   ★   ★

As Heath jogged forward, he managed the anxiousness that flooded through him when he thought about the danger he'd placed Bekah in. It had been his choice to have her patrol in this area. But she wouldn't have wanted him protecting her. That would have brought out her ire; he was sure of that.

*Let it go. When she's out here, she's a Marine. If you treat her any differently, even for a second, you're doing her and yourself a disservice, and you won't be fit to command these Marines.*

But thinking of her as one of the other Marines was hard. Thinking of female Marines as regular squad mates was difficult to begin with. His first inclination was to protect them. Most male Marines had to squelch that reaction when they were partnered with women on a line. That was one of the reasons the SEAL teams didn't allow females. Men got torn between fighting and protecting. Women made brave, good soldiers, but for the men, undoing generations of genetic and social hardwiring was a challenge.

With difficulty, Heath shelved that line of thought once more. He scanned the streets and listened to the progress of the men he'd ordered into the surrounding buildings. There wasn't much al Qaeda resistance. Pike had become a lethal force with the machine gun.

The dead littered the street. Men, women, and children lay scattered and bloody, some of them missing limbs and unrecognizable from the damage. The sight sickened Heath even after everything he'd seen in his previous tours. A soldier didn't get used to this. If he was lucky, he developed a means of setting it aside, but it still affected him. A lot of soldiers dealt with posttraumatic stress disorder. Heath had seen a number of those men since his first active tour.

As Heath approached the Humvee, Pike clambered down from the vehicle with his M4A1 in one hand. Although Pike was a couple inches shorter than Heath, his shoulders were broader and he was more powerfully built. Pike was a guy who couldn't be overlooked when he made himself known.

At present, the man looked hard-pressed. His camo was torn and tattered in several places. Blood streaked his stubbled face beneath his nonregulation sunglasses. But he moved like a big cat on the prowl. In his football career, Heath had seen linebackers who moved like Pike did—hungry, hunting, restless, always a danger because they intuited so much and moved with lightning quickness.

Heath nodded to Pike. "You good?"

Pike's lips tweaked in a slight smile that never looked quite genuine or at ease. "I am."

Once again, Heath wondered at Pike's background. The man never said much about where he'd been and what he'd done before becoming a Marine. "Nice work with the fifty."

"I aim to please."

Then Heath's attention centered on Bekah as she emerged from the building sporting bullet-pocked walls. A feeling of relief washed over him, followed immediately by guilt. He shouldn't feel any differently about her than any other Marine, but he did—and he felt differently about her than he did about the other female Marines as well.

He just didn't know how those feelings were going to shake out. In fact, he wasn't sure how she'd react to them if she knew they were there. She wouldn't like the confusion inside him at all. Of that he was certain.

Bekah was almost as disheveled as Pike. In a couple places her body armor showed through her camo, and he knew she'd taken rounds or gotten hit by shrapnel.

"Are you all right, Corporal?"

"I'm fine, sir."

*Sir.* The word defined their relationship in this time and place. He was an officer and she was a noncom. Not only was there not supposed to be any fraternization between male and female Marines, but there wasn't supposed to be any between officers and noncoms.

That was two strikes.

He looked into her eyes, thinking maybe she wanted him to say something else, but he didn't know what he was supposed to say. He remembered how awkward things had gotten the last time he'd seen her in the park. Her granny had been playing matchmaker, not knowing that was the last thing Heath or Bekah could afford in their military careers.

They were in dangerous circumstances. Both of them needed to be focused.

Gunney Towers stepped into the awkwardness. He waved over at the Humvee. "Looks like the tangos shot the crap out of your vehicle, Corporal Shaw. I count three flats, and that surviving tire don't look to be in much better shape."

Under the layer of dust that covered Bekah's face, she blushed a little and looked uncomfortable. "Actually, Gunney, the tangos aren't responsible for all of that damage. I tossed a grenade under the vehicle."

The big sergeant cocked a surprised eyebrow at her. "Nobody told you not to do that?"

"The tangos were using the Humvee as cover. I parked a frag under there to flush them out. I figured the blast plates would save the vehicle."

Gunney Towers turned to frown at the dead al Qaeda warriors around the Humvee. "You probably figured right, Shaw, but the people in the motor pool ain't gonna be any too happy with you for all the extra work you're throwing their way."

"Probably not."

Towers switched his gaze back out over the street. "Luckily, you ain't gonna be having to explain that anytime too soon. We still got a lot of work here to do."

★   ★   ★

In an effort to get the city back to normal more quickly—even though Pike didn't think Kandahar had seen anything close to normal in years—the Marines were tasked with helping watch over the citizens while they took to the streets to claim the bodies of their family and friends.

Pike stood guard with Cho, but he couldn't just hang around and watch as those people grieved over their losses. He got bloody helping gather the bodies and place them on flatbed trucks and pickups that were commandeered by the Afghan National Police.

One of the victims had been close to ground zero when an RPG warhead had gone off. The blast had shredded the man's body and torn off his legs and one arm.

A young private from back east stared down at the dead man. He spoke in a flat monotone and sounded out of it. "'We can rebuild him. We can make him better than he was.'"

Pike looked at the man. "You doing okay, Marine?"

Startled, the young private took a step back and looked at Pike. He hadn't known Pike was there. His eyes were red, and Pike suspected it wasn't just from fatigue and the dust. The guy looked like he was flying on something, wired tight. He shrugged. "Yeah. I'm fine."

"You don't sound fine."

"It's just this guy." The private jerked a thumb at the dead man. "Reminded me of Steve Austin. You know, the Six Million Dollar Man? Lost both of his legs and an arm in a plane crash. Government rebuilt him. Made him into a cyborg."

Pike vaguely remembered the television show. "Nobody's gonna make that man into a cyborg."

"Guess not."

"You're Hutchison, right?"

The private hesitated, then nodded. "Trevor Hutchison."

"Some advice, Hutchison." Pike stepped over to the man—intimidation through proximity. "Maybe you want to chill with the pop-culture references around these people and show a little respect."

Hutchison's hand tightened on his assault rifle. "Maybe you want to chill with the advice. I didn't ask for none, and I sure don't need it."

"You don't need whatever you're flying on either. I catch you using again while you're on patrol, I'm gonna throw you a beat down myself."

Heat showed in Hutchison's face, and for a minute Pike thought the man was going to act rashly. That was fine with Pike. He'd spent the last three hours picking up pieces of things that used to be individuals. He could use the distraction.

Suddenly, like he'd blown in on a quiet breeze, Gunney Towers was there, looming over them. "Do we have a problem here, Marines?"

"No, Gunney." Hutchison looked at the big man. "Just looking for the pieces. Pike volunteered to get this one." The private turned and walked away.

Watching the man go, figuring the last thing Towers needed was to deal with a stoned Marine in the middle of all this carnage, Pike let out his breath, then squatted and took hold of the dead man lying at his feet. He hooked one hand under the man's armpit and fisted his shirt in the other. Even wearing surgical gloves to prevent skin-to-skin contact, Pike could feel the coolness of the dead man's flesh. The sensation was alien, wrong. The corpse rolled in his grip, feeling as heavy as wet cement.

Towers went to the man's truncated hips, grabbed hold, and lifted. "Want to tell me what that was about, Pike?"

"Difference of opinion." Pike walked backward over the blood-drenched street.

"What difference? What opinion?"

"It's nothing to cry over." Pike lifted the body out of Towers's grip and stowed that half of him on the truck. Two other Marines stood on the flatbed and helped shift the bodies that arrived.

"Didn't look like you were gonna cry over nothing. Looked like you were 'bout to stove that guy's head in."

Pike didn't bother to deny it. He went back to where they'd collected the corpse and picked up one of the legs. The other leg was twelve feet away. He hadn't found the arm yet.

Towers picked up the other leg and followed Pike to the flatbed. "Folks deal with this stuff in their own way."

Listening but not taking it in, Pike went into his neutral zone, that place he'd created as a kid to shut down his emotions. Nothing mattered there. Nothing could touch him. He was a rock. This—and the private—didn't matter either.

"I've seen you clean up bodies before, Pike. You've never let it bother you."

"Not bothering me now, Gunney."

"That kid's attitude lit you up."

"Nah. I was just looking for a diversion. My bad." Pike strode over to a woman's body that lay against a delivery van. He knelt down and took her by the shoulder, deliberately not seeing the bloody mess the shrapnel had made of her back. If he didn't take those sights in, own them, he didn't have to remember them. He pulled the body away from the vehicle.

Underneath the van, a small boy who looked like he was seven or eight lay on his side. Blood oozed from a wound in his stomach. Scrapes and bruises on his face, arms, and hands offered mute testimony that he'd gotten beneath the van under his own power. The woman's hands showed the same kind of wear and tear, and Pike suspected that she'd tried to shove the boy underneath the van to protect him. It hadn't done any good.

The sadness of the moment stole through Pike's defenses, surprising him. But he knew it was because the boy was so close to Hector's age and wore the same innocence on his face. Pike couldn't help thinking that the two boys could have been friends if they'd known each other. Children didn't carry the same kind of baggage adults did, unless their parents forced it on them.

And then he couldn't help thinking that maybe Hector could be this boy. The part of Tulsa where Hector lived was dangerous too. Step off the wrong street corner at the wrong time, Hector could catch a no-name bullet from a drive-by and end up just as dead.

The thought left Pike cold. He didn't want that vision of Hector lying dead on the street mixing with what he was seeing now. That would make it too real, too permanent. There was a reason soldiers kept their lives in battle separate from the world back home.

The boy's eyes popped open and he looked right at Pike.

For the first time, Pike realized they hadn't been open the way so many of the dead's eyes were. He hadn't even thought about it until he was looking into the boy's eyes.

The boy spoke in a thin, dry voice. Pike had just enough of a command of Pashto to understand that the boy was asking for help, for water.

"Gunney!" Pike shoved the dead woman away and scrambled under the van. "I need a corpsman over here. This boy's alive." He reached for the boy, managing to shove one hand under the back of his neck and one under his thighs. Gently Pike began extracting the wounded boy.

Towers bawled for a corpsman in his best voice, and the command rang between the buildings.

By the time Pike had the boy resting in his arms and was getting to his feet, two Navy corpsmen had joined him. Pike looked around and spotted the triage truck that had been set up half a block away. He started walking toward it, holding the boy tightly against his chest, reminding himself again and again that it wasn't Hector—and trying to forget how easily it could have been.

# 22

**"TAKE A MINUTE, PRIVATE."**

Pike handed off a dead man to two Marines loading the back of a pickup. Turning, he spotted Towers standing only a couple feet away. The sun had crept down in the west, stretching cooler shadows across the urban battleground. Clouds of flies had descended upon the scene as well and flitted from place to place. Pike wore his scarf over his mouth and nose to keep from sucking flies up when he breathed.

"Sure." Pike pinched his scarf to hike it higher on his nose. His back and shoulders burned from all the lifting. "You heard anything about the kid?"

"Last I heard, it was still touch and go. Let's grab some space." Towers strode through the street. He kept his M4A1 in his fist and his gaze moving as he watched over his people. He'd worked alongside the Marines, pitching in and offering moral support to some of the guys who were still green and needed a break from the horror around them. "Kids have a way of pulling through stuff that would kill an adult."

Pike didn't say anything to that. He didn't know why Towers had singled him out. Pike had worked steadily, even skipping some of the breaks the other Marines had taken. There was no reason for Towers to pull him aside.

Towers halted at the opening to an alley. He took out a pack of spearmint gum, offered it to Pike, who took a stick, then took one himself. "Gotta admit, I'm kinda worried about you. Surprises me 'cause that's something I'd never thought I would be."

Unflinching, still cold and hard, Pike met the gunney's gaze full-on. Pike unwrapped the gum and put it into his mouth. Out of habit, he folded the paper and shoved it into a pocket. He spent a lot of time on recon, and training to not leave a trail stayed with him. Of course, he'd first learned that when he and Petey had gone into business for themselves.

"Aren't you even going to ask why I'm worried about you?" Towers chewed thoughtfully.

"No. You decide to worry, you'll worry. You want, I'll tell you you're wasting your time."

Towers grinned and shook his head. "This is what? My second tour with you?"

"Yeah."

"When I saw you in Somalia, you had all kinds of bark on you. Never let nothing or nobody in. Never hung with other Marines by design. Drifted in some, but you didn't let anybody close. Except maybe Bekah Shaw."

Pike chewed his gum and kept his gaze roving as well.

"How are you sleeping?"

"Horizontal, when I can."

Towers frowned. "I'm trying to help here, son."

"I ain't your son." Pike spoke before he knew he was going to. The quick, hard response came out of the past, out of those days he'd spent in foster homes listening to men who acted like they wanted to be his dad but were really only taking him and the other kids in for the money. The women had been just as bad, but Pike hadn't been able to stomach the guys who thought he somehow owed them thanks and respect for taking him in. Everybody had their own agendas. Even Petey had concentrated on his own there at the end, which had been a surprise and had taught Pike that final lesson. It was just how people were.

Towers's eyes narrowed somewhat, burned a little with anger, but he nodded in understanding. "Got daddy issues too, Marine? On top of everything else?"

For just a moment, Pike thought about punching Towers. It would have meant spending some time in the brig, but he was willing to do that. He'd done it before. Except that it might also have meant the end of his career in the Marines, which he wasn't ready to let go of. And he liked Towers for the most part. Admittedly, he liked the man more when he was yelling at him to get something done instead of trying to get into his head.

Towers had shifted as well, and Pike realized that the man had gotten prepared for a punch to be thrown. In fact, Towers seemed more surprised that Pike *hadn't* reacted violently. A trace of disappointment showed on Towers's face, then was gone just as fast as it had manifested.

"I got a lot of issues, Gunney. I think we both know that from the way I've been busted in rank."

"Yeah. Yeah, I guess we both know that." Towers adjusted the strap of his assault rifle over his shoulder. "But this isn't about a lack of respect for authority. This is about what I seen in you this tour and what I seen in your eyes when you hauled that boy out from under the van."

"Wasn't nothing to see."

"There was something there. For just about a minute."

"You didn't see nothing except fatigue."

Towers studied Pike for a quiet moment. "What'd you leave undone back home, Pike? 'Cause you sure didn't show up with the Marine mind-set here and your past back there."

"I'm fine."

"Who you got waiting on you?"

Pike was silent for a moment. "If you're expecting some kind of warm fuzzy to come out of this, you got another think coming."

"I'm not expecting that." Towers's dark eyes bored into Pike. "I'm just trying to figure out the name of that devil that's riding your shoulder."

"Ain't no devil on my shoulder. If you think you're seeing devils, you should consider checking in with the chaplain. Or the corpsmen. Bet they got something to fix that." Even as he spoke, though, Pike knew Towers didn't believe him.

For a time, Towers held Pike's gaze; then he finally nodded, more to himself. "Contrary to your rank and the way you handle authority, you're a good Marine, Pike. I seen some of that back in Somalia. Seen me some of the bad, too. Ain't gonna say I didn't. I figured there was something in you worth saving in Somalia, but could be I was wrong. If I find out I was, that'll go in the after-action reports I file on you."

Pike didn't like getting threatened, but he bit back a hostile reply.

"You got two men inside you, Marine. One's a man I could call a friend, but the other one?" Towers shook his head. "I don't wanna know that one. Don't wanna see him showing up out here neither. Hutchison, he just about got to see that side of you up close and personal."

Pike kept chewing the gum and watching the street. "Whatever you say, Gunney."

"Yeah, it is what I say." Towers's nostrils flared and Pike thought maybe it was out of anger, but he figured it might have been out of frustration, too. "Like I said, you got two men in you. And a devil riding your shoulder. You figure out which one of them men you wanna be and let me know."

That hit too close to what Hector had said, and the memory ghosted through Pike's mind before he could shut it down.

"Am I dismissed, Gunney?" Pike hooked a thumb over his shoulder. "The dead ain't gonna bury themselves."

"Not just yet, Marine. I been in the corps for a lotta years. I'm just about old enough to be your daddy. I seen a lotta things during that time." Towers nodded at the carnage in the street. "Seen things that was worse than this, believe it or not. Back home in Alabama, growing up in them swamp towns where my momma raised her kids, I seen a lotta bad things too. This war ain't got no monopoly on grief and evil. There's plenty of that in them small towns. A whole lotta bad people that's got bad ways. They carry scars, and some of them scars they ain't even got names for.

"You ask me—and I know you ain't, but I'm gonna tell you anyway—you got a pain in you that you ain't let go of yet. Something that's anchoring them two men inside you. Kinda the way twins share their momma's womb until they're born. That's what pulled that devil to your shoulder. It's just sitting there, feeding on everything that's festering inside you. You figure out how to deal with that pain, maybe you can let go of the evil inside you and hang on to the good."

Pike just stood there the way he had when he was a kid listening to foster parents that he knew weren't going to be more than a speed bump in his life. He held everything in tight, letting Towers see nothing.

Despite that, though, Mulvaney's words echoed inside his head. *"I am certain that God, who began the good work within you, will continue his work until it is finally finished on the day when Christ Jesus returns."*

Pike pushed the thought away, angry at himself for even being able to remember what Mulvaney had told him. What made Mulvaney think God would ever start something in Pike's life, especially when Pike didn't want any part of it? How he felt, whatever

Towers thought he saw in him, none of that had anything to do with any God Mulvaney claimed existed.

Towers sighed. "This was supposed to be a positive talk, not a rag session. I apologize for that." His dark eyes flashed. "But make no mistakes: I meant what I said. You get your head screwed on straight before you get one of my people killed." He nodded toward the street. "Get on back to what you were doing, Marine."

Pike turned and went, but he didn't like the way he felt bad leaving Towers standing there. He wasn't supposed to feel anything. That was when he handled things the best.

★　★　★

Hours later, Pike stood under a lukewarm shower in the barracks. Soap stung the cuts and abrasions he'd picked up during the day. Blood sluiced down the drain. He lathered up twice, enjoying the smell of the soap, shaved by touch, then reluctantly turned the shower over to the next man in line.

He dried off outside the showers, dressed in fresh camos he'd brought from his kit, and bagged his dirty clothing. He stood, relishing the feel of fresh socks inside the boots he'd scrubbed as clean as he could of dirt and blood.

Hefting his duffel and his M4A1, Pike headed for the door.

Outside, one of the regular Marines stood guard, leaning against a Humvee while he watched the grounds. Night had fallen, and Kandahar had grown quiet with it. Earlier, the loudspeakers had called Muslims out for final prayers, and their voices had sounded everywhere. Now the city seemed at peace, which was as far from the truth as it could be.

"Hey, Marine. Pike." A Navy corpsman walked toward the facility. She was young and lean, close-cut and clean, wearing tidy camos.

Pike waited but said nothing. The woman came to a stop in front of him. She smelled like a hospital, strong whiffs of Betadine clinging to her, but there was something else, too. A floral fragrance that carried a hint of lemon. She was pretty, dark-blonde hair and green eyes, five and a half feet tall. Her nose had a slight bump in it, like it had been broken at some point and hadn't healed correctly, but it gave her character and Pike liked the look on her.

"It is Pike, right?"

"Yeah."

"Things get crazy like they did today, I don't always remember names. But I remembered you because you brought that boy in." She shrugged. "Mostly I remember we had a hard time prying him away from you." She smiled. "Kind of hard to do our job while you were hanging on to him."

Pike didn't remember it that way, but it wasn't worth the argument. "How's the boy?"

"Doing good. I saw him earlier. Bullet went through his abdomen and missed everything vital. God was watching over him."

Pike resisted the impulse to point out that if God had truly been watching over the boy, he wouldn't have gotten hurt and his mother wouldn't be dead. "Good to know."

The woman offered her hand. "I'm Julie. Julie Meadows."

Pike took the proffered hand and felt the smooth strength of her grip. "You know me."

Julie smiled at him. "You just go by Pike? Just one name? Like Cher?"

"Most everybody just calls me Pike."

"All right, Pike." She nodded. "You're one of the new arrivals for Charlie Company."

"Yeah." Pike was conscious of the Marine by the Humvee watching him.

"Big wake-up call today. You guys barely got on the ground."

Pike shifted his kit over his shoulder and wished the woman would get to whatever it was she had on her mind.

"I've got a confession to make." Her green eyes sparkled. "I didn't just happen by. Your gunney told me where to find you."

"He sent you?"

"No. I came looking for you."

"Why?"

"To tell you about the boy, for one, and for another, I thought you might like company for dinner."

"Why me?" It wasn't unusual for women to hit on Pike. He knew part of it was he never intended to be stopped by one. They were just diversions as he rolled along.

The question gave her pause, but only for a moment. "I need to have a reason?"

"Yeah."

She placed her hands on her hips and gazed steadily up at him, a slight smile on her lips. "I have to say, your gunney warned me away from you. Told me you were antisocial. I know I'm not a supermodel, but generally when I offer to spend time with a guy because I want to know him a little more, I get a better reaction." She shrugged. "No foul. I guess I'll see you around, Private." She turned and started to walk away.

Pike watched her leave. Turning a girl down wasn't a big deal. Over the years when he'd been running with Petey, there had been a lot of girls.

But he thought of how the woman had taken the boy from his arms, the professional way she'd started taking care of him, and the way she'd checked Pike over when she had the chance. She was good at her job. She'd had a rough day too.

So maybe her attention was nothing more than somebody looking for something new so she wouldn't have to rehash the horror of the day. She just wanted a distraction from earlier events. Pike didn't owe her that. He didn't owe anybody anything.

He reminded himself of that even as he called out to her. "Doc. Hey, Doc. Gimme a sec."

Ten feet away, Julie looked back at him. "You don't have to call me Doc."

The address was one of respect. Marines only used it for corpsmen they had been under fire with.

"Yeah, I do." Pike walked over to join her. "I want a do-over."

"A do-over?" She had crossed her arms and kept herself distant. "What if I said I didn't believe in do-overs?"

"Then I wouldn't blame you. I rarely ask for them. So the ball's in your court."

The smile peeked out again. "What do you want a do-over for?"

"For dinner. I'd like to take you up on that."

"My offer's been withdrawn."

Pike grinned, liking her moxie. "Okay, so let me ask you to dinner."

"Why?"

"I need a reason?" Her defenses almost cracked at that one. "So we can eat."

"Not interested. Believe it or not, Private, there are a lot of Marines I can eat with." Julie turned to go.

"Doc, I'm sorry. And that's something I try to never say. So if you're not gonna accept it, that'll be it."

She stopped and looked at him. For a moment he thought she was going to still walk away, and he told himself he didn't care. That would just be the end of a bad day. No sweat. He'd have another one tomorrow.

"Lucky for you, I'm hungry now and don't want to eat by myself or go looking for more tolerable company."

"Understood."

"And for the record, I came looking for you because I was impressed by the Marine I saw who was taking care of that little boy today. A lot of guys like the idea of being the hero, but all you were concerned with was that boy. I liked the selflessness I saw."

Her words made Pike feel awkward, and he started thinking maybe he should have just let her walk away. "Maybe you saw wrong."

She smiled and shook her head. "I've had my share of bad boys, Pike. I know you're one of those too, under the right circumstances, when you're pushed or backed into a corner. We're not going to visit those circumstances tonight. I didn't come here looking for that guy. I'd rather be with the guy I saw carrying the boy earlier today. This is dinner—and maybe a chance to get to know someone else. My life's open to new experiences. I learn more that way. And since I'm in the people business in the medical field, I want to learn more about people. You're a person."

Despite his misgivings and the way her words echoed Towers's earlier comment, Pike smiled. "As simple as that, huh?"

"Life can be pretty simple when you get in there and learn to accept things. I have." She shrugged. "Plus, I like your ink. What is that?" She peered at his shirt collar. "A dragon?"

Self-consciously, Pike pulled at his shirt. The Marines were strict about ink. If it wasn't covered by a blouse, Marines had to get their ink removed or leave the corps. His neck tat, barely covered usually, must have shown through at some point. "Yeah. A dragon."

"Cool. I like dragons." Julie nodded to his duffel. "Why don't you stow that and let's get dinner?"

"All right."

"We could eat in the mess hall, but I figure a guy who wears a dragon around his neck probably has an adventurous spirit. If you do, I know a couple places that will be open tonight. No beer, since we're in a Muslim country, but you can sample the native cuisine. Ever been to Afghanistan before?"

"I have. Helmand province."

"We've got a few places with Indian food if you like it hot. You go to the Mumtaz Restaurant, it can be pricey. Especially after today. But I know a few small cafés where we can eat for a reasonable price."

"Sounds good." To his surprise, Pike was looking forward to the meal.

# 23

**"GOOD EVENING, GENTLEMEN.** My name is Gerald Benton. I'm the point man for the Central Intelligence Agency regarding three agents who have gone missing and are believed to be in the hands of Zalmai Yaqub. To add to that, earlier today Yaqub kidnapped an American journalist named Jonathan Sebastian. Together, we're going to track down and lock down Yaqub."

Seated in the fourth row of the conference room, Heath Bridger watched the CIA agent with increased interest. Heath knew the reporters had been targeted during the al Qaeda attacks. He'd helped recover some of the bodies of those men and women. There had even been whispers that other reporters were taken during the attack on the Noor Jahan Hotel.

Heath also knew Sebastian from television news. The man was a die-hard right-winger, as close to a war hawk for operations in the sandbox as any politician was. Sebastian held the opinion that the United States should finish cleaning up the mess in the Middle East, including a heavy drop into Syria and Iran to quiet those areas as well. The reporter constantly railed against the dangers of the Arab Spring and how it was going to upset political stability around the globe. Heath was of the opinion that the "political stability" Sebastian championed was thinly veiled economic interests.

Benton was average-looking. His hair was neither too long nor too short, and the color was hard to figure out even when looking at it. His face was long and didn't show much expression. He could have been anywhere from his midthirties to his midfifties. Gerald Benton probably wasn't his real name. Most of the guys in the CIA had cover identities. There was nothing memorable about him. He was the kind of man who could enter a room or leave it and never be noticed.

He wore camos so he could blend in with the local military populace, but he didn't wear them like a military person. His gig line wasn't straight, and any Marine worth his salt would have been set up right when addressing an audience.

Benton pointed a remote control at the projector on a table in front of the big screen. "Video from the hotel provides more than enough to identify Yaqub and some of his associates."

Heath brought up the files he had on Yaqub on his iPad. Intel had already come down on the man. Yaqub was known as one of the major players in Kandahar province. Heath matched the photos of the man with the video from the hotel. There was no doubt as to his identity or to the fact that Yaqub had shot several people in cold blood.

The footage paused a half-dozen times as Yaqub and his entourage strode through the hotel and killed the reporters. Each time the footage froze, a graphic popped up, matching Yaqub's features to similar photos from military intelligence archives. Heath had seen most of the images before. What those images hadn't been able to show was the cool dispassion that Yaqub exhibited while gunning down helpless people. The man was ice cold and totally lethal.

Other graphics popped up to identify a few of the victims of the shooting.

"We believe Yaqub had someone inside the hotel." Benton continued the briefing without emotion. "As you can see from this video, it's apparent that Sebastian was the target."

The footage, still without audio, showed more people going down under the al Qaeda guns. Although Heath had seen similar footage on other occasions—sometimes from military operations and sometimes while acting as third or fourth chair on one of his father's trials when the firm represented drug cartels—the silent killing still unsettled him worse than being shelled by mortars. The sound and fury of war crashing around him was more understandable than the eerie quietness of the scenes on the monitor.

The video cut to another camera, this one in a hallway. Yaqub and his men walked down the hall and disappeared into one of the rooms.

The men around Heath shifted uncomfortably as the video sped up and the numbers showing the time and date flickered in a whir. Several minutes later, Sebastian walked out of the room behind Yaqub.

Downstairs, the other cameras picked up the procession as they walked through the front door, overlapping in quick cuts to follow Yaqub and his entourage. Outdoors, the exterior cameras trailed them to waiting SUVs where they loaded up and took off.

"The Afghan National Police made contact with Yaqub and his people once more, to no avail." Benton's voice was flat and empty as he relayed the information.

The lethal confrontation on the street played out, and there were a few shots of Yaqub's vehicle disappearing.

"We lost Yaqub, but now we're going to get him back." Benton used his clicker and changed the image on the screen. "You're all familiar with Sebastian and his work. The man's a powerhouse in the media. Yaqub seized him so more attention would be drawn to his campaign here. As most of you know, we recently lost three agents in Pakistan."

The screen flickered again, and the faces of three men were displayed there. All of them looked calm and controlled, office photos of men who had nothing to fear.

Heath knew that when—or *if*—those men were found, they would look nothing like the images on the screen. They'd been prisoners for days, and Yaqub and his associates wouldn't have been gentle about their care.

"We're operating on the assumption that Yaqub wants to make an object lesson of these men."

The object lesson was an easy one to figure. Public execution at the hands of al Qaeda remained a preferred standard. Heath had seen a few of those videos and had come away shaken each time. Seeing men die like that was hard.

"I want those men back, and I want Yaqub brought down. He's just pushed his way to the top of the Pentagon's and POTUS's most wanted lists. You'll be given the particulars on these agents, and that information is *not* to be leaked to the media. If the time comes that Yaqub broadcasts that information to the press, you are to neither confirm nor deny the kidnappings of those men." Benton used his clicker again.

Another image of Yaqub filled the screen, this one of the man at a much younger age. Holding an AK-47, he stood in the shadow of a taller man. The older man's face was a war map of past engagements, lined and scored by violence. A scar bisected his right eyebrow and tracked down across his right cheek. When it had healed, it had pulled up the corner of his mouth. The left side of his face was pocked with scarring that looked like it was the result of a fragmentation explosive. His beard was shaggy and graying.

"This is Sabah al Hadith. He is Yaqub's father. This picture was taken in 1992, one of the earliest we have of Yaqub and one of the latest of Sabah."

More pictures cycled across the screen: Sabah as a younger man, leading warriors and talking to Americans.

"When the Cold War was in full force in the 1980s, the United States intelligence circle cultivated Sabah as an asset. In those times, the enemy was perceived to be the Russians. Sabah was a hero to his people, and he'd been listed on Russia's TOS agenda for years because of his ability to lead his men into battle."

Heath studied the man's features, respecting the force that Sabah must have become in order to achieve terminate-on-sight status. The fact that the man had remained alive throughout the Russian military campaign was even more impressive.

"When Sabah shifted his loyalties to al Qaeda, he remained on the Russians' TOS orders and swiftly rose in our target lists. But he also brought with him a large number of experienced warriors. Our agency has only identified some of them, but we have confirmed that those men and their sons continued to follow Sabah." Benton flicked through several images of Taliban warriors in the Kandahar mountain ranges.

The image shifted to a bombed-out metro area. Flames and smoke trailed from nearby buildings, but the one centermost in the picture had been reduced to rubble. American military units were closing in on the site.

"Based on intelligence given to us by one of our agency assets, we believed we had tracked bin Laden to this site. We hit the target with a Predator drone, then followed up immediately with ground troops."

Another image flickered into view, this one of a windowless room with several bodies lying on the floor or scattered on furniture. Maps and photos covered the walls.

"Bin Laden wasn't there when we hit the premises, but we only missed him by hours. The intelligence teams that covered the site confirmed that the location had been an intelligence center for the al Qaeda cell that was operating in the area—and that it was seeking primary military targets." Benton gazed at the scene. "Breaking that site allowed us to save the lives of several military personnel and claim a few of bin Laden's elite warriors as well."

More pictures scrolled across the screen. Heath checked his iPad, making sure the information was reaching him as well.

"We also believed we'd killed Sabah at that time. The intelligence teams that went over the premises found blood and tissue samples that matched the DNA we had on file on Sabah. We also found one of his arms and one of his legs."

The newest images showed those limbs encased in ice chests. For Heath, the visuals were too reminiscent of the horror that had taken place in Kandahar's streets earlier.

"No one believed Sabah could have survived the attack. We didn't close the book on him, but we felt reasonably certain that he'd been terminated.

"After Sabah was believed killed, some of his warriors returned home to sit out the current war, leaving the conflict up to bin Laden and al Qaeda. Bin Laden and his people lost a significant weapon in their arsenal. That brings us to Yaqub."

The new image on the screen showed a much younger Yaqub smoking at a small outside café. Text at the bottom of the photograph listed the location as Paris.

"Until his father's apparent demise, Yaqub had been attending the Paris-Sorbonne University. As it turns out, he wasn't there to get an education. He was being groomed, learning the mind-set of his father's new enemies, exposing himself to Western ways and culture, and firming up partnerships outside Afghanistan. Our agency kept tabs on him at that time, but he was a small fish. No one expected Yaqub to become a major player. Then, after his father was targeted, Yaqub vanished.

"Since that time, Yaqub has been back here shoring up his strength, committing himself and his followers to al Qaeda, recruiting those old warriors down from the mountains, consolidating their power base. Every time we chipped away at al Qaeda, taking down one leader after another, we've made it easier for Yaqub to make his power play. The inroads we've made in this country, the foundations for freedom, are being threatened on several levels. The Afghan people know that America is making preparations for pulling out and leaving them on their own. Too many of the Afghan politicians, military, and police are backsliding and attempting to align themselves with the Taliban and al Qaeda. You people already know that. Some days you're taking your life in your hands by working with the ANA and ANP."

One of the captains at the front of the room raised a hand. Benton recognized the man, and he spoke. "We're not going to be able to control what the Afghan people do once we're gone, Special Agent Benton, and controlling the people in this country has never been the goal."

"You're right." Benton nodded agreeably.

"Then, other than this attack and the hostages that have been taken, why is Yaqub so important? I understand the need to rescue those people if at all possible."

"We have two objectives in addition to the search and rescue operation. One: we see Yaqub as a threat for consolidation in the area. If we take him out, then some of the command structure he's put into place will fragment. Some of those hard-liners from the mountains will pull back, hopefully sitting out any further involvement. His people aren't as structurally sound as the rest of al Qaeda. But if he's left to his own devices, our intelligence tells us that he'll become a major factor in the future of this country. Whatever the future of Afghanistan holds, we prefer it not have Yaqub as one of the components."

Benton's face hardened and his gaze was more bleak. "Two: our intelligence also indicates that Yaqub is a larger threat than we'd first believed. The three agents we had across the Durand Line in

Parachinar were there to assess the threat level the Pakistani government is going to pose as the military shuts down more operations in Afghanistan. While they were there, they picked up on a Russian arms dealer in the area who has been supplying al Qaeda. Prior to those men being captured, they had pushed information on to our agency that Yaqub had become a client." Benton paused. "We're not sure of the exact nature of the weapons Yaqub and his people have gotten their hands on, but we do know that a lot of it is high-end offensive weaponry. We want that controlled, and we want Yaqub's source shut down."

Heath took that in. Like the military men around him, he wasn't surprised by the news. Al Qaeda had a lot of money backing them. That was how they had been able to embed themselves in several nations when they pulled back from the initial American intervention in Afghanistan.

But the prospect of all the civilian casualties, which the tangos were all too ready to spend, left him feeling sick. Several of today's victims had been women and children. Back home, people talked about the war and the cruel nature of the enemy they were up against, but the media kept most of the horror away from the American audience.

Some of that violence had been kept in check by American and Western military personnel putting themselves on the front line. Now that line was growing thinner. The Marines left on the ground inside the country were at increasingly greater risk.

And right now, his team was part of that vulnerable contingent.

The screen changed once more, this time to the hard, mountainous terrain where Afghanistan butted up against Pakistan.

"We're going to get Yaqub, gentlemen, and we're going to shut him down. But we've got to do it before he gets back across the Durand Line and into Pakistan."

One of the young lieutenants seated beside Heath shook his head and snorted derisively. "Yaqub's probably headed for Pakistan like his tail is on fire. He knows we're going to be gunning for him."

Using a laser pointer, Benton indicated the distance between Kandahar and the Durand Line. "He's got a lot of ground to cover. Tomorrow morning we're going to begin sending teams into the mountains to start running a grid. We're going to pick up Yaqub's trail, and when we do, we'll close his operation down. Permanently."

# 24

**WITH A LONG STRIDE** and rolling muscles made strong from years of walking through the mountains, Yaqub reached the top of the range and peered down into the stone valley where snow lay in drifts. This high up, the land stayed gripped by winter. Permafrost gleamed in the early morning sunlight, and Yaqub's breath spilled out of him in gray patches of fog.

After leaving Kandahar, they had abandoned the SUVs when they could no longer hold the trail that wound up into the mountains. Then they'd covered them with tarps and snow and dirt so they couldn't be easily tracked by the drones Yaqub was certain the Westerners had launched. He had prepared for that, though, arranging for other outbreaks of violence that would occupy the attentions of his enemy.

That morning, at first light, Yaqub had taken out his prayer rug and given thanks that his mission had borne the fruit that it had, and he asked that he be kept strong enough to pursue his goals. Finished, once more filled with the certainty that he was upon the chosen path, he'd rolled his prayer rug and gotten his caravan into motion.

Only an hour into their journey on foot, they'd been met by warriors with donkeys. The pack animals carried food and ammunition. The only donkey in Yaqub's party carried Jonathan Sebastian. The journalist clung to the surly little beast like a man holding on to a life raft in a rugged sea.

When Sebastian had first seen the donkey and been told he would be riding, he'd been thankful. The man was used to the soft life, to sitting in furnished quarters and pontificating on whatever story or angle he'd been given. His days of being in the field were long behind him. The hour or so of walking that he'd had to endure since leaving the vehicles had sapped much of his strength and endurance.

Now, given the grimace on his face, Yaqub was willing to wager that Sebastian was torn between believing the donkey was a blessing or an even worse torment than walking through the frozen mountains. The journalist was also not a rider. He sat uncomfortably on the donkey and shifted in an effort to find better seating.

"Is that where we're going?" Sebastian pointed down into the valley, where small mountain homes occupied the relatively flat lands. All of the homes butted up against the mountains.

Yaqub shifted the AK-47 on his shoulder and peered at the journalist. "Yes."

"What's down there?"

"The reason we have come."

Sebastian grimaced and shifted again, then started to dismount.

Yaqub held up a hand, freezing the man in place. "Stay on the animal. If you get off now, you will not have the strength to get back on."

Looking pained, Sebastian adjusted himself. Bored, the donkey flicked its ears. "I can't guarantee that I can ride much longer. I'm too old for this."

"If you fall off, we'll put you back on and tie you in place. You will make this journey one way or another."

Sebastian cursed.

Looking forward, Yaqub spied Wali, then waved, and they moved forward once more, heading down into the valley. Heaviness stirred in Yaqub's heart because he knew it would be the last time he would make the trip.

★　　★　　★

Men and young boys tended the goats sheltered inside lean-tos built into the foothills of the surrounding mountains. Others carried rocks to build the recent fortifications that Yaqub had insisted on. For years the valley had hidden those who lived within its walls, but those days were soon to be over. The women and female children had already been evacuated from the site.

As Yaqub and the rest of the caravan came down out of the mountains, the men and boys abandoned their chores and picked up the rifles they'd been issued. All of the weapons were modern. For every old single-shot rifle, there was now an AK-47 or a Dragunov sniper rifle. But trust was a hard thing among the mountain warriors, and they didn't easily abandon the old ways. Even though they were grateful for the new weapons, the men still hadn't discarded the rifles they'd carried for so long and knew how to make ammunition for.

Wali loped ahead of the caravan and shouted to the men as they took up arms and settled into position behind the rock walls. Even after Wali reassured them, the men didn't put away their weapons. They had hidden their secret as carefully as had the surrounding mountains.

Sahebi, one of the men who had trained Yaqub from the time he was a boy, stood at the forefront of the group. In his sixties, the old man was wiry and quick. His long beard was more gray than black these days, and he looked as weathered as the mountains.

"Zalmai, it is good to see you."

Stepping forward, Yaqub allowed himself to be briefly swallowed in Sahebi's strong embrace. "It is good to see you too."

Sahebi released him and stared at the caravan. His iron-hard face was implacable. "You have brought a visitor."

"Yes."

A somber look lent an edge to Sahebi's features. "This is the man you sought in Kandahar?"

"Yes."

"Then God has blessed you with success."

"I have so been blessed."

Sahebi nodded, but he didn't look pleased. Both of them knew what that success meant—and the loss that both of them were about to experience. "Your father will be proud."

"Perhaps, but he will know—as I do—that this is the will of God. I am merely an instrument. Soon we will drench our blades in the blood of the unbelievers."

"Please. Go in and make yourself comfortable." Sahebi waved to one of the stone homes. "Get out of this cursed chill and warm yourself. We will take care of your animals and the goods you have brought."

The caravan hadn't been organized just to transport Yaqub and his group to the valley. It also carried fresh water, wood, food, and clothing that the people who lived there could use. Living in the mountains was harsh and demanding.

"Thank you." Yaqub headed for Sahebi's home.

Like all the other houses around it, Sahebi's resembled an organized pile of stones stacked against the surrounding mountain walls. The homes were much bigger on the inside than they appeared on the outside because their builders had widened and shaped the natural caves inside the mountains.

At the front of the home, Yaqub pulled aside the heavy tarp that blocked the freezing wind and stepped gratefully out of the unforgiving perpetual winter weather and into the warmth of the home. The previous night, he and his men had swaddled themselves in sleeping bags and thick layers of clothing to stave off the chill they'd ascended into. Though he'd grown used to hardships over the last few years, Yaqub still hated the cold.

On the other side of the tarp door, the large room held a fireplace hacked into the wall. A chimney carved through the stone led the smoke away from the room while leaving the heat behind.

Yaqub swung his AK-47 around and grasped the weapon's pistol grip in his right hand while he waited for his eyes to acclimate to the dimness.

Firewood, always a precious commodity this high in the mountains, sat stacked neatly beside the fireplace. Burning logs crackled and spat embers. A heavy pot hung from an iron bar near the flames, just close enough to keep the contents warm. The familiar robust scent of *shorwa e ghosht*, beef and bean soup, tantalized Yaqub's nose. His stomach growled in response.

A young boy sat near the fireplace and tended the fire and the soup. He gazed up at Yaqub with dark-brown eyes. "Would you like something to eat?"

"Perhaps in a while." Yaqub divested himself of his thick outer coat, throwing it into a pile near the door. "Is he resting?"

"Yes."

Yaqub stepped through the doorway on the left and into another room. He paused there at the entrance to study the room's lone occupant. Despite the smell of the soup and woodsmoke that permeated the dwelling, the strong odor of death also hung over the other room. In his heart, Yaqub believed no other man could have clung so fiercely to life. That kind of strength demanded a special conviction and desire for revenge.

On the thick pile of sleeping bags and bedding in the center of the room was a frail, incomplete stick of a man. Despite the number of blankets, the way they clung to the sleeping figure revealed the absence of the man's arm and leg on his right side. His left arm lay over the top of the blankets, a gnarled, scarred, and bony testament to the life of violence its owner had led.

Years and infirmity had turned the old man's beard and hair white as snow and paled his features. His face had withered away to an edged, hawklike profile. Burn scarring tracked his right cheek and temple, so thick that the beard and hair no longer grew in those areas, and his ear was a burned and twisted thing that no longer worked. A black patch covered his right eye, and fluid wept continuously from the socket.

The left eye opened; then the hawklike face turned toward the door. Despite the man's weakness, his gaze was fierce and unforgiving. "Zalmai?" The voice was a hollowed-out croak that sounded as if the man still carried with him the smoke from the fire that had burned him so badly.

"Yes, Father."

A smile curved Sabah's scarred face, and he waved to Yaqub weakly. "Come, my son. I have been awaiting news of your efforts in Kandahar."

Retreating long enough to pick up a tallow candle from a box near the fireplace, Yaqub lit the wick and set the candle inside a lantern. He crossed the uneven stone floor to his father's side. The people who lived in the valley had chopped stone from within the caves and left tracks across the floor. Most of the tool marks had been worn smooth over the passage of time. The yellow light revealed the uneven surfaces, painting them in shadows.

Kneeling beside his father's bed, Yaqub set the lantern to one side and took the emaciated claw the old man held up to him. The candle flame played over Sabah's ravaged face. Years of frailty and sickness had eroded the flesh of the old man's hand, leaving only skin over tendon and bone, but Sabah maintained a supernatural strength.

"It is good to see you, my son."

"It is good to see you too, Father." Every time Yaqub had left the mountain village since his father's tragic wounding, he'd expected that to be the last time he would see the man. On each occasion, he felt convinced that he would return only to find a grave that marked his father's passing.

"Your mission?"

"God has blessed me."

A ghost of the old smile, pulled out of shape by the burn scarring, twisted the man's lips. Seeing the expression only served to remind Yaqub of the strength his father had at one time commanded, and the disparity between then and now shoved through his heart like a hot knife.

"I told you that God would see you through this. We will crush our enemies." Tears of infection tracked down the side of Sabah's face. Other infection had dried there, leaving crusted paths behind.

"Yes, Father." Yaqub laid his AK-47 to one side, then picked up the cloth on a corner of the bedding. He wet the cloth in a small bowl of water and gently cleansed his father's face.

Sabah relaxed under Yaqub's ministrations. The old man kept his hand on Yaqub's wrist, and Yaqub tried not to notice how cold and thin the fingers were. He took back the cloth and rinsed it in the bowl.

"Thank you for this last chance to enact vengeance upon our enemies, Zalmai."

"You are welcome, Father."

"A man should not have to go to his grave without striking back at those who killed him."

"I know." Yaqub put the cloth aside. "Let me get you a bowl of soup."

Sabah shook his head. "I am not hungry."

"You must eat to keep up your strength."

"My faith sustains me, my son." Sabah fixed his remaining eye on Yaqub, and a hint of the old sparkle showed there despite the jaundiced color. "God will keep me alive till I can do my part."

Yaqub silently hoped that was so.

"The American journalist is here?"

"Yes."

"Then help me get dressed so that I may see him. We have much to do to prepare, and our enemies must be nipping at your heels like hounds."

"Of course." Gently, Yaqub pulled back the bedding and covers to reveal his father's crooked and wasted body.

Since the attack, Sabah had never been the same. The loss of his arm and leg were only the most apparent of the injuries that the old man had suffered. Burn scarring covered a lot of his body, especially his other leg, charring into the musculature to leave the limb withered and twisted, unable to support his weight. His breath came hoarse and ragged, and he often got lung infections that left him wheezing for days until antibiotics fought the fluid from his airways.

Yaqub did not know how many times his father had nearly died over the past years. The doctors whom he had brought to see Sabah always left amazed at the old man's resolve and seemingly bottomless reservoirs of recovery.

Sometimes, during his weaker moments that he was not proud of, when he'd sat at his father's side and listened to him fight for his breath, Yaqub had thought of picking up a pillow and pressing it down over Sabah's face. He wouldn't have had to hold it there long, just until his father slid from this life into the paradise that Yaqub was certain awaited him. The temptation was great. In God's grace, in *Firdaws*, Sabah would once more be whole, and he would live among virgins in a house made of gold and silver and pearls. It would be a magnificent dwelling.

Then, when Yaqub had finished his war with the Westerners, he would join his father there.

But such a sin would surely have left him bound for *Jahannam*, also known as "That Which Breaks to Pieces" and "Blazing Fire."

Now, though, his father's course was nearly run, and he would end it as a warrior.

Quietly, gently, Yaqub dressed his father and prepared for him to meet Jonathan Sebastian.

# 25

**PIKE, WITH CHO AT HIS HEELS,** fell into position along the alley wall only a short distance from where Bekah and Zeke were locked into place. The sun baked into them, and sweat coated Pike's body under his camo and armor. He held his M4A1 canted at the ready and maintained radio silence.

Since yesterday, Marine visibility in the city had picked up. The word coming down from the brass had promised nothing but long days ahead and an escalated threat level. The Marines had been ordered to push back—and push hard. Pockets of terrorist activity continued to flare up around Kandahar like spontaneous combustion. There was too much of it to assume it was coincidence. Whatever had started yesterday was still rock and roll in the city.

Several of the Marine units had been detailed to round up and investigate suspected tango sympathizers. The list was long, and the work had turned into a logistical nightmare for the American military. The Afghan people knew that the American soldiers would be pulling out soon, leaving them with whatever problems remained, and many of them had resented the Marines' heavy-handed intrusions into their affairs from day one.

The Marines' police action had, so far, triggered a half-dozen shoot-outs as tangos either got caught red-handed on the premises or took advantage of the situation to attack small groups of American military. The violence was mounting, turning more swift and bloody. The day hadn't even reached noon yet.

Pike paused beside the scarred metal door to a small-engine repair shop midway down one of the long alleys in Kandahar. A covered peephole was the only feature on the door. The business was located behind a butcher's shop, and the alley was filled with the stench of spoiled death in the nearby trash bins.

Cho fell into position on the other side of the door. Clutching his weapon tightly, Cho looked nervous, but he was holding it together well. A lot of the sass and vinegar had left him since the action yesterday. Picking up corpses could do that to a man.

Pike glanced at Cho.

The other Marine nodded.

Looking past Cho, Pike held up a hand to Bekah and Zeke. Another team was behind Pike, ready to provide immediate backup if things turned ugly. Afghan National Police contingents waited in support positions at either end of the alley.

Bekah waved Pike to continue.

Pike tried the door and discovered that it was locked. He checked the sign posted on the alley wall beside the door. He couldn't read the particulars, but the business hours were easy enough to decipher. The shop was supposed to be open. Clattering and clanking and voices inside the shop offered proof that several people inside were working.

Bunching his left hand into a fist, Pike banged on the door. The work and the voices quieted on the other side. Pike banged again, with more authority this time.

A voice spoke on the other side of the door, but the words were in Pashto and Pike only understood a few. He translated "Go away" just fine.

Holding his assault rifle in one hand, Pike pulled a small plastic explosive charge from his ammo rack. He figured he already knew how this was going to go down.

"American soldiers. Open up."

The man repeated his command, more insistently this time.

"Back away from the door. Do it now."

The peephole slid open just enough to reveal the man's eyes briefly; then the wicked snout of a small pistol shoved through. The man fired at once, but the angle was wrong and the bullets only thudded into the opposite wall.

Pike swept the M4A1's barrel against the pistol barrel and knocked the weapon away. He slapped the explosive charge onto the door, sealing the adhesive side against the metal. He toggled the three-second detonator and dodged back, turning to shield his face.

"Fire in the hole!"

The shaped explosive was small, and the resulting blast was sharp but quickly faded. A few metal fragments clinked out into the alleyway, but Pike knew more of them had ripped inside the room. The door sagged on its hinges, coming partially open. Pike shoved the muzzle of the M4A1 into the gap and flung the door open.

Peering inside the room, Pike spotted three men down on the floor. The one nearest the door had caught the majority of the blast. Shrapnel gleamed across his bloody back, and he wasn't moving— either dead or rendered unconscious from the explosion. The other two men tried to get to their feet. Blood covered the face of one of them. The other appeared to be only shaken up because he tried to point a pistol at Pike.

Taking aim, Pike squeezed the trigger and put a three-round burst into the man's chest. The man staggered back into some kind of drill press. Man and machine went down in a tangle of limbs and electrical cords. Pike got off another clean shot just before the second man finished taking aim.

Sweeping the room with his gaze, Pike noted that at least ten men had been working inside the shop. The survivors had split up, three of them running to the north end of the building and four to the south. Pike entered the room behind his weapon, staying low and taking cover from the surrounding lathes and other machinery. The dull hum of electrical motors vibrated through the room.

"Bekah." Pike reached for a section of three-inch pipe lying on a nearby table. When he upended the pipe, nails, screws, and broken glass tumbled out along with a mixture of coarse, ash-colored gunpowder.

"Here, Pike." Her voice sounded like it was being filtered through cotton, and Pike knew that was the result of the explosion.

"They were closed for business today because they were making bombs. You've got gunpowder and other ordnance scattered through this place. You'll want to be careful."

"Roger that."

"Tangos split up. Three north and four south. I'm leaving two dead in this room. Third guy's incapacitated."

"We've got your back."

Pike knelt next to the unconscious tango, then pulled a zip tie from his gear and secured the man's hands behind his back. He took the M4A1 into his hands as he stood. Cho was behind him, holding a solid covering position, showing no signs of stress.

"We're headed south," Pike announced into the radio.

"Roger that."

Pike moved forward, staying behind his rifle, following the gun sight as he hunkered down. He reached the open doorway at the back of the room, pressed up against the frame, and peered through. A narrow hallway separated the machine shop from the furniture shop at the other end of the long building.

Footsteps sounded to the left and he gazed in that direction, spotting a short flight of stairs that led to the second floor. Ambient light from the door gleamed from the oily black finish of a machine pistol in the hands of the tango crouched at the top of the stairs.

Pike yanked his head back an instant before a stream of bullets chewed into the doorframe and scattered wood splinters like confetti. Dropping to one knee, Pike waited till the firing stopped, guessing that the man had run through his weapon's magazine. Leaning around the door, Pike aimed at the top of the stairway, found the tango shoving a fresh magazine into his machine pistol, then fired two three-round bursts into the man.

Caught by the rounds, the tango flopped backward and the weapon spilled down the stairs. Pike ejected his partially spent clip and swapped it out for a fresh one so he would be at full capacity when he went up the stairs.

"You can scratch one of the four we're pursuing."

"Roger that." In the machine shop, Bekah and Zeke were closing in on the north door. The third team of Marines occupied the machine-shop doorway in a holding position.

Staying crouched but moving fast, Pike entered the hallway and started up the steps. At the top, he paused briefly to place his fingers against the downed tango's throat. There was no pulse.

The stairwell opened into another hallway lit by a single window at the far end on the east wall. Two doors were on the north and three on the south. No one was in the hallway. Curtains fluttered in the open window.

Pike moved rapidly down the hallway, shifting the assault rifle from side to side slightly, staying loose and ready to lock onto any target that presented itself. He kept to the left side of the hallway so Cho had a clear field of fire on his right.

Cho's voice was whisper-thin and tight when he spoke. "Nobody's up here."

"Keep your eyes peeled. These guys didn't just disappear." Pike tried the doors as he passed them, turning the knobs, but none of them were open. Cho did the same on his side but got the same results.

At the window, Pike peered out. A fire escape ran like a crooked snake up the side of the building, reaching from the alleyway to the fourth floor and the rooftop beyond. Across the alley, a few people stared from the windows of their apartments at Pike and at the rooftop. Evidently something up there had captured their attention.

The blowing curtain brushed against Pike's face and scraped at his stubble. Sharp reports of gunfire came from below. He briefly worried about Bekah and Zeke, then put them out of his mind. He had his own mission to deal with, and he knew from past encounters that she was capable of taking care of herself.

"They had to have gone out the window." Cho stood to one side, covering the window and their backs.

"Yeah, but you gotta wonder if anybody's laying back waiting for us." Twisting, turning his back to the window, Pike leaned out backward so he could peer up through the fire escape.

No one lingered at the rooftop's edge, which meant the men he was chasing were enhancing the lead they'd gotten.

Pike stepped out onto the fire escape and started up just as a group of Afghan National Police rounded the alley and caught sight of him. Some of them brought their rifles to shoulder and took aim.

# 26

CURSING, PIKE POUNDED up the fire escape and hugged the side of the building as he shouted, "American! American! Marine!" He cursed again, over the radio frequency now because a handful of bullets peppered the stone wall nearby. "Captain Zarif, tell your men on the east side of the building to stop firing. They're shooting at friendlies."

A command in Pashto immediately followed, and the Afghan National Police in the alleyway lowered their weapons.

"My apologies. Many of the men, they are still nervous under fire."

Pike ignored the captain and continued up the fire escape. He checked the windows on each floor as he passed them. All of them were closed and locked, but verifying that cost time, potentially putting him farther behind his quarry.

At the top of the fire escape, Pike remained hunkered down and peered out onto the roof. Beyond the other side of the building, two men fled across the adjoining structure while a third man was getting to his feet.

"Bekah, I'm in pursuit of the last three." Pike heaved himself up and onto the roof. "They're escaping across the building to the west." He ran, Cho following him immediately.

"Roger that. I'm sending Nathan and Jelani after you."

Pike ran, driving himself forward. Dressed in full battle armor, he hoped he didn't hit a soft spot in the roof. He'd heard stories of other Marines who had ended up in someone's living room while in pursuit of a tango. "They're going to have to catch up in a hurry."

The third man on the other side of the building caught sight of Pike and Cho and started yelling at his companions. A moment later, he whirled around with a rifle in his hands.

"Affirmative." Bekah sounded distracted. Gunfire blasted into her broadcast, burying her continued response.

Pike dropped to one knee next to the rooftop's edge and took shelter from the thin wall that ran around the building. Bullets from the tango's weapon ripped through the air and tore through the thin wall. One of the rounds glanced off Cho's body armor, causing him to stagger to one side.

With the open sights centered over the tango, Pike squeezed off three rounds one at a time, following his target as the man moved in search of shelter. Pike was certain he hit the tango with all three rounds, and one of them had to be the kill shot because the man crumpled to the rooftop and lay still. Pike pushed himself up, surveyed the eight-foot gap between the buildings, then backed up a few feet to give himself a running start.

"Come again, Bekah. I lost transmission." Pike slung the assault rifle across his shoulders to free up his hands.

"I said we need to take one of these men alive if possible. You copy?"

"Copy that." Pike wasn't happy about it, but he understood. The Marines were severely lacking information about Yaqub's operation. He sprinted forward, knowing the eight-foot distance wouldn't have been a problem normally, but carrying a full pack and weps made the jump potentially disastrous.

At the roof's edge, Pike planted his right foot atop the low wall and pushed as hard as he could. The wall broke beneath his weight, crumbling into pieces and costing him leverage, and he knew his jump was going to come up short.

As Pike hurtled through the air, he couldn't help thinking of all the times he and Petey had dodged death when they were kids out on their own. In those days, death had seemed to sit on their shoulders, waiting for the slightest misstep so they could be pulled down. No matter how close it got, they'd always laughed about it later, acting like they had never been scared at all.

The day Petey had died, though, he had been afraid. Pike remembered that now as he threw his hands out in an attempt to reach the other building before gravity claimed him and pulled him to his death. That fear in Petey's eyes had been the worst thing Pike had ever witnessed. He had seen Petey drunk and flying on mushrooms at different times, had seen him angry, and had even seen him lost in painful memories from his childhood. All of those things Pike remembered. They were all pieces and parts of Petey, things that had gone into the making of his friend.

But the fear in Petey's eyes was what Pike remembered most sharply. That memory cut hard and deep as a motorcycle chain, and it was in Pike's mind as he fell. He thought that was the final straw, that the weight of the memory would drag him down, just short of the other building.

*"No pain without gain."* Petey had changed the old saying around to suit him. It had been his way of telling Pike that he wasn't going to take chances unless there was a profit involved. *"You don't put your head on the chopping block for free, bro."*

Pike felt certain that if Petey could see him now, his friend would laugh at him and tell him he was an idiot.

Pike's fingers closed over the rooftop's edge. The building had the same kind of low retaining wall as the structure he had leaped from. As his chest banged into the wall and his chin painfully scraped the stone, the wall tore away under his left hand. Pieces of wood dropped into the alley.

Grimly, feeling as though his right shoulder was about to separate, Pike held on and desperately flailed with his left hand till he secured purchase. He was dimly aware of Cho sailing over him and thudding onto the roof a few feet ahead of him and to one side. By the time the other Marine had gotten to his feet, scrambling to get back to Pike, Pike had levered himself onto the roof.

Cho stared at him. "Oh, man, I thought you were going to eat it when I saw that wall give way underneath you."

Adrenaline still thrummed through Pike, but it was an old friend and his drug of choice. He pulled his assault rifle into his hands and scanned the roof. "Talk about it later. Move out now." He ran forward.

On the other side of the building, the two surviving tangos had taken the fire escape.

With his shoulder burning as if it were on fire, Pike ran. "Bekah, the tangos are heading down the fire escape on the adjacent building. North side. Do we have anybody there?"

"I'm getting someone there now."

Captain Zarif cut into the channel. "I have men headed there now."

"Roger that, Captain." Bekah sounded out of breath. "Remember, our orders are to bring in prisoners to question."

"I understand, Corporal Shaw." The ANP captain sounded put out. He hadn't been happy to learn that he would be taking orders from a corporal. But the local police were working as support, not taking charge of the operation. "Rest assured, you will have our full cooperation."

Reaching the fire escape, Pike peered down and spotted the two men already on the second-story landing. A few men and boys were in the alley, all of them evidently from surrounding businesses and curious about the nearby gunfire. Pike figured they were probably wondering if they should take cover or vacate the area before they got caught up in the violence.

When the gawkers spotted the two Marines clambering down the fire escape in pursuit, they immediately pulled back inside nearby buildings or to recessed doorways. By that time, Pike was in motion, rapidly descending the steps.

Closer now, Pike noticed that one of the tangos wasn't a local. The coloration of the man's skin was too fair. His black hair was cropped short, and he wore a neatly trimmed goatee. His Western-style clothes marked him as different too.

What was he doing with the tangos? That thought barely registered in Pike's mind before the two men reached ground level. The man with the goatee turned and pointed a pistol at Pike as he reached the second-floor landing. The pistol spat three quick shots. One of them spanged off the fire escape railing. The other two slammed into Pike's chest, flattening against his armor but still feeling like hammer blows over his heart.

The guy was good. Pike swung over the railing and made the ten-foot drop to the ground. His knees screamed from the height with all the extra weight he was carrying, but he remained standing. The move caught the guy with the goatee off-balance, but he tracked his pistol onto Pike. A bullet split the air beside Pike's head and skimmed off the side of his helmet.

Holding his position, Pike opened fire from twenty feet away. His rounds chewed into the man's lower legs, knocking his feet from beneath him as a group of Afghan National Police came into view at the end of the alley fifty feet away.

The other man tried to stop before he reached the police. Realizing that he had no chance, the man started to throw his pistol away, but a hail of gunfire slammed into him before the weapon left his fingers. He fell to the ground on his back, sightless eyes staring up at the midday sun directly overhead.

The man with the goatee had a Russian accent, or it might have been Eastern European. The intonation was something definitely from that neck of the woods. He cursed and reached for his fallen pistol, but his fingers remained just short of reaching it.

Stepping forward, Pike kicked the pistol away. Still cursing, the man held up his hands in surrender, staring hard at Pike with wide blue eyes. Blood from the man's wounded legs spread over the cobblestones. None of the wounds appeared to be gushing, so Pike felt certain he hadn't hit the femoral artery. There was little chance of the man bleeding out.

Cho joined Pike just as the Afghan policemen surrounded them.

Pike took a step back, away from the arriving policemen, and waved to Cho. "Keep an eye on that guy."

Cho nodded.

Turning to face the alley, splitting his attention between both ends while staying alert, Pike keyed the radio. "Bekah."

"Yes."

"We're secure here."

"Good. We've got these men too."

"Are all yours Afghan?"

"They look like it. Why?"

"Got a guy here that sounds Russian. Doesn't fit in with the locals. Didn't Heath mention in his debrief that Yaqub was doing business with some Russians?"

"Yes."

"Maybe we got one of the guys that—"

"Hey! What are you doing?" Cho sounded angry and defensive. "Back off! Back off now!"

Pike turned around just as Captain Zarif shot the Russian between the eyes. The Russian had been struggling against the Afghan National Police, but his body went slack and those blue eyes stared vacantly.

"Why did you do that?" Cho moved toward Zarif, but one of the policemen standing nearby grabbed his arm and prevented him from reaching his target.

Stepping forward, his rifle resting across his body so he could pull it into play, Pike grabbed Cho's shoulder and tugged the Marine back.

"He shot him!" Cho pointed at Zarif. "Guy shot him and there was no reason to do it!"

Captain Zarif was in his early forties, a hard-faced man carrying extra weight from living well. His hair and beard were salt-and-pepper. Four small, irregular scars lined the right side of his round face. He turned his flat, hard-eyed gaze on Cho and held the pistol pointed at the Marine.

"Back away, American. You should thank me for saving your life."

"Saving my life?" Cho shook his head. "No way. The guy didn't have a weapon. He was just lying there."

"Really?" Zarif sneered contemptuously. "Then how do you explain this?" He nudged the dead Russian's left arm aside to reveal a short fighting dagger lying on the ground. "Like I said, you should thank me for saving your life."

"That guy didn't have no knife." Cho shrugged free of Pike. Pike let him go, but he pushed Cho back slightly with his body. The Marine was scared and mad and embarrassed, a volatile concoction that was just waiting to make an even bigger mistake. "One of your guys put that there."

Zarif spoke coldly. "Careful with what you say. I will have you brought up on charges. You may not be under my supervision, but you will respect my position."

"I know how to deal with a—"

Pike stepped in front of the other Marine. "Step off, Cho. Watch my six."

Furious, Cho quieted and moved back. "I got you, Pike."

Moving slowly, Pike closed on the dead Russian. The Afghan National Police remained in place, blocking the way, but Pike never broke his stride. He locked his eyes on the captain. "That's our prisoner. We're not leaving here without him."

One of the soldiers spoke up hotly. "You will not tell us what to do, American. This is our country. You will remain respectful."

Pike kept walking and held Zarif's gaze. "Our. Prisoner." From the corner of his eye, Pike saw a Marine Humvee roll into the alley. A machine gunner stood on deck behind the big .50-cal.

Zarif spoke quickly in his native language. His men stepped back, leaving the dead Russian and the other man.

Pike gazed down at the Russian, aware of Zarif and his men walking away.

A moment later, Bekah joined Pike. "What's going on?"

Pike pointed to the dead man. "Zarif killed our prisoner to keep him from stabbing Cho."

Face stained with sweat and dust, Bekah looked up at Pike. "You don't think that's what happened?"

"The Russian was right-handed. We closed on him, he drew on us, fired real quick, real accurate." Pike touched his body armor, reaching through the material to dig out one of the flattened rounds. He juggled it in his palm, still feeling the residual heat. "You tend to remember somebody like that shooting at you. He was right-handed. The captain claimed he was pulling the knife with his left hand."

"Doesn't mean he didn't."

"Yeah, I know." Pike pointed at the dead man, indicated the way the man's pocket had been turned inside out and a few coins littered the alley. "I don't think he picked his own pockets before the captain shot him either. Would have been even harder after he was dead."

# 27

**YAQUB SAT ON A MAT** in his father's room while Faisal brought Jonathan Sebastian to him. During Yaqub's conversation with his father, Sebastian had been fed and kept isolated.

The reporter looked grave and frightened, but he strove to maintain his composure. A man didn't negotiate from a position of weakness, and Sebastian had obviously learned that during his career. The fact that Yaqub had gone to some trouble to bring him into the mountains made him feel somewhat more confident. Yaqub saw that confidence in the man and quelled the impulse to quash it. For the moment, he needed the reporter. Tired and wan, Sebastian stood at the foot of the bed and gazed down at Sabah.

"Hello, Sabah. It has been a long time."

"Yes. From one war to the next." Sabah gestured with his hand. "Please, sit. The present accommodations are not much different from the last time we met."

Sebastian smiled at that. "I remember. First time I'd ever eaten goat. I remember it being warmer, though."

"We were younger men in those days."

Yaqub sat quietly by and watched his father. The old man acted stronger than he was. Evidently Sabah viewed the interview with the American journalist as a battle and summoned his strength.

Awkwardly, with some pain, Sebastian sat on a rug. Even with the padding, Yaqub knew the other man could feel the cold stone floor. Sebastian made himself as comfortable as he could, sitting with crossed legs, his elbows resting on his knees. He wore the suit coat, but his tie had been shoved into a pocket. Yaqub had made certain the man hung on to it.

"You have met my son." Sabah lay swaddled against the wall behind him. His clothing had been arranged to cover his missing limbs.

"I have. He was much younger the first time. I didn't recognize him until he mentioned his name. Then I saw you in him." Sebastian nodded and smiled a little like he was talking with an old friend, not to someone who held his life in his hands. "You must be proud of him."

"I am proud of all the warriors who are around me. The men you see in these mountains? They are those who fought the Russians to a standstill in the 1980s. They are the warriors who taxed the Soviets to death, taking down helicopters with single-shot rifles and picking off tank crews when they became mired in the canyons and against the mountains."

The pride Sabah spoke with touched Yaqub's heart as it always had. He'd heard the stories around the campfires, and the tales had mingled with the cries of the wounded and those who lay dying.

"They were called *dukhi* in those days."

"They still are. The Russians I've talked to who were involved in that war still whisper about the 'ghosts' they faced in the mountains. None of them ever saw you or your men. At least, they didn't live to speak of it."

"Those battles were hard, fierce, and they wore away those of us who were weak, till only the bravest and hardest to kill survived. We became an elite few, Mr. Sebastian." Sabah smiled. "And we stand ready to rise once more from these mountains, those warriors that yet live and their sons and grandsons after them. We are the *mujahideen*. We are those who first gave example to the Taliban and al Qaeda in their holy wars. We are the first iron God pulled forth from his holy forge."

"I know who you are, Sabah. I covered those stories too."

Sabah nodded. "Back in those days, you were an ally. You brought attention to our cause, and you brought patronage from the West to our fight against Soviet occupation. In those days, our battles seemed to be your battles."

"We had a common enemy."

A small smile pulled at Sabah's wrecked face. "The battle still rolls on here in Afghanistan. We have not changed sides. But now we find ourselves battling those who once aided us."

"That's not true. The United States came here to destroy bin Laden and his people. Not you."

"I am lacking an arm and a leg because of American military efforts."

Sebastian was silent for a moment; then he said what was on his mind. "You allied yourself with people who are our enemies. There was no other choice."

Not "America's enemies." He'd said "our enemies." Sebastian had taken sides in the interview. Yaqub quietly respected the man for having the spine to do that.

"In that war against the Soviets, we fought to be free. Then, after they had gone, the West continued to be an influence in our country."

"We were trying to help."

"The United States was quietly undermining our country. Every day, our children looked to Western ways, wished for lives like those of American children." Sabah shook his head. "Such a thing would have taken them far from God. That could not be tolerated. A line had to be drawn. We found ourselves fighting to preserve our faith, and we could not fight on the same economic battlefield as the West. You tempt our young with a different lifestyle. The only choice we had was to charge a blood price for your efforts in the hopes that you would leave us be. Even then, even with your soldiers dying by the hundreds over here, you insist on spreading your lies and treachery."

"We wanted peace. We still do."

"You say peace. I say you want subjugation. Idolatry to wealth, to living a life without honor or responsibility, without an understanding of God."

Sebastian remained silent for a moment. "Yet you sent your son to school in France. You deliberately exposed him to Western ways."

"Yaqub is strong in his faith. I knew that he could be among Western ways and return to us whole and more knowledgeable about our new enemies. What he and other young men have learned has been invaluable to us."

"Has it?" Sebastian's face hardened. "I saw him killing defenseless people only yesterday—"

"The death of an innocent has a stronger impact than the death of a warrior."

"—and he has been trading with the Russians. Selling opium he's been getting from raiding other Muslims."

The fact that Sebastian knew these things surprised Yaqub, but it explained what the CIA team had been doing in Pakistan. He had known from the beginning that his operations wouldn't go long unnoticed.

A brief flicker of irritation showed on Sabah's face; then it was gone. "He has conducted business with men who had weapons he needed. They are Eastern Europeans. Criminals."

That caught Sebastian's attention, telling Yaqub that the American media didn't know everything. "What weapons did Yaqub need?"

"We are not here to discuss that." Sabah waved the question away. "As for the opium, it is here in our country. The spoils of war. It is merely another resource open to a warrior following *fard al-'ayn*, his holy duty. When we have united Afghanistan again under God, then we will purge the drugs from our lands."

"Those drugs are used to fuel the war against the West."

Yaqub's hand slid down to the hilt of his *pesh-kabz*, and he almost drew the blade from its sheath. He would not have killed Sebastian, but he would have hurt the man. His father's hand was there atop his own before he knew it.

"The Americans chose to allow the warlords to continue harvesting the cursed fruit of the poppies in order to gain their cooperation. They left that weed in place to buy the loyalties of those who have no honor, and it is a certain sign that your people and the warlords act upon the devil's wishes. Do not seek to throw stones over that. When it comes to the opium, your country's hands are not clean."

Sebastian looked at the old man. "Why was I spared when so many were killed? Why bring me here?"

Sabah took his hand from Yaqub's and relaxed against the stone wall behind him. The old man spoke gently, as if to a child. "You are a storyteller. You are here to tell a story." He smiled. "Some of the greatest stories the world has ever known have come from these lands. You are here to tell another."

"What story?"

"You will spread the message of the rise of the new blood that will wash over Afghanistan, of the warrior who will reignite the holy war and raise it to new levels, of the master who will unite the true believers who follow Muhammad's blessed teachings, and the one who will drive the infidels from our borders. Yaqub will carry that tide, and all before him will be changed. Those who embrace faith and the word of God will be reborn and join him in his holy battle. Those who stand against him will be broken and washed away." Sabah closed his eye for a moment while the other wept infection from beneath the black patch. His pulse beat rapidly at the hollow of his throat.

Yaqub knew his father's frail strength was fading. He pushed himself to his feet and gestured to Sebastian. "Father, if you will allow me."

Sabah nodded. "Go, Mr. Sebastian, and do your job well. Listen well to my son's words. God watches over him."

Yaqub gestured to the reporter. "Come. I will show you what you are here to do."

With some trepidation, Sebastian rolled over to his hands and knees, then awkwardly got to his feet. Whatever pain he thought he was feeling today from the donkey ride, it would be worse tomorrow, and the cold would only make it more difficult.

Yaqub bade his father good-bye and was not certain if the old man even heard him. He led the way out of the home, pausing at the door only long enough to pull on a heavy, hooded coat. Sebastian pulled on one as well.

When he stepped outside, Yaqub was surprised to learn that it had snowed. A few more inches of fluffy whiteness had filled the valley. Snow mounded up on the newly constructed walls, but the men and boys had already walked muddy trails through it as they continued their work to build the defenses.

Tramping through the snow, feeling the biting chill against his nose and cheeks, Yaqub walked toward the home where the three CIA agents were being held. The wind whistled down over the mountains and sent gusts of snow dancing like dervishes.

Two guards fell in behind Sebastian, making themselves noticeable as they followed. There was nowhere for the reporter to go. He could not make it down the mountain without dying, and Yaqub was certain Sebastian knew that.

At the other home, Yaqub swept aside the heavy tarp and stepped inside. Warmth greeted him, pushing into his face with a doughy consistency and the sharp odor of burning wood.

The home was small compared to the one where his father dwelled. Four armed men sat on rugs in front of the fireplace. Candles flickered amid pools of melted wax in niches carved out of the cave walls.

Two of the men got up with weapons in hand and walked to the wooden door that opened into another cave behind this one. The heavy door had been specially cut to occupy the space. It was held in place by crossbars anchored in the stone wall.

On either end of the door, two of the men removed the rope restraints to lift the door up and out of the way. The other two covered the space with their AK-47s.

Yaqub paused at the doorway to pick up a candle lying in a pile on a narrow shelf of stone. He lit the candle from one of those nearby, then ducked under the door and entered.

The strong scents of unwashed bodies and fear and blood filled the small cave. Yaqub could reach up and easily touch the roof. The candle flame danced briefly, but it remained true and lit up the cave.

On the other side of the space, the three CIA agents sat shivering under thin blankets. They were gaunt and hollow-eyed. All of them had grown weaker since their capture. Their hair and beards were uncombed and unshaven, infested with lice that had caused sores on their faces and necks. Bloody rags wrapped the hand of one of them.

Sebastian saw the men and froze.

One of the men spoke in a phlegmy voice. "You're an American."

The reporter said nothing till Yaqub nudged him; then he nodded and took a step forward. "I am."

"Did you come to help?"

"No, I'm afraid I'm not in a position to do that."

The man cursed foully, summoning up the last fragments of his courage. Yaqub would break that soon enough, and he looked forward to it.

"Are they going to get us out of here?"

Sebastian shook his head. "I don't know."

"They can't just leave us here. Did they make a deal?"

"No deal has been struck." Yaqub used the candle he carried to light four others inside the cave. The ambient yellow glow bathed the interior and left a skein of shadows traced across the walls and roof.

"You can't keep holding us like this."

Yaqub removed the hooded coat. "You are wrong. I can do anything I wish to. You're only alive now because I wish you to remain so. You will not get to live long."

The man's face crumpled. "What do you mean?"

Reaching to his waist, Yaqub drew the *pesh-kabz* in a fluid motion. The razor edge whispered along the leather sheath, but the sound was loud in the small cave.

Flinching fearfully, the CIA agent drew back.

"You will do as I tell you to do." Yaqub held the flat of the blade against his thigh. "As long as you do, you will live." He gestured to one of the men who had followed them into the cave.

The warrior produced a small camera and turned it on. Light sprayed over the huddled CIA agents.

One of the men summoned a brief bit of daring and spoke rapidly, leaning toward the camera. "We're somewhere in the mountains. Can't be far from the Durand Line. We didn't travel long. We're being held by Zalmai Yaqub."

The other warrior in the cave crossed the distance to the prisoners and kicked the man. The American agent had just enough time to get his manacled hands up to protect his face. The force knocked him over backward into his comrades and he groaned.

"Silence, dog! You will speak only when you are told you may."

The American agent came up snarling viciously, but he kept his manacled hands in front of his face. The warrior drove his rifle butt into the man's hands and knocked him to the floor again. This time he lay there, panting and spitting blood.

"That is enough, Kadeem." Yaqub spoke in a quiet, authoritative voice. "I would suffer him to live for now. He has a use."

Kadeem stepped back.

"Do you have the paper?"

Kadeem reached into his clothing and took out a rolled copy of the *Surghar Daily* from a pocket. He unrolled the newspaper and handed it over.

Yaqub passed the paper to Sebastian. "Hold this in front of yourself when you speak." The paper was a current edition, offering proof that Sebastian and the CIA agents were still alive.

The reporter took the newspaper and looked tentative. "What am I supposed to say?"

"Introduce yourself. Tell the listeners that the American spies are all still well."

Sebastian waited for a moment, then frowned. "Is that all?"

"For now."

"Don't you have demands?"

"I will. In time. Not at the moment. For now, we will only open negotiations."

"Where should I stand?"

Despite the tension inherent in the situation, Yaqub almost smiled at the question. Sebastian would do nicely. The man was used to taking direction.

"Over there. In front of the spies."

The camera's light remained focused on Sebastian as he moved. He stood in front of the men. "Can you get the sound from here all right?"

Yaqub glanced at the warrior holding the camera. He was young, one of those who had been to school in the West for a time, and he was good with technology. The man nodded. Yaqub turned back to Sebastian.

"The sound is fine."

Sebastian started to speak, then pulled off his long coat and set it aside. He straightened his clothing and ran a hand through his hair in an effort to make himself more presentable. Then he began speaking in a well-modulated voice.

"This is Jonathan Sebastian. Currently I'm being held . . ."

# 28

THE DEAD RUSSIAN LAY stripped on a table inside one of the military buildings occupied by Charlie Company. Images in bluish ink tracked his upper body, but some of the tattoos were symbols and Cyrillic words. All of them looked unrefined, not like the art Heath had seen on other people. Some of his father's criminal clients were walking tapestries for skin artists.

"Man, that's some ugly ink." The young Marine assisting the corpsman shook his head. He was dressed in surgical scrubs and stood just behind the woman performing the examination.

Another Marine stood nearby, holding a video recorder and capturing the procedure. The bright light played over the corpse, making his flesh look fish-belly white and the tattoos stand out even more acutely.

"Prison tats." Pike stood to Heath's right and spoke up absently. His gaze was on the dead man, but Heath got the sense that Pike's mind wasn't totally on the corpse. "Guy got them when he was locked down. In Russia, criminal organizations use tats to mark their allegiance and their history. If you know how to read them, those tats can be a walking confession."

"Sounds like you know a thing or two about this, Private." Captain Benjamin Hauser stood to Heath's left. In his forties, the captain was six feet tall and maybe ten pounds overweight. His hair had turned prematurely gray, but his ruddy complexion suggested that at one time he'd had fair hair. His hazel eyes carried a gray tint that made them look like chips of dirty ice.

"Yes sir."

"Maybe you'd care to elaborate, since we're here in an effort to understand why Captain Zarif saw fit to execute this man." Hauser had called for the examination after hearing the circumstances of the man's death.

"Sure. Can I approach the body?" Pike wasn't asking the captain. He was talking to the young corpsman.

She glanced at Pike, and her eyebrows rose over the surgical mask, indicating surprise. But there was a hint of familiarity in there as well. "Be my guest, Pike."

*Pike. First name basis at that.* Heath checked his iPad, noting the woman's name. He wondered where Pike had crossed paths with Julie Meadows.

"Prison ink like this always shows up blue." Pike pointed at the symbols, words, and images. "That's because when they're in lock-down, the ink they use is from a ballpoint pen. It's not the same as tattooing ink. It has a tendency to fade to this color." He pointed to an image on the upper right side of the man's chest.

Heath wasn't quite certain what the image had been. It looked like maybe it had been a flower, but scar tissue from some kind of burn had distorted it.

"This rose indicates the guy used to be part of some Russian Mafia group."

Hauser took a step closer and peered at the tattoo. "You're sure that's a rose?"

"Was a rose. Yeah. I'm sure. Probably his first tattoo. They usually get a rose when they're accepted into one of the gangs."

"What's the significance of the rose?"

"Don't know. Never asked."

That statement indicated that Pike knew someone either in the police or in a Russian gang. Given a guess between the two, Heath was pretty certain it was the latter. He felt a little guilty about making generalizations, but he couldn't help it. Pike was a curiosity, made so because the man didn't fit into the corps in many ways yet kept coming back activation after activation.

Then there was the violence that Pike seemed to thrive on. Heath had never met another man so inured to the atrocities on the battlefield. No matter how bad things got, Pike seemed to roll right through them.

Back in the law offices, Heath had run a background check on the man, something he'd never done on another Marine under his command. The results had been less than spectacular, and the cool, calm warrior Heath had seen on the battlefield didn't match up with the paper tiger in the report.

Pike never sought out the company of others. He didn't walk away from fellow Marines, but he didn't look for companionship. Except evidently something was in play between Pike and the corpsman Julie Meadows. Heath made a mental note to follow up on that when he had the chance.

Pike continued. "Guy got kicked out of the Mafia, though."

"How do you know that?"

"Somebody tried to burn away the rose tattoo. The criminal gangs do that when someone betrays them. Guy's lucky he didn't get a bullet between the eyes before Captain Zarif parked one there."

"So he's ex-Mafia."

Pike nodded. "That would be my guess. Whoever went after that tattoo used acid. Had to hurt." He pointed at a cathedral inked onto the man's stomach. "People think when they see a church on a Russian criminal that it has some kind of religious significance."

"I gather it does not."

"No sir." Pike pointed to the spires above the structure. "Tells you how many years the guy has served on lockdown. This guy's got six, so he's been in prison for six years."

"Then I'd further suppose that the crucifix on this man's chest doesn't signify any religious preference either." Drawn by the story, Hauser had moved in closer. Heath had moved up as well.

"No. A crucifix means the guy was a thief."

"That's how he betrayed his gang? He stole from them?"

Pike shook his head. "Thief was this guy's occupation in the gang." He pointed to a smaller tattoo on the dead man's side. It was of a Madonna and child. "The image of the Virgin Mary means that he'd been a thief since he was young. Probably since he was a kid."

Heath used a stylus to add notes to those he'd already written down.

"Can you tell me anything else about this man's history?" Hauser glanced at Pike.

Pointing to the stars tattooed on the man's knees, Pike nodded. "These mean that this guy wouldn't kneel to anyone. Wouldn't take any crap." He indicated the stars on the man's shoulders. "Those mean that he was a captain. A leader in his crew."

"I see. Is there anything else you can tell me?"

Stepping away from the body, Pike shook his head. "No sir. The tats are all from a culture you'd have to be part of. I get some of it, but not everything you see there."

"You mean the Russian culture?"

"I mean part of this guy's crew. They tend to make up their own languages, their own symbols. Some of the bigger tats, like those I showed you, translate across the board for the Mafia, but not all of them. That's why the police agencies have trouble figuring them out."

Hauser thought for a moment. "We have a Russian criminal who was kicked out of his own gang and who was also working with suspected al Qaeda sympathizers. Do we know what he was doing with those people?"

Heath fielded the question, knowing Hauser intended it for him since he'd been heading up the investigation so far. "The machine shop was churning out IEDs and other explosives."

"Good thing we shut that down, then."

"Yes sir. Gunney Towers and Corporal Shaw have been inventorying the premises. They've found a significant amount of Russian ordnance."

"Well then, we know what the Russian was probably doing there, don't we?"

"Yes sir."

"But we don't know why Captain Zarif took it upon himself to shoot this man."

Pike folded his arms across his broad chest. "We don't know what Zarif and his boys took out of this guy's pockets either."

"Do we know that anything was taken?" Hauser looked at Heath.

Heath shook his head. "No sir. Neither Pike nor Cho saw anything taken from the dead man's pockets."

The captain grimaced. "Seems to be a lot we don't know."

"Yeah."

Hauser swung his attention to Pike. "Good job today, Private. You're dismissed."

"Yes sir." Distracted, Pike started to walk away, then remembered he was in the presence of an officer. He fired off a salute and headed out of the building.

"What's going on with Pike?" Heath sat in the small office he'd been assigned. Gunney Towers and Bekah sat across the desk with their field reports in their hands. Empty food cartons stood in organized stacks awaiting removal. Dinner had been a working meal.

Outside the building, on the other side of the windows that were hung with Kevlar armor to block potential snipers, night had fallen. Heath could see the darkness through the small cracks around the windows.

Bekah looked up. Fatigue hollowed her eyes. "Nothing that I'm aware of. Why? What have you noticed?"

Heath shifted in his chair. "He seems distant."

"Pike keeps himself distant. He never fully integrates with the unit."

"I know." Heath rubbed his stubbled chin and stifled a tired yawn. "But he seems more pulled back than ever."

Towers shrugged. "Man's quiet waters. Runs deep, and you ain't gonna see nothing till he's ready to show it to you." He paused. "Thought he got a little stressed yesterday when we were doing cleanup after that action in the street."

"Stressed?" That caught Heath's attention instantly. He'd never seen Pike stressed.

"Yeah." Towers pulled out a package of Doublemint gum and offered it around. Heath took a stick to help keep himself awake. Bekah passed. "One of the other Marines made a comment that Pike didn't like. Thought Pike was gonna hit him for a minute; then he cooled back down."

"That's not the first time Pike has had to wade through something like that."

"No, it's not. First time I seen it bother him, though. Thing that bothered him most was the boy."

Heath remembered the dead children he'd helped take from the street. The work had been brutal and hard. Seeing people reduced to bloody and charred hunks of meat took a lot out of a soldier.

Especially when those pieces had once been children. In an instant, a soldier could see years of innocence that would never be spent.

"Dead kids hurt."

"Kid wasn't dead, though. When Pike found him, he was alive. Still is. But the corpsmen just about had to pry that kid outta Pike's arms." Towers chewed his gum. "I seen Marines go through trauma like that before, but I never seen Pike like that."

"You talk to Pike about it?"

Towers leaned back in his chair. "Tried. He wouldn't have none of it. Went back to being Pike, closemouthed and surly. I got the message. Left him alone."

Someone knocked on the door; then it opened and a private shoved his head into the room. "Lieutenant Bridger?"

"Yes, Private?"

"Captain Hauser says you should get to the communications center ASAP."

Heath stowed his iPad, pulled on his armor, and hooked his helmet up from the floor by the chin strap. Towers and Bekah followed him.

Television reporter Jonathan Sebastian stood in front of a stone wall. He looked worse for wear, but he seemed healthy enough.

Heath stood at the back of the crowd in the communications center, taking it all in and dialing down the feeling that thrummed inside him—the need to do something. This was the CIA's show at present, but he knew the Marines would be sent in soon. They always were. He wanted to know as much as he could before that happened.

The broadcast was coming in over a link the Marines had to the Kandahar channels. CIA Special Agent in Charge Gerald Benton stood to one side of the large screen that carried the television station. Like Sebastian, Benton looked tired.

"So far we are still alive." On the monitor, Sebastian gestured to his left.

The camera view tracked in that direction and focused on three men huddled on the floor. A moment passed as the cameraman cycled through the magnification and stripped away the fuzzy softness till the image was clear. Bearded and fatigued, the prisoners sat at the back of the cave. Faded bruises showed on their faces, and one of the men had his arm and hand heavily bandaged.

Another monitor showed the faces of the three missing CIA agents from the agency's files. It only took Heath the space of a drawn breath to verify the three men with Sebastian were the CIA agents taken by Yaqub in Pakistan.

Sebastian spoke calmly, but tension tightened his voice. "I am told that our good health will continue as long as our captor is certain he has the attention of the United States military and the Kandahar government. This presentation is designed to open a dialogue."

The camera shifted back to Sebastian, who unrolled the newspaper he was holding. The cameraman zoomed in on the paper and brought it into sharp focus, centering on the date.

"The paper is to prove that we are still alive."

Several computer operators in the room worked frenziedly at their stations. Another CIA agent walked through the cyber team.

"C'mon, guys. Get me that signal. It's not originating at the Kandahar station. It's coming from somewhere else. Find it."

One of the technicians, a young woman whose fingers flew across the keyboard, read screen after screen of numbers faster than Heath could follow. "It's coming from outside the city. Up in the Safed Koh mountains."

The agent crewing the cyber effort wheeled on her, sliding into place to peer over her shoulder. "That's a lot of open area, Agent. Narrow that."

"I'm working on it."

Grid after grid flashed onto the computer screen, flipping into place and magnifying the mountainous terrain. Heath felt himself tensing up as he watched the search even though he didn't know what was taking place. He knew that men's lives hung in the balance. If the CIA could narrow the search enough, Charlie Company could get fire teams into the area and put boots on the ground. They'd have a chance to bring those hostages home safely.

"I have been told that negotiations will begin soon." Sebastian rolled the paper up and held it in a fist. "I am hopeful that we will all get out of this alive."

The broadcast suddenly ended and the screen went black.

"No!" The female CIA operative leaned more closely over her keyboard, and her fingers almost became a blur as she typed. As impressive as her speed was, though, the images on the screen stopped cycling and sat over the same area.

Judging from what he could see, Heath knew the area was too large to be a viable target for a search and rescue operation. They'd been stymied.

"Did we get the location?" Benton walked from the front of the room to the computer stations.

"No." The computer tech shook her head. "We didn't. I'm sorry. I've narrowed the parameters, but not enough."

Anger tightened Benton's face, but he remained professional. "We'll get it next time. Yaqub isn't going to stop talking now that he knows he has our attention." He turned and walked back to stand beside the screen. "I know you Marines are still working the streets, still gathering intel, and I know that some of your comrades were killed in today's sweeps."

Heath hadn't lost any of his troops. He'd been fortunate.

"I want you to know that your sacrifices are appreciated. More than that, they're needed. This isn't just about those three hostages. This is about Zalmai Yaqub. We need to run him to ground and put him down . . . one way or another."

Towers spoke softly at Heath's side, putting into words what every Marine in that room was thinking. "Give us a target and we'll get it done."

Heath knew that they would . . . if they could. So far Zalmai Yaqub had remained one step ahead of them. And they still didn't know what the man's true game plan was.

# 29

**"WHERE'S YOUR MIND?"**

Puzzled, Pike swung his gaze from the booth where a crowd of Afghan National Police sat and looked across the table at Julie Meadows. They were seated at a local restaurant the Marines frequented when they were outside the zone.

The corpsman was easy on the eyes. He could tell she'd gone to some effort to make herself look presentable in the uniform, which wasn't an easy thing to do. But Julie had pulled it off.

"What?" he asked.

She smiled at him and didn't seem angry. Always a good sign. "Exactly. You're somewhere else, Pike. Not here, not right now."

Pike didn't know why he'd agreed to another dinner. He didn't need the company. In fact, most of the time he preferred his own company. "I didn't know I wasn't paying attention."

"If I wasn't as confident as I am in myself, that could hurt."

"I'm not very good at this."

"What? Eating dinner?"

"Eating dinner *with* someone."

"You eat dinner with Marines all the time."

"They don't expect you to hold a conversation."

"I didn't know a conversation was going to be a problem." Julie's tone remained light, but Pike knew he was on dangerous ground.

"It's not you. It's me."

She sat back from him a little, and he felt the distance between them widen.

"When I'm out in the field, I stay switched on. I always notice stuff."

"Except for dinner partners."

Pike ignored that and pointed his chin at the Afghan National Police gathering. "Over there."

Julie sipped her water and casually glanced at the other table. Her eyes glinted and her mouth hardened. "Captain Zarif and his cronies."

"Cronies?"

"You have another word?"

Pike was thinking they were more like a gang, not policemen, not anything as genteel as cronies. "I do, but I try not to use it around women."

"Well, I feel relieved. At least you noticed that part, even if you weren't keeping track of the conversation."

"Yeah, it's been tough to concentrate when I'm looking straight at the guy who killed the Russian prisoner I took into custody." Pike focused on the other table. "So you've heard of Zarif. What do you know about him? And his . . . *cronies*?"

"Just rumors. None of 'em flattering. But sounds like the brass have their hands tied."

"So they leave him in play?"

"Zarif is connected. Having him arrested would be an embarrassment to the Afghan National Police and the US military. I've also heard he can be counted on to monitor tango activity, that he has connections to more sources than a lot of his fellow policemen do."

"I'm starting to wonder if it's because he's doing business with them."

"It's a case of the devil you know," Julie said. "Looks like Zarif knows just how far to push things, and the Afghan National Police and the US military let him take it to the limit."

Pike sipped his tea. "Could be that someone should take a closer look at Zarif."

"You?"

Pike looked at her. "Could be."

"Because he murdered the Russian?"

"That caught my attention. Zarif didn't kill the Russian just to put points on the board. He was covering up something. Or taking advantage of the situation somehow."

"How?"

"I don't know yet. But I suspect that not all of the ordnance the Russian munitions dealers brought into the city has been found. I think that's what Zarif is hiding."

"You could tell someone."

Pike shook his head. "If people are already looking the other way for this guy, he's going to have to be caught with his hand in the cookie jar to change the status quo."

Zarif glanced at his cell phone on the table, then picked it up, excused himself, and stepped away from the table to talk.

Pike watched the Afghan National Police captain. "He's talking in Russian."

Julie's eyes narrowed. "You can hear him?"

"I can read his lips. You get raised in foster homes, it's a skill you pick up. Like learning to read body language."

"You were raised in foster care?"

Too late, Pike realized that he'd revealed more about himself than he'd intended to. He'd carefully kept the conversation loose, talking more about what was going on in Kandahar or the mechanic work he did with Monty in the garage back in Tulsa. "Yeah. It's something I don't talk about a lot."

Thankfully, Julie left that alone.

After a moment, Zarif returned to his table, talked to the men there, then departed with a few of them in tow.

Pike looked at Julie. "I'm sorry, but I gotta go. To me, that conversation looked like business, and I need to find out what Zarif's up to. If there are still munitions floating around out there, we need to nail those down."

Julie nodded. "I understand."

Zarif disappeared through the door.

Pike stood and grabbed his rifle and helmet. "Can I get a rain check on dinner? Next time I'll be better company, I promise."

Julie smiled. "I'd like that." She rested a hand on his forearm. "Be careful, Pike."

"Always." Pike gave her a wink and walked through the tables, only a short distance behind Zarif.

★   ★   ★

*"You should stay out of this. What's done is done, and you getting riled up over what happened ain't gonna do no good. You listening to me, Pike? No, you ain't. I can tell. You got that mad on. It's gonna get you killed one of these days."*

As Pike moved through the shadows, he didn't know if the voice was Petey's or his own common sense. He'd told Petey that same thing whenever Petey had gotten bent over something they couldn't do anything about. On occasion, he'd given himself the same advice. And sometimes Petey had thrown the warning in Pike's face just to get his attention.

However, even after all the bad things Pike had seen during his biker days and during tours in the sandbox, Captain Zarif's cold-blooded execution of the Russian cut Pike bone deep. Pike objected to being made a fool of on general principle, and he didn't like the idea of a helpless man getting killed like an animal. But the thing that bothered Pike most of all was not knowing what was going on around him when it concerned Zarif. The Afghan National Police captain was privy to too many Marine operations inside Kandahar.

Not knowing things could get a man killed. Not knowing his best friend was working a piece of drug business and betraying the people he was dealing with could get that man killed. Not knowing what was going on in the sandbox could get a Marine and his whole squad killed.

That wasn't going to happen on Pike's watch. So he was going to figure out what angle the police captain was working. At the same time, Pike resented the fact that he felt so responsible for everybody. This wasn't his thing.

Only he couldn't stay out of it.

With his M4A1 slung over his left shoulder and his M9 riding at his hip, Pike followed Zarif and three of his hardcases through the shadowed streets.

The strident ring of a cell phone reverberated over the street, sounding out of place. Zarif reached into a pocket and withdrew the instrument. The glow of the phone played over his cheek and beard as he pulled it to his ear.

Zarif halted and looked along the street. With catlike reflexes, Pike stepped into the shadowed recess of a nearby shop door. The business was closed, as were the others along the block. He slid his M9 free and kept the pistol out of sight behind his leg.

Speaking quickly, Zarif replied in Russian.

While Pike and Petey had been in California, they'd done some business with the Russian Mafia in Los Angeles, and Pike had picked up some of the language just by observing. In the foster homes, he'd learned that a kid who couldn't pick up on the words between words and the nonverbal communication of caretakers sometimes stepped into a threshing machine. He understood enough of the exchange to know that whoever was on the phone with Zarif wanted a meeting. The guy also wanted his *property* back.

Zarif grinned and said that arrangements could be made. He gave an address not far away and said he would be there in twenty minutes.

Anger flowed through Pike as he got under way again. Pike wanted to know what Captain Zarif had, and he needed to find out before the Russians arrived. He kept the M9 in his hand.

On the next block, Zarif and his men stepped into a small hotel. Darkness filled the windows of the building, and shadows loitered at the entryway. Only a weak yellow light shone inside the office area.

Pike went through the door and ignored the small man reading a newspaper on the other side of the check-in counter. The clerk glanced up only for a second, then quickly looked away.

Treading on the outsides of the stairs to make less noise, Pike went up. He watched ahead of himself, but he listened behind. He didn't want to get caught on the stairs.

Down the hallway on the third floor, Zarif and his men walked into a room on the right.

The building primarily housed small businesses. Signs on the doors on either side of the hallway were marked in Pashto and English. Evidently the last few years of Western military operations in the area had brought about English language concessions.

Intending to simply walk past the doorway, Pike was listening intently. But the door sank inward, and one of Zarif's men popped out with a gun in his hand.

"Do not move, American."

The man shoved the barrel of his pistol into Pike's neck. Pike had to resist the impulse to take the weapon away from him. No matter how much it was emphasized in training, too many guys didn't understand the lesson about touching an enemy with your weapon. Doing so made the gun wielder especially vulnerable.

Pike froze and slowly lifted his hands. "Hey. I'm not looking for trouble."

The man wrapped a fist in Pike's collar and shoved him toward the room. Stumbling, Pike went through the door. Another man caught Pike by the lapels and swung him up against the wall.

The room was small but held four desks and accompanying chairs. Books and computers occupied the tops of the desks. City maps and Post-its covered a bulletin board on the rear wall, but the walls were otherwise barren, offering no clue as to what type of business took place there.

"Who are you?" The man holding Pike's lapels stared into his eyes.

Behind this man, the first man checked the hallway, then retreated back into the room. He glanced at Zarif, who was sitting in an overstuffed chair beside the room's only window. A breeze ruffled the thin, worn curtains.

"He is the only one in the hallway." The first man lowered his pistol, but he didn't put it away. "No one else is with him."

Zarif glared at the man. "Go downstairs and watch. These Americans don't travel alone."

The man nodded and let himself out the door, closing it behind him.

A third ANP officer stood slightly to one side so that he had a clear field of fire with his pistol. Holding Pike with one hand, pinning him against the wall, the second man searched him quickly. He took the M9 and the M4A1, slinging them to the man behind him, who placed them on a desk.

Zarif stared at him more intently. "I know you."

Pike said nothing.

"Of course I do. You are the American who found Evstafiev."

Pike filed the name away and stared back at the Afghan National Police captain. His captor's breath pushed against his face and stank.

"What are you doing here?"

Pike kept silent.

Zarif's face turned to stone. He glanced at the expensive watch on his wrist. "We do not have much time. What you say in the next few minutes could save your life."

Pike smiled. He didn't believe a word the man said. He and Petey had dealt with too many guys like Zarif. They lashed out when they were threatened, and Pike's presence there was a definite threat.

Pike spoke softly, shifting slightly to cause his captor to shift with him. The fact that the man wouldn't kill him until Zarif ordered his death was something he intended to take advantage of. "You murdered Evstafiev. I want to know why."

Zarif relaxed somewhat and rested his pistol on his thigh. "I did not murder him. I shot him before he could kill your squad mate."

"Sure you did, and the only reason I figure you did it was because there was something in it for you." Pike shifted again. This time the man holding him took a fresh grip on his shirt and pulled a combat knife from his belt. The man pressed the sharp edge against Pike's throat. The knife slit the flesh just enough to sting.

"You do not know what you are talking about."

Pike grinned. "Really? Then why are you meeting more Russians here tonight?"

A frown etched into Zarif's face. He glanced at his watch again. "Kill him."

Pike had already known the command was coming. He'd read it in the captain's body language. Even as Zarif spoke, Pike reached up and caught his captor's right wrist in his strong left hand and kept the knife from biting any deeper. Jamming the heel of his right palm into the man's chin, Pike hit him hard enough that the man's teeth clipped off the end of his tongue. Blood dribbled down his chin as his eyes started to roll back into his head. Pike kept hold of him, using him as a shield while the man behind him jockeyed for a clear shot.

Bracing himself against the wall for extra leverage, Pike shoved the knife wielder backward and drove the man with the pistol like a football tackling dummy toward the desk with his weapons. All three of them smashed into the desk, and it broke under the impact.

Pike tracked his M9 as he dropped to one knee. The two ANP officers were down in a heap, the knife man mostly unconscious but the other one trying to heave his comrade's slack weight from him. He fired his pistol twice, but the bullets went wide of Pike.

Scrambling, Pike closed his fist over the M9, brushed the safety off with his thumb, and fired two rounds into the gunman's face as he brought his weapon around. A bullet tore through Pike's collar, letting him know how close he'd come to dying. With the adrenaline singing through him, thinking about the times he and Petey had ended up in similar situations, Pike couldn't stop a smile from spreading across his face.

He turned his weapon toward Zarif. The captain stood with a two-handed grip on his pistol. The man didn't look so calm and controlled now, but he didn't freeze up. Two bullets came close enough to Pike's face that he felt the heat, and a third ripped through the material over his right shoulder.

Pike sighted by instinct, aiming for Zarif's chest the way he'd been trained in the military. Both rounds ripped into the Afghan National Police captain's center mass.

With a shocked and pained expression on his face, Zarif stopped firing and looked down at the blood spreading across the front of his shirt. Then he forced himself to fire again, managing to get off two more shots before Pike put a round between his eyes.

Zarif stumbled back and sat down in the chair behind him. The pistol slid from his nerveless fingers and thumped against the floor.

The man with the knife started to come around and retrieved a gun just as Pike was getting to his feet. Pike brought his pistol to bear and fired a single shot. The man lay still. Grabbing his M4A1, Pike slung the assault rifle over his shoulder and crossed the room to Zarif. The Afghan National Police captain sat in the chair with unseeing eyes.

Shoving the pistol into its holster, Pike knelt and quickly searched the dead man, knowing the gunfire would draw someone. At the very least the other Afghan policeman would return to the room.

*"You don't have time for this. You gotta get out of here."*

Pike still didn't know if the voice in his head was Petey's or his own. Those times with Petey didn't seem so far away right now, not when he was playing in the sandbox. Death could lie on the other side of the next heartbeat.

He went through Zarif's pockets but didn't find anything that looked like it might have come from the dead Russian. Zarif's contact on the phone had seemed to want his property back, though. There should have been something.

*"Doesn't mean it was small enough to be on this guy, Pike. Get moving."*

Despite the ringing in his ears from the gunshots confined to the office, Pike heard running footsteps out in the hall. Cursing in frustration, knowing tonight's events had gone a lot further than he'd thought they would, Pike abandoned the search and went to the window. He peered into the street. The drop wasn't far. He shoved his head and shoulders through, holding on with his hands, and flipped himself outward.

Arcing his body, Pike propelled himself away from the building so he wouldn't get ground to hamburger against the rough exterior. He hit and went down at once, rolling to dissipate his momentum, coming to his feet effortlessly.

Only to be blinded by a sudden flare of lights. He reached for the M4A1, but an American voice brought him up short.

"Stand down, Marine." The command came from the Humvee that rolled out of the alley. The powerful searchlight plucked Pike out of the inky darkness.

Releasing his assault rifle, Pike started to dodge to the side, thinking he might still get away. Only two Marines stood there as well. Both of the men were young and had their weapons to shoulder. He knew that if he moved, they would shoot him.

Slowly Pike raised his hands over his head and dropped to his knees. There was nowhere to run—and a whole room full of dead people he couldn't explain.

# 30

**"THIS IS A MESS,** Lieutenant Bridger."

Standing in that business office with the dead Afghan National Police lying where they'd fallen, Heath had to agree. "Yes sir. It is that."

Major Lee Hollister glared at the carnage. He was in his forties, a short, powerful man with angular features and prominent cheekbones. He was liaising between the Marine Corps and the Afghan National Police.

"And I've got to clean it up because our allies among the Afghan National Police are *not* happy with Marines gunning down their people." Hollister glared at Heath as if he were responsible. "Which means you're going to do your best to help me."

"Yes sir." Only Heath didn't know how he was going to do that. He'd been laying out plans for tomorrow with Bekah and Towers. Now it technically *was* tomorrow, and the day promised to be much different than he'd envisioned.

"This private, he belongs to you?"

Heath's gut reaction was to point out that Pike didn't belong to anybody, but he quelled that because it wasn't an answer Hollister was looking for. And Heath wasn't going to sell a member of his team down the river. If Pike was in the wrong on this—and it looked like he was—Heath, as Pike's commander, was still prepared to stand beside him. "Yes sir."

"What was he doing with Zarif?"

That was news to Heath. He'd been summoned, then pulled into the room while Hollister's investigative team took over. No names other than Pike's had been mentioned when he'd gotten the notice to come running. But the man's name struck an immediate chord.

"Zarif?" Heath pulled out his iPad and flicked through his after-action reports. "Captain Ashna Zarif?"

"Yes," Hollister growled irritably. "Stay up, Lieutenant."

Heath curbed an impulse to point out that this was the first time he'd heard Zarif's name and that he'd never met the Afghan National Police captain. Having him not prepared was Hollister's choice. Heath wasn't there to argue, and doing so could put him in the same brig as Pike. "Yes sir. I will, sir. Which one is Zarif?"

Hollister pointed to the dead man seated in the chair near the window.

Heath approached the man and took a couple pictures with the iPad for later comparison. "There was an altercation between Zarif and a group of our people earlier today." He paused. "Correction— yesterday."

"What kind of altercation?"

"Zarif executed a Russian male our Marines had taken into custody." Heath used *our* as a subliminal reminder to Hollister as to whose side he was supposed to be on.

"Executed?" Hollister frowned.

"Yes sir. The Russian had been taken into custody following a raid on a site that turned out to be a bomb-making facility. A lot of the ordnance was Russian." Heath left it up to Hollister to connect the dots. An attorney learned not to oversell the logical parts of an argument. Of course, it didn't hurt to underscore parts of that logic, either. "I've been told some of the assembly also showed Russian influence."

That was a little leading because no one had reported anything about the techniques employed to put the bombs together. Then again, if someone used Russian ordnance, it only stood to reason that some form of Russian technique would creep in.

Hollister cursed. "Do we know anything about the dead Russian?"

"He's a member of a criminal organization."

"How do you know that?"

Heath brought up pictures, then tilted the iPad so the lights in the room didn't glare off the screen. He let the tattoos speak for themselves. "My specialist says this guy was probably on the outs from the organization." He didn't mention that the specialist had been Pike.

Hollister grimaced and wiped his face with a big hand. "I've seen tats like that before. And I've seen Russians in Kandahar before too." He heaved a sigh. "Do we have a name for that man yet?"

"No."

"So your private wasn't out here on your orders?"

"No." Heath had decided to tell the truth, but he also wasn't going to let Pike swing in the breeze.

Hollister swiveled his attention to one of the men supervising the evidence collection team. "Lieutenant Simms, what did Zarif have on him?"

Simms, a slim African American, gestured to one of the desks. "Got it all bagged here."

Hollister stepped toward the desk. Heath followed discreetly behind, then took a couple images of the contents on display.

Zarif had been carrying a thick wad of local currency and one nearly as thick that had American, Chinese, and Russian notes. Keys, spare magazines for his pistol, change, breath mints, and a smooth stone completed the personal effects.

"The captain was carrying a large bankroll." Hollister riffled through the currency with a ballpoint pen, spreading the bills out.

Heath didn't say anything, but he knew that both of them recognized that the presence of so much cash offered mute testimony to the fact that Zarif was conducting some kind of business on the side.

Hollister put the ballpoint pen back in his pocket. "It appears Zarif might have been doing some business on the side."

Heath didn't say anything.

Hollister addressed Simms again. "What did the private have when you took him into custody?"

Simms guided them to another desk.

As he studied the desk, Heath noticed immediately that Pike didn't carry much other than essential equipment, and all of that showed evidence of well-tended care. The only thing that caught Heath's eye was the compass. That wasn't regulation Marine equipment, and Heath didn't know what to make of it.

"I don't see anything incriminating, Lieutenant Simms."

"Nor do I, Major."

"When you took the Marine into custody, was there any indication of alcohol or drugs?"

"No sir. Straight as a board."

"Except that he came in here and killed these men." Hollister waved a hand around.

Heath took pictures of the bullet holes in the walls and the weapons lying on the floor next to the dead men. "Did Pike fire all the rounds?" He knew that Pike hadn't done all the shooting unless he'd deliberately shot in every direction. Judging from the wounds on the dead men, Pike hadn't wasted a bullet.

Hollister looked at Simms for the answer.

Simms shook his head. "No sir. The Afghan police got off some rounds too. You ask me, from what I'm reconstructing here, Pike was fighting for his life. He was just better than these guys. *Way* better."

"Did Pike say anything when you took him into custody?"

"No. The sergeant who caught him said once Pike knew he wasn't getting out of the situation, he gentled down immediately."

Heath figured he could make a point of that in Pike's favor. "Pike didn't want to hurt any Marines."

Hollister cursed. "Or maybe he just knew he was going to get shot."

Resisting the impulse to offer a quick rebuttal, Heath bit back an observation. Thankfully, Simms couldn't keep his own thoughts to himself.

"Begging the major's pardon, but this guy, sir, he wasn't afraid of getting shot. These ANP guys had him cold." Simms pointed to the wall by the door. "Looks like they had Pike here, probably held him at bay with this knife." The lieutenant indicated a combat blade on the floor nearby. "Only he didn't stay put." He pointed to the bullet holes in the wall. "This second guy shot at Pike." He approached one of the dead men, squatting down to point out a bullet wound high on the man's right shoulder. "He shot his own guy in the process. Then Pike got loose." He stood and looked around the room. "My guess is that it was over pretty quick after that." A small smile flickered across the lieutenant's lips. "Three-on-one odds, sir, and they had their weps locked and loaded. Impressive."

That was Pike all right. Heath studied the dead police officers. The problem wasn't what he knew about Pike. It was what he didn't know about the man.

Hollister cursed again, then focused on Heath. "Lieutenant Simms is going to work the scene re-creation here. Even if he's right, which I think he is, that still leaves the question as to what brought Pike here. I want that question answered. So do the Afghans."

"Yes sir. Can you clear it so I can talk to Pike?"

"It'll be done before you can get there."

"Thank you, sir. If you would, I need to clear another person to talk to Pike."

"Sergeant Towers? Not a problem."

"Actually, I was thinking Corporal Shaw."

Hollister thought for a moment, then shook his head. "I don't know him."

"*Her*, actually."

Hollister's eye twitched. "Her."

"Yes sir."

"The Marines aren't any place for a woman. Someone should have told her that. Still, I suppose you need someone to talk to the Afghan women."

Heath held his irritation in check. There was a lot of controversy over women in the military, but they'd been there since Vietnam. Not as many had volunteered for service in hot spots back then, but he knew an Air Force colonel who had been excellent at *her* in-country post. "Corporal Shaw is a good Marine, sir. And I think she can be of help with Pike. She's got a way of getting people to open up."

"It's your call, Lieutenant."

"Thank you, sir."

"You're dismissed."

Heath fired off a salute, then turned and headed for the door.

"Just get back to me the minute you find out what went on here. I've got to talk to these people, and if I don't have an explanation for this mess, heads are going to roll. Starting with your private's."

"Yes sir."

# 31

**LYING ON A THIN MATTRESS** in the brig, Pike slept with one arm folded over his face. Only faint streams of light bled through the grille on the door. He still smelled the gunpowder on him from the encounter with Zarif and his men, and the odor made him restless, tainting his dreams as fragments of memories wove in and out of his imagination.

"Hey, bro. About time you got here. I've been telling our new friends all about you." Petey sat at a table in the back of the bar. He was grinning and acting like he didn't have a care in the world. In reality, he was eight thousand dollars short on inventory for a delivery to the man seated across the table from him.

Pike didn't say anything. Road dust from south of the border covered him. Early that morning, they'd closed the cantinas in Juárez after crossing the border the hard way to bring in a load of merch for the local banditos.

For the last few months, Pike had been rebuilding engines and doing other mechanic work on sleds over in Austin. He'd been doing fine for himself, staying off the outlaw trails and making a legitimate living. Pike hadn't planned on the semiretirement from the criminal life. It had just happened.

A guy in a shop had loaned him the tools he needed to fix his Harley, then talked to him about a project bike he'd been having trouble with. A conversion for a guy who'd lost the use of his legs but still wanted to feel the wind in his face.

Curious and maybe a little challenged, Pike had hung around. Petey was off hanging with some chick he'd found, spending the money they'd made on their last transport job. Every now and again, Petey would call and check in, surprised that Pike was still working at the garage. Petey told Pike about the work he was doing with a guy who specialized in identity theft, told Pike there was a position open for him if he wanted.

Pike didn't want. Petey liked the tech jobs. He had a head for hacking and stuff. He'd learned that at one of the foster homes he'd stayed in. Before the man and wife got carted off for identity theft. They hadn't made any other mistake than to leave the computer where Petey could get to it. Petey hadn't known as much back then. He'd only been twelve. He still had a lot of learning ahead of him.

He'd told Pike about it, about the way the cops had broken in and thrown the foster 'rents on the floor, handcuffed them right there while some of the other kids screamed and cried like it was the end of the world. Petey had laughed when he told the story. Pike had laughed too.

But Pike hadn't been feeling it then. He was getting over a whaling by his latest "father figure." The guy didn't like the way Pike looked at him, but he'd ordered Pike to look him in the eye when he was talking to him. There was no winning a deal like that. So Pike hid his bruises and laughed at Petey's stories because that was what Petey expected. Petey always wanted people to join in the fun.

Petey was laughing that day in the bar too. And Pike wasn't feeling that either.

"Got a problem, bro." Petey shook his head and kept his hands on the table in front of him. "Franco—this guy—" he nodded toward the guy across the table—"he thinks we're short on the merch."

That was when Pike knew they were short on the guns. He remembered the underground casino not far from the hotel where they'd crashed. He noticed the dark circles under Petey's hollowed eyes. It didn't take a rocket scientist to put the pieces together.

Petey had a thing for long odds, and it almost always got him on the wrong side of the balance sheet. That was what had ended the "job" working the identity-theft ring too. One morning he'd shown up at the bike garage five minutes ahead of a hard crew looking to make an example out of him. They'd warned Pike to stay out of it, but it was Petey, and nobody worked Petey over on Pike's watch.

Pike grabbed a set of tire tools and waded into them. Minutes later, after he'd pulled them off Petey and put a couple guys in critical condition, he and Petey were on the road again. Juárez, Petey had said, because he knew a guy there who needed somebody to run contraband into Mexico. They'd done work like that before.

Pike missed the bike shop, and he missed the old guy who ran it. He'd seen the old man in the shop while he helped Petey back to his bike. The old man knew the score. Judging from the tats on his forearms, he'd ridden the outlaw trails himself.

"You don't gotta go, brother." The old guy, Jonas, talked softly. "You don't gotta run."

Pike shook his head. "Got no choice. Cops'll be here soon." He jerked a thumb over his shoulder. "These guys are connected to somebody. They won't stay beat down. The trouble Petey gets into usually has long arms and an even longer memory."

"There's another way." Jonas tapped the blue lines of the cross tattooed on the inside of his left forearm. That tat was the last one he'd gotten, the last he was ever going to get. "You just gotta wrap your head around which way you want to go."

Pike smiled. "Got the church message before. Didn't take then.

It's been good working with you." Then he'd climbed on his bike and ridden out of there with Petey.

Now, four days later, he was looking at Petey across the table from Jorge Franco, a guy who didn't take prisoners and had a habit of leaving people who'd betrayed him scattered across highways for buzzards to feed on.

"You *are* short on the merch." Franco spoke Spanish. He was a thickset man with big hands and a broad face. Mirrored sunglasses covered his eyes. A neatly trimmed goatee and mustache framed his mouth. His teeth were big, and there was a lot of gold in his grill. Pike had never seen a man with so much gold in his mouth. Franco's hair was jet black and hung to his broad shoulders. Silver chains glittered at his throat.

Two other men, both of them big as well, stood on either side of the table, young guys who would do whatever they were told to do. They operated maybe a step above the guns they carried, and there would be no mercy at their hands despite their youth.

Pike had seen burnouts like them in the foster homes and the orphanage. Humans had the capacity to teach their young to feast on them and on each other.

"What I want to know is what you're going to do about it." Franco stared a challenge at Pike.

All of them knew what was going down. Franco was going to make an example of Pike and Petey. He was going to leave them spread across some street or alley. Franco thought Pike was there to beg for his friend's life, knowing Pike wasn't going to have the money either. Petey thought Pike was going to save him, betting on one of those small chances that he couldn't resist.

Pike told himself that. The thought crossed his mind that Petey just hadn't wanted to die alone, but that was more selfish than Pike was willing to believe.

Staring into Franco's dark eyes, Pike spoke in a soft monotone. "I'm gonna ask you to let my friend go. He made a mistake. He won't be doing business with you anymore, and you can afford to lose eight grand."

Franco had laughed at that. "You're out of your mind. I'm gonna kill both of you—" He didn't get to finish his threat because by then Pike was in motion.

They'd frisked Pike for weapons. The problem was they didn't realize anything could be a weapon. Pike snatched a longneck beer bottle from the table with his right hand, smashed it into the face of the man on his right. As the unconscious man spilled toward the floor, Pike rammed the broken end of the bottle up under the other man's jaw and sliced his windpipe.

Franco only had time for a single shot that glanced off Pike's side, cracking a rib before Pike had the man's pistol in his hand and put three rounds into Franco's head.

Rib burning, having to force himself to breathe because it hurt so badly, Pike swung to stare around the bar. People were already hustling outside. Nobody there owed Franco anything, and probably some of them were glad he was dead.

Crowing loudly, probably jacked on something, Petey came from behind the table and clapped Pike on the back. "I knew you wouldn't let me down, bro. You never have."

"Gotta get out of here, Petey." Pike knelt and picked up another pistol, shoving it under his belt at his back. "Cops'll be here any minute."

"Sure, sure. Just lemme get his stash." Petey rummaged through Franco's bloody clothes, taking money and drugs. "Okay. I'm ready."

Breathing shallowly in an effort to keep the cracked rib from hurting too much, Pike followed Petey out of the bar.

Only this time they didn't make it. Two police cars full of Diablo bikers waited outside. Dust covered their cracked road leathers, and a few of them were just grinning skulls with the flesh pooled around their necks. They raised their weapons to fire, and Pike knew he and Petey were going to die this time.

"Told you, brother. Told you there was another way." Jonas stood to one side, out of the field of fire. The tat of the cross was clearly visible on the inside of his arm. "You stay on that road you're riding, Pike, you're gonna die."

The Diablos opened fire, and Petey staggered as the blood poured out of him.

★   ★   ★

Pike woke in a rush, heart pounding, and he could feel the phantom pain of that long-ago cracked rib lancing through his side. He blew the air out of himself, knowing he'd hyperventilate if he didn't.

He sat up on the side of the bed, and his head spun like he was coming out of a bender. *Just a dream. Not real, bro. Keep it together.* He rubbed at his face, feeling the calluses wear against the stubble.

He stared into the darkness around him. Thoughts of Hector and the garage got all tangled with the memories of what had happened to Petey and the shooting with the Afghan National Police. It was getting hard to sort them out.

*Gotta make life simple again. Things are getting too heavy. It's time to drift. Just let it go and find a piece of the highway you ain't been down before.*

He settled back on the bed, putting his back against the wall like he used to do when he was in foster care. If anyone—any*thing*—came at him, they'd have to come at him from the front. Sitting there quietly, he listened to his heartbeat and worked on keeping it at a measured rate.

He was going to survive this. All he had to do was get back to the

States and let the witness protection people find him a new place. He'd crawl out of the sandbox one last time, maybe even crawl out of the protection program too, then get good and gone.

# 32

**"OPEN UP."** Heath nodded at the brig door and handed over the orders Major Hollister had issued for him. "I'm here to see the prisoner."

"You'll have to leave your weapons here, sir." The MP was young, but he was thorough. His partner stood ten feet away and watched with bright interest.

Heath put the paper bag he was carrying on the desk to one side of the brig door, then passed over his assault rifle, M9, and combat knife. The weapons were stored in a metal ammo box beside the desk.

"What's in the bag?"

"Breakfast."

"I gotta see it before you go in."

"Sure." Heath scooted the bag across the desktop.

The MP took a moment to go through the two Styrofoam containers filled with lamb chops, sticky rice, yogurt, and grapes and apricots. There were also slices of naan—covered in poppy seeds and still warm and fresh from the oven—and two bottles of water.

"Looks good." The MP returned the bag. "Beats the breakfast I got this morning." He peered through the bars at the occupant. "Hey, Private. Stay away from the door. Do that and we're all good."

"What if I don't want any company?" Pike's voice was a ragged, sleepy roar.

"You stopped getting a choice last night when you got stuck in here. Just stay back from the door." The MP peered through the bars again, then opened the locks and pulled the door to one side.

Pike sat against the back wall, knees drawn up, his elbows resting on them. He looked at Heath with an unreadable expression.

"Step inside the cell and immediately to one side."

Heath nodded, reminded of how the security was when he went to see Darnell Lester. The strange thing was that there was something in Pike's face that reminded him of Darnell, the same kind of resolute acceptance of his fate.

As soon as he stepped inside and to the side, the MP slammed the door behind him. The lock grated, and Heath was suddenly more aware of being inside the room alone with Pike than he'd thought he would be. The feeling was primitive and wary.

"Did the brass bust you down to kitchen patrol?" A slight smirk twisted Pike's lips.

"No." Heath placed the bag on the bed. "I didn't do anything wrong. Get your breakfast. Half of that is mine."

For a minute, Pike didn't move. Heath knew the man was just being stubborn and prideful. Then Pike reached into the bag and took out one of the Styrofoam containers and a bottle of water.

Pike waved to the small cell. "You'll have to figure out your own seating arrangements. Place didn't come fully furnished."

Heath took the bag and sat on the floor, stretching his legs out before him with his back against the wall. He refused to let the lack of accommodations bother him—or the lack of ease. On a good day, Pike was prickly to deal with.

Opening the container, Heath looked over the contents and inhaled the fragrant aroma. "You're going to have to eat it with your fingers. They're not even going to let you have plastic silverware."

"Too bad. You should see what I can do with a spork."

"Maybe another time." Heath took the sarcasm as a positive thing. Of course, that could work against him too.

"You don't know what you're missing."

"I'll take your word for it." Heath dug into the meal with relish. He folded chunks of lamb into the naan. He seasoned the makeshift sandwich with some of the sauces provided, then took a big bite and chewed. He didn't try to talk. Pike wasn't going to talk until he was good and ready.

Pike outlasted Heath, though. The man sat cross-legged with his meal between his knees and focused on consuming the food like the task was the only thing on his mind. When he was finished, he closed the Styrofoam container and put it aside. He nursed the bottle of water and stared at a spot on the wall.

"We're going to have to talk about it." Heath set his container aside and drew his knees up.

Pike spoke without looking at him. "Is that an order?"

"No." Heath regarded the man openly, thinking back over the little he knew about Pike. Heath had made an effort to get to know every member of his unit, through their paperwork as well as during exchanges on deployments.

To say Pike had been reticent was an understatement. The man never gave anything away, never discussed his life outside the Marines.

"I can help you, Pike."

"I don't need any help."

"You killed those men."

"I've killed a lot of men, Lieutenant." Pike folded his hands behind his head and leaned against the wall. He kept his focus on the door.

"You killed Captain Zarif."

"Yeah."

"Why?"

"He needed killing."

"Why?"

Pike didn't answer.

"Did you kill Zarif over the dead Russian? Because Zarif killed that man while he was in your custody?"

For a minute, Pike didn't answer. "I didn't know the Russian, if that's what you're thinking."

"I don't know what to think, Pike. I came here to figure out what I'm supposed to tell Major Hollister. He's heading up the investigation of the shooting."

"What do you think?"

"I don't think you're a murderer."

Pike grinned, but there was no humor in his dark gaze. "I trailed Zarif and his men last night. That looks like premeditation, Counselor. Ain't no other way you're gonna sell that. The Marine Corps will convict me or at least kick me out."

"Does it make a difference to you?"

Pike took in a deep breath. "I don't want to die, and I don't want to be locked up for the rest of my life."

"Then let's improve on that."

Pike shook his head.

"Did you intend to kill Zarif and his men?"

"You representing me in this?"

"Do you want me to?"

"You can't. The Marines will appoint an attorney when they decide to prosecute me. And they *will* prosecute me. They don't have a choice. The relationship with the Afghans is deteriorating. The military will have to have their sacrificial goat. I don't want it to be me, but it looks like that's how it's gonna be."

Heath knew that what Pike was saying was right. Even if he wanted to represent Pike against the coming charges, he wouldn't be able to. Heath wasn't signed up as a military attorney, and the Marines would go to their own legal staff first.

"This ain't your deal, Lieutenant, so breathe easy on that score. I chose to roll the dice. This wasn't you. Didn't have anything to do with you."

Heath knew that wasn't exactly true, though. As standoffish as he was, Pike took care of his fellow Marines. The man had risked his life several times, put himself in harm's way to protect those he served with. Heath wasn't going to ignore that kind of dedication.

Pike continued in a soft voice. "I screwed up last night. Got into a bad situation and shot my way out of it. Turned out even worse when I got taken down by other Marines. If it'd been anybody else, I would have shot my way out of that, too." He slowly shook his head. "Just bad luck. That's all it was. Bad luck all the way around." He paused. "But you need to keep your eyes open. The Afghan National Police ain't all on the up and up."

"Was Zarif doing something wrong?"

Pike smiled. "You see? That's one of the main differences between my world and yours. In your world, you need proof that a guy's bad before you can do anything. In my world, you only need to know you know. I know Zarif was bad. I just didn't get the chance to find out how bad because things turned sideways on me."

"Tell me about it."

"Can't. That's the problem. I blew up Zarif before I could get a handle on it." Pike took in a breath and let it out. "I can tell you this. Zarif has a connection to the dead Russian, and there are more Russians out there."

"What do you know?"

"That's it. I was hoping to find out more. That wasn't in the cards."

Listening to Pike, Heath got irritated. "You tailed Zarif because you thought he killed the Russian to protect someone?"

"Why do you think he killed the Russian?"

"His report says that the Russian had a hidden weapon."

"That guy wasn't holding nothing. I put him down. Didn't have nothing on him."

"Do you think Zarif was involved in the anti-American factions in the Afghan National Police?"

Pike shrugged. "Don't know." He folded his arms over his chest. "I had to guess, I'd guess that Zarif was an opportunist. Saw a chance to grab something for himself and went with it."

"Grab what?"

"Like I said, I don't know. Our conversation never got that far."

Heath pushed himself to his feet and picked up the Styrofoam container. He gestured to Pike for his and took it as well. "I'm going to dig into Zarif's background and see what I can find."

"You'd be better off just letting it go. You stick your neck out, the Marines are liable to chop it off for you. They want to get out of this as clean as they can, and letting me take the fall would be the easiest way."

"That's not the right way."

"Don't be a Boy Scout." Pike's tone made his words a sarcastic accusation. "You don't get to fix everything, no matter who your daddy is. Leave this alone. This ain't your problem. It's mine." Pike looked up at Heath. "I don't have clean hands. I'm not the kind of guy you want to put it on the line for. You need to stay focused on keeping the guys in the unit alive. Whatever Yaqub is cooking up, you can bet there's a big price tag involved. Don't let any of your people get cashed in while you're distracted with me. I'm not worth it. Those people are."

Looking at Pike, Heath was again reminded of Darnell Lester and how the man had come to accept his own fate. Heath had changed that, though. "Pike, there's not a person out there who's not worth

saving. Just some keep refusing to find something good in them."
He reached into his shirt pocket and took out the compass he'd spotted in Pike's things. He showed the compass to Pike, then tossed it across the room. He still didn't know what had prompted him to bring it with him, but he had gone along with the feeling, trusting his instincts.

Pike caught the device in one big hand and held it in his closed fist, deliberately not looking at it.

Heath resisted the impulse to smile. "Who have you got waiting on you back home? Somebody I can get in contact with for you?"

"Nobody." Pike's answer sounded brittle and hollow.

*Yeah, keep telling yourself that.* Heath knocked on the brig door.

Gunney Towers and Bekah were waiting in Heath's office when he returned. Both of them were involved with the paperwork he'd left them to handle during his absence.

Heath placed his coffee on the desk and stowed his weapons before sitting down.

"So how's Pike?" Towers pushed a fresh stick of gum into his mouth.

"He's fine." Heath frowned. "Not talking much, though."

"He don't seem to be a fan of conversation."

"No, he doesn't. But that's only part of the problem."

Towers lifted an eyebrow. "What's the other part?"

"Pike thinks Captain Zarif killed the Russian to cover something up."

"Cover what up?"

Heath shook his head. "The conversation last night didn't go that far."

Towers tapped a finger on his clipboard. "Way I hear it, Major Hollister is wanting to clear this situation quick-like."

"And he'll hang Pike out to dry to do that."

Towers nodded.

"So we have to do an end run around the major if we're going to look into this."

"Well, I've always felt that what top brass didn't *have* to know, top brass didn't *need* to know." Towers smiled. "You have a starting place in mind?"

"I do. Russians. The ones operating under suspicious circumstances. Men who have no visible connection to the city, transients. We find them; we watch them. In the meantime, I want to know who Captain Zarif was running with."

"Getting around the brass should be easy right now. They're all watching Yaqub, trying to get information on him and his buddies. As long as we're out of sight, we'll be out of mind."

"Yeah, I figured that too." Heath turned his attention to Bekah. "How much do you know about Pike?"

She thought about that for a moment, then shook her head. "Not much."

"See what you can find out."

"Why the interest in Pike? I thought you were trying to get him out of trouble."

"I am. But I also want to *keep* him out of trouble." Heath sipped his coffee and felt immensely tired. "He's been part of this unit for a long time, Bekah, and we still don't know much about him. It's time to change that."

Towers nodded in agreement. "So you figure if Pike won't come to you . . ."

"Then I'm going to get to know Pike one way or another. I want to know once and for all if he lines up in the asset or liability column."

# 33

"**GET UP.**" Yaqub kicked Jonathan Sebastian's feet, startling the reporter awake.

Bleary-eyed, Sebastian peered up from his rumpled bed. His hair lay in disarray, and he hadn't shaved during the last four days. His clothes were wrinkled and unkempt. The thin pallet he used for a bed was scarcely better than the cold stone floor of the cave. He hadn't looked comfortable before being awakened. Now he looked even less so.

Sebastian brushed hair out of his eyes. "What's going on?" His voice was a dry croak. The altitude would do that.

"It is time to get up."

"Are we going somewhere?" The man gazed around, then down at his wrist, obviously seeking the watch that Yaqub had taken away from him. Inside the cave, he had no way of telling time. That way his mind was as great a prison as the mountain around him.

"Do not ask questions. Get up or I will have one of these men get you up."

After a quick glance at the hard-faced men accompanying Yaqub, the American sat up and reached for his shoes. His movements were slow and jerky, his coordination not quite together. Concentrating, he pulled one shoe on and tied the laces.

Yaqub waited patiently nearby. Once Sebastian was on his feet, the man picked up his suit coat and pulled it on. His tie hung out of one pocket.

"I'm ready." Sebastian's voice quavered.

Yaqub knew the man feared death, terrified that each day was certain to be his last, but his ego was too strong to allow him to accept that. The possibility tortured him. Taking the newspaper from the man nearest him, Yaqub handed the periodical to Sebastian.

The reporter's relief washed across his face, softening some of the worry lines. He slid the paper in his pocket, then fished out his tie and put it on. He straightened his wrinkled shirt as best he could, tucking it inside his pants. Using his fingers as combs, he tamed his hair but didn't achieve his usual neatness.

"Showtime, huh?" Sebastian sounded grateful.

"Yes." Yaqub led him to the holding area where the CIA agents were imprisoned.

"What do you want me to say?"

"Today you will threaten the Americans with the deaths of these agents if they do not release al Qaeda prisoners I will name for you." Yaqub stepped into the holding area. He gave Sebastian the names of the twelve men he wanted to include in the broadcast. The reporter only took two attempts before he'd memorized the list, pronouncing each correctly. He was very quick and good at his job.

Two armed men stood guard in the room. They held pistols in their fists.

The three American agents sat along the rear wall. For the last four days, their treatment had become more severe. First food and water had been withheld to weaken them, and then only enough sustenance had been provided to keep them alive.

They had not been fed or given water that day. They looked at death's door, and they were closer than they even knew.

Sebastian stepped into the center of the room and took his place where he'd stood last time. He took the newspaper from his pocket and unfurled it. He glanced at the CIA agents.

"Good morning, gentlemen."

The agents didn't say anything.

Sebastian ignored them, then cleared his throat and nodded to Yaqub. "I'm ready whenever you are."

Yaqub waved to the man carrying the camera. The man held the unit to his shoulder and started filming. The bright fountain of light filled the small cave.

★   ★   ★

Filled with excitement and trepidation, Heath followed the other Marines to the comm center and walked in on Yaqub's most recent broadcast. Everyone in the room was silent. The squads had been stretched thin the last few days, handling everything in Kandahar as well as searching for Yaqub and the kidnapped agents and reporter.

In addition to that, the Joint Chiefs of Staff had an inspection scheduled four days from now. That information was only now starting to disseminate through the ranks. The in-country brass had tried to talk the Joint Chiefs out of the visit given the present unrest, but the Pentagon wasn't going to pull back. The visitation was a show of strength, proof to the Taliban and al Qaeda that the United States was withdrawing units, but it wasn't relaxing its posture. After the recent attacks, the Department of Defense was even more determined that the visit would take place.

Heath had been pulling double duty to get his assigned tasks done as well as pursue leads that might spring Pike from the brig. Hollister's investigation into the shooting was all but done according to the scuttlebutt that reached Heath. So far, Hollister was pinning the blame squarely on Pike, saying that revenge was a possible motivation or letting the rumors fly about a drug buy gone bad. Either way it played, the major was distancing the Marines from Pike, circling the wagons and pointing the finger.

Heath didn't blame the man. No matter what reason had drawn Pike to Captain Zarif, he hadn't belonged there. Any follow-up on the Afghan captain should have gone through channels. Only Pike didn't believe in channels. And maybe, in this instance, Pike had been right. Unfortunately he'd also been wrong.

As it turned out, there were a few other rumors circulating about Captain Zarif's connections to the opium trade and the warlords. People Heath had talked to indicated that Zarif was the man to go to in order to get illegal goods, and the Afghan National Police captain had connections to the black market as well as stolen military equipment. There were some who claimed the captain had been sitting on a small fortune at the time of his death.

On the large screen, Jonathan Sebastian looked haggard and worn. His features were pale, but Heath knew that was probably as much from not wearing makeup for the impromptu shoot as from his incarceration. Sebastian held up the newspaper with the current date on it. Heath relaxed a little, knowing that the men were still all alive at this moment.

"Today." Sebastian shook the newspaper emphatically. "*Today* I'm here to give you the names of men our captor wants freed from the prison there in Kandahar."

"'There.' He said, 'There in Kandahar.'" One of the CIA's cyber team unit sounded suddenly excited. "That confirms they're being held outside the city. The signal isn't just being bounced around."

The man next to the speaker shook his head warily. "If he's not lying. If he really knows where he is. You know how these guys operate."

All the men and women at the computer stations worked quickly, tapping keyboards and scanning screens of data. Heath recognized their anticipation but didn't buy into it. Zalmai Yaqub wasn't going to make it easy for them to find him, and they'd already known the man wasn't in the city. Heath didn't think they'd gained anything.

One of the men operated a one-handed yoke. The imagery on his monitor raced by. "I've got a drone in the air. We've got eyes over the target area."

Gerald Benton stayed behind his team, flicking his gaze from monitor to monitor. Heath wondered if the man could tell anything more about the information pulsing across the computer monitors than he could, then supposed Benton probably knew a lot more about the ongoing operation than he did. Heath didn't work with any of the drone operators other than in the field. He rarely saw this end of the work.

"We're vectoring in on the signal."

Benton rocked on his toes slightly. "Stay with it. Don't lose it."

On the large screen, Sebastian waved toward the CIA agents in the back of the cave, where they were being held. Today the hostages seemed even more listless than before. Heath wondered if they were being drugged.

"As you can see, we're all still alive." The camera turned back to Sebastian. "But I've been told that if the al Qaeda prisoners aren't freed in four days, these men will die." He paused. "I will die."

"Almost there." The tech holding the control yoke jockeyed the Predator drone miles away through the mountains. He leaned into the controls, stiffly alert. "We've triangulated the signal to ten square miles, Special Agent Benton."

The craggy faces of mountains flashed by the Predator's vid array. Since the last transmission, Marine teams had set up around the mountains and erected a communications array designed to track the electronic signature of the broadcasts.

Benton leaned in closer. "Ten square miles is a lot of area to cover."

*Especially if you're trying to get an extraction team into the area without being seen.* As daunting as the task seemed, Heath knew he wouldn't have hesitated for a moment. All he or any Marine needed was a location and a chance of success.

Jonathan Sebastian spoke the names of the al Qaeda members in a strong voice, giving listeners time to write them down, though that wasn't necessary because the broadcast was being recorded. When he spoke the last name, the broadcast shut down.

"Did we get the location?" Benton asked.

The drone pilot shook his head. "No sir. Best we can come up with is a ten-square-mile area."

Benton cursed. The constant stress of the situation was taking its toll on him as well.

Heath followed the drone's flight, noting all the mountainous terrain and potential hiding places. When American forces had first arrived in Afghanistan after 9/11, they'd fought in similar mountains, uncovering al Qaeda bases and the long tunnels that connected them. By the time rescue teams located Zalmai Yaqub, the tangos could have repositioned.

It was still a needle in a haystack.

As the cameraman put down his camcorder, Yaqub drew his *pesh-kabz* and stepped forward. Jonathan Sebastian cowered away from him, dropping the newspaper in a flutter of pages. The long, curved blade glinted in the candlelight that illuminated the cave.

Ignoring the news reporter, Yaqub walked toward the three CIA agents. They had outlived their usefulness, and his desire to spill the blood of his enemies had grown more restless and stronger. In four days' time, the Americans would not release the al Qaeda members

he had named because Yaqub would not be there to continue negotiations. The agents had been bait, nothing more. Even dead, they
could still fulfill that function. They would just be more manageable.

The agents evidently saw their fates written in his eyes. Weakly,
they pushed themselves to their feet. Their manacles clinked as the
short chains drew them up into an uncoordinated mass of bodies and
limbs. They shouted curses and tried to defend themselves.

Sebastian cried out behind him. "Wait! What are you doing?"

"Silence."

The reporter staggered, then started to come forward again only
to have one of the guards intercept him and push him against the
wall.

Yaqub turned off his emotions, thinking only of the sacrifices
he and his father were making to maneuver him into a position of
power. He grabbed one of the men by the hair and yanked.

Swinging the *pesh-kabz* fiercely, Yaqub powered the blade through
the man's throat, stopping his litany of curses at once.

Yaqub swung again, this time at the back of a man's neck.

Yaqub trapped the last man, stepping onto the center of his chest.
The agent grabbed Yaqub's leg, but his grip was too weak to manage
any kind of leverage. Mercilessly Yaqub drove his fighting knife into
the insides of the man's thighs, cutting the femoral arteries and assur-
ing him of a quick termination as well.

Satisfied with his handiwork, Yaqub stepped back and watched
them die, looking forward to the day when he could do the same to
all of his enemies. In four days' time, though, he would add consider-
ably to those numbers.

When the last of the three agents stilled and slipped into death's
embrace, Yaqub leaned down and cleaned his knife on the thin blankets the CIA agents had been given. He sheathed his weapon and
turned to his men. "Get the bodies out of here."

"It will be done."

Yaqub stopped in front of Sebastian.

The reporter swallowed hard and looked as though he was about to pass out, but he was too proud—or too terrified—to beg for his life.

"Do not worry, Jonathan Sebastian. I still have need of you." Yaqub turned away from the American. "Take this one back and guard him. See that he is fed."

★    ★    ★

Outside the cave, Yaqub stood in the new-fallen snow that came up to his knees. The air tasted thin and sharp. He studied the fortifications the men there in the village still prepared and felt satisfied with what had been done. The stone walls would slow those who came for him, and they would cost the American military lives. The snow would further impede the would-be rescuers who could only arrive too late.

And then die.

Yaqub intended that many of them die. His only regret was that he would not be here to see it happen.

Turning back to the cave where his father lay, he traipsed through the snow, following a path made by a donkey carrying firewood that still stood out of the wind near the entrance. He passed the guards where they sat in front of the fire and went to his father.

Quietly, without a word, Yaqub sat beside his father and listened to his hoarse, irregular breathing. The last few days' excitement had been too much for his father. The strength he'd saved for so long was finally giving out on him. He was dwindling, slipping away. It was a terrible way for a warrior to die.

As he sat there, Yaqub contemplated the broken shell of the man, contrasting sharply with the warrior who had trained his son to fight and plan and kill his enemies. He missed the shaggy old warrior he had grown up with. But he did not miss the dangerous man his father had been; that had *never* gone away. Sabah was still dangerous, and Yaqub was putting teeth back in his father's bite.

After a moment, Yaqub grew aware of his father's single eye staring at him. That fierce anger still burned within him, banked into coals that would not extinguish till life itself was ripped from his body.

"My son." Sabah's voice was a hoarse croak, thick with phlegm.

"Father."

"Things are well?"

Yaqub took his father's withered claw into his own hand, feeling the frailty and the merciless strength of it at the same time. "Things are well, Father." He took a breath. "I have dispatched the CIA agents."

Sabah smiled. "Then the time of my revenge is upon us."

"Yes."

The old man's smile went away. "You are troubled."

"Only a little."

Sabah took back his hand and patted his son's hand gently. "Do not take that burden upon yourself, Yaqub. I would die as a man, striking at my enemies. Not as a cripple gasping for my last breath."

"I know, Father."

"And know that I will not die before my part in this is played. I gave you my word."

"I do not worry about that, Father."

"I am proud of you. You have found a way to put a weapon in my hand after all these years. I will make you proud of me."

"I have always been proud."

Sabah squeezed Yaqub's hand. "Then, when you leave, know that you have provided me this thing, and know that you are stepping into your destiny."

Yaqub bowed his head. "I know this, and I look forward to the day when I drive the Westerners from Afghanistan." His voice thickened. "When I do, I will make certain your name will always be remembered."

"Kill our enemies, my son. This is your heritage, and it will be their doom."

# 34

**PIKE WAS LOUNGING** on the thin bed in the brig for the fifth straight day since his arrest. He was plowing through a copy of a history of the Mongols that Heath Bridger had brought by. The book had been part of a stack the lieutenant had brought in. There'd been no comment, just the delivery.

When he'd seen the books, Pike knew that Heath had been poking around into his personal life. Not many people knew he read or that he preferred histories over anything else when he did read. Pike had never really cared for fiction stories because after the life he'd had in the system and in the orphanage, he knew those stories never happened. Good endings belonged in fiction.

History was different, though. Those things, most of them, had happened. Of course, there was some conjecture about what *really* happened. One book would put forth an idea, and another book would tear the first one down. Pike enjoyed the arguments, too—that sometimes historians and research people weren't certain what truly took place—because then he could figure out what he thought about an event or the people involved.

Pike had read about the Mongols before. Genghis Khan was a favorite subject. The Mongols had lived outside of the growing cities and civilized areas, and they had instilled a fear in the Chinese that was big enough to cause the Great Wall to be built. That was something, a fear that big and that deep. On their stout little ponies, always traveling from place to place and taking what they wanted or needed, the Mongols weren't that much different from a motorcycle gang. In fact, one of the outlaw biker gangs had even named themselves after the Mongols, but they weren't anywhere near as fierce as their namesakes. Genghis Khan had changed the face of Asia and beyond.

Stretched out on the bed, Pike wore camo pants and an OD green tank top that revealed the tattoos normally covered by his BDUs. Usually he wasn't so open with his ink around the Marines, keeping that side of himself private. But since his arrest, some of the old rebelliousness had returned to him. He'd decided to fly his freak flag. If he was going to be treated like a criminal, he was going to look like a criminal. He'd let his beard grow too, and it was coming in heavy, darkening his chin with sandpapery stubble.

His head was clear, and his heart beat steadily. Before he lay down to read, he'd done an hour of calisthenics to burn off the excess energy and to keep himself in shape. Strength and speed were everything to a guy on his own. They were the only assets a survivor truly had, and once they were gone, it was hard to get them back.

*"Gotta keep the tools sharp, bro."* Once again, the ideas in Pike's head were exactly what Petey might have said. *"If you get the chance, you gotta bust outta here. No matter where you go, here or in the States, you can make it on your own. Just get out, get away, and get gone. There's an open highway out there. You never shoulda gotten complacent. Not in Tulsa. Not in the Marines. You don't belong anywhere. You're a rolling stone, bro. You've been fooling yourself."*

Pike had been thinking about that. Provided he could get away from the base, which wouldn't be all that hard during a transport detail, he could slip across the Durand Line and into Pakistan. Once he was there, he could set himself up any way he wanted to. All kinds of illegal operations were going on in Pakistan that were open to foreigners willing to get their hands dirty, and not all of them involved terrorists. People needed muscle there, someone who could stick when things got tough and pull the trigger when it came to that. He figured he could cut himself in somewhere, get some money together, and get to wherever he decided to go.

He didn't have to return to the States. In fact, the more he'd thought about it, the more he felt certain he'd limited himself by staying in the US. There were a lot of places he'd read about in Europe but had never seen. He thought maybe he'd like to see Russia and Asia too.

It was a plan, and he liked it. Getting caught killing Captain Zarif and his flunkies had been the best thing that could have happened to him. It was a double bonus. He'd woken up from the stupor he'd been in since Petey's death. He'd dropped Zarif, and he had an out planned from the hole he'd dug for himself. He'd played the game with the witness protection program only to get stymied and stuck in Tulsa. Once he got himself set up, once he was ready, he knew he could slip back into Texas long enough to kill the men who had killed Petey.

Then that debt would be off his head. After that, he could get back to living life on his own terms.

The only thing that nagged at him was that little secondhand compass. He'd tucked it under his pillow so it would be out of sight, but it wasn't out of mind. Apparently not thinking about it was impossible. And once he started thinking about the compass, he started thinking about Hector, wondering how the boy was, whether he was okay, if anybody was helping him with his math homework.

*"You're thinking about math homework? Bro, you ain't domesticated. You ain't even civilized. You're a beast. A caged animal waiting to get out. You need to remember that. Eye of the tiger, bro. That's you."*

Mulvaney's voice cut into his thoughts too, though, and it haunted him. *"I am certain that God, who began the good work within you, will continue his work until it is finally finished on the day when Christ Jesus returns."*

Pike still didn't know what that meant or even if it applied to him, but touching on it for a minute left him unsettled, like he needed to do something. Only he didn't know what he was supposed to do.

Pike was trying to focus on his book again, knowing he'd read the same paragraph at least four times, when the knock sounded on the door. He closed the book and put it away, determined that Heath wasn't going to catch him reading it.

One of the MPs peered through the grille at the top of the door. "Stay back, Private."

Pike remained prone on the bed and folded his hands behind his head. He didn't even look at the door. He didn't want company, and he planned to make that clear to whoever stepped inside the holding cell.

Only it wasn't Heath Bridger who entered the brig. It was Bekah Shaw. She looked at him lying there on the bed and smiled.

The smile irritated Pike. He resisted the impulse to sit up or make space on the bed. Her unexpected appearance made him feel uncomfortable and slovenly. "You see something funny, Corporal?"

"For a guy looking at getting charged with murder in the first degree, and getting tried in a military court at that, you seem awfully relaxed."

Pike shrugged and kept staring at the ceiling. "I am relaxed. This ain't no thing. Been here before." He'd noticed the brown bag she carried into the cell, and now the aroma of freshly baked food and spices tickled his nose. His stomach growled noisily, embarrassingly loud. The tips of his ears burned, and that irritated him even more.

"You're also hungry."

"I'm not hungry."

"Well, I am. I'm on my lunch break." Bekah sat cross-legged on the floor and opened the bag. "I also have enough for two. Actually, I have enough for three, but it should share out okay for both of us."

"What are you doing here?" Pike refused to look at her. It was childish and he knew it, but some mannerisms from the orphanage and foster care stayed ingrained forever.

"Like I said, lunch break."

"They got other places around camp where you eat."

"Yeah, and those places are a lot more welcoming and festive. So I was thinking to myself, who needs that crap?"

Despite Pike's mood, her unabashed sarcasm made him smile. She wasn't shy about eating, either. She opened a Styrofoam container and dug into some rice and meat dish that smelled absolutely fantastic. His stomach growled again.

Bekah didn't say anything. She just kept eating.

Pike frowned. "You're just going to sit there?"

"I'm eating. And I'm enjoying the silence. You know, most places around the camp get noisy. Everywhere you go, people are talking. I can see how the quiet in the brig fits that alpha-male thing you do so well."

Pike snorted. "I don't *do* anything."

"Yeah, you do. Most guys do. They reach for some tough-guy facade, and they do it mostly when they don't know what else to do. Like when they get in over their heads."

"Maybe you don't know as much as you think you do."

"Of course I do. I know I know stuff. I'm a woman. I think about stuff, about the way people go together, about why some guys talk and why some guys go dark, and because I think about them, I know stuff about them." Bekah took another bite. "You know stuff too."

Intrigued, just a little, Pike looked at her.

"You knew about the Russian, that Zarif had killed him and stolen some evidence . . . or just to shut the man up. You knew about the tattoos. I didn't know any of that. Neither did Lieutenant Bridger or Gunney Towers. So, yeah, you know stuff."

Feeling uncomfortable with all the closeness inherent in the conversation, Pike looked at her and decided to push her back to create distance. "You call him Lieutenant Bridger when you guys are alone?"

Bright spots of color appeared on Bekah's cheeks, and her eyes wouldn't meet Pike's. He'd decided he wasn't pulling any punches. He wanted her out and gone.

"I mean, since we're on the topic of stuff I know, I thought I'd point out that I'd picked up what's going on between the two of you."

"Nothing's going on between the two of us."

"But you wish it was." Because he wanted to hurt her for invading his privacy, Pike kept going. "He's out of your league. That guy? He's used to flashy society women, cut his teeth on cheerleaders and sorority girls. You're from some hick town and you've got a kid. You're nothing but a lot of headaches. You think you're anywhere on his radar?"

Bekah picked through her rice for a piece of lamb. Her lower lip trembled a little, but she got it back under control again pretty quickly. Pike was impressed because he knew he'd hit the target dead center.

"Don't want to talk about the stuff I know anymore?"

Bekah lifted her eyes to his and returned his gaze full measure. "If I knew for sure what was going on, and if you were civil, maybe I would talk to you about it. But since you're not being civil and I don't know what or if anything is going on—*or even if I want anything like that going on*—we're not going to discuss that particular topic."

Pike wanted to strike back and hit her again, push her away, but he heard the emotion buried in her words and knew the subject was a tender one.

Sighing, knowing he didn't have the heart to hurt her more and that he was being weak, he pushed himself into a sitting position and looked down at her. "The offer for lunch still open?"

"You're lucky you're not wearing it." Bekah passed the other Styrofoam container over.

Pike took the container, then nodded at the other end of the bed. "I got a seat up here if you want."

She was stiff and not so open, but she wasn't leaving either. "I'm perfectly comfortable where I am."

"You're stubborn." That was something Pike respected. It was a survivor skill.

"And you're a jerk."

In spite of the situation, Pike laughed. He opened the container and sorted through the food, picking out a piece of lamb and popping it into his mouth. The juice was delicious. "The Marines pay for this?"

She looked at him in puzzlement.

"If you paid for this, lemme know what my part is. In fact, I'll buy lunch since you brought it. You got a kid to feed. I don't want to be taking nothing off his plate."

"My son is just fine, and I'm just fine. I can afford to buy you lunch."

"You shouldn't have to."

"I didn't have to."

Pike rolled up a ball of rice and ate it. "You're here because you were told to be here."

"Actually, I'm here because I wanted to be. I could have gone to Lieutenant Bridger and let him handle this."

"Handle what?" Pike didn't really care. He already had his game plan in place, waiting to put it into play. But he was a little curious.

"Briefing you on the investigation."

Pike shook his head. "MPs already do that. I hear them talking. A couple of the young ones act like they're holding some kind of international terrorist in here."

"You've got a reputation as a dangerous guy."

Pike didn't say anything to that.

"And I wasn't talking about Hollister's investigation into the shooting. That's pretty cut-and-dried. I was referring to the investigation Lieutenant Bridger, Gunney Towers, and I are making into Captain Zarif."

Pike kept eating.

"As it turns out, Captain Zarif is a component in the local black market. He's been accused, but not successfully, of *misplacing* military ordnance that later turned up in the hands of people who shouldn't have had it. The Russian guy?"

In spite of his decision to remain aloof, Pike nodded.

"His name was Emile Evstafiev."

"Where'd you get the name?"

Bekah looked at him. "Did you know his name?"

Pike gave her a look and didn't say anything.

"I'm not here to give anything other than lunch away for free, Pike. It works like this: I tell you something; you tell me something."

For a long minute, the silence stretched in the cell and Pike occupied himself with his meal. The food was good and he was hungrier than he'd thought. He didn't think Bekah could wait him out. The women he'd known weren't much when it came to patience. They knew stuff—or even *thought* they knew stuff—they generally had to tell it or explode.

Bekah didn't show any signs of that. She worked at her meal too and didn't look at him.

Grudgingly, Pike gave in to his curiosity. "I knew the last name. Evstafiev. Didn't know the first one."

"You'd never seen him before that day in the machine shop."

"Nope."

"You went looking for Zarif because you knew he took something from Evstafiev."

"Thought he did."

"Did he?"

Pike hesitated again, remembering Petey's constant advice. *"You can't trust anybody outside your skin."* Pike closed his mouth and saw his friend. This time Petey was dying in his arms, bleeding out, and there wasn't anything Pike could do about it. *"Can't trust anybody. Don't be stupid."*

"I don't know. Maybe there was something. Maybe Evstafiev was just carrying information."

"How do you know that?"

Pike shook his head. "I've been doing all the giving."

Bekah nodded. "Lieutenant Bridger has developed some contacts within the black market."

"How?"

"Bribery."

Pike laughed. "Not exactly in the Marine Corps playbook."

"The lieutenant says he learned that working court cases with his father. Anyway, during the investigation, he turned up another name that connected to Evstafiev's. A guy named Deyneka." Bekah struggled with the pronunciation.

Pike pronounced the name correctly.

She looked at him with renewed interest. "You know that man?"

"No." At that point, Pike knew Bekah had deliberately stumbled over the name. He mentally kicked himself. "I've been around Russians. Heard the name before. So who is Deyneka?"

"A munitions dealer handling Russian ordnance. The same kind of ordnance we turned up in the machine shop."

Pike picked up another piece of lamb and chewed thoughtfully for a moment before swallowing. "There was a Russian that called Zarif. I overheard the conversation. If it was Deyneka, he was after some merch that went missing."

"'Merch'?" Bekah looked puzzled.

Pike chuckled and licked juice from his thumb. "You're new to this cops and robbers stuff, ain't you?"

She flushed slightly but didn't say anything.

"Merch. Merchandise. Deyneka was looking for goods that got misplaced. Maybe the tangos weren't the only people Evstafiev was supplying."

"Deyneka thought Zarif had his missing . . . *merch*?"

Pike shrugged. "If he was the guy on the phone that night, yeah."

"I'll let Lieutenant Bridger know." Bekah pushed herself to her feet and bundled up her trash. She put Pike's in the bag as well. "This still doesn't mean we can get you out of here."

"I never thought it did."

"But the lieutenant wanted me to tell you not to lose faith."

"Sure. Maybe I'm not as big a believer in the system as Bridger is."

Bekah eyed him, hesitating. "Faith's an important thing. Living without it makes a hollow life. I've just recently learned that. Could be something you need to think about."

Pike had noticed this deployment that Bekah seemed changed, more accepting and less fretful. She'd always been a good Marine and a solid person, but he'd noticed the difference.

"I'll keep that in mind."

"Oh. Something else." Bekah reached into a pocket and took out a letter. "Mail call."

That surprised Pike. He'd never gotten a mail call. He accepted the small letter but didn't look at it, thinking maybe it was from

Mulvaney, but that would have been a serious breach in witness protection protocol.

Bekah glanced at it. "You got a son you've never mentioned?"

"No." Pike figured he knew who the letter was from now, but he didn't know how Hector had written to him.

"That's from a young boy." Bekah smiled. "I recognize the handwriting. I get letters that look a lot like that one. Usually has crayon pictures."

Pike nodded, not saying anything.

Bekah knocked on the door and left.

Heart beating a little faster, emotions tangled in a goopy ball in his stomach, Pike glanced at the letter. It was addressed to Private Pike Morgan, USMC, and the Marine address was underneath it. After all the time spent helping the boy with his homework, Pike would have recognized the handwriting anywhere.

He opened the letter carefully.

*Hi Pike!*

*I hope you are okay. I am okay. I miss you. I pray evry nite that God will keep you safe. He sees you all the time, you know. So I asked him to look out for you becuz I am here and I cant look out for you. I am doing the best I can with math, but I hope you get back soon.*

Pike kept reading—there wasn't a lot because the message got repetitive—and when he finished, he read the letter over again. For the first time since he'd been arrested, Pike truly felt caged. There was another life out there, and he couldn't get back to it.

Or away from it.

He leaned his head against the wall, closed his eyes, and tried not to feel the emptiness that echoed within him.

# 35

TWO DAYS LATER, Heath caught up with Illya Deyneka. The Russian black marketer had pulled out of sight even more in the wake of Evstafiev's death. Heath and Gunney Towers had been hard-pressed to find the man even with the money Heath had spent looking for him. Bribery was a secondary and desperate economy that flowed through Kandahar.

Finally, though, an informer came up with the intel that Deyneka was staying at a small warehouse in one of the industrial sectors of the city. Heath assigned his unit to cover the area, then closed in on the warehouse early in the morning before dawn.

"You roust them this early, they're gonna know straight off this ain't nothing they want to hang around for." Gunney Towers stood beside Heath in an alley across the street. He held binoculars to his eyes and studied the warehouse through the predawn dark.

"Deyneka's already on edge." Heath adjusted his gear, tightening the straps on his ammo rack. "He's going to run as soon as we hit the door, but we're ready for him."

Towers lowered the binoculars. "How do you want to do it?"

"During the morning prayer session." That was only moments away. "Things will be loud and busy. The Russians will ignore the prayers because they're used to them. They'll have their guards down. We'll take advantage of that."

Nodding, Towers put his binoculars away. "Sounds good to me."

"Then let's do it."

★  ★  ★

Heath sat in the passenger seat of the Humvee while Towers drove. Two more Marines sat behind them. Towers pulled the Humvee to a stop at the warehouse next door to the one they'd targeted.

As he climbed out of the Humvee, Heath felt the eyes on him. He adjusted his helmet, making certain his chin strap was tight. Then, when the ululating call to prayer rang out over the city, he headed toward the target warehouse.

"I've got movement inside the building." Bekah's voice was calm and controlled. She was in the alley across the street, keeping watch through binoculars.

"Make sure we contain anyone who leaves the building." Heath unlimbered his M4A1 and picked up the pace, jogging toward the warehouse door. At his side, Towers already had a shaped C-4 charge in his left hand ready to go.

"Roger that."

At the door, Towers slapped the charge into place beside the door lock. "Fire in the hole." He rolled away from the door as Heath backed off and raised his assault rifle.

Towers triggered the detonator, and the small explosion barely made a dent in the call to prayer that echoed over the city. A fist-size hole appeared in the door where the locking mechanism had been. Smoke climbed swiftly into the air and dissipated.

"Move in." Heath grabbed the door in his gloved hand and yanked it open. He shoved the M4A1 inside, then followed the weapon. Towers came at his heels. From the corner of his eye, before he stepped inside, he spotted the other Humvees racing forward to close the cordon around the building. The two Marines who had accompanied Towers and Heath held their position at the entrance to provide an extraction point if it became necessary.

Heath hoped Deyneka was on the premises and that the Russian would agree to tell what he knew. Otherwise Heath was going to be in a lot of hot water for the unauthorized raid.

The warehouse held several crates, but with a lot of empty space too. Evidently the goods Deyneka dealt in didn't have much of a shelf life. Then again, with all the renewed attacks within the city, munitions were cycling quickly.

Heath kept moving forward, working through the stacks of crates. He'd gotten blueprints on the building, but even though the structure was fairly new compared to the rest of the city, the layout inside the warehouse wouldn't necessarily match the original schematics.

Towers covered his six, never more than one long stride away. Radio chatter over the mission freq let him know some of the warehouse's occupants had already stepped outside into the Marines' trap.

Although he knew he couldn't afford the distraction, Heath kept listening for Bekah's voice. As long as he could hear her, he knew she was okay. He was still surprised at how she'd gotten Pike to open up to her. Unfortunately some small part of him wasn't happy about that for reasons he couldn't quite put his finger on. He also knew he didn't want to go exploring that particular unease too much. *Keep your head in the game.*

A man peered around the corner of the stack of crates ahead.

"United States Marine Corps." Heath made his voice loud and strong. "Stand down. Get on your stomach."

Before the man could move, gunshots sounded. Behind Heath, Towers cursed and staggered away.

Swiveling, Heath aimed at the head and hands of a man lying atop crates ahead and to the right. Heath squeezed the trigger and watched as splinters leaped up from the crates. The man fired again. Heath's next burst tattooed across his face and he went slack.

The man at the corner in front of him started shooting a pistol. Heath stayed where he was, covering Towers, who had taken a round in his back. Heath fired two more bursts and plucked the shooter from the corner as Towers started shoving himself back to his feet.

"I'm okay." Towers grimaced, his dark face etched with pain. "Armor stopped the bullet. Got the wind knocked out of me for a minute."

"When you're ready, Gunney."

Towers nodded and adjusted his helmet. "I'm ready. Let's go."

Heath led the way, taking longer strides now, eating up the distance and listening to the crackle of gunfire outside the warehouse. As he passed the dead man beside the crates, he kicked the pistol away and the weapon slid under a forklift in the next aisle.

Deyneka and three of his men were at the rear door, peering out anxiously, weapons in their hands. They didn't see Heath or Towers closing in on them until it was too late.

Twenty feet away, one of the men turned and started to pull away from the door. He spotted Heath and yelled what Heath believed was a warning in Russian, then opened fire.

Heath spaced a burst across the man's chest and watched him fall away as the other three men wheeled. Deyneka stood to the left, a large-caliber Israeli handgun in his fist. The Russian was thin and dark. His salt-and-pepper hair was buzzed close to the skull and he had a short-cropped salt-and-pepper beard as well. Tattoos coiled around his neck, creeping up from the sweater he wore. One was in the middle of his forehead, and Heath knew from Pike's discussion of Russian crime tattooing that Deyneka had probably gotten it when he'd been ousted from some Mafia organization.

"Deyneka." Heath held his assault rifle centered on the man while Towers covered the other two. "Put down your weapon and you get to live today."

"Why are you here?" The Russian's English was heavily accented.

"The United States Marine Corps wants to talk to you about ordnance you've been helping deliver to al Qaeda operatives in Kandahar. We've got proof of your involvement. You can live or die in the next minute." Heath paused. "You decide or I'll decide for you."

Towers's voice was thick with threat and boomed inside the warehouse. He was in full gunnery sergeant mode. "You heard the man. Me? I've got an itchy trigger finger and you been supplying guys that have been killing my men. I might not be able to wait long."

The two men beside Deyneka tossed their weapons aside and held up their hands. Deyneka cursed, then tossed the big pistol aside as well.

Heath let out a tense breath and moved forward. "Get down. Down on your stomachs, hands behind your heads."

Sullenly, the three men obeyed. Heath moved among them, securing each man in turn with disposable cuffs while Towers watched over them. The gunfire outside had tapered off to occasional pops.

"Bekah." Heath pulled Deyneka roughly to his feet.

"We're here. We got them."

"The team?"

"Standing up. We're all good here."

Some of the tension in Heath unraveled and went away. He put a hand against Deyneka's back and pushed him into motion. "Roger that."

"Who is that man?" Major Hollister stared through the grille in the brig door. The major wasn't happy, and it had taken Heath two hours to get the man to break his schedule.

Inside the room, Deyneka sat on the bed.

"Illya Deyneka. He used to be Russian military back in the eighties." Heath flicked through the images on his iPad, showing Deyneka in a Russian military uniform. The man had been young and earnest. Heath had gotten the images from a helpful CIA agent who'd done background research on Deyneka. "Then, in the nineties, Deyneka joined up with the Russian Mafia." More images followed, police reports from three different countries. "Somewhere in there he ended up working on his own here in Afghanistan."

Hollister looked away from the door and focused on Heath. "The Mafia? Like the Russian your team turned up at the bomb-making facility."

"Yes sir."

"What does this man have to do with me?"

Heath cycled through the scanned pages of a document on his iPad. "What I have here is a signed confession from Deyneka. He had an arrangement with Evstafiev, the Russian that Captain Zarif executed after my team discovered and shut down the bomb-making facility. Evstafiev had brokered a deal for munitions, which he was selling to al Qaeda and to Deyneka. Evstafiev hadn't delivered the weapons to Deyneka before he was killed."

"Do we know where those weapons are?"

"No sir."

"Well, that's unfortunate."

"Yes sir." Heath paused, then got back on track, knowing he had to keep his explanation short, the same way he had to in the courtroom to keep a jury focused. "When Captain Zarif killed Evstafiev, he recovered contact information for Deyneka. Deyneka says that Zarif called him and said he knew where the weapons shipment was. It was going to cost him to recover it."

Hollister's eyes narrowed in understanding. "Zarif was black-mailing Deyneka?"

"Trying to, yes sir. The night that Captain Zarif was killed, Deyneka was on his way there to finish negotiations." Heath pointed to the iPad screen. "He admits to that in this. Says he was outside the building when the Marines arrived."

"Deyneka was there to take possession of the weapons."

"Yes sir."

Hollister considered that. "Zarif didn't have a weapons cache with him that night."

"No sir."

"And we didn't recover any information regarding those weapons."

"No, we did not."

"Then I don't understand why I'm here. Unless you're wanting congratulations for capturing this man and getting a confession out of him. You could have written that up in a report. This is just part of your job, Lieutenant."

"Yes sir, it is. So is taking care of my unit." Heath put his iPad at his side and gazed into Hollister's eyes. The play was on the table, and he wasn't about to back away. "I want Pike out of the brig, sir."

Hollister frowned and shook his head. "The man killed three Afghan National Police officers."

"Pike killed men who were planning to resell the munitions Evstafiev brought into Kandahar."

"Alleged weapons. As you said, you didn't recover any of those."

"No sir, we did not, but we did recover a lot of Russian ordnance from the site where Evstafiev was initially taken into custody before Captain Zarif murdered him. I'd say the circumstantial evidence for the existence of the munitions is strong. Deyneka tells a believable story. If Pike hadn't been there, that transaction might have taken place and those weapons would be out there in the streets."

"You don't know that they haven't ended up there already."

Heath took a breath. "No sir, I don't. But I do know that Pike's presence there that night exposed the operation for us. Deyneka is cooperating, naming names. We've got more targets to hit over the next few days. I'm confident that the situation we have now will enable us to make a difference in pursuing al Qaeda and those weapons."

Hollister's frown deepened and his displeasure was palpable. "Private Morgan isn't an innocent, Lieutenant."

"I didn't say he was." Heath paused to set himself. "But he's one of my Marines. That night Pike was following Captain Zarif, a man suspected to be corrupt, in an effort to find out what had triggered the execution of a Marine prisoner."

"He went there to murder Zarif."

"With all due respect, sir, I'm going to have to disagree with you there. If Pike had wanted to kill Zarif, he could have done that in the street and walked away clean. Instead, he nearly got killed exposing a situation that led us to the capture and confession of Deyneka. In addition to ending Captain Zarif's participation in munitions dealing—" and that was as nice a face as Heath could put on the Afghan National Police captain's death—"Pike's involvement was also instrumental in uncovering Deyneka and his people. And the pipeline that we'll be following up on. The way I see it, Pike is responsible for both of those results. That's the way I'm putting it into my report."

The last was a challenge and Heath knew it. In the future, Hollister would remember that Heath wasn't exactly a team player. That was fine.

"That man doesn't belong in the Marines." Hollister spoke forcefully, but without the conviction he'd had.

"Again, with all due respect, sir, I'm going to have to disagree with you on that as well." Heath hadn't known he was willing to go that far with Pike's case until he'd been standing at the edge of the cliff and jumped. His commitment surprised him, but he knew he was willing to stand by what he'd said. Pike was different, and maybe he'd never make a conventional Marine, but he looked after his unit.

And for whatever reason, Heath knew Pike needed a second chance. Just like Darnell Lester.

Hollister glared at Heath, but Heath didn't flinch. The judges he'd faced were more stern, and even they paled when compared to his father's displeasure.

"Fine, Lieutenant. Get your man out of the brig, but find a way to keep him out of my sight."

"Yes sir. Thank you, sir." Heath saluted as the major turned and walked away. Then he headed back to Pike's cell.

# 36

"**WHAT YOU GONNA DO** with your newfound freedom, Private?"

Standing outside the barracks, Pike had been watching the sun go down. He hadn't realized how much he'd gotten used to seeing it and how much he'd missed that over the last few days. Back in Tulsa, he and Monty would crack open a couple beers some evenings and watch the sun sink as the cool crept into the city. That small thing had meant a lot. Now it almost seemed like a celebration.

Another thing Pike had learned was that he never intended to be in lockdown again. No matter what it took, he wasn't going to be that vulnerable. The road was calling him, and he'd never felt its pull so strong before. Petey's memory was whispering in his ear constantly.

But he also felt the weight of Hector's letter and that secondhand compass sitting in his pocket.

Pike turned and faced Towers, who was pulling out a pack of gum. "I was thinking maybe I'd go out to eat."

Towers snorted and shook his head, grinning as he shoved the stick of gum into his mouth. "Nah, you can forget that. Grab something and go is what you're gonna do. You're standing guard tonight. Got a lot of Marines that were pulling double duty to get your sorry self out of the hoosegow. You can cover for them some, let them catch up on rack time and downtime."

For a minute, Pike got angry and wanted to argue; then he let it go. If he was standing a guard post somewhere, he could be gone anytime he wanted to be. By morning, they'd never find him. He could leave all his problems behind, and he could leave Tulsa behind too.

*"Time to do that, bro."*

So instead of arguing, he just nodded. "Sure, Gunney."

Pike stood at one of the perimeter posts around the camp and gazed out into the dark night northeast of the city. He'd fallen back into routine without a problem, and he felt better geared up again. The M4A1 rode in the crook of his arm as he scanned the area.

Boots crunched on pavement as someone walked toward him. Warily, Pike turned and spotted Bekah approaching with a Styrofoam cup of coffee in each hand.

"Coffee, Pike?"

"Sure." Pike took one of the cups and sipped. The burning liquid nearly scalded his tongue. He turned back to face the perimeter, feeling more than a little uneasy at being there with Bekah. He stood so he could see the Marines on the left and right of him, and every now and again he spotted the squad sniper on one of the buildings behind him. "Thanks."

"You're welcome." Bekah didn't walk away. She stood there and sipped her coffee as well. She didn't talk, didn't say anything to let him know what was on her mind, and that bothered him.

"You come out here to bring me a cup of coffee?"

"That wasn't the only reason."

When she didn't continue, Pike's irritation grew. "You gonna tell me or you gonna make me guess? I'm not much into games."

Bekah took a drink and stared out at the darkness leaking into the perimeter. "Lieutenant Bridger went the distance for you today."

Pike looked away from her and clamped down on the guilt that stirred within him. He didn't like guilt, but he knew that it was only something other people offered. He didn't have to accept it. So he walled himself off from it and sipped coffee that almost burned his tongue again. "He did that because he wanted to."

"He did that because he takes care of the people around him. Whether you deserve it or not, you're one of those people he takes care of."

Pike glanced at her then. "One of us don't want him taking care of him."

Bekah's features hardened. "And that's the other thing I wanted to talk to you about. Whatever's going on between me and Lieutenant Bridger—and whatever you *think* is going on—that's a no-fly zone. I gave you a free shot because you were in the brig and I thought maybe you didn't have your head on straight. Like you said, I ain't one of those high-society women or a cheerleader. I'm small town to the bone. You push me, I push back. So if you bring up mention of some *imagined* relationship between me and the lieutenant again, you try any derogatory comments with me, I'll have you on KP and latrine duty till you go blind. You'll never get rid of the smell and you'll have dishpan hands the rest of your life. Is that understood?"

The harsh forcefulness of her words surprised Pike, but they also triggered that immediate impulse in him to lash back at any show of authority. He shut his anger down just before the torrent of cursing was set free. He nodded and shifted his attention back to the perimeter. "Crystal."

"When you get off duty, grab some rack time. It's gonna be the last you get for the next couple days. In the morning we're leaving to help with the S & R for those CIA agents. Scuttlebutt is that our unit got picked for the detail because Major Hollister is seriously tweaked that you're no longer in the brig. A lot people in our unit aren't happy about leaving the comfort and safety of the camp here for roughing it. Nights are gonna be cold and drafty up in the mountains."

Pike nodded and shelved his thoughts of making a break before morning. Out in the mountains, it would be even easier. He'd also be that much closer to Pakistan.

"And you owe me the price of a cup of coffee too. You can settle up in the morning." Bekah was already headed back before he could think of anything to say.

Pike swallowed his resentment and embarrassment with the bitter black coffee and looked out into the darkness. *"Don't worry about it, bro. Gonna be gone soon enough."*

That wasn't entirely true, though. Pike knew he couldn't get gone soon enough.

★　★　★

Coming down out of the mountains at night was difficult, but the new-fallen snow helped more than it hindered. With the moonlight flashing through the scudding clouds, it was bright enough to see pretty well. The cold was another factor that ate into Yaqub and the men with him. He pulled his cloak tighter around him to block the knife-edged wind and walked through the gray fog of his own breath.

He thought of his father back at the village. Sabah had almost looked strong when Yaqub had said his good-byes. The old warrior was definitely a shadow of his former self, bereft of his limbs and his strength. The fire had returned to his father's eye, though. Sabah had held the device Yaqub had provided him in his clawlike hand.

As far as final images of his father, Yaqub had to admit that it was one worth keeping. His memories of his father as a younger man were better, but they were so distant now.

The sadness that touched Yaqub was a weakness. He forced his mind away from it and focused on the walk ahead of them. They had to cross sixteen miles of torturous mountain terrain to reach the vehicles they had waiting.

They had been walking since first dark, following donkeys that broke a trail through the hip-deep snow. The men—twenty of his best, all handpicked—marched with him. Wali led the way. Faisal walked just behind Yaqub.

A shadow passed over the snow-covered terrain, and Yaqub's grip tightened on his AK-47. Rags covered the assault rifle, protecting it from the cold. He stared up, searching the star-filled sky between the heavy clouds. A moment later, he discovered the shadow had been made by a passing cloud, not one of the Americans' drones.

Over the last few days, Yaqub's men had seen a few of the observation craft crisscrossing the sky. Yaqub had known to expect the Predators. The spy vehicles were the greatest threat to his operation, but he was also counting on them to provide distraction when the time came. The Predators could cut both ways.

The ground was uneven, and the rolling hills of snow made traversing it even more problematic. Yaqub stayed focused on his goal and kept moving, wishing he could run to arrive at his destination more quickly but knowing that it was better to err on the side of caution. So he kept walking.

Ahead, the lead donkey breaking through the snow suddenly stumbled and went down. The animal brayed loudly and struggled to get to its feet. The line stalled as Wali knelt beside the squalling beast. The men hunkered down and made personal tents of their cloaks to break the cutting teeth of the wind.

Impatient, Yaqub went forward. Despite the scarf and his beard, his face felt stiff and frozen. He trudged through the deep snow and reached Wali's side.

"What is the matter?"

Wali caught one of the donkey's legs and held it so the animal couldn't kick him. "Broken leg."

Irritated at the setback, Yaqub drew his *pesh-kabz* in one hand and placed the other on the donkey's head, pinning it against the snow with his knee. He drew the knife across the animal's neck, and hot blood spurted out to splash over the snow. The blood melted the snow and caused brief flurries of fog to rise before the wind swept them away.

Yaqub cleaned his blade on the donkey's thick coat as it kicked through the final moments of its life. "We have more donkeys, Wali. Get another."

"Of course." Wali called to one of the men leading the string of donkeys, ordering him to bring up another animal.

Yaqub slung his AK-47 and dug his hands deeply into the snow. He shoveled quickly, digging a hole for the donkey. Faisal helped him, and within minutes they had created a depression. They grabbed the donkey and pulled the animal's corpse into the space, then covered it over with snow so the drones wouldn't spot the dead creature the next day and perhaps track it back to the village before they were ready. Possibly the dead thing wouldn't be found for months.

When the corpse was covered and the new donkey was in place at the head of the caravan, Wali urged the beast into motion and they resumed the trek down from the mountain.

Hours later, shortly before dawn, Yaqub arrived at the village where he'd arranged to have the vehicles that would take them back into Kandahar proper. The vans and trucks had been hidden under a camo net amid trees only a short distance from the village, where more of his men had stayed to supervise the care of the vehicles.

The people in the village gazed on fearfully as Yaqub and his men clambered aboard. The vehicles carried work tools. With all of the attacks that had gone on in Kandahar, seeing such vehicles had become commonplace. They would be, for the most part, invisible.

Despite being fatigued from the long hike through the mountains and the cold that had constantly plagued them, Yaqub felt alive and ready to go as he took his place in the passenger seat of a plumber's van.

"Here." Wali handed over a thermos of tea and a sack of rice cakes to eat during their final journey into Kandahar.

Yaqub accepted the items and poured the tea into two cups while Wali slid behind the steering wheel. The younger man handed his rifle and pistol back to the men seated in the cargo area of the van. They lifted the false bottom and secured the weapons. In the well space, the missile launchers Yaqub had bought in Parachinar stood out among the rifles and pistols.

The cover was replaced over the weapons as Wali started the engine. After a few moments to make certain the other vehicles had started, Wali engaged the transmission and pulled onto the one-lane road that led farther down the mountains to the highway that snaked into Kandahar.

Forcing himself to eat despite his excitement, Yaqub bit into one of the rice cakes. He glanced up into the mountains, at the snow-capped peaks where his father lay waiting for his final battle, thought briefly of the old man as he had been when fighting the Russians and later the Americans and the warlords.

He would always remember his father's face being as cruel and harsh as the mountain landscape. The Americans would remember Sabah as well, and Yaqub knew they would fear him.

Pike sat in the driver's seat of the Humvee and gazed out at the inhospitable land around them. The Marine convoy raced through one of the valleys in the Safed Koh mountains. The temperature had cooled slightly since they'd left Kandahar, but Pike knew it would be much colder in the ridges.

He kept reminding himself that Pakistan wasn't that far away. A couple days' walk, he'd be in Parachinar. That was as far as his plan went. After that, he'd have to see.

Cho and two other Marines rode in the Humvee. In the passenger seat, Cho gazed in silence at the land around them. He whistled tunelessly. The two Marines in the rear had sacked out, sleeping sitting up with their heads lolled back and rolling with the uneven gait of the Humvee across the rough road.

Radio chatter was sporadic. The Marines weren't happy about leaving the camp, and Pike was certain they blamed him for their misfortune. No one dared get in his face, though. That was a bonus for having killed Captain Zarif and his men.

Cho glanced at the GPS. "Should be coming up on the marker in the next few minutes."

Pike nodded.

"If it wasn't for GPS, man, I don't know how they'd tell one section of these mountains from the others." Cho nodded toward the mountains. "How bad do you think it's going to be up there?"

Pike gazed at the white-capped ridgeline. "With Zalmai Yaqub and his men?"

Cho shook his head. "No. The cold. Wherever Yaqub is, I don't think we're the guys who are going to find him. But we're going to freeze our butts off while we're up there."

"Maybe." Pike turned his attention back to the road.

"Hey, Pike." Cho had turned to face him. "Not everybody's going to be on your case about you blowing up Zarif and his boys. Me? I think you're some kind of hero taking those guys on by yourself like that. A lot of the guys do. I heard that the information we're getting out of that other Russian is going to save a lot of lives."

"Good to know."

Cho sighed. "You're a hard guy to get to know."

"I'm okay with that."

"Wouldn't hurt you to lighten up. If you'd told people what you were doing that night, you might have been surprised how many Marines would have gone with you."

"Yeah, 'cause that would have really helped out with the whole stealth part of following Zarif."

"Dude, take a compliment."

Ahead, a line of pickups and vans approached the Marine vehicles. Pike kept his left hand on the steering wheel and reached for his M4A1 with his right. His stomach tightened in readiness. Out here in the wilderness, a lot of things could happen on the road.

Gunney Towers's deep voice came over the frequency. "Hold steady but be alert."

A minute later, the vans and trucks whipped by the Marine convoy. Pike watched them go, staring at the equipment racked on the tops of the vans and occupying the truck beds.

Cho peered at the passing vehicles too. "Guess all the repair work in Kandahar has drawn laborers out of the sticks." He shook his head. "Wonder how much they're going to get paid to risk getting shot or blown up."

"Probably about the same as you."

Cho frowned at that. "Man, you can be a total buzzkill."

"I thought you weren't looking forward to the camping trip."

"I'm not." Cho folded his arms over his chest. "But I'm figuring at least out here our chances of getting shot or blown up are probably less than they are back in the city."

"If you want to stay alive, you won't even start thinking like that." Pike checked the rearview mirror and watched the caravan of laborers disappear over the distant hill.

# 37

**DURING HIS CAREER** reporting from battlefields around the world, Jonathan Sebastian had sometimes entertained the idea of being KIA. Of course, the killed-in-action tag wasn't really a designation for journalists, but dead was dead. He hadn't thought about how he would be killed, though he knew most of the ways. He had seen bodies scattered all across the Middle East and in South America.

Rather, he'd mostly envisioned how he would be eulogized after he was dead. He'd won a lot of awards, gotten to meet a lot of important people, been in a lot of hot spots. He was certain he was a man whose death would not go unnoticed.

But even after everything he'd seen, he'd never once thought he was going to die locked in the throat of some wintry mountain so far from the main action. Now, though, he knew that was what was going to happen. He tried to focus, determining that the next time he got in front of the camera on a live feed, he would tell the world that Zalmai Yaqub had betrayed them, that the CIA agents everyone wanted to rescue were already dead.

Making such a broadcast would be heroic, and he had no doubt Yaqub's men would exact immediate vengeance. Jonathan Sebastian would go out in a blaze of glory, sticking it to his Muslim captors and saving dozens of lives. Now that was an epitaph he could live with. Metaphorically speaking.

He couldn't save those three CIA agents, though. Couldn't even save himself.

Except that he kept flirting with the idea that the Marines or the CIA or someone would arrive in the nick of time and take him out of the mess he was in.

He liked that idea, even though he knew the odds of such a rescue happening were infinitesimal.

He sat huddled under a thin blanket in the corner of the cave he'd been assigned to and wondered what time it was. This was the fourth day after his last broadcast. This was the day Yaqub had threatened to kill the CIA agents that the world didn't know were already dead.

One of his captors approached him with a pistol in hand. "You will come with me now."

"Where?"

"To make broadcast." The man waved his hand impatiently.

Sebastian looked around. "Where's Yaqub?"

"That is of no concern to you. Come." The man waved again.

"I want to talk to Yaqub."

The man lashed out unexpectedly, smashing Sebastian across the face with the pistol barrel. Pain exploded inside Sebastian's face and curled up inside his skull like a dying rat. Blood trickled down to his chin from the corner of his mouth.

Shoving the pistol into Sebastian's face, the man grabbed his shirt collar and slammed him into the wall behind him. "You come make broadcast—" he mashed the pistol into Sebastian's cheekbone under his left eye—"or you *be* broadcast. You decide. Either way, they get message."

Fear quickly eroded the pain, and Sebastian pushed himself to his feet despite the dizziness swimming in his head. He followed his guide to the other room.

Even though the bodies of the CIA agents had been removed, Sebastian could still smell the death clinging to the stone walls. On autopilot in front of the camera, he started straightening his clothing and his hair. The actions were ingrained habits but this was the first time his hands had shaken so badly since he'd first gotten up in front of a camera in junior high school journalism class.

"Here is the paper." The man handed Sebastian a copy of the newspaper.

With shaking hands, Sebastian opened the paper. He peered at the front page, at the date, and did the math. He'd been correct; today was the deadline day. He also scanned the paper, hoping for news of prisoner releases.

There were none. A sinking sensation opened up in the pit of Sebastian's stomach.

"Are you ready?" The hard-faced man stared at him.

"Ready?" Sebastian had to struggle to get his voice to work. In the past, he could count on one hand the number of times his voice had failed him—and have fingers left over.

"Yes. To report." The man passed over a paper filled with compact writing. "You will read this as it is written. If you fail to do this, I will shoot you."

Sebastian clung to that idea. If he failed to read the paper, he would die. So it stood to reason that if he did as he was instructed, he would live. He studied the writing, realizing that he was going to be delivering Zalmai Yaqub's promise of death to the enemies of his God and the man's call to other believers to strike down the Westerners.

"Yes. You are ready. Begin." The man waved to the cameraman.

Bright light bathed Sebastian, and he unconsciously stood a little straighter. "This is Jonathan Sebastian, and I am here to deliver Zalmai Yaqub's promise of vengeance." He thought briefly of telling whoever was listening that no rescue should be tried and it was too late for all of them. But he desperately hoped someone was coming. And he hoped that if he did as he was instructed, he would live. He clung to that. "You have failed to release the prisoners. Now you are going to see the costs of your decisions. . . ."

★　★　★

Standing in a waist-high snowdrift that was covered with a crust not quite thick enough to support the weight of a full-grown man, Heath studied the mountains ahead of him. He and his team had been marching since early morning after leaving the Humvees at a secure location. A lot of the terrain ahead of them had to be covered on foot.

Last night had been physically demanding. Despite their cold-weather gear, he hadn't ever truly gotten warm, and he was willing to bet that none of his Marines had either. He'd scheduled regular breaks to accommodate the fatigue created by the harsh climate, and he also made sure each Marine was hydrating. The cold-weather climate was as severe as a desert.

He'd been assigned a platoon, three squads under two sergeants and a corporal. Bekah Shaw and three other female Marines had been attached primarily in support positions to speak with any Afghan women they encountered in the villages during their search. Female Afghans wouldn't talk to male Marines because of religious convictions or fear of reprisal from their men.

Heath had split the squads up, working the grid he'd been assigned to search. Thirty-six Marines, two Navy corpsmen, and an attached weps specialty unit operated under his command. He kept the squads moving, covering as much of the western face of the mountains as he could while keeping them safe.

So far since their insertion, they'd had a couple close encounters with local Afghan caravans that Heath suspected were ferrying opium into Pakistan across the Durand Line. None of the men involved had admitted to seeing Zalmai Yaqub. Maybe that was true, but Marines had tagged one of the animals on each caravan with an electronic tracker so they could be traced by the Predator drones that patrolled high above.

Using his iPad, Heath pulled up the recent topographical maps that the intel division had put together. They had satellite access, and he flicked through his platoon's progress with a few hand gestures.

When he finished, he scowled. *It's too much and we're too little.* The only solace he had was that none of the other S & R teams in the mountains had turned up anything either. But that was cold comfort. It was as if the Safed Koh range had simply opened up and swallowed Zalmai Yaqub, like Ali Baba and the forty thieves.

Heath's MBITR crackled for attention. "Indigo Leader, this is Indigo Two."

Heath turned so the wind wouldn't interfere with the mike's transmission. "Go, Two."

"Checked out that village. Nobody home. Nobody's been home in a long time. Place is a ghost town."

"Roger that, Two. Leader confirms no joy." Heath marked the map, adding one more confirmed area to his grid. One of the caravan leaders they'd talked to had told them about the village. Heath hadn't held out a lot of hope, but it had been a more defined target than their other blind searching. "Proceed to your next twenty."

"Roger that, Leader."

Heath glanced farther uphill and spotted Pike seated on a rock that jutted up from the snow. He'd assigned Pike to his squad, keeping the man where he could watch over him. Since his incarceration, Pike had drawn apart from everyone even more than he'd already been.

Heath had kept Bekah in his squad as well, but that had been for different reasons, and he wasn't entirely comfortable with the preferential treatment he was showing.

Pike sat with an M40 bolt-action sniper rifle across his thighs. He carried a Remington 870 12-gauge shotgun as well for close encounters. He was a qualified sniper, and the assigned position allowed him to act as scout and gave him distance from the other Marines. He didn't seem to have a problem working with Private Cho, his primary assigned partner, but some of the other Marines harbored resentment over the S & R assignment.

Hollister had let it leak through the grapevine that the posting had been punitive, directly related to Pike, but Heath knew that his team was also up in rotation. The major had just claimed the assignment as his own bit of justice.

"Indigo Leader, I have a communication directive from Command." The voice was flat.

Excitement flared through Heath. That was the first time he'd had contact with Command since taking the field. "Roger that, Command. Switching to Tach One." He made the freq change to his MBITR. "Indigo Leader here."

"Be advised that we have confirmed the location of your target, Indigo Leader. Another television transmission is currently in progress and we have identified the source. We're sending encrypted transmission to your device."

"Roger that." Heath opened his iPad link to Command and watched as downloads initiated.

"The source is two klicks from your present location."

The announcement startled Heath, jerking his attention from the iPad to the ridgeline. They'd almost reached another summit, but there was no indication that anything was there.

However, the map that unpacked on his iPad showed the target area was somewhere in that rise. A red dot pulsed in the midst of a narrow valley.

"We're scrambling a team, Indigo Leader, but the air gets thin up there. Can't reach your present twenty with helos."

"Roger that." At their current altitude, a helicopter wouldn't be able to function well, and the wind shears clinging to the mountains would make an accident probable.

"We have decided to send you people in and follow up with a secondary unit we can mount from here. Our best estimation is that the support group will only be five or six minutes behind you. Indigo Six will intersect with both your group and the support team thirty-seven minutes after that. Given the fact that your target has promised to get bloody in this, you're to get inside that area and lock it down as quickly and as safely as you can. We want those people out of there safely if possible, and we want that tango leader put down or locked down. You're cleared to engage."

"Roger that, sir. We're on our way." Heath clicked out of the freq, then called for Towers and his squad leaders. Less than a minute later, Indigo Team was en route, pushing through the tall snowdrifts and closing on the target.

★   ★   ★

Yaqub got out of the van dressed in stained work clothes. He walked to the rear of the vehicle and opened the doors. Faisal handed him a toolbox that contained an AK-47, a pistol, and magazines for both weapons instead of tools. The box was heavy and hung at the end of his arm.

Faisal and another man emptied a wooden crate that had contained plumbing hardware and slid in one of the Russian missile launchers he had purchased with the opium shipment.

As they crossed the street, an Afghan National Police truck rolled past. For a moment Yaqub worried that his plan might be discovered early, but the ANP vehicle kept rolling. Perhaps the men in the truck knew who he was and what he was doing, and perhaps they only believed he was a plumber. The corrupt Afghan National Police officials had assigned al Qaeda sympathizers to the area as support. If the American military attacked, the Afghan National Police would fire on them.

Normally the area outlying the airport would have been subject to Marine security, but as the United States military had pulled back, more and more of the areas had been given over to the Afghan National Police to patrol and protect. With the recent attacks inside the city, as well as the capture of the journalist, Jonathan Sebastian, the American forces had concentrated more on containing the violence there. Their men were stretched thin, and the search up in the Safed Koh mountains taxed them further.

Yaqub knew there were still Marines in the area, and they would come after him as soon as the attack began, but he felt that not only would the attack be successful, but his chances of getting away were good. After all, this morning had been filled with distractions for his enemies, assorted blows that would render them bloody.

Even now attacks had sprung up again in Kandahar, and Jonathan Sebastian had captured the attention of the world with his plight and that of the CIA agents.

Feeling confident, wanting to see the rest of his mission through, Yaqub boldly headed into the apartment building he had selected days ago.

The four-story building was in one of the hardest-hit areas outside of Kandahar. The city lay eight miles to the northwest from this pocket neighborhood, but this was one of the small areas that serviced nearby businesses. One of those businesses, only two miles away, was the Kandahar International Airport. Over half of the units were uninhabitable, but that hadn't stopped squatters from moving in.

A few of the residents noticed Yaqub and his people, but they quickly retreated from the purposeful strides made by the group.

Yaqub took the stairs up, following Wali, who had a silenced pistol in hand.

On the third floor, they approached the first unit that faced the Kandahar airport. Wali opened the door and walked inside.

Two men sat at a small table in the center of the floor. Both got up and started to protest. Wali lifted his pistol, put two rounds into each man's chest, and kept moving into the next room before the corpses hit the floor.

With his own pistol naked in his fist, Yaqub followed Wali through the apartment.

No one else was present.

Crossing the room to the window, Yaqub stood to one side and cautiously shifted the curtain. The Kandahar International Airport lay in the distance two miles to the southeast, well within operational distance for the Russian 9K38 Iglas. Seeing the airport was difficult because a haze of dust constantly hovered over the area.

Yaqub knew it was there, and that was enough.

Wali and Faisal uncrated the missile launcher and readied the weapon. Two other men set up a small laptop computer and portable satellite dish, equipment that had been stolen from American military provisions.

Taking the cell phone from his pocket, Yaqub called a preprogrammed number.

"Hello."

Yaqub scanned the blue sky over the airport. "Are the planes still en route?"

The man at the other end of the connection answered immediately. "Yes. They are running on time." The man was one of the liaisons in the Afghan National Police who interfaced most with the American military. After today, his position would be compromised and he would be running for his life. But that was fine because

Yaqub had promised him enough money to keep him living well for years.

Yaqub glanced at the men working on the computer. One of them nodded. "Send the identification of the planes," Yaqub ordered.

"It is on the way."

A moment later, the computer screen revealed a sweeping view of the airspace over the Kandahar airfield. When the American planes reached Kandahar airspace, they would show up on the computer. In addition to the American military leaders, the planes also carried more military supplies and equipment.

"Let me know when the aircraft begin their final approach."

"Of course."

Yaqub punched the cell phone off and put it back in his pocket. He kept watch over the airport. The United States Joint Chiefs of Staff's surprise visit was about to turn more surprising than they had planned. Sabah would have been proud to watch the American planes explode.

Sadness touched Yaqub then. Not because he was certain his father was dead or would surely be dead in the next few minutes, but because his father would not live to see the death he would inflict upon their enemies.

Once news of the attack got around Afghanistan, and perhaps even in Pakistan, more true believers would rise to take up the fight against the Americans. The al Qaeda forces would battle with renewed belief and vigor.

And Yaqub would take his place as their leader once they learned what he had accomplished.

# 38

THE COLD ATE into Pike's chest as he slithered across the snow. He gained the top of the ridge, planting himself behind a hide he'd picked out on his way up the mountain. The shelf of rock blocked view of him from anyone below. He kept the M40 in a protective wrap to keep the sniper rifle from the snow and the cold. Despite the scarf that covered his face, the wintry chill scoured his cheeks and nose.

He left the M40 lying on the ground beside him and fished his binoculars from his chest pack. He scanned the ground, noting the snow-covered fortifications that created a maze across the valley floor.

In addition to the low stone walls that made irregular lines, there were several tangos taking up positions behind the barriers. He counted fifty-three tangos, but he knew there were more inside the caves.

He clicked the MBITR as the wind stirred small snow flurries over his position. It was like sitting in his own personal snow globe. He contacted Heath and spoke just loud enough to be heard over the connection. "I count fifty-plus tangos on-site. There are at least seven caves in the valley, so I'm betting there are more tangos on the premises."

"Roger that."

"On top of that, the tangos have constructed a kill box across the open ground. New fortifications. Walls. They planned on us coming." Pike gazed at the no-man's-land, knowing that the Marines were going to get hurt taking the valley. There was no way around that.

*"So let the Marines deal with this, bro. This is their thing. Not yours. Me and you, we can get out of here. Get gone while we've got the chance."*

Clearer than ever, Pike heard Petey's sibilant voice in his head, just as conspiratorial as he'd ever been, but Pike wasn't certain that vanishing in the mountains was ideal at the moment. The hike into Parachinar would take days. He didn't have the supplies on him to get that far. But the pull to step away was upon him. He didn't want to watch those Marines die.

That thought surprised him. In the past, on different missions, he'd accepted death as a constant companion. Warriors fell. It was a basic truth in any battle, and that hadn't changed in thousands of years. The Marine Corps trained their personnel that the deaths of comrades in arms happened. No one ever got used to the idea, but they dealt with it.

For the first time, Pike thought he didn't have the stomach to watch those younger Marines die. They were only a handful of years younger than him, but they were kids in his view.

Pike made himself breathe out. Losing fellow Marines had always hurt in the past, but he'd been able to keep himself distanced from it. Memory of the street battle that had taken place days ago played through his mind, making him realize how close he'd come to losing Bekah Shaw, Zeke, and Cho. None of them deserved to die today.

And Bekah had a kid, not much younger than Hector.

Thinking about Hector reminded Pike of all the things that could happen to the boy on any given day. A drive-by shooting, a predator in the neighborhood. *Anything* could happen, and it was all out of Pike's control.

Panic welled up inside him, and he had to force it away. He'd never felt anything like it before, not even when he was in the worst of the foster homes. Back then, he'd learned to be in control of himself and, gradually, his life around him. When he and Petey had escaped the system, they'd controlled their lives through violence and crime and whatever else was necessary to get by. They hadn't drawn any lines, hadn't backed away from whatever it took.

No matter what he did, Pike realized he couldn't protect the boy from everything that was out there. In fact, he *was* one of the things out there that Pike wouldn't have wanted Hector to cross paths with.

Last night he'd dreamed of the fight inside the diner, and he remembered the shocked expression on Hector's face when he'd thought Pike was going to kill that man. The trouble was, Pike knew he'd have killed that man and done it without hesitation. That was the kind of man he was. Kill the threat and it was never a threat again. And that was what Pike had intended to do.

Except that Hector had been there. As long as Pike stayed around Hector, as long as he stayed around the Marines, Pike knew he was going to deal with worrying about other people. He didn't want to do that. He wanted his life to be simple. He didn't belong in either place. He needed to get back to being on his own. If any of them knew what he'd truly done in his life, they wouldn't want him with them either. He was as big a threat to them as anything else. Hector's view of the world had already been altered because he'd been there with Pike that night in the diner. He'd already changed that boy's life, and it hadn't been a change for the better. He wasn't good for Hector.

That was a fact. It was time to move on.

Just as soon as he finished up here. Afterward, if he was alive, in the confusion he could choose his own exit strategy.

"Okay." Heath's voice was soft when he spoke, but it sounded brittle at the same time. "Hold your position and provide sniping cover as long as you can. We're going to soften them up with grenade launchers and suppressive fire, then pop smoke and go at them. We locate and secure the hostages, put down everybody who gets in our way."

"Roger that." Pike picked up the M40. He unwrapped the rifle, uncapped both ends of the sniper scope, and settled in behind the weapon, selecting his targets in order of preference. Things would have to happen fast if they were going to rescue the CIA agents.

Pike Morgan was also going to happen fast.

Jonathan Sebastian looked at the paper in his hands in disbelief. He'd reached the end of Zalmai Yaqub's demands and accusations before he'd known it. Now he stood there, holding on to the paper with shaking hands. His time onstage was almost at an end.

He stared at the camera, for the first time in years not knowing what he was supposed to say next.

Then the hard-faced man in front of him raised his pistol and took deliberate aim.

"No!" Sebastian's voice was hoarse and filled with panic. His heart thudded against his ribs and he felt a scream rising in his throat. He wanted to move but couldn't, frozen right where he stood.

The gun flashed, very bright, and something hard and unforgiving slammed into his face.

Grenades arced into the valley, fired from the M203 launchers equipped on some of the Marines' M4A1s. The resulting explosions caught the tangos by surprise.

Craters opened up in the snow and the defensive walls sagged in places, turning the barriers into stone shrapnel that took out more tangos. The thunder of the rounds detonating filled the valley with shock and awe.

Pike stayed with the M40, calmly and systematically sighting targets and working the bolt as he emptied the magazine. He picked out one of the men stationed at a machine-gun nest as the weapon opened up in full-throated roar. When the crosshairs dropped over the man's face, Pike took up trigger slack and squeezed off the round. Trusting his marksmanship, Pike worked the bolt to eject the spent cartridge and used his left eye to select his next target, never moving his head from where it rested against the rifle stock.

The machine gunner's partner reached for the weapon and became Pike's next target. Shifting his vision back to his right eye, Pike placed the crosshairs over the second tango and squeezed the trigger again, laying him out next to his companion. An instant later, a 40mm grenade wobbled through the air and took out the machine gun, scattering smoldering-hot parts across the snow.

Smoke grenades followed the high-explosive grenades, and red smoke carpeted the valley floor. The color looked stark and menacing against the snow. Not only would it serve to blind the tangos on the valley floor, but it would clearly mark the area for the drones that Pike knew were flying overhead.

Pike slammed a fresh magazine into the M40, then slung it and took up the 870 as Heath gave the order for his squad to move in. He rose from the ground at the same time Cho did only a few feet to one side. The younger Marine was focused and tense, but he didn't falter. He'd come a long way the last few days, and Pike took some pride in that. Cho was going to be a good Marine.

Charging downhill, Pike slammed through the snow. He tripped over rocks masked by the white powder, put out a hand to get his balance, and skidded briefly. Then he was on his feet again, racing toward the valley floor.

Ten feet up, the smoke thinned a little, but at ground level it was thick as soup. Tangos staggered inside the red mist and fired blindly up into the mountains. Without breaking stride, Pike pulled the shotgun to his shoulder and took aim at a shadowy figure. He squeezed the trigger, staggered briefly as the butt slammed almost painfully into his shoulder, then recovered as the double-aught buckshot hammered the tango backward.

Pike pumped the shotgun, and the smoking cartridge spun from the ejector port. The fresh shell barely had time to seat properly before he pulled the trigger again. The second burst sent another tango spinning away.

Gunfire echoed all around Pike, caught in the valley and made alien by the thin mountain air. He struggled to breathe, more winded from his exertions than he normally would have been, but he knew it was because the altitude was making him struggle.

He reached the valley floor with Cho at his heels. Ahead and to the left, a tango popped up with an AK-47 blazing. The large-caliber rounds buzzed through the air like a swarm of angry bees.

Pike threw himself down beside the stone wall the tango was using for cover and yelled to Cho. "Down!"

Cho went to ground immediately, and Pike was at first worried that the man had gotten shot. Then Cho rolled back against the stone wall, taking cover and swapping out magazines. "I'm okay."

Switching his attention to the tango, Pike crawled on his elbows and knees, getting to the end of the short wall. The tango was holding his position, taking cover behind the wall.

When he reached the end of the wall, Pike curled around the barrier and pulled the shotgun into his shoulder while he rolled over onto his side. The tango spotted him at the last minute and tried to bring his weapon to bear. Pike fired once, aiming at the man's legs and taking them out from under him, then pumping the shotgun and firing once more.

"Clear!" Pike got to his feet and fed four more shells into the shotgun to replace the ones he'd fired. The 870's capacity was eight, but he'd been trained to reload every chance he had.

Cho stood and looked around, his rifle to his shoulder. "I'm good."

Taking the lead, Pike saw Bekah and Zeke off to the left, working along the barriers in tandem. Bekah spotted Pike and nodded. Pike matched her speed as they moved toward the caves.

The tangos tried to hold their positions, but they died quickly. They were dedicated, but they weren't skilled. That bothered Pike. Al Qaeda used cannon fodder on attacks, but it would have figured that something like this would demand a better-trained group.

Ahead, a tango burst out from behind one of the walls. He screamed defiance and called on God in his language. His cloak flapped around him and revealed the explosives strapped to his body.

"Bomb!" Pike shifted the shotgun to cover the man and squeezed the trigger, aiming at the head, hoping to take him out before he could trigger the explosives, thinking that maybe shooting him in the chest would trigger the blast anyway.

The double-aught buckshot caught the man in the face. His knees folded and he went down, unconscious or dead—Pike wasn't sure. Before the man hit the ground, though, the explosives detonated.

The concussive force slammed into Pike, picking him up and knocking him backward like he'd been hit by a bus. He flew through the air, barely hanging on to consciousness. If the air hadn't already been knocked out of him, his lungs would have emptied when he smashed against one of the stone walls.

The combat helmet kept his skull from fragmenting on impact, body armor kept him from taking any serious damage, and he was loose enough to keep from breaking anything. His head bounced off the barrier and his vision blurred as his lungs refused to work. He flailed weakly, struggling against his own body like it no longer belonged to him. His vision had gone gray, and all noise had dulled to almost mute. Then everything reconnected in a heartbeat. His vision returned in a rush of bright colors, and the noise around him was suddenly a deafening din.

"Pike!" Hunkered down, Bekah was coming back for him as bullets chopped into the frozen ground around her.

Pike wanted to tell her that he was okay, that everything would be great if he could just breathe, and he wanted to tell her that he was sorry for the things he'd said when he'd been in lockup.

But he couldn't.

She caught hold of his armor and started trying to haul him out of the way as tangos rushed toward them. She was only half Pike's size, though, and pulling him was almost impossible. That size differential was one of the main reasons men didn't want women serving in fire team capacities. Women didn't have the same upper-body strength.

Bekah kept tugging Pike, though, refusing to let him go as the tangos swarmed their position and bullets plowed into the snow all around her.

Forcing himself to move, not quite back to optimum performance, Pike helped Bekah move him. He drove his legs, knocking her off-balance as he swung awkwardly from side to side. Together, they rounded the corner of the nearest wall and tumbled in a sprawl.

Bekah recovered first, hauling her M4A1 up and rising to a kneeling position. Pike finally managed to suck in air and tried to ignore the pounding in his head. He gripped the 870 and pulled it to his shoulder as he fought his way to his feet.

He rose from behind the stone wall. Four tangos stood before him. Two of them poured bullets into the barrier, maybe thinking they were going to get a lucky round through the pile of rocks and snow to the Marines on the other side.

Pike shot the first man in the chest, blowing him back into the second. Before either of them recovered, he pumped two more rounds into them, killing both. The third man went down under Bekah's fire, and the last man was caught in a cross fire from Cho and Zeke.

Bekah looked at Pike. "Are you okay?"

"Yeah. Thanks."

She was moving before he could say anything else, headed toward the caves. Other Marines were already swarming over the entrances, swapping fire with tangos still inside.

Pike didn't look forward to entering the caves. Based on previous experience he'd had, there would be a rat's nest inside the mountain, and all of it would be dangerous. Still, he followed Bekah as they plunged into one of the entrances.

Heat filled the interior of the cave, pressing in against Pike's face. He stayed on Bekah's flank, using his peripheral vision to scan the cave till his pupils adjusted to the change in light. Shadows draped the cave, making it hard to see, but the tangos' movements made them stand out against the darkness. The bright splashes of muzzle flashes revealed the shooters in quick, jerky images.

Swiveling, Pike aimed at those muzzle flashes and fired again and again. A bullet flattened against his body armor, eliciting a shock wave of pain that was barely noticeable in the cocktail of throbbing soreness that vibrated through him.

The shotgun cycled dry, the last expended shell spinning loose and catching the firelight, before Pike stopped. He held the 870 in one hand and drew his M9 with the other as he searched the cave.

Nothing moved.

He crossed the room to the bodies lying against the far wall. He slung the shotgun and used his flashlight to verify that their opponents were down. All of them were dead.

Outside, the gunfire was slowing and the radio chatter confirmed that the Marines had gained control of the valley and the caves.

Heath called over the radio. "Does anyone have eyes on Yaqub?"

Pike kicked over two of the dead men at his feet. Neither of them was the tango leader. Nor were any of the other tangos lying on the stone floor.

A chorus of negatives rolled over the freq.

"Keep looking. The man's got to be here somewhere."

"Indigo Leader, I found the reporter dude."

"Where?"

"Guy's toast. Somebody put a round through his head."

Pike wasn't surprised. The window for getting those people out alive had been small.

Heath hesitated only a moment. "What about the CIA agents?"

"Not here."

Pike put more rounds in the shotgun, filling it to capacity, and followed Bekah to the back of the cave. Another entrance barely stood out in the firelight. She advanced with her rifle at the ready.

"I got the CIA guys, Leader." Another Marine cursed. "They're over here. They're dead. Looks like they've been dead for a couple days at least."

*A couple days?* The news didn't sit well with Pike. That meant the whole operation was a suck, a setup designed to draw the Marines into the kill box. It hadn't worked out that well for the tangos, so what had Yaqub hoped to achieve?

At the entrance at the rear of the cave, Pike peered over Bekah's shoulder as she shone her flashlight into the chamber beyond. The sweet fragrance of rot clung to the area.

The flashlight beam settled on an old man in a bed. Even from the distance and in the poor lighting, Pike could see the man was missing an arm and a leg. His crippled body lay exposed on top of the bedding.

"Americans, I am Sabah al Hadith, and I am here to deliver your moment of reckoning in the name of the one true God." The old man raised his only hand, and Pike spotted the electronic device in it.

Reacting instantly, Pike pulled his shotgun up and fired. The double-aught blast tore through the old man's forearm. His shriveled hand, still holding the remote control, flew backward and bounced off the wall behind him.

For a moment, Pike thought that everything was all right. Then he heard the explosions starting, reverberating throughout the mountain. The cave shuddered and shook, suddenly rolling like a ship's deck on a storm-tossed sea. Rocks tumbled from the ceiling.

Pike grabbed Bekah and shoved her toward the cave mouth. "Move! *Move!* They mined the mountain!" He followed at her heels as a tumbling rush of rock filled the cavern where the old man had been, drowning out his final cries.

They barely cleared the door, sprinting across the shivering earth, as more and more explosions detonated.

Outside, Pike stared at the changing landscape of the valley. Rock and snow came down in powdery avalanches. He had only a moment to look at the hopelessness of it all before something slammed into his back and he was buried in a rush of moving earth and snow.

# 39

**COUGHING, BATTERED AND BRUISED,** Pike shifted beneath the debris that covered him. Rocks and snow slid off him, and he managed with effort to get his head and shoulders above the rubble. His hearing was thick, like he had cotton in his ears, and blood wept down the side of his face. Snow had fallen inside his blouse, chilling him and turning to water within seconds.

He fisted the shotgun and brought it up with him. He didn't know how many of the tangos were still alive, or if they'd weathered the blast any better than he did. Bracing the shotgun on its butt, he used the weapon to leverage himself to his feet.

Dust and powdered snow drifted over the valley. Dead men lay strewn across the countryside. Some of them were the tangos the Marines had killed to take the valley, but many of them were Marines.

Incredulous, Pike gazed out at the damage. Yaqub had set up the valley as a kill box, but the kill box was far more dangerous than Pike had surmised. Much of the architecture of the surrounding mountainside had changed. Landslides covered the valley in several places.

Pain throbbed through Pike's head. He couldn't quite connect with himself. How many of those dead Marines had he fought with and eaten with? How many of them did he know?

Then his mind snapped back to him, and he remembered he'd been with Bekah. Fear stabbed him in prickling bursts, somehow penetrating the daze that filled him to overflowing.

Pike looked around, searching for Bekah and Zeke and Cho. Only snow and rock and rubble met his gaze. In the distance, other Marines began searching for teammates as well.

"Corpsman!" The cry was ragged and barely snaked through Pike's muffled hearing. *"Corpsman!"*

Dropping to his knees, Pike tried to remember where everyone had been when he'd come out of the cave.

Suddenly the area in front of him heaved, creating a molehill. Abandoning the shotgun, Pike dug into the snow and rock, scooping it away with his hands, bruising his fingers in the process. Within seconds, he'd found Bekah and started clearing away the rubble covering her.

She came up wheezing and hacking. Her left eye was nearly swollen shut, and a large knot had formed along her eyebrow. She had her M4A1 in her hand. Covering her mouth with her elbow, she coughed several times and studied the nearby ground. "Zeke and Cho?"

Pike shook his head.

"They were right here. They've got to be under here somewhere." Bekah started digging, clawing at the earth.

Renewing his efforts, Pike dug too. Cho should have been to his right. That was the best that he could recall.

"Here." Bekah kept digging, revealing the boot she'd found.

Pike joined her. Together they uncovered Zeke. The young man was unconscious but breathing. They left him on the ground and continued the hunt for Cho.

A few minutes later, Pike found Cho's hand. He'd had to move out five feet from where he'd expected to find Cho. Either the man had tried to throw himself out farther, or he'd been propelled by the blast.

Cho's hand was loose, nonresponsive as Pike pulled on it. Working quickly, Pike uncovered the man. Cho had been lying on his back. When they had his head clear, Pike knew at once they'd gotten to him too late. Dirt filled Cho's eyes, but Pike could see that the man's pupils were dilated in death. More dirt filled his mouth.

Bekah yanked on Cho. "Help me, Pike! Help me! We've got to get CPR started!" She kept fighting, struggling to get Cho free.

"Bekah." Feeling hollowed out, like he'd been gutted, Pike caught Bekah's hands and tried to calm her. She was still half out of it herself, her coordination not quite back to normal. "Bekah."

She fought against him, yanking and shoving. "Stop. Let me go. We can help him."

"No." Pike kept his voice gentle. "We can't."

"We just need to start CPR. Get him breathing again." Bekah tried to pull away.

"Bekah, it's too late. It's too late." Pike held her hands in his. "He's gone."

Bekah looked down, took a deep breath. "All right." She wiped her face on her forearm, then got to her feet. "Let's go see if anyone else needs help."

★　★　★

The secondary team of Marines had arrived in the valley just in time to get caught up in the blast. They'd missed out on the gunfight, then lost nine men in the suicidal ambush.

Pike's team had lost seventeen Marines, almost half. Three had been killed during the brief battle, and nine had lost their lives in the explosions and the ensuing avalanches. Five were still MIA, presumed buried in the debris or in the caves that had collapsed.

Pike helped pack the dead into body bags. He knelt, staring into the open bag that contained Johnny Cho. For a moment, as he gazed at the man, it wasn't Cho. It was Petey. And Pike felt like he was losing his best friend all over again.

That was the problem with caring about people outside his own skin. He couldn't protect them, couldn't be there for them the whole time. Just like he hadn't been able to be there for Petey. Cho and those other Marines had slipped right through Pike's fingers.

"Pike."

Someone laid his hand on Pike's shoulder. Pike swung around, pushing himself to his feet and bringing the 870 around, swinging the weapon for the man's head.

Gunney Towers caught the shotgun barrel in one big hand and halted it only inches from his face. Towers stared into Pike's face. "You okay, Marine?"

"Yeah." Pike pulled his weapon away from Towers. "I'm peachy." He turned back to Cho and zipped the bag, trying hard not to think about Petey or Cho or Hector, but all of them were mixed up in there and it was difficult to think of nothing at all when he was carrying dead men.

"Let me give you a hand." Towers stepped in beside Pike.

"I can get it."

"I can help you."

Pike surrendered and stood there.

Towers searched Pike's face. "Who'd you lose, Marine? Who you thinking about while you're looking at this man?"

Pike didn't speak.

"'Cause I know you're thinking 'bout somebody. I seen that look before. Saw it the day we were cleaning them people up out of the street. So now, right this minute, you and me are gonna talk."

"There's plenty of other people for you to bother, Gunney."

"I 'spect I'll get around to bothering them soon enough. Got a lot of grief heaped on us today, and we still got to secure this area so the CIA can go through everything, see what they can find out." Towers locked eyes with Pike. "So you tell me who's weighing so heavy on your mind."

Pike considered refusing, using language graphic enough to land him back in the brig, but the old pain from Petey's death, the fresh pain from Cho's death, and the fear of what might happen to Hector swelled up like a balloon in him and felt like it was going to burst.

"Had a friend. We came up together in foster homes. Just the two of us, you know?"

"Had each other's backs." Towers nodded.

"Yeah. Always. Just me and Petey. We took care of each other the best we could. When we got the chance, we cut and ran. Then it was just him and me out on the streets." Pike stared into Towers's eyes, but he didn't really see the man. He was back in the past. "We did things we shouldn't have. We did *everything* we shouldn't have, Gunney. We were hunted by bad people, and we were no friends to law enforcement."

Towers didn't say anything, just listened.

"Petey took chances. He always pushed a situation. Always figured he had an angle. Always figured he was smarter than everybody else."

"Till one day he found out he wasn't."

Pike nodded. "Yeah. Guys he went up against killed him. I wasn't there. He didn't tell me he was going. Just lit out on his own. By the time I found out about it, it was too late. I got to him just in time to watch him die."

"You're still carrying that hurt around with you."

Pike's voice got tight and he had to force the words out. "It won't go away."

"Never lost nobody close to you before."

"Never *had* nobody close to me."

Towers was quiet for a minute. "You're gonna lose people every now and again, Pike. That's how this life is. Ain't nobody forever. And it hurts 'cause it's supposed to. The pain reminds you how much you loved them."

Blinking his eyes, Pike had to look away. "I'm not gonna feel like that, Gunney."

"Kinda hard to decide that."

"Not so hard. All I need to do is go back to living life the way I used to."

"Just be you, huh?"

"Yeah."

"You can do that, maybe, but it would be a hard thing to do, and in my opinion, the life you'd live would be a lot harder than what you're trying to get away from. God put us here on this earth to take care of each other. Made it so we care about each other so we ain't alone. And that means sometimes losing somebody's gonna hurt 'cause that's just how it is."

Pike didn't say anything.

"You think about that some, Pike, before you start walling yourself off from people. You think about what you'd be giving up. You ask me, that pain just makes having them people in your life worth even more."

"I don't see it that way."

"I see you don't, and I think that's a shame." Towers wiped his face with his hand. "I'm sorry about your friend. The one you lost then and the one you lost today." He glanced at the body bag that contained Cho. "Now, come on. I'll give you a hand."

Together, they bent and picked up Cho's body.

Trying not to dwell on the dead Marines who littered the snow-covered battleground, Heath tramped through the area again, picturing it in his mind the way it had been before the attack and the way it was now. He skirted a mortar crater that had blown black earth over the pristine whiteness and headed into one of the caves his scouts had discovered. That man's report about his findings had intrigued Heath.

The cave was small and deep. Hay covered the floor and animal dung spotted it in places. He knelt beside a pile of it and waved to Bekah, who was overseeing more investigation nearby.

She trotted over, breath fogging out in patches before her. "Something wrong?"

Heath pointed at the pile of dung. "Do you know what that is?"

Bekah frowned in confusion and answered without getting any closer. "You can stand off a ways from it and know what it is. You don't have to be right up on top of it."

"Yeah, I got that. But where did it come from?"

"The other end of the animal than the one you feed. This isn't hard."

Heath shook his head. "Not the point. What animal would you say this came from?"

"Big apples like that, probably a horse. A cow would have left a pie behind, and sheep would leave small pellets."

"And goats?"

"Pellets. Same as a sheep or a rabbit. Granny calls them goat berries."

Heath ran a hand over his chin, knowing something was wrong. "They had goats up here. We found some of those in caves, along with a few chickens. But I haven't seen any horses."

Bekah's gaze grew more interested. "They don't care for horses much up on the mountain. Caravans through here use donkeys."

"That's what I was thinking."

Kneeling, Bekah used a strand of straw to push the poop around. "This is fairly fresh. Hasn't been here long. With the altitude and the cold, it would be either dehydrated or frozen. It's neither." She tossed the straw away and stood. "This reminds me of that old joke. The one about the little girl who got a box of horse poop for her birthday and kept digging around inside because she was sure there was a pony in there somewhere."

Heath stood as well, surveying the cave and the animal spoor. "There were a lot of donkeys in here at one time. So where are they now?" He looked at Bekah and shook his head. "Yaqub's not here. We're wasting our time trying to find him."

"We haven't cleared out all the caves. We don't know that."

Heath shook his head and strode from the cave. "*I* know that. Yaqub drew us in here, gave his father one last chance to play the unconquerable hero and become a martyr for the cause, and hoped to kill as many of us as he could. He's thinking we're going to spend our time focused on this place, looking for a body we'll never find to confirm the kill, while he's off doing . . . what?"

Bekah gave the question some serious thought. "Yaqub's not just going to slink away. The guy's not wired like that. If he didn't have something better to do, he would have stayed here and died with his father."

"Yaqub wasn't planning on dying. This was for his father, a last hurrah. Yaqub's after something, and he wanted us focused elsewhere." Heath thought furiously, then locked on to a thought that left him shaken. "There's a flight coming in today. The Joint Chiefs are arriving for a meet and greet." He took off at a near run, heading for Gunney Towers standing tall on a hill overlooking the mountainside. "Gunney!"

Towers left his post and came over at once. "Yes sir."

"Get the men up and ready to move out. We're leaving in five minutes."

"Goin' where?"

"Back to Kandahar. That's where we'll find Yaqub."

Towers frowned. "You sure about that, sir?"

Heath pointed back at the small cave. "You get the men ready. I'm going to square our departure with Command." He glanced at his watch. If they hurried, they might make it back to Kandahar before the Joint Chiefs arrived.

If they didn't make it, he was certain it would be too late for a lot of things. If he was wrong, he was pushing a lot of tired Marines for no reason. But he was more afraid of arriving late than of being wrong. He was sure he wasn't wrong.

★   ★   ★

Tired and aching from the rapid deployment following the mountain battle, Pike sat behind the wheel of the Humvee and pressed down hard on the accelerator. The Humvee raced along the two-lane highway. Behind him, the other Marine vehicles trailed in a tight formation.

*"What do you think you're doing, bro? You're just heading back into the problems you're trying to get away from."* Petey's voice had been nagging Pike the whole way down the mountain.

Pike wished Petey would shut up and leave him alone, let him think, but he knew that wasn't going to happen until he figured out what he was doing. And why he was doing it.

Thoughts and memories and hurt raged inside Pike's skull, all of it threatening to break loose. He didn't know what would happen if those emotions threw off the shackles, so he kept a tight hold on all of it. He told himself he wasn't coming unraveled at the seams, but the truth was that he didn't know. The last few days in the Marines had been difficult, and the desperation to get out from under an emotional overload had become a fierce push inside him.

The Marine in the passenger seat had tried talking to Pike, asking what all the hustle was about, but Pike had shut the guy down, not wanting to listen to him. It should have been Cho in that seat, but it wasn't, and Pike wasn't ready to deal with that either at the moment.

After Heath had briefed the Marines, letting them know what he was thinking about Yaqub doubling back to Kandahar, Pike had told Heath about the caravan he'd seen hours ago. The Predators hadn't had any footage of the area at the time because they hadn't been looking for a feint.

If that caravan had been Yaqub and his warriors, they were hours ahead of the Marines.

*Doesn't matter how long Yaqub's been in Kandahar. The plane with the Joint Chiefs isn't going to land till it lands. There's time to get there and do something about this.* Pike kept telling himself that.

Command had listened to Heath's theory, and they'd agreed that they were going to bulk up the security details around the airfield, but the arrival was going as planned. If the United States military backed off, the retreat would be seen as a loss of conviction, a weakness. People would stop believing in the help that was supposed to be there. And after all the losses incurred from Yaqub's troops in the city, the supplies were needed.

Pike put his foot down harder on the accelerator when they reached a straight stretch. In the distance, he could see the outskirts of Kandahar. He knew that Yaqub would be somewhere around the airport if the Joint Chiefs were his target, but finding the terrorist leader was going to be like looking for a needle in a haystack again.

# 40

**"HEADS UP, MARINES,"** Heath called over the radio. "Command says that tangos have launched attacks on military units and buildings inside Kandahar. We're going to be entering a battle zone."

Pike peered through the Humvee's dirty windshield. The Kandahar airport lay ten miles southeast of the city proper. The military would be deployed all over the airfield. The terminal's main building looked like a row of interconnected M's. Glass filled the curved space. Humvees and Marines were in position all around the airstrip, but they were stretched thin trying to hold the airport and the city.

Everything in Kandahar had turned to chaos. In the distance, in the direction of the city, dark smudges left bruises in the sky.

Scanning the surrounding countryside, Pike noticed Predators roaming the air. The drones were photographing the flat scrubland around the airfield, relaying intel to the spotters in-country and the oversight operation stateside. Pike felt certain no one could be hiding out there.

So where was Yaqub's attack coming from? What capabilities did the man have?

Pike keyed the MBITR. "Heath, this is Pike."

"Yeah?"

"Look, Yaqub's not gonna be here. If he was, the drones would have picked him up by now. When you've got them out looking for something, they don't miss much."

Heath was quiet for a moment, and the silence almost frustrated Pike. Then Heath came back on. "If you want to say something, say it."

"We know Yaqub's been doing business with the Russian arms dealers. I'm betting he's picked up something he can use from a distance." Even as he said that, Pike knew it was true and his stomach turned sour. "He's planning on hitting his target and walking away a winner. That's what this guy does. He's not fighting for a draw here. He's fighting for the brass ring. He wants to come back as leader of the terrorist forces. He can't do that if he's dead, and he can't do it if he doesn't make a big strike against us."

"If that's true, where are we going to find him?"

"Hiding somewhere in plain sight."

"There's no way to know that. We've been tasked to help hold the airfield."

Pike tried to stem the black anger that surged within him. "Listen to me! We can't do anything here except maybe help pick up the pieces if this thing goes wrong. We need to get out in front of Yaqub."

Heath's hesitation was a lot shorter this time. "How do we do that?"

"We find one of Captain Zarif's playmates and put the squeeze on him. Wherever Yaqub is holed up, those turncoat Afghan National Police guys will know where he is."

"We don't know who those people are."

"No, but the Russians will, and they're not going to be feeling any too friendly toward them. That munitions dealer you picked up—Deyneka? He hasn't told you everything he knows. You can bet he's been holding information back. Any gangster with common sense would. You gotta have cred to leverage your way out of a situation."

After a pause, Heath said, "All right, let's chat up Deyneka."

Pike glanced at his watch. The Joint Chiefs were still a ways out. But they were running out of time.

★　　★　　★

"How do I know I can trust you, Lieutenant Bridger?" Handcuffed and wearing leg irons, Illya Deyneka peered at Heath through the smoky haze of his cigarette. He sat at a plain table in one of the interview rooms at the camp.

Heath stared back at the man. He hadn't gone through channels to get the interview with Deyneka. He'd just ordered the man brought before him.

"You're not going to know until you walk through that door a free man."

Deyneka shrugged and took another hit off his cigarette. "Then you see my dilemma." He squinted against the smoke as he expelled it. "For that matter, how do you know you can trust me?"

Heath thought back to the interviews he'd watched his father conduct. Lionel Bridger had cut several corners to get his high-rolling criminal clients off in court, and he'd done it by railroading middlemen like Deyneka. The trick was to bait and switch. Make them think they were giving up one thing when they were really giving up something else entirely.

"We both want something," Heath said. "I want to put an end to Zarif's network, shut it down once and for all. You want the men who betrayed you dead."

"Maybe dead is too harsh. Yaqub is good customer."

"Maybe the terrorists are good customers, but the Afghan National Police guys who have turned thieves are getting in the way of good business." Heath laid down images of Emile Evstafiev lying on a stainless steel table. "I read your jacket. Says you were a friend of Evstafiev. Captain Zarif put your friend on that table. Shot him down in cold blood."

Smoke drifted up from Deyneka's cigarette. "I have heard this."

"One of my Marines went after Zarif because he killed Evstafiev while he was in my Marine's custody. That's why Zarif is dead." Heath let that sink in. "What I'm offering, besides your freedom, is a chance for the Marine Corps to do what you would like to have done."

"You mean taking down Zarif's network."

"We don't know all of them. If we did, we would shut them down. That would create a vacuum in the power structure for a while, and we would consider that a win."

"I see. But you know others would come along to take Zarif's place."

"For now, I'll be happy to take these guys off the board," Heath said. "Guys like you will always exist because a market will always exist for your product."

"For the moment, though, all things will be equal."

Heath shrugged. "The way I see it, the munitions dealers will still have an edge. We'll look for you harder, maybe even stop a lot of you, but we can't stop you all."

"True."

"And for every munitions shipment we stop, the demand for the others will increase. As will the profit margin."

Deyneka smiled and smoked his cigarette again. "You know crime very well."

"I do." Heath folded his arms across his chest. "Do we have a deal or not?"

"You should understand that I do not know everyone Zarif deals with among the Afghan National Police. I do know that there are— how do you Americans put it? Bonuses?"

"*Bonuses* works for me."

"Yes, bonuses. These are kicked up to Zarif's commanders as well, but I do not know them so much. I know some of the names of the police officers in the streets."

"I'll take that."

Deyneka ground out his cigarette in an ashtray. "Very well. We have a deal."

Heath took out his iPad and stylus. "Give me the names."

Anxiously, seated in the passenger seat of the Humvee Gunney Towers drove, Heath watched as blue dots lit up on his iPad screen, overlaying the Kandahar street map.

Towers focused on his driving, but he spared a glance every now and again as he drove. "All those blue dots are Zarif's people?"

"The ones Deyneka believes were on Zarif's payroll."

"And people who we're thinking might be in cahoots with Yaqub now."

Heath glanced at Towers.

"Somethin' you didn't understand, sir?"

"Did you just say *cahoots*?"

"It's a word." Towers looked defensive, firming his jaw as he swerved to dodge a stalled car that was on fire.

Overhead, the M60 suddenly roared to life and chased back a group of tangos that had massed in an alley.

"I know it's a word. I've just never heard anyone say it before."

"A situation like this, what are you going to call it?"

"*Cahoots* it is. And yeah, these blue dots are the ones that are supposed to be terrorist sympathizers and were known to congregate with Zarif."

"Looks like a lot of 'em are congregating right now."

That was true. Most of the Afghan National Police were equipped with US military communications devices. Heath had negotiated a signal ping on the suspect devices to reveal their locations.

Hopefully the tactic had paid off. They'd know soon. Heath checked the time. The planes were due to land in the next twelve minutes. Their own ETA was eleven minutes. They had a brief window to operate in.

And there was no guarantee that Yaqub would be anywhere near Zarif's people. It was a slim chance at best. But it was all they had.

★   ★   ★

Rounding the corner and seeing the Afghan National Police jeep parked sideways in the street in front of an apartment building that Heath had designated, Pike ignored the brake and laid on the horn, not slowing his approach at all. He pulled his gas mask into place with his free hand.

One of the policemen inside the vehicle got out and waved Pike to one side. Pike ignored the policeman, swerved hard to the left, and wove behind the parked car before the driver could react. Pike roared across the street and slammed on the brakes, bringing the Humvee to a rocking halt at the front door.

"Move it!" Pike unclipped the 870 from the dashboard and threw the door open. He got out, joined by the other Marines assigned to his unit—three men whose lives were in his hands just the way Cho's had been. He pushed that thought away. *Get the job done, Marine.*

*"Get out of there, buddy. This isn't your fight. You don't have nothing at risk here. You don't gotta prove nothing to nobody."*

Pike knew it wasn't about proving anything, and he did have something at risk here. However complicated it was, this was the life he'd chosen. All of it. Surviving foster homes with Petey, deciding to get into the witness protection program, staying at the garage with

Monty and helping Hector with his math—all of those had been choices that had shaped him.

*Get out of my head, Petey. I gotta cut you loose. I did everything I could by you, but there are other people depending on me today. I'm not going to walk away from that.*

Pike tried the front door, but it was locked. Out on the street, more Humvees pulled into place. A loud-hailer barked orders to the Afghan National Police. "This is Lieutenant Heath Bridger of the United States Marine Corps. We are here upholding the peace-keeping efforts. You men stand down and you will not be harmed. Put down your weapons and step away."

Someone out there started firing, the M4A1 pop-pop-popping, but that was cut short by the full-throated roar of an M60 machine gun.

Stepping back from the door, Pike waved his team to the side, then pulled a CS grenade from his ammo rack. He yanked the pin, held the spoon, and braced his shotgun, aiming at the door lock. When he pulled the trigger, the shotgun recoiled against his shoulder and the locking mechanism fell to pieces.

Pike rammed a boot against the door, knocking it open with a shuddering *crack!* Instead of going in, he tossed the grenade in under-handed as bullets pocked the door and whizzed by him.

Counting down, Pike stepped to the side of the door in front of a large plate-glass window and waited as tear gas filled the room beyond. He peered inside. Three men in street clothes fired Russian machine pistols at the door. One of them caught sight of Pike at the window and started turning.

Pike aimed the shotgun and squeezed the trigger. The glass shattered as the double-aught buckshot tore through it. When the tight pattern of shot hit the tango, the impact knocked him backward. Racking the slide without hesitation, Pike advanced, knocking glass out of his way with the shotgun's barrel. As he strode into the foyer, more of the glass dropped onto his helmet and shoulders. He ignored it and took aim again, never stopping, walking forward as he approached the tangos.

The next shot caught another man and dropped him in his tracks, temporarily drowning out the rapid chatter of the machine pistols. Swiveling, racking the slide again, Pike tried to pick up the third man, but the tango was in motion, plunging through the CS gas, disappearing into the white smoke.

Pike locked on the stairwell and started up.

Someone on the radio yelled, "I spotted the tangos! Visual confirmed on Yaqub on the southeast corner, third floor. Could not get the shot. There are at least four other men inside that room."

"Close in," Heath said calmly. "Keep it tight. Let's shut them down."

Pike fed extra shells into the shotgun as he ran up the stairwell. By the time he reached the first landing, eyes sweeping the stairs, the shotgun was fully loaded again.

At the second-floor landing, two tangos took up positions behind the railing and unlimbered their weapons. Bullets stitched the wall behind Pike. He didn't break stride, twisting to bring the shotgun to bear and squeezing off three rounds.

One of the rounds missed the two men, going high and wide, but the next two were on target. Buckshot chewed through the flimsy railing and tore into the two tangos. One of the men fell backward and sat down against the wall, unmoving.

The other straightened and tried to run but only succeeded in falling over the railing, dropping immediately to the first floor and passing close enough to Pike that he could have reached out and touched the tango.

He fed more rounds into the shotgun, pushing himself forward and up, feeling the weight of his gear trying to hold him back. His calves and thighs burned from the effort of sprinting up the stairs. He turned at the next landing, kept moving. Below, more gunshots sounded, letting him know the second team through the apartment building door had engaged the enemy as well.

Pike reached the third-floor landing, oriented himself in a heartbeat, and headed for the corner apartment.

# 41

**HEARING THE GUNSHOTS** ringing in the streets below, Yaqub took his eyes from the binoculars and glanced down. American military vehicles flooded the streets, taking down the Afghan National Police standing guard over the operation. A few of the policemen engaged the Americans, but most quickly surrendered. Those who decided to resist the Americans did not last much longer, and they did not fare well.

Aware of the possibility of snipers lurking in the surrounding buildings, Yaqub pulled back from the window and drew his pistol. He looked at the man sitting at the laptop computer.

"Where are the planes?"

"They are beginning their final descent."

"Good. Then we may still have our victory. Ready the weapons." Yaqub stood to one side of the window, moved the curtain, and peered through. Holding the binoculars to his face, he studied the approaching planes.

The aircraft were Boeing C-17 Globemaster IIIs, each capable of transporting nearly eighty tons of cargo. From what Yaqub had learned, most of the deliveries were vehicles and heavy equipment to reoutfit the American effort. The attack today would not only deliver a message written in blood but also destroy millions of dollars of American investment.

According to the figures on the laptop computer and the Afghan air controller who was working with them, the three C-17s were a little more than eleven kilometers out and closing quickly.

The Igla missile launcher system was good for five kilometers. The apartment building was a little over three kilometers from the airfield. There was precious little room for error.

Gunshots sounded out in the hallway, growing closer. Yaqub steeled himself and looked at four of the men at the back of the room. "Go. Kill whoever is coming toward us."

The men readied their weapons, opened the door, and charged into the hallway.

Yaqub waved to Wali, who stepped to the window with one of the Igla launchers on his shoulder. Yaqub spoke over the cell phone connected to the other four fire teams. "Select your targets. You will fire on my signal." Excitement burned through him as he watched the computer screen and saw the distance to the airfield rapidly shrink.

Wali shifted slightly as he held the launcher. "I have target lock ping."

Watching through the binoculars, Yaqub studied the approaching planes. Their silver color reflecting the sunlight made them almost invisible in the blue sky.

Only two of the other teams declared that they had target lock as well. The remaining two were unable to secure the necessary ping to assure a hit. Knowing the Americans were closing in, that the men might not hold for long in the hallway, Yaqub realized he could wait no longer.

He glanced at the laptop, hoping the distance had shrunk to the acceptable five-kilometer mark. It hadn't. The planes were still nine kilometers out, but maybe that was close enough. He was out of time. "Fire!"

Wali triggered the launcher, and the missile filled the room with noise and flame and hot wind. Arcing through the air, the missile sailed over the surrounding buildings and shot toward its target.

From other buildings, two more missiles cleaved through the sky as well. Two more missiles leaped from the highway nearer the airport.

Faisal manned the phone that connected them to the Afghan air controller. He looked up at Yaqub. "Our contact says that the Americans have seen the missiles."

"It does not matter. They cannot escape." Yaqub watched through the binoculars, feeling his excitement growing. His father was doubt-less dead by now, but he would have accounted for several of their enemies as well. Both of them had claimed a significant victory today.

A detonation flashed in the sky, well short of the airfield.

"The Americans have intercepted one of the missiles," Faisal said.

A second detonation followed on the heels of Faisal's words.

"They have taken out a second missile."

Yaqub remained focused on the airfield, telling himself that his efforts would be rewarded, that his father had not died in vain.

Only a short time later, despite efforts at evasion, one of the C-17s became a roiling ball of orange-and-black flame. Another airplane lost a wing and began an erratic descent.

The destroyed C-17 hit the ground in a haze of black smoke spreading out from the debris that rained down on the countryside on the approach path to the airfield. The second plane managed to land on the tarmac but quickly skidded out of control and flipped over. Yaqub waited for the aircraft to explode, but he was disap-pointed. Still, one of the planes had been demolished, and the other had to have suffered tremendous damage.

*It is enough to impress those who need to be impressed.*

Yaqub grinned, feeling that God was with him. He lowered the binoculars. "Come. Now we must leave so that we can amass our army. Many will come to follow us now." He sprinted to the next room.

In the adjoining room, a section of the flooring had been cut away, leaving a rough rectangular hole down into the apartment under it. In that apartment, a hole had also been cut, creating access to the first floor. A third hole had been cut to the underground utility tunnel.

Yaqub clambered over the side, hung from his fingertips for a moment, and dropped to the floor, then made for the second hole. By the time the Americans figured out his escape route, he would be long gone.

★   ★   ★

At the third-floor hallway, Pike spotted the men waiting ahead. He threw himself into the narrow cover of a doorway as he waved his team back. "Take cover!"

Bullets tore along the hallway, gouging holes in the wall and chewing up the floor.

Splinters ripped from the doorframe where Pike took up a position. A bullet glanced off the body armor covering his abdomen, knocking the wind out of him for a moment. He grabbed a grenade from his ammo rack, pulled the pin, and yelled, "Fire in the hole!" He counted off two seconds and flipped the grenade down the hallway, hunkering back into the doorway with the shotgun raised vertically, waiting.

The explosion filled the hallway, and all the sound went away for a moment.

Pike whirled around the doorframe and leveled the shotgun. At the end of the hallway, four dead tangos lay sprawled across the floor. Pike sprinted toward the apartment door, fired a round into the lock, and kicked the entrance open, quickly dodging to the side.

When there was no return fire, Pike looked into the room. Smoke from the grenade poured in after him.

No one was there. Only a laptop and an Igla missile launcher remained.

"Heath," Pike called into the radio as he strode into the smoke-filled room.

"Go, Pike."

"I found the room Yaqub was supposed to be in. He's gone." Pike walked to the window and peered outside.

"He can't be gone."

"Have you got eyes on the building?" Pike knew it was a stupid question, but he couldn't think of anything else to ask.

"Yes. Yaqub has to be there."

"He's not." Pike spotted the adjoining room and found the hole cut into the floor. "He's escaped."

"How?"

Pike slung the shotgun over his shoulder and let himself down to the apartment below. "Cut the floor out of the room."

"Then he's still in the building."

Pike dropped through to the first floor and peered down into the utility tunnel. "Negative. He made his way into the sewer under the building. I'm taking my team after him."

"Roger that. Watch your six. I've got teams coming, and I'll see if we can get blueprints on the access tunnels."

Pike dropped into the utility tunnel and ripped away his gas mask because it interfered with his vision in the darkness. The stench of the sewer gagged him for a moment, and he breathed through his mouth to lessen the odor.

Stone-and-mortar walls stood rough and uneven, obviously older construction, not quite six feet tall. Pike had to crouch to move along the tunnel. He took his Maglite from his combat harness and turned on the bright beam, trying to figure out which way Yaqub and his people had gone.

Wet footprints stood out on one of the ledges on either side of the sewer.

"East, Heath. Yaqub's headed east. I'm in pursuit." Pike took off running with his head ducked down, but his helmet still scraped along the low stone ceiling.

"Roger that. Watch yourself, Pike. I don't want to lose any more people."

Pike saved his breath for running. Twenty yards farther on, he spotted what looked like a pile of debris on the opposite ledge. His light gleamed off the wire strung across the tunnel.

Holding his team back around a curve in the tunnel, Pike aimed his shotgun at the pile of debris and pulled the trigger. The IED exploded immediately, either from contact with the buckshot or because of the trip wire.

With the sound of the detonation rolling over him, Pike resumed the chase, more watchful now and cursing the need to be. At an intersection, the wet footprints were fading but still visible.

They stopped at the bottom of metal steps that led up to a manhole cover that was just sliding into place.

"Heath."

"Go, Pike."

"I'm on top of them." Pike halted, readied the shotgun, and climbed the three steps, hunkering down under the manhole cover with his left hand splayed against it. "Do you have my twenty?"

"Roger, Pike. Reading your GPS. We're headed that way."

Pike braced himself and shoved the manhole cover up and over. The thing weighed more than fifty pounds, but he cleared it with one shove. Above, a tango pointed an AK-47 down into the tunnel. Pike fired his shotgun and blew the man backward, racked the slide, and climbed out of the manhole. He swept the street for more targets but found his immediate surroundings empty of civilians.

Fifty feet away, a black SUV rolled out of an alley and accelerated down the street.

"He's got wheels, Heath. Black SUV heading west." Desperately, Pike gazed around for some means to continue the pursuit.

"He's headed back into the city. If he reaches the city, we're going to have a hard time finding him again."

"I'm working on it. What about a Predator strike?" Pike ran along the street, chasing the SUV and looking for a vehicle he could use.

"Even if I could call one in that quick, they can't effectively target a moving vehicle. I'm coming, Pike."

"Roger that." Pike ran along a row of abandoned cars. Evidently the owners had taken cover in nearby buildings when the hostilities broke out.

None of the cars had keys in them.

Pike was considering hot-wiring one of them, but none of them looked capable of catching the SUV. Then, between a panel truck and a dented sedan, he spotted a motorcycle.

It was a Japanese make, set up for trail riding, and it was simple to hot-wire. Pike slung the shotgun, then righted the motorcycle, threw his leg over, and took out his knife. He bared the ignition wires and touched them together. Sparks flew and the engine caught. Feeling the familiar vibration of a motorcycle beneath him, Pike smiled.

He pulled in the clutch, kicked the gearshift into first, and twisted the throttle, easing off the clutch and picking up speed instantly. "I got wheels, Heath. I'm in pursuit." He focused on the dirt cloud following the SUV nearly a quarter mile ahead of him.

"We're almost there."

Pike became part of the motorcycle, feeling that return to who he had always been, fierce and reckless and free. He realized then that no matter what he gave himself to, no matter what unwanted responsibilities he took on, there would always be a part of him that was unbridled and wild. He couldn't stop being who he had been, but he was more than that now.

The motor roared as he opened the motorcycle up. He raced through the rooster tail of dust the SUV left. In the vibrating mirrors, he just caught sight of a Humvee turning onto the street.

Reaching over his shoulder with his left hand, the motorcycle redlining as he pushed it to the limit, Pike unlimbered the shotgun and laid it on the handlebars. He stayed bent low over the motorcycle, eating dust but knowing that the debris was working for him too, helping him stay hidden.

One of the tangos in the back spotted Pike when he was fifty yards out. He turned and yelled for the driver. Yaqub sat in the passenger seat up front. A look of disbelief tightened the tango leader's face.

By the time the driver started taking evasive action, Pike could almost have reached out and touched the SUV's rear bumper. One of the tangos leaned out the window with his assault rifle.

Pike blasted the man. Shifting the shotgun to the SUV's rear tire, Pike fired again.

The tire shredded immediately, ripping to pieces, and the SUV sagged, dropping to run on the rim. A shower of sparks mixed with the dust as the vehicle wove from side to side. Pike kept zipping forward, faster on the motorcycle than the SUV. Beside the driver's door, he leveled the shotgun and fired again.

The window disappeared in a bloody rush, and the SUV floated out of control. Pike shot the front tire out as well and the vehicle swung violently to the left, narrowly missing him. In the next instant, the SUV turned sideways and flipped over and over, finally coming to a rest right-side up.

But it wasn't going anywhere. Radiator fluid pooled beneath it in a green puddle. Steam poured from under the hood. All of the windows were broken out.

Pike pulled the motorcycle to a stop, killed the engine, and stepped off. He reloaded the shotgun as he rounded the back end of the SUV and headed for the passenger side.

Yaqub sat dazed in the passenger seat. Blood trickled from a cut on his forehead.

Pike leveled the shotgun at the tango leader. "We can do this the easy way or the hard way."

The door behind Yaqub jerked open, and a young man stepped out with a pistol clenched in his fist. Pike tried to turn, but he knew he was going to be too late. The man was as fast as anyone he'd ever seen. Two bullets hammered Pike's body armor over his heart, and a third ricocheted from his helmet, knocking his head back. Pike pulled the trigger at the same time, though, and the double-aught buckshot lifted the tango from his feet and pitched him backward.

By that time, Yaqub had an assault rifle pointing out the window. Pike stood his ground, knowing there was no time to run—and he wasn't going to run anymore, not even from himself. He swung the shotgun around and pulled the trigger, staring death in the face, feeling the heat of the bullet kiss his right temple, then felt the impact of the 12-gauge thudding against his shoulder.

The buckshot caught Yaqub in the head and shoulders, knocking him back inside the vehicle.

The Marine Humvee skidded to a halt as it locked down. In the next instant, Heath swung out from behind the steering wheel and Gunney Towers stepped out on the passenger side.

"Yaqub?" Heath asked.

Pike jerked a thumb over his shoulder, feeling suddenly dizzy and noticing he had double vision. "You can have what's left of him."

Gunney Towers took Pike by the shoulder. "Let me have a look at you, Marine."

Pike stood still and shook his head, regretting that instantly. "I'm fine."

Towers examined him for a moment, then took a gauze pad from his chest pack and pressed it to Pike's head. "You are all right, Marine. Gonna be right as rain. But that there's gonna leave a mark."

Pike looked at the older man, meeting his warm brown gaze. "Everything I've gone through in my life has left a mark, Gunney."

Smiling knowingly, Towers nodded. "I suppose it has."

# EPILOGUE

**WEEKS LATER,** when the deployment ended, Pike returned to Tulsa. Carrying his duffel, the scar on his forehead still pink and shiny, he got off the bus at the street corner near his apartment. For a minute, he just stood there and breathed in, letting the city sink into him. He was surprised to discover how comfortable he felt, how much he had missed the familiar streets. Instead of going to his apartment, he headed to the garage.

Monty greeted him with a grease-smeared smile, sliding out from under a pickup up on the rack. "You're back."

"I am."

Monty sat up on the creeper and wiped his hands on a red rag. "It's good to see you, Pike. Real good." He paused. "I got the feeling there at the end before you deployed that you thought some about not coming back."

Feeling a little embarrassed that he could be read so easily, Pike shrugged. "I'm not much for staying."

"I knew that. I lined up another mechanic to help me here because you've brought in so much business. Had to have somebody."

Disappointment hit Pike harder than he thought it would. "It's no sweat, Monty. I understand. You did what you had to do." He was surprised at how much he'd been counting on having a job when he got back. "I had a great time working with you."

Monty stood and shook his head. "You planning on going somewhere?"

"I'll be around."

"Pike, you still got your job here. The mechanic I took on works at another shop. He was just moonlighting here. Another pair of hands when I needed them, and I needed them. Your job is your job, brother. For as long as you want it."

Pike smiled. "I appreciate that, Monty. You don't know how much."

Monty stared at him and smiled back. "I know. Believe me, I know. My wife and kids may make me crazy every now and again, but I love knowing where I belong. And right now, you belong here too. You can get started anytime you're ready. I got both bays full."

Glancing at the clock on the wall, Pike saw that school would be out. "Gimme a minute to go scarf a burger and I'll be back."

"Sure. Whenever you're ready."

Pike held up his duffel. "Mind if I leave this here for a bit?"

Monty took the duffel. "Let me handle that for you. Lemme guess: you're going to the diner."

Pike shrugged. "Thought I'd check and see if the kid was doing his homework."

"He is. He'll be glad to see you."

Pike crossed the street and walked into the diner. Hector was at one of the back tables, working diligently, but when he spotted Pike at the door, he got up and raced over as quickly as he could. He wrapped both his arms around Pike, hugging him fiercely.

"You're home!"

"Yeah, I am." Pike Morgan hugged the boy, and for the first time in his life, he felt like he truly was home.

# ABOUT THE AUTHOR

**MEL ODOM** is the author of the Alex Award–winning novel *The Rover*, the Christy Award runner-up *Apocalypse Dawn*, and the Called to Serve series, which includes *Deployed* and *Renegade*. Odom has been inducted into the Oklahoma Professional Writers Hall of Fame (at the age of 37—otherwise mentioning such an award makes him sound very old and retired). He lives in Moore, Oklahoma, where he coached Little League for years, and teaches professional writing classes at the University of Oklahoma. Since first being published in 1988, Mel has written more than 160 books in various fields, which he blames on his ADHD, desperation (five children), and opportunity.

## CALLED TO SERVE
### SERIES

Watch for the exciting conclusion
★ **COMING IN 2014!** ★

# GO MILITARY.

Best-selling author **MEL ODOM** explores the Tribulation through the lives of the men and women serving in the U.S. military.

### APOCALYPSE DAWN
The end of the world is at hand.

### APOCALYPSE CRUCIBLE
The Tribulation has begun, but the darkest days may lie ahead.

### APOCALYPSE BURNING
With lives—*souls*—on the line, the fires of the apocalypse burn ever higher.

### APOCALYPSE UNLEASHED
In the earth's last days, the battle rages on.